ANCESTRAL MACHINES

Pyke faced Khorr.

'So, just taking hostages wasn't enough.'

'I want to be certain that your every thought and action is focused on carrying out the mission to the end, to the final blow.'

'Oh, we're focused, all right. You can be sure of that.' Pyke's thoughts were full of violent imaginings, smashing an elbow into that throat, a fist into that face. Instead he spread his hands. 'Let's waste no more time – let us get on with this black business.'

BY MICHAEL COBLEY

Humanity's Fire

To me old mate Graeme Fleming,
AKA the mighty Progmeister General!

ANCESTRAL MACHINES

MICHAEL COBLEY

www.orbitbooks.net

ORBIT

First published in Great Britain in 2016 by Orbit
This paperback edition published in 2016 by Orbit

1 3 5 7 9 10 8 6 4 2

Copyright © 2016 by Michael Cobley

Excerpt of *Ancillary Justice* by Ann Leckie
Copyright © 2013 by Ann Leckie

The moral right of the author has been asserted.

A CIP catalogue record for this book
is available from the British Library.

ISBN 978-0-356-50178-9

Typeset in Sabon by M Rules
Printed and bound by CPI Group
(UK) Ltd, Croydon, CR0 4YY

Papers used by Orbit are from well-managed forests
and other responsible sources.

MIX
Paper from
responsible sources
FSC® C104740

Orbit
An imprint of
Little, Brown Book Group
Carmelite House
50 Victoria Embankment
London EC4Y 0DZ

An Hachette UK Company
www.hachette.co.uk

www.orbitbooks.net

PROLOGUE

The drone Rensik Estemil was in the middle of an intelligence-gathering mission down on Tier 104 when the peremptory summons reached him. It took him forty-three hours to stealth-exfiltrate Problematic Area 3 and ascend through hyperspace to Tier 49, home of the *Garden of the Machines*. Even so, on arrival he insisted on being recased in one of the new Iterant-9 varidroid shells before complying with the summons and going in search of the Construct.

He left the faceted blue reshell chamber and glided out along one of the hundreds of black-mesh walkways that coiled, curved and intertwined around the new and heavily armoured *Garden of the Machines*. From a distance, the Construct's stronghold had resembled a dark webby cloud through which a thousand tiny pinpoints crawled between the bright clusters of test and trial bowers. Up close, there was a sense of the jungle about it.

Rensik found the Construct's command proximal in a gazebo positioned among the outermost walkways. A pale gauze-canopied archway afforded a generous view of the Slegronag Interval, an askew expanse on hyperspace Tier 49, a cavernous opening half a million miles wide and about three million long, its floor a vast plain littered with the split, cracked and smashed ruins of entire worlds, gargantuan heaps of planetary wreckage strewn in all directions. A dead, airless and abandoned graveyard over which the *Garden of the Machines* drifted on a course that zigzagged slowly along the length of the Slegronag.

'You took your time. A lack of promptness is scarcely a quality one expects from an Aggression field supervisor.'

The Construct's new proximal was a hovering nine-sided unit from which a variety of tentacles and articulated arms sprouted. Before it, on a long low cradle, there sat what at first glance looked like a large black and green drone of unfamiliar design. It had a blunt-nosed blimp configuration with a number of what were probably weapon blisters dotted around its battered hull. Blackened, twisted thrust nozzles jutted at the stern. A dozen or more sections lay open while the Construct's tentacular tip-tools prodded at the innards. Twinkly gleams from the shadowy interior indicated the presence of remotiles, scanning hard-to-reach niches, sending back rich datastreams.

Rensik Estemil's newly acquired varidroid was a marvel of nano-compression and multi-function shield technology, and was comfortingly well armed. Yet he was dwarfed by this bulky, inert mass. The aura of lapsed millennia was almost tangible to his sensors.

A segmented tentacle tipped with a cluster of purple lenses snaked towards him.

'I've seen the reports of the Julurx operation,' said the Construct. 'Risky strategy, allowing the second-stage colony to develop unhindered, yet your engineering of a counter-horde turned out to be highly effective. Most creative. All the local legacy civilisations will be greatly relieved.'

For the Construct this was the equivalent of a triumphal welcome-home parade, but then Rensik had been faced with a predicament freighted with the potential for ghastly consequences. A flotilla of Hodralog nomads had been scavenging through an eroded tiltway on the periphery of Tier 103, when they disturbed the hibernating mekspores of a replicating machine horde called the Julurx. The Hodralog, and their ships and AIs, were swiftly overwhelmed by the spores, which wasted no time in switching over to building the stage-two horde, using their newly acquired stores of organic and refined materials. Rensik and his wing of battle-hardened Aggression destructors, responding to panicky alerts from Tier 103's spire-city civilisation, reached the tiltway several hours after the last Hodralog was slain. But comm despatches from the ill-fated nomads had been relayed earlier to the Construct drones and by the time they arrived Rensik Estemil had a plan.

'Replicating machine hordes don't place much value on retaining nuanced data from previous outbreaks,' Rensik said. 'Otherwise they would have known how to counter my brilliant strategy of capturing unactivated stage-one spores and using them to engineer an anti-horde dedicated to eradicating the Julurx.'

'How long?'

'Thirty-one-point-four hours.'

'The Julurx must have reached one of the later stages after that space of time.'

'Stage six,' Rensik said. 'Its first gigatropolis was partially complete when our anti-horde launched its main attack wave. Afterwards, we repeatedly beam-scorched the vicinity, and a network of scanner-probes were left on-station.'

'Good,' said the Construct proximal. 'Well summarised, if a little self-satisfied. And how would you describe the progress in Problematic Area 3?'

'Progressing satisfactorily.'

'Droll. And I notice that you've changed your name again.'

'I thought that minor individuations were permissible,' Rensik said. 'Has that changed?'

'Not at all. It is merely noteworthy to observe that since your involvement in the Darien Conflict you have changed your name nine times. Did you know that certain Human leisure-class subcultures pursue similar alterations in designation? They vie with one another to come up with the most outlandish forms of nomenclature.'

'Fascinating,' Rensik said. 'When I arrived I was sure that you were going to explain why you were investigating this rusting relic – I had no idea that my name would prove to be of such interest.'

'Perceptive,' said the Construct. 'Pithy and ironic.' The lens-tipped tentacle swung in a bit closer. 'We here in the tiers of hyperspace exist in a kind of sediment of relics, the debris of past universes compacted upon one another. Yet even up there, in the prime continuum, you cannot escape the undying fragments of the immemorial past, lingering gracenotes of vast symphonies of destruction, the heirlooms of bygone insanities.' Another tool-tentacle tapped on the hull of the ancient drone. 'This war machine is indeed, as you say, a relic. Until very recently it was preserved in the deep permafrost of a world on the spinward boundary of the Sendrukan Hegemony. Possibly the only intact example of a Zarl Imperium combat drone known to exist ...'

'The Zarl Empire,' mused Rensik. 'Collapsed about a million years ago?'

'Indeed, although this device dates from the tyranny's high-point a little further back. Most of the materials used in its construction were anti-entropic, otherwise it would have crumbled to dust by now. But this is not the reason I asked you to see me. Have you ever heard of an exotic megastructure known as the Great Harbour of Benevolent Harmony?'

'Yes, I have,' said Rensik. 'Began as some lofty altruistic collaborative project over in the Greater Shining Galaxy about a hundred thousand years ago. Ended as the lair of several psychotic species hell-bent on slaughter, and was hunted down and destroyed by the Just Reprisal Alliance or something similar.'

'It was more like fifty thousand years ago,' the Construct said. 'Archive documentation about the Greater Shining Galaxy's deep history is fragmentary with few details, except that it was apparently a massive macro-engineering achievement. And now it seems that it was never destroyed. Despite concerted massive attacks it survived and escaped.'

A moment or two of silence followed, which from past experience Rensik knew was to be filled by a leap of understanding from the listener. There was really only one possible extrapolation to all this and it was a disturbing one.

'Has this thing arrived in our galaxy?' he said.

'Well done! Guess what emerged from hyperspace several hours ago near the border between Earthsphere and the Indroma Solidarity? On the Indroma side, no less, hiding in one of those huge starless gulfs that diplomats have been wrangling over for decades.'

In one of his dynamic memory niches Rensik ran a swift scenario model, pitting the regional powers against the potential of something like the Great Harbour. The outcomes were not encouraging.

'We will need a serious magnitude of firepower to stop this thing,' Rensik said. 'An assault fleet of five, no, six thousand Aggression units, plus support tenders, would provide the necessary deployable force, especially if I were in command.'

'We would not be able to assemble such a fleet in the very short term,' said the Construct. 'Based on third-hand reports from our galaxy's outlier stellar clusters, this intruder can be expected to move in the very short term against any isolated worlds in the area. Therefore I am sending you, and I'm even letting you use one of the upgraded shimmerships.'

'I see, a solo mission,' Rensik said. 'Covert observance, monitoring comms, gauging capabilities and weaknesses, sending regular reports—'

'No, not solo – you'll be accompanied by a Human operative from Earthsphere's military intelligence.'

Rensik groaned. 'Humans—'

'Your experience in that field should be of considerable utility.' The Construct paused as one of its tentacles snaked into some cranny within the ancient Zarl drone and a bright light stuttered for a moment. 'While the assignment includes covert observation and intel gathering, your first task is to find out who commands and what their purpose and strategy are. I suspect that the regime, or regimes, will be despotic or tyrannical to some degree so the existence of resistance groups is practically a given. Your main task, you and your Human coagent, is to seek out the most effective of these rebel movements and offer what assistance you can. Feel free to be creative.'

'How creative can I be while babysitting a ...'

A priority data object pinged into Rensik's entry buffer. Decoiled, it turned out to be sparse background details on the Great Harbour and the personnel file for one Lt Commander Samantha Brock.

'I don't imagine that she'll require much in the way of baby-sitting,' said the Construct.

'It seems that she might be useful,' Rensik conceded after flash-reading the Lt Commander's file. 'Although in my experience Humans usually find a way to complicate matters.'

'And while the pair of you attempt to foment revolution among the downtrodden, I shall be working to keep both Earthsphere and the Indroma Solidarity from sending in their fleets. The imponderables of the Great Harbour are too great and some of the surviving accounts are too horribly suggestive to take the risk of triggering full-scale hostilities. The complications would be ...'

The Construct paused as clusters of symbols began to pulse and slow all over the Zarl drone's battered hull. Cold blue flashes of light were visible inside the crowded interior. The Construct retracted its questing tentacles with alacrity just before most of the gaping panels slid or flipped shut. A strident bellow, half deep brazen roar, half rasping howl, blasted out at shattering volume. The Zarl drone tore free of the cradle's perfunctory restraints, rose up and whipped round to bear down on Rensik Estemil.

Rensik's defences surged into battle-readiness. With all tac-combatives ramped up to optimal, the initial moves and countermoves of sensor probes, feint targetings and shield shifts were taking place in fractions of a second. Rensik's sensors were also picking up a cascade of energy-state changes from within the Zarl machine which revealed previously undetected arrays of hideously powerful weaponry. Sections of its carapace were bulging to permit the extrusion of barrel snouts and to create launcher apertures while Rensik readied his own defences, starkly aware of how outgunned he had suddenly become but unwilling to back down ...

And just when a convulsion of destruction seemed inevitable, the cryptic symbols glowing all over the Zarl drone's hull faded and died away. There was a chorus of muffled clunks, the war machine wobbled in mid-air for an instant then fell to the floor with a loud, sharp thud, rocked back and forth a couple of times and was still.

Rensik scanned it, found no energy sources, no datastream activity, nothing apart from vestigial ionisation around four points on the hull.

'Excellent!' said the Construct, drifting in closer. 'Most informative.'

It took Rensik no time at all to figure it out.

'I see. So you decided to unleash this grisly old killing machine, knowing that it would go for the most threatening target present – me. But all the time you had a cut-out of some kind rigged and ready ...'

'A specifically exotic ultrafield, generated between four nodes previously attached to the drone carapace,' the Construct said. 'It scrambles coherent energy patterns, which effectively deactivated our antiquated friend here. Sometimes only a live trial can reveal the subject's essential nature.'

'So glad to be of help.'

'You have and will be again, I have no doubt. You should leave now. The shimmership is prepped and ready for you in Bay 14 – taking into account the ascent through hyperspace to the prime continuum, you should reach the vicinity of the Human home system in under nineteen hours. High-level approval has been granted so Brock's commanders will have received notice of her secondment to the joint mission by the time you arrive.'

Even as the Construct finished the sentence a trio of caltrop-like lifter modules glided into the gazebo, fixed themselves to the Zarl drone, which then rose from the floor and in one smooth movement returned to the cradle.

'Safe journey,' the Construct said as it resumed its study, flexing tentacle tips tugging open panels and hatches.

It certainly seems more talkative than before, Rensik thought as he left the gazebo and headed for the vehicle bays. *Still just as maddeningly eccentric, but definitely chattier . . .*

CHAPTER ONE

Through Brannan Pyke's slow-waking mind, thoughts stole like foggy ghosts ...

Death came ...

He felt cold, lying on something soft, something weightless.

Death came whispering ...

Cold, yes, but not soft, not lying on anything.

Death came whispering orders ...

Just hanging in zero-gee, he realised drowsily, hanging in the dark, with something glowing faintly red off to one side. Those words about death whispering seemed familiar somehow ... then he remembered. It was poetry, something that Dervla had been singing yesterday ...

Then Pyke awoke with a curse on his lips as it all came back in a black, bitter rush, the rendezvous with Khorr, the handover, the sleepgas ambush ... and now here he was in some shadowed corner of the *Scarabus* where he spun lazily amid a cloud of angular objects that caught faint red glimmers from ... from a solitary emergency lamp over the hatch.

'Lights,' he said, voice hoarse in a dry throat. Nothing happened. 'Scar – can you hear or respond?'

Silence reigned in the gloom, which meant that the comms and/or the AI was offline.

Pyke coughed, swallowed, and realised he was in Auxiliary Hold 3, the place where they stored stuff that wasn't pointless and wasn't crucial but might be later. A variety of containers, plastic, card and fabric, drifted all around, some agape and surrounded by their contents, components, silver-wrapped edibles, unidentifiable disc things webbed together in tangled nets, trade goods maybe.

Well, he thought. *Still most definitely alive. But why would that pusbag Khorr do that? Why leave behind witnesses that could identify him . . .*

His imagination provided a variety of answers in shades of sadism and horror, and it was impossible not to think about the rest of the crew, Dervla especially. He had to get out of here, find out what had happened, whatever it was.

Several unsecured storage straps hung from the ceiling, drifting like strands of plaslon kelp. He stretched out and caught one with his fingertips, drew it into his hand, then hauled himself up to the ceiling and used the sling loops to get to the nearest bulkhead. Loose boxes and tubes and bags hung in his way, reminding him of the number of times he'd asked Ancil to sort through this guddle and clear out the really useless tat.

Racks lined the bulkhead. Pulling himself across them he steered towards the hatch, anchored himself with the metal handle and prodded the panel of touch controls. As expected, they were dead so he reached down and twisted the manual release. The doorseal popped and he felt a brief but definite puff of air as pressures equalised. Wedging his arm between the hatch handle and the doorframe he slowly forced the unlocked hatch open. With a sigh of relief he floated out into the ship's starboard passageway, glanced either way and saw the same emergency lights shedding meagre red halos amid the murk. There were no sounds, just a muffled quiet. He hooked one arm around a wall stanchion and paused to think back.

The trade rendezvous had been set for the environs of a snow-bound world called Nadisha II, in an unexploited system right on the border between Earthsphere and the Indroma Solidarity. The *Scarabus* had been in orbit for over an hour when Khorr's vessel finally arrived. The meeting had taken place in the *Scarabus*'s main hold, and was Pyke's first face-to-face with the client. Over subspace comms Khorr had claimed to be the descendant of higrav workers but in the flesh he was clearly much more, humanoid in appearance though possibly lab-coded for what headhunters referred to as non-civilian applications. Garbed in worn, leathery body armour, Khorr was easily seven feet tall, bald, and had a fighter's brawny physique, as did his two slightly less imposing henchmen. With the body armour and the heavy boots they resembled extras from the set of an exceptionally ultra-gothique glowactioner.

Pyke had taken the usual precautions: apart from Punzho and Hammadi, the rest of the crew were on hand to provide the deterrence of an armed welcoming committee. Khorr and his men had climbed out of their squat shuttle and strode leisurely over to where Pyke stood next to a waist-high crate on which sat the merchandise, resting within its shaped padding, a state-of-the-art milgrade subspace scanner-caster. When the three stopped a few feet short and crossed their arms, Pyke had heard one of Dervla's trademark derisive snorts from behind. Ignoring it, he had given a bright smile.

'Well, now, here we are, meeting at last. Very nice.'

Khorr, face like granite, grunted. His dark eyes had flicked right and left at the rest of the crew for a moment before fixing on Pyke again.

'This is the device?'

Pyke gave the scanner's case an affectionate pat.

'You see before you Sagramore Industries' latest and finest

scanner, factory-fresh and field-ready, conveyed to your waiting hands by my professional services. Which don't come
cheap.'

Khorr nodded, reached inside his heavy jacket and produced
a small flat case just the right size for holding a number of
credit splines. He held them out and waited until Pyke's fingers
were prying at the release button before saying, 'Here is your
payment!'

Now, floating weightless in the half-lit passage, Pyke remembered how his danger-sense had quivered right at that moment
but his hands had had a life of their own and were already
opening the small case. A faint mist had puffed out and even
though he had turned his face away from it he still caught a
whiff of something sweet. He had felt cold prickles scamper
across his face as he turned to shout a warning, but saw Ancil
and Win crumpling to the deck a second before grey nothing
shut down his mind.

And yet I'm still alive, he thought. *And that skagpile Khorr
really doesn't seem like the type to leave behind loose ends.*

Grabbing handholds on the bulkhead, he launched himself
along the passage towards Auxiliary Hold 4. He slowed and
floated over to the hatch window, gazed in and swore at the
sight. Hammadi's corpse hung there, adrift amid blue and
green spares boxes. Dead. The jutting tongue and noticeably
bulging eyes spoke of suffocation by depressurisation, gradual
not explosive, otherwise there would have been webs of burst
blood vessels and more grotesque damage. Hammadi was – had
been – chief engineer, a genius in his own way who had made
the *Scarabus*'s drives sing like a chorus of harmonised furies.

But all Pyke could think about was Dervla. *Dear god, please
no!*

Pyke pushed away from the hatch, turning towards a side
opening, the midsection lateral corridor which led to the

port-side passageway and the other auxiliary holds. He launched himself along it, driven to get it over with.

The quiet was eerie, unnerving. No mingled background murmur of onboard systems, no whisper of a/c, no low hum of micropumps, no faint sounds of crew activities, no music, no chattering news feeds. Just a numbed silence. But the air ... he sniffed, breathed in deep, and realised that it was not as stale as it should be. Some backup ventilation had to be running somewhere, but how and why? More unanswered questions.

It was just as gloomy over in the port-side passage. From the T-junction he glided across to Auxiliary Hold 2, grabbed the door stanchion and peered in through the hatch window. There was movement, and the surprised, bandito-moustached face of Ancil Martel glanced up from where he floated, crouched next to the manual override panel.

'Hey, chief,' came his muffled voice. 'It's jammed on this side. Can you ... ?'

Pyke nodded, pried aside the outer panel and after several sharp tugs the hatch seal gave with a familiar pop. A moment later the hatch was slid aside enough for Ancil to squeeze through.

'Those ratbags chumped us, chief.'

'I know.'

'But why are we still alive ... ?'

Pyke ground his teeth and shook his head. 'Hammadi's in Hold 4, dead from air-evac. I think that's what that gouger Khorr had in mind, for us all to be in our quarters and dead from some massive failure of the environmentals. But something must have interrupted the scum ... or he just made a bollocks of it and didn't know.' He glanced along at the next hatch. 'What about Hold 1? D'ye know if there's anyone in there?'

Ancil shrugged. 'Only came around a short while ago. Banged on the wall a few times but I didn't hear anything.'

'Better find out, then, hadn't we?'

So saying he pushed off along to Hold 1's hatch, grabbed its handle and swung in close to the window and ...

'Feck and dammit!' he snarled.

Inside, near the rear bulkhead, the bulky, brown-overalled form of Krefom, the Henkayan heavy weapons specialist, drifted a few feet off the deck, still as a statue, sightless eyes gazing out of that craggy impassive face. In Pyke's mind he imagined Khorr and his men moving through the ship, dragging the unconscious crew along, imprisoning them one by one.

'That son of a bitch is going to pay!'

With the last rage-filled word he slammed one palm and upper arm against the flat bulkhead, making a sudden loud bang which reverberated along the passage. Then he gasped as he saw the Henkayan's still form jerk convulsively, eyes staring wildly around him for a moment or two. Then he spotted the disbelieving Pyke and Ancil at the window, gave a big grin and pointed.

'He was sleeping?' Pyke said. 'Sleeping ... with his eyes open?'

A frowning Ancil shrugged. 'Maybe Henkayans can do that, chief. I've never seen him asleep.'

Then Krefom was at the hatch, knocking on the window with a big knuckly fist.

'Can't open this side, Captain-sir,' came his deep rough voice. 'Broke the emergency handle. Sorry.'

'We can crack it from here, Kref,' Pyke said.

Moments later the lock-seal was released and Krefom pushed the hatch aside with a single push of one mighty forearm. As the big Henkayan shouldered out of the hold he gave a gravelly chuckle and slapped palms with Ancil. Pyke intervened before they started swapping stories.

'Kref, I need to know what you have stashed in that cabinet up by the crew quarters.'

'Some good stuff – shockbatons, trankers, concussion and smoke nades, some light body armour ...' The Henkayan frowned for a moment. 'And a tangler. You think them skaghats is still on board, Captain-sir?'

'Dunno, Kref,' he said. 'But I'll not be taking any chances. Let's go.'

Together they floated back along the lateral corridor to the midpoint where a panel was yanked out to reveal an interdeck access shaft. Pyke went first, hand over hand up the cold alloy ladder. Near the top, where a hatch led to an alcove near the crew quarters, he heard voices and slowed. He made a silencing gesture to Ancil and Kref below him while listening intently. One voice was female and after a moment he smiled, recognising the unflappably sardonic tones of Win Foskel, their tactics and close combat expert. Pyke proceeded to snap open the hatch catches without trying to mute the noise, then gripped a ladder rung and pushed the hatch upwards.

'Stop right there!' came Win Foskel's voice. 'Surrender your weapons – toss them out, no smart moves or I'll drop something down that shaft that'll fry you from the inside!'

'And what would that be?' Pyke said. 'One of those grit-burgers from the galley?'

Ancil laughed further down as Pyke pushed himself up and into the corridor. A rueful Win tilted her tranker away and nodded, then grinned as Ancil was next to emerge. Her glittered dreads wavered as she drifted over to him. Out in the corridor proper, Pyke found Mojag, a skinny Human, Punzho the Egetsi, and Dervla who seemed oddly calm when her eyes settled upon him. He was about to ask how she was but there was something in her features, in fact something in the demeanour of them all. Then he realised what was wrong – three Humans, one Egetsi, but no portly, middle-aged reptiloid Kiskashin.

'Where's Oleg?' he said abruptly, even as he guessed.

Dervla floated over to him, grey eyes staring intensely from her pale face, her back-tied red hair looking almost black in the redness of the emergency light. She leaned in close and kissed him.

'That's for being alive,' she said. Then with disconcerting suddenness she slapped him. 'And that's for Mojag, because he's far too polite!'

'So you thought you'd take it upon yourself to act in his stead, is that it?'

Her gaze was full of smouldering anger but Pyke could see the hurt behind it. Oleg had been Mojag's copartner but in the four years since they joined the crew Dervla had built up bonds of friendship with the Kiskashin.

'You led us here, Bran,' she said.

'Where is he?' Pyke said.

'And it was your idea, your deal.'

'Where?'

Before she could answer, Mojag spoke from where he floated further along the darkened passage.

'Our cabin,' he said in a quiet voice. 'They must have sealed him in there then set the environmentals to evacuate. I don't know if he knew what was going on but when the temperature and pressure fell the hibernation reflex must have taken over.' Mojag breathed deeply for a moment and rubbed his face. 'He looks peaceful – he was probably in hibernation fugue when the air ran out.'

'But they could only do that if they got into the enviro controls first,' said Ancil, who then paused, and snapped his fingers. 'The auxiliaries in the main hold.'

Pyke nodded, anger leashed. 'You're right.'

'Wouldn't be any of them still aboard, would there?' said Ancil.

'No – once the deed was done, the filthy gougers would have left us for dead and scarpered, although we better be sure.' By now the crew were gathered round, listening. 'So what we're going to do is this – empty that armoury cabinet, make sure everyone's got something harmful and a torch, and maybe some armour, then we split up. Two groups, one sweeping the ship from bows to stern while the other heads for Engineering to see about getting the power and the environmentals back up and running. Okay? Let's get to it.'

The crew seemed subdued, faces masked with sombreness and ... something else. Sorrow over the loss of Hammadi and Oleg, certainly, but Pyke could sense some kind of reserve. Perhaps Dervla wasn't the only one laying blame at his door.

The armoury cabinet had only been partially looted. Unearthed from a carrycase was a solitary pulse-stunner which Kref passed to Pyke, who looked it over, checked the charge, then pulled out the extendable stock, locking it in place. It was an ugly, stubby weapon done up in a horrible mud-brown colour scheme but for shipboard skirmishing it was highly effective.

Pyke chose Kref and Win to go with him to Engineering, while the others accompanied Dervla forward to start at the bridge. The *Scarabus* was a small ship, yet the journey back along grav-less, low-lit passages to the aft section was tense, almost nerve-jangling. Pyke's group checked from the main hold back to the storerooms, the little machine-shop, the lower and upper generators and the aft maintenance niches, ending up at last in the narrow, split-level chamber that served as Engineering Control. It had taken twenty-odd minutes, and Dervla's group arrived just moments after them.

'Nothing,' she said, balancing a black-handled shockbaton on her shoulder. 'Not a sign, not a sound, not a soul.'

'Just as well,' said Pyke. 'Then first order of business is getting the gravity back on. Ancil, you think you can manage that?'

Ancil screwed one eye half shut thoughtfully. 'Eh, if Mojag lends me a hand.'

Mojag gave a wordless nod and climbed up to join Ancil at the long console where he sat, prodding boards awake.

'Time we got as close to the deck as possible,' he told the others. 'Don't want anyone copping a sprained ankle or worse.'

Lying flat out with his head propped up on one hand, Pyke thought about Mojag. He was a skinny guy in his middle years, dark brown eyes and short brown hair lightened by encroaching greyness. He and the Kiskashin, Oleg, had only joined the crew a year ago but the story went that back in his twenties, before he met Oleg, he had suffered head injuries so serious that nearly half his brain was replaced with a pseudo-organic cortical prosthesis. While the injury and subsequent operation erased great swathes of memory, the prosthesis permitted the replacement of fact and images as supplied by members of his family. Whenever the subject arose, Mojag insisted that before the injury he had been something of a planet-skipping, bed-hopping playboy, a claim most of the crew found amusing since the Mojag they knew was calm and meditative and self-possessed to the point of unreadability. Even now.

Once everyone was on the deck, Ancil gave a five-second countdown before bringing the grav-system back online. The return of body weight elicited a collective *oof!* a moment before the sound of crashes and clatters reverberated along the corridor outside and undoubtedly throughout the ship.

'The sound of our worldly goods rediscovering which way is down,' said Dervla as she got up on shaky legs.

With a dry laugh, Pyke forced himself upright. 'Right, then, Ancil – can you activate some sort of comms?'

Sitting slumped in one of the bucket seats by the monitors, Ancil frowned. 'Without oversight from Scar? I might be able to rig an open channel using the corridor voker network. You might have to shout, though.'

Scar was the name Pyke had conferred upon the ship's AI.

'Aye, do it,' Pyke said. 'We'll get Scar back online, and then maybe we can find out what's keeping the air breathable.'

'Bet it's another legacy system,' said Dervla. 'Y'know, the stuff that Voth dealer promised that he'd wiped from the substrate nodes. Six years since you bought this heap and we're still getting weird events like this.'

'Well, aye, but this time it's kept us alive,' he said. 'Perhaps yourself and Win could go up to the main hold and restart the enviros from up there?'

'What about Oleg and Hammadi?'

'We'll deal with them once the *Scarabus* is up and running, and we have the sensors and weapons primed and ready, not before.'

Dervla regarded him. 'Should we go to the bridge afterwards, relight the boards?'

'No, I'm heading there myself in a moment or two.' He offered a thin smile. 'Get Scar woken up and bright-eyed.'

'You and that AI are too close for my liking,' she said, arching one eyebrow. With that she headed out of the hatch, followed by Win who smiled and rolled her eyes before leaving.

Watching them go, Pyke thought, *Well, if I didn't know any better* ...

He turned to the others. Mojag and Ancil were still working at their elevated workstations, prodding and flicking screen glyphs and webby data arrays. Krefom the Henkayan was doing stretching exercises to firm up his relaxed muscles, while the Egetsi, Punzho Bex, was still slumped on the floor by the wall. At two and a half metres he was average height for an Egetsi, a lo-grav biped species whose homeworld lay in the confederal alliance of Fensahr.

Pyke squatted down beside him. 'How are you doing, Punzho?'

'I have been without gravityness for some time, Captain,' the Egetsi said in his soft, double-larynxed voice. 'I am with embarrassment at my body's incapacity. I should be aiding the recovery of our vessel.'

'Don't you worry yourself about that – you'll be right as rain in a short while. I just need to ask you something about when that Khorr and his goons came aboard; did ye sense anything from them at all, any kind of threat?'

The Egetsi's narrow features were a picture of anguish. Pyke had hired him a year and a half ago on account of his voluminous knowledge of rare and valuable trade goods (especially arts and antiquities). He also possessed some low-level psi abilities that had proved useful now and then.

'Captain, I am with sorrow. I detected nothing from them, nothing at all. They were very calm—'

'Might have been shielded,' chipped in Ancil from above.

'Or mind-trained,' Pyke said, frowning. *Which would make for a very interesting skillset for a bunch of supposed smugglers.*

He patted Punzho on the shoulder and stood.

'Look, if they were able to shield their minds then there was nothing you could have done. Doesn't matter how they did it. So don't be getting bent out of shape over it, all right?'

Punzho raised one long-fingered hand, reached inside his pale green overtunic and took out a small dark blue pouch. He loosened its ties, opened it and tipped out a number of small, intricately detailed figurines. Sorting through them he picked out one and returned the rest to the pouch.

'You are right, Captain,' he said. 'I must winnow out the true guilt from the false, and in the enduring time regain my strengths. Gst will help me see the path.'

Punzho was a follower of the Weave, a religion derived from the lives of nine holy seekers who lived at a time when the Egetsi had reached a tribal level of development. Believers memorised the Three Catechisms, the Three Inspirations, and the Three Obligations, and carried on their persons a pouch containing effigies representing the Nine Novices. The little figurines served as a focus for meditation on a wide range of topics, either on their own or in specific arrangements. Out of curiosity, Pyke had once asked Punzho if he ever employed the effigies as stand-ins for the crew but the Egetsi insisted that according to orthodoxy such a use amounted to allegory and was therefore inadvisable. Pyke wasn't sure how much of an answer that was.

'Good,' he said. 'And now I'm off to the bridge to get things humming there ... oh, and Kref, would you check the aft storage booths for breakages and damage? The sensors on some of the stackerbots are crocked so we may have to straighten the booths out by hand.'

'I can do that, Captain,' Kref said. 'There'll be some good lifting in that.'

Pyke grinned and left, following the starboard corridor to where a companionway led up to an offdeck up on a level with the high gantries that ran along either bulkhead of the main hold. A viewport gave a view down into the hold where he could see Win Foskel inspecting the innards of a tall, hinged maintenance panel. Of Dervla there was no sign. Turning, he glanced at the smaller, thicker viewport in the bulkhead which was part of the hull; there was only a dozen of them scattered around the *Scarabus*, and all were double-sealed by the shipwide shutdown. Getting them open again was high on his list, serving his need to see the stars. The Great Star-Forest, as his Granny Rennals used to call it, saying that there were many trails through the forest and not all of them were safe.

Well, you were right enough there, Gran. If I ever get back to Cruachan I'll have a few stories to tell you.

A couple of weak red emergency lamps scarcely pushed back the gloom on the bridge, otherwise broken by a scattering of glowing amber pinpoints. But Pyke moved with the ease of familiarity from station to station, switching on the six retrofitted overhead holomonitors. Silver radiance 'lit up the vacant operator couches and patches of the deck, while brighter luminance bloomed from console lamps and readouts as he started to bring the secondary systems online.

Moving over to the command console, he sat in his battered, leathery chair with the tilt-gimballed drink holder and watched the system indicators go green on his main holoscreen and felt a measure of satisfaction. The *Scarabus* was a Type-38 Ombilan transport, well known for its ruggedness, but the modifications he'd put in down the years had changed it from a reliable work-horse into a tough, fast multipurpose vessel capable of giving as good as she got. Now she practically amounted to an extension of himself and this shipwide reactivation was like a part of himself reawakening.

The AI Scar had not yet reached full-run status. From a standing start it was always the slowest to reach functionality, but since most of the secondary systems were now online Pyke decided to unseal the viewports, starting with the ones on the bridge. Three yard-long, foot-wide curves of lattice-toughened u-glass capable of withstanding direct hits from pulse and beam cannon. Now the outer seals retracted into their hull apertures, revealing the world they were orbiting, a large planet banded in shades of dark blue and grey and adorned with a thin and perfect, almost delicate-looking orbital ring.

That's not Nadisha II, he thought. *I should be looking at a pale blue world in the grip of an ice age, not this ... whatever it is.*

'Captain, where are we?' Win Foskel was standing in the entry hatch, staring in shock at the viewport. 'That's not the ice planet—'

'I know that, Win,' Pyke said calmly. 'Now, if you sit your-self down at the nav-station we'll work on finding out what the situation is, okay?'

'Okay,' she said shakily, going over to one of the couches. 'But that's a gas giant, and we were orbiting a class P habitable before—'

She was interrupted by a brief, tinny fanfare.

'At last,' Pyke muttered in relief. 'Win, I have a feeling that we're still in the same system but I'm sure the expert can figure it out. Scar, y'back in the saddle yet?'

'Hello, Bran. Cognitives are at 98 per cent ... now at 100 per cent.'

Pyke smiled. The AI's voice was composed and purposefully synthetic, yet with a feminine undertone.

'Excellent, Scar. Priority request – verify astrogational location.'

'Still trying to initialise main sensors, Bran. Crash power-down has damaged several low-level data conduits ... sensors initialised ... scanning now.'

Pyke glanced over at Win and said, 'Wait for it ...'

'Astropositional anomaly!' said the AI in a more urgent tone. 'Rebuilding stellar context array – gathering system comparators – matching with last known coordinates – Bran, I can confirm that the *Scarabus* is still in the Nadisha star system. However, we are now 594 megaklicks from our original position, in orbit around Nadisha IV, a mid-range gas giant—'

'What's our orbital status?'

'Ecliptical intermediate, high stability.'

'And just how long were we out?' Pyke said, thoughts racing.

'Seventeen hours and twenty-four minutes have elapsed since the crash powerdown event.'

He uttered a low whistle. 'That's quite a span of time – whatever they were up to they'll be long gone by now, I reckon.'

Seated in her couch, Win Foskel looked over her shoulder at him. 'Chief, I don't get it – if they wanted us dead why not just blow the drives instead of hauling us halfway across the system . . .'

'Look at it from their twisted, psychopathic side,' he said. 'Those scum wouldn't have known what precautions we might have taken, or who knew we were coming here . . . eh, Scar, was the ship ident still active through all that?'

'Yes, Bran, it was.'

Pyke nodded. 'Yes, they might have looked like low-brow brutes but they had some smarts among them. So anyone who came looking for us would lock onto our ident, follow it here only to discover that we were all victims of a tragic enviro-system malf. Which would keep attention away from the planet we were originally orbiting.'

He sat back in his high-backed couch, enjoying the creak of the blue tove-leather as he thought for a moment, wondering why the ship had been moved and what might be happening back at their original location. Then he said:

'Scar, what's our general status? Are we fit to fly?'

'Hull integrity is optimal, as are shields and secondary propulsion units.'

He gave a little nod and leaned forward to prod up a comm-link on the holoscreen.

'Ancil?' In the holoscreen Ancil Martel looked round. 'Ancil, I'm thinking we should set a course back to that wintry world we were orbiting before, see if we can find out what happened to our cargo and that gang of scum-sucking jackers. How are the drives behaving?'

'Sweet as a bell, chief. Field matrices should be ready in about ten minutes. Will we by any chance be making a microjump?'

'That's my thinking,' Pyke said, pausing when he realised that the seat next to Martel was empty. 'Where's Mojag?'

'Well, once the generators were up and running, everything was on track. Mojag knows his stuff, must have picked up a lot from, y'know, Oleg. So he says he has to take care of his quarters and I told him that's okay 'cos I'm on top of everything.' Ancil frowned. 'He seemed quieter than usual, but not himself.'

'What do you mean?'

'When I glanced over a few times I saw him shake his head slightly or make that agreeing sound he makes, but nobody was speaking to him, and once I definitely heard him mutter to himself.' He shrugged. 'Never saw him do that before.'

Pyke nodded. 'Mojag has a different load to carry than you or I. Got that chunk of hardmem in his head which makes dealing with grief complicated.'

'Mojag is a very mellow fellow,' said Ancil. 'He's usually a calming influence.'

'And I am sure that in time he'll find a way to cope with his loss,' Pyke said. 'In the meantime, how are those fields coming along?'

'A few minutes yet, chief, then we can shake the dust and be on our way.'

'Good man.' Then, sensing something he spun his chair round to see Dervla watching him from the port-side bridge hatch.

'You're really taking us back to the ice-world?' she said. 'Could be risky, going by what we've just been through.'

'I don't take kindly to being trussed and chumped by a bunch of overmuscled leatherboys,' he said.

'Ah, so this is about your ego. Mmm, glad we're clear on that.'

Smiling, Pyke poked one of the comm buttons. 'Scar, set a microjump course back to Nadisha II, if you please.'

'Yes, Bran. I shall be ready to commence a shipwide thirty-second countdown in two minutes.'

'Thanks.' He met Dervla's gaze. 'And no, my flower, this is not about my ego. I take on jobs for business reasons, not thrills, and I think I'm quite entitled to remedy the situation.'

'And get us into . . .' She shrugged. 'Okay, so what's the plan?'

'Well, as we are in possession of neither the comm-scanner nor the payment we were due from that pus-stain Khorr, the idea is to return to the scene of the crime and see what clues we can find, ion trails, any stay-behind pieces, that kind of thing.'

In the background Scar's voice announced the imminent hyperspace microjump and started counting down.

'So we're going after the scumbucket,' Dervla said. 'While not having any idea of what force he might have at his disposal. Y'know, there is such a thing as cutting your losses.'

'And there's such a thing as self-respect!' he came back. 'In any case, we actually need the money to keep the *Scarabus* operational . . .'

At that moment the ship's hyperdrive kicked in, bending the subquantal structures of space-time in very specific ways. Pyke felt the familiar squeeze-vertigo effect as it swirled through him, but he only paused for a moment or two.

' . . . and . . . AND – it might be nice to buy some of that stuff they call "food". I'm led to believe that it actually has a taste, unlike that cyclo rubbish we've been . . .'

He stopped when Dervla, wide-eyed and uneasy, pointed over at the bridge viewports.

'Is that really . . . ?'

Even as Pyke swivelled his chair to look, the ship AI spoke.

'Planetary anomaly detected – stat conflicts across all main parameters – full macroscan in progress.'

Nadisha II was a pale blue world, its continents buried beneath snow and blizzards that weren't due to start receding for another half a millennium. But what Brannan Pyke was seeing through the viewports was something completely different, a darkened world, swathed in angry cyclonic weather patterns. As he stared he felt a strange urge to laugh.

'Scar, what the devil are we looking at?'

'Scan results are incomplete but preliminary assessment is confirmed – although this planet occupies exactly the same orbital location as Nadisha II, and possesses the same angular velocity, it is another planet altogether.'

Pyke nodded judiciously.

'Well, you don't see that every day.'

CHAPTER TWO

Half an hour later everyone was on the bridge, seated at the workstations, heads tilted back to regard the ceiling-mounted holodisplays, apart from Pyke who was watching the one at his own console.

'Ready when you are, Scar,' he said.

'Very well, Bran. I shall begin.'

All the holodisplays switched from webby anims to the brighter standard planetary summary. A pale blue world spun at the centre, flanked by stat tables, atmospheric analysis, biosphere data, climactic overviews, mean temperature gradients and other parameters.

'This is Nadisha II,' the ship AI said. 'A habitable world currently deep in the trough of an ice age that recurs every seventy thousand years – the world about which this vessel assumed orbit some twenty-point-eight hours ago.'

Abruptly the image changed to show a different world, its ashen face mottled with dull brown patches and dark grey streaks and overlaid with a violent, cyclonic weather system, angry swirls of storm surging across the seas and land masses. The stat summaries were dynamic and augmented by supplementary columns which moved forward every thirty seconds or so, providing additional info from air, water and soil analyses.

'This, however, is the world around which we are orbiting

now. It is 7.9 per cent larger by overall surface area than Nadisha II but has 21.3 per cent less oceanic surface—'

'Is that a city?'

Win Foskel was indicating a section of the planet's surface that she'd magnified, and which Scar quickly shared across the other displays. Pyke leaned forward and saw, half obscured by a bank of cloud, the unmistakable regular shapes and grids of some kind of metropolis. Also highly evident were the clusters and lines of bomb craters.

'Yes,' said Scar. 'Image analysis reveals the remains of extensive areas of advanced development, patterns of usage consistent with standard models of residential conurbations and built-up urban centres, as well as transport conduits and hubs. Similar habitation nodes are widespread but deserted, at least in the swathe of planetary surface I have been able to scan.'

Punzho Bex raised a long finger to point at the unfolding desolation.

'It looks as if war has wrecked this world,' he said. 'Scar, have the usual delights of battle been unleashed here?'

'If you refer to environmental degradation, that is correct. I despatched a small disposable probe as part of the macroscan, and the data recovered is undeniable. Not only is the environment highly irradiated but the air is almost a stew of lethal biological agents. Yet the long-range biosensors have picked up lifesigns of small creatures, mainly in scattered packs, probably scavengers. Most prevalent form of vegetation seems to be a type of clinging creeper. Rivers, lakes and coastal water stretches are highly polluted—'

'Scar, have you come up with any ideas to explain why this radioactive ball of mud is here and Nadisha II ain't?' Pyke frowned. 'Y'know, any idea backed by what you've discovered so far.'

'Sorry, Bran, but thus far I have insufficient data with which to construct a reasoned hypothesis. Speculation would seem to be the only method open to us.'

'Fine, speculate away.'

'I would still require parameters within which to evolve such a conjecture.'

Pyke drummed his fingers on the console. 'Okay. So tell me, are there any signs of sentient beings still alive down there, communities, bases, anything?'

'Thus far I have directly scanned less than 18 per cent of the surface area. I have detected no transmissions, no subspace casts, no power generation signatures, no variations in the surface temperature that would indicate outlets from hidden habitats, and no lifeforms that meet sentient behaviour profiles.'

'So, essentially it's a lifeless, radioactive ball of mud,' Pyke said. 'Just what I needed. Scar, have you also scanned for drive traces in the immediate vicinity?'

'Several vessels have been operating here, and there is one thrust emission profile that matches that of Khorr's ship. But all drive traces in the greater gravimetric shell are fragmented or dispersed. Any explanation would be speculative but I have detected a strange residual resonance on the subspace boundary, implying that something capable of generating immensely powerful inertial fields was manoeuvring through this system, causing a muddying of the nearby real-space locale ...'

Pyke's mood slumped on hearing this. 'You're saying there's no way we can track down that scumbag Khorr?'

'I'm afraid that there's no trail to find.'

Not good, Pyke thought. *Damn – are we going to have to go back to Tajnap Orbital? We might pick up some leads on Khorr and his ship, if we're lucky, but the docking and fuelling fees would really eat into what's left of the funds. Dear mother of god, if we come up empty-handed I could be faced with having to sell off the loaders, maybe even the shuttle ...*

He suddenly became aware that the others were watching him.

'So, Scar, about this planet – are you saying that it's totally uninhabitable, not a chance of finding real, living intelligent life?'

'My sensors have now scanned 19.3 per cent of the surface without finding evidence of such, Bran. However, it cannot be ruled out.'

'You know, I can't help thinking about how that gobshite Khorr went to a fair bit of trouble to divert attention away from here, so' – he swung his gaze across the crew – 'I say we let Scar finish her survey and see what crops up.'

There were nods at this, a couple of shrugs, and Dervla giving him a thoughtful look.

'Good,' he went on. 'Scar, how long will it take to complete this scan of yours?'

'Two hours and fifty-five minutes, maintaining current level of detail analysis.'

'Fine, you go ahead and finish it.' Pyke got to his feet. 'In the meantime, we can get on with putting the stores in order.'

'But chief,' said Ancil. 'Shouldn't we try and figure out how the original Nadisha II turned into that poisonous hell?'

Now halfway to the hatch, Pyke paused. 'Thought it was obvious,' he said. 'Someone came along, swapped that nice, clean icy world and left a toxic, bombed-out heap of rubble in its place. Why – do you have a different notion?'

'Well . . . no, but aren't you interested in who did it and why?'

'Not especially. Anyone slinging around that kind of tech is someone whose way I plan to stay out of. Khorr on the other hand tricked us and tried to kill us, and I intend to get hold of what's rightfully ours.'

'And what if Khorr is involved with these planet thieves?' said Dervla. 'What then?'

'Can't see it myself. Why would ultra-high-tech planet-jackers hire a thug like Khorr to get hold of a gadget from a less developed civilisation? No, my bet is that he's working for a gang of ware-runners looking to stay one step ahead of the Earther-uglies. Either way, we're all going to have to be just a bit extra-deadly!

'So while Scar is working, I suggest that we do the same and find some useful chores to occupy ourselves for the next couple of hours. Kref, you're with me – we really need to sort out the storage booths.'

Minutes later Pyke and the Henkayan were back aft, trying to get a reckoning of what needed attention. He had Kref do some restacking of the lighter crates while he worked on the stackerbot in the armoured storage where heavy-duty items like hull plates, drive couplings and weapon mountings were kept. About half an hour later Mojag appeared at the open hatch and said, 'Captain, can I have a word?'

'Of course – step into my office.'

Mojag picked his way around an angled heap of dislodged hull plates while Pyke upended a crate for him to sit on. He sat down, legs together, hands on his bony knees, his sombre gaze angled down at the deck. Pyke, tinkering with the innards of the stackerbot, waited. After a moment Mojag cleared his throat.

'Captain, there's something I need to tell you ...'

'If it's too upsetting to deal with Oleg's remains, I can get Kref or Ancil to—'

'Oh no, I've dealt with that already,' said Moja. 'Wrapped it in poly and stuffed it in a stasis drawer in sickbay. It's something else that you need to know. About Oleg.'

About Oleg? Pyke had thought that Mojag was about to ask for severance when they next hit port, but now he was puzzled.

'Okay, I'm listening.'

Mojag smiled faintly. 'Do you remember when you hired us nearly two years ago?'

'During that stopover at Darien Orbital, yes, I remember.'

'I made my hire-us pitch, and gave you a summary of our skills, and those involving my data implant.' He tapped the side of his head. 'Everything I told you about the prosthesis was absolutely truthful, but I didn't really go into detail on the full range of its functions. Sure, there is a huge amount of storage in there – I have all the high European classical music of the eighteenth and nineteenth centuries, for example, and it takes up a tiny fraction of the main store.'

Pyke regarded him. 'I'm assuming that this omission has not been the cause of any difficulties in our dealings.'

Mojag's eyes widened. 'No, no, Captain, not in the least!'

'Okay, so what's this got to do with Oleg?'

Mojag's gaze wandered off a little and he gave a faintly sardonic half-smile. 'Remember that cargo of genadapt cow zygotes we smuggled to Floresta about a year ago?'

Pyke smiled wryly at the memory. The zygotes had been stored in waist-high stasis canisters, 400 of them, which they'd collected from a secluded biolab on a grey-law world in the 4th Modynel and ferried across the Earthsphere border to a comparatively new Human colony world called Floresta. All went smoothly after the pickup, no hitches at all until they touched down on Floresta. The agreed drop-off point was near the mouth of a wooded valley and they had offloaded about a third of the consignment when unseen hostiles opened up with small-arms fire. Mojag and Oleg had been driving the loaders and were forced to take cover while rounds and beam pulses flew either way with the *Scarabus* caught in the middle. Boundary disagreements between their client and his well-armed neighbour had erupted into a full-blown range war earlier that day and it took a nerveracking hour before the return fire persuaded the neighbour's forces to withdraw.

'Yes, that was a touch more arduous than I would have cared for,' Pyke said. 'But we were still well paid for our trouble.'

'And I knew, and Oleg knew, that risk is part of the job,' Mojag said. 'But not long after, Oleg sat me down and asked me for a favour, a very specific favour that only I could fulfil.'

'With your data implant?' Pyke said.

Mojag nodded. 'After that little episode you diverted to a system on the Gerlan border . . .'

'Erjef-Sessax, that amalgamated habcity in the asteroid belt.'

'Yes, big maze of a place,' Mojag said. 'Me and Oleg asked around and eventually found a corto-services vendor who agreed to deepscan Oleg's brain and create a meta-fractal copy of his mind-state—'

'Wait a second—'

'—which was then transloaded into my data implant.' Mojag regarded Pyke warily. 'So strictly speaking, Oleg is still alive. In a sense.'

Pyke stared at him for a moment or two then burst out laughing, his thoughts caught between surprise, disbelief and a momentary dash of the absurd.

'Sorry, Mojag – not making fun or being disrespectful,' he said. 'But you're serious – you've been walking around all these months with a copy of Oleg in your head? Why would you – why would he do such a thing? Did he think he was going to die?'

'He wasn't expecting death, Captain, despite the inherent risks, and he knew that you always kept our safety in mind.' Mojag gazed upwards and sighed. 'He just wanted to increase the chances of finishing his Spursong.'

'And what would that be?'

'A long poem describing all the key moments of a Kiskashin's life. The Kiskashin are an ancient race with several distinct branches and Oleg's branch, the Idekri, are scrupulous about maintaining the Spursong tradition.'

Pyke was nonplussed. 'This copy of Oleg you've been carrying around all this while – it's been writing poetry?'

'Not just that,' Mojag said. 'We converse on many subjects—'

'How?' Pyke said. 'Are you talking with him now? Is he listening to us?'

'He can observe what I observe, and we usually meet and chat in a virtual meeting place I've set aside in my data implant.'

Pyke smiled and nodded, despite a continuing puzzlement. 'Well, I can truthfully say that I never imagined that I would ever have a conversation like this with, well, with anyone. I mean, I know about the AI companion implants they have on Earth, although I haven't seen many lately.'

'They went severely out of fashion after the Battle of Darien and the failed AI coup in the Hegemony,' said Mojag.

'Just as well,' Pyke said. 'Gives me the crawls just thinking about it.'

'This is nothing like that, Captain,' Mojag said. 'Oleg was – is a friend.'

'Yes, I get that. Have you spoken to Dervla about it?'

'Not yet. I'm unsure of how to proceed.'

'Be straight with her – that usually works. And I'm glad that you came to tell me as well – although I should warn you that I won't be paying you two shares!'

Mojag grinned. 'Furthest thing from my mind, Captain.'

At which point Scar's voice spoke from the vokers out in the corridor.

'Captain Pyke to the bridge – this is a command alert.'

Stackerbot repairs forgotten, Pyke got to his feet. 'Scar,' he said loudly. 'What's new?'

'A few moments ago my sensors picked up a compressed communications burst from a location on the planet's surface. Linguistic subsystem is currently analysing . . . '

'Right, I'm on my way.'

With Mojag hard on his heels Pyke left the storage booth and hurried along to the companionway leading for'ard. A minute or two later he was striding onto the vacant bridge.

'Any luck with that translation, yet, Scar?'

'The comm-burst is a verbal message but the syllabic groups have no match in my database. The syntactic analysis, however, strongly implies a plea for aid. The voice-stress evaluation corroborates.'

'So what's happening around down there?' Pyke said as he dropped into his leather couch, which creaked in protest. 'Any sentient lifeforms?'

'No Bran, but there is a group of lesser creatures gathered around a hillside structure which could be shielding occupants from being scanned. From the same location I am also detecting what could be energy-weapon discharges.'

Suddenly Pyke was back on his feet, feeling invigorated.

'Right, rescue mission.' He thumbed the shipwide on his console. 'Kref, Win, this is the captain. Get yourselves to the shuttle bay and break out the heavy gear.' He looked up. 'Scar, how dangerous is the environment down there?'

'The hillside structure is sited on the periphery of a ruined city which seems to have avoided being hit by nuclear weapons. The weather system, however, still blows around a variety of toxic risks, weak residues of aerosolised biochem agents, even pulverised dust carrying motes of radioactive material. I should recommend full hazmat rigs, Bran, but if you decide to use just face-breathers and ensure to leave no skin uncovered you should suffer no ill effects. As long as planetside activity is kept as brief as possible.'

'Got it. Anything on that translation yet?'

'Sorry, Bran – I'm not any further forward. I need to converse with a native speaker in order to gain a basic understanding.'

'See what I can do about that.' Pyke turned to Mojag who had been peaceably observing the developing situation. 'Mojag, don't forget to let Dervla in on the secret.'

Mojag looked reluctant. 'How do you imagine she might react?'

Pyke shrugged. 'Ah, the mysteries of a woman. I'll tell you this, though – if you don't tell her and she finds out later it might not go too well for you.'

'I take your point with gratitude.'

Pyke grinned and headed for the bridge hatchway.

When he reached the main hold he encountered Dervla coming out of the double sliding doors.

'Scar tells me that you're taking the shuttle down to the poisonous mudball on some daft rescue mission,' she said, the hardness in her eyes belying her composed smile.

'I cannot tell a lie,' Pyke said, hurrying past her. 'There's folks down there who need help, our skilful, well-armed help!'

Inside, the shuttle had been lowered from the shadowy fuel and refit area above the launch ramp. Close by, Kref and Win were standing next to a big pull-out rack, trying on pieces of body armour.

'I thought about getting at you for putting your own crew in mortal danger,' Dervla said, following him in. 'But truth is, they're just as crazy as you are.'

'What a thing to say about your crewmates,' said Win Foskel as she snapped a magazine up into an assault rifle.

'Well, naturally I meant crazy in a good way.'

Kref paused from filling a backpack with extra ammunition, his broad forehead creased with a frown.

'Am I crazy? Why does Dervla think we're crazy, Captain?'

Pyke shook his head. 'It's okay, it's not you she thinks is crazy. However, I would certainly be crazy to go on this mission without those Lewison heavy pistols which are hanging right next to you.'

The Henkayan chuckled. 'With the explosive rounds?'

'More firepower is better than less.'

By now Pyke had strapped body armour onto his torso, arms and legs. The holstered guns that Kref tossed to him were claw-bonded to either hip. He almost felt invulnerable, encased in all this gear, but he knew that he would be slower on his feet.

Yeah, well, looking like Captain Dangerbad is one thing, staying alive is another.

'Okay,' he said. 'Time to go. Scar, until we get back Dervla is in command.'

'Understood, Bran.'

Dervla crossed her arms. 'So do I get to keep the ship if you don't come back?'

As they reached the shuttle's gaping hatch Pyke glanced back over his shoulder. 'Sorry, that's not what it says in my will.'

'You have a will?'

He laughed. 'Keep an eye on things on the bridge, dear heart. Don't want to be caught by any surprises.'

With that he tugged the heavy hatch down and thumbed the autoseal. Bolts clunked and the hydraulics made the hatch airtight. Then he turned to regard Kref and Win, the hulking Henkayan standing over the diminutive, almost elfin Human, yet from past experience he knew that it would be difficult to say who was the more deadly in combat.

'Ready to ride to the rescue, you crazies?'

Kref snorted, and Win shrugged.

'As ever,' she said.

Out in the hold, the pre-launch systems screened off the shuttle bay with layered forcefields designed to prevent atmosphere leakage while shielding against any thrusters backwash. From a monitoring recess in the hold bulkhead, Dervla watched the underside bay doors part and the wedge-nosed shuttle swing down on the guide rails. Grips snapped open, rear manoeuvring thrusters emitted bright, half-second bursts, and the craft was gone.

'They should be okay, do you think?'

She glanced up to see Mojag standing between the open entry doors.

'Well, they're lugging enough heavy weapons for a small war.' She paused. 'But this hunt for Khorr is cracked. I think that bastard is connected to this planet-jacking operation somehow, and Bran is going to get us all killed.' She shook her head, reining in her temper.

'Hopefully not today,' Mojag said.

'Yeah, just a day's worth of good luck is all I'm asking for at the moment.'

'Eh, Dervla, was wondering if you can spare a few minutes – there's something I need to tell you.'

'Well, I have to get to the bridge to monitor the feeds for Bran and bear witness to his mighty triumph over some mutant radioactive mouse or the like – eh, can you tell me about it on the way?'

'I can certainly do that.'

So he did. By the time they reached the bridge she was listening with uneasy fascination to the explanation of how the Oleg in Mojag's head was just as aware of events as he was. And how when the real Oleg was found dead, the Oleg-copy had wanted his existence announced straight away, thinking that this would forestall grief and upset since he was actually still alive, in a way. Mojag, however, had thought this inadvisable.

'I felt at first that our crewmates would need time to come to terms with the loss of the flesh-and-blood Oleg,' he said. 'And then, after a while, we could reveal the copy's existence. But in the light of the changing situation we decided to let the captain in on our secret, and he said to tell you.'

By now Dervla was seated at Pyke's console, trying to clear away some of the cans, food trays, schematic flexis, miscellaneous components and trick-tools.

'I think your instinct was right,' she said. 'The others wouldn't see a copy of him as being the same as the original.' She frowned. 'And of course, he's hearing all this from me as well ... just how like him is it?'

Mojag's smile was a little sad. 'It was a highly detailed scan down to the meta-fractal range – in my mind it sounds and speaks and thinks exactly like him.'

'But doesn't he feel—'

The AI Scar's voice interrupted her.

'Dervla, there is an incoming comm-feed from the shuttle.'

'I'll take it here, Scar.'

The command console's holodisplay winked on to show a side view of the shuttle's cockpit. Pyke was closest and gave a rakish smile while Win waved from the copilot's station.

'So glad you could join us,' Pyke said. 'In the interests of fast engagement, we opted for a plunge re-entry so we should reach the target location in about twenty minutes.'

'Plunge re-entry,' Dervla said. 'I bet that was fun.'

In the display, Win Foskel rolled her eyes. 'You have no idea.'

'If we could keep the mutinous commentary for later,' Pyke said. 'We have a mission to carry out, so, while we manoeuvre for approach, Dervla will coordinate with Scar on the wider picture, using her judgement to spot any potential hazards.'

'Yes, my captain,' Dervla said, giving a quick salute. 'Dervla shall.'

'I'll be remembering this mockery when it comes to reckoning the bonuses,' Pyke said. 'Now can we get on with it?'

Glancing round, Dervla saw Mojag perched on the edge of the command console, smiling and shaking his head. Sharing the smile, she shrugged and went about the task in hand. Scar provided additional screen layers detailing environmental and lifeform readings at the target location as well as local and regional overviews. Also, there were sensor scans from both the planet's near-space environs and the wider system – and as far as she could see there was no threat-level activity, no sign of intruders or anomalous presences. If something sinister was happening, it was happening somewhere else.

'Nothing to report,' Dervla said on the open comm-link. 'No contacts.'

'Any change at the target location?' said Pyke.

'The local scan says that the predator pack lost a few to weaponsfire but others have joined.'

'Sounds shady. Right, we're still some minutes out so while we get the masks and headcams ready I'll need you to stay on-station.'

'Not got anything else to do,' she said. 'Don't worry, we got you covered.'

As attention within the shuttle shifted to landing prep, Punzho and Ancil arrived on the bridge together. A muttered exchange between them was cut off by Ancil with a palm gesture and the word 'later'. The tall Egetsi nodded then came over to kneel by the command console, long hands folded and resting on the edge of the desk surround. Ancil stood back a few feet, leaning against the bulkhead.

'Shuttle is seventy-three seconds from touchdown,' said the AI. 'Switching to headcam feeds.'

The single steady view of the shuttle cockpit was replaced by three bleached, grainy, jerky visuals from the headgear cams. Dervla had had to deal with these feeds before and adjusted their filters individually before arriving at a measure of shared clarity.

'I'll be taking point,' said Pyke, now looking into Win's cam. 'Kref and Win will be on rear flanks.' He fiddled with his mask, setting it firmly into position, then gave a thumbs-up.

'Sensors show four of the lesser lifeforms gathering around the shuttle, Bran,' said Scar.

'Okay, time we chased off the wildlife,' Pyke said, punching the release code into the hatch controls.

The hatch was hardly open when a slender, long-necked scaly head thrust itself through the gap, closely followed by a skinny taloned limb, and a second.

The view from all three headcams jerked about while everyone started shouting, Kref and Win urging Pyke to just shoot the thing, shoot it now. Pyke was yelling back that he didn't want to wreck the hatch while holding it shut on the snapping, lashing beast. Through the clamour, Dervla heard Win say, 'Screw this!' as the cam-view ducked under Pyke's arms and angled up at the intruder. Then she raised her laser carbine, shoved it against the bottom of the creature's neck and pulled the trigger. With the first hot white burst the thing shrieked and with the second it writhed in agony as it tore itself back outside. Dervla thought that Pyke would then tug the hatch shut – instead he pushed it open and dived through, guns blazing.

She exchanged an appalled look with Mojag before going back to the headcam displays.

That first frantic encounter set the tone for the intense minutes that followed. Pyke's assault left two of the scaled creatures blown apart and scared any others off into the cover of smashed buildings. The shuttle was parked on level ground at the foot of a cracked, rubble-strewn road that swept up a hillside past yet more near-levelled ruins. Pyke pointed with one of his heavy pistols at what looked like a curved canopy jutting from a rocky outcrop shouldering out of the hill halfway up.

'That's the place,' he said. 'We better hurry . . .'

'Hostiles,' said Win, who was looking at a handheld tactical sensor. 'The two we missed.'

The two that Pyke had killed both had six long jointed legs, which strongly suggested that they were ground dwellers. The next pair launched themselves from atop crumbling sections of wall, gliding to the attack on stretched-out membranes. Kref and Win were quick enough to burn them down in mid-flight, and at Dervla's request Win went up close with her headcam, revealing that they had four limbs and shorter necks.

They fought more of the lizard things on their way uphill, and almost every encounter introduced another variety. Some had four legs and a long, lashing tail; others had two small grabbing forelimbs and muscular rear legs that allowed them to make huge leaps (a sub-variant had longer, more powerful legs on which it could run with unnerving swiftness). Other types had two front legs and a serpent-like body, or bony horns jutting from shoulders or spine, or ...

Teratogeny had clearly run riot through the lizards' gene pool, whether via radioactivity or some vile bio-vector engineered to weaken and distort the bonds of DNA. Dervla had seen the effects of something similar on some Gomedra nomads who unsuccessfully tried to hire Pyke and the *Scarabus* during a job-stop at Blacknest a couple of years ago. Their forebears had been victims of a mutagen attack, the consequences of which had been terrible, as was their hunger for vengeance.

These mutated lizards, while fast and savage, were also stupid enough to be shot or burnt down before they got too close. The anxiety shared by Dervla, Mojag, Ancil and Punzho eased as their shipmates saw off all attacks and drew close to the hillside refuge where the distress signal was coming from. All three cam-feeds swung in watchful arcs to left and right, although Pyke's was the first to show just who they had come to rescue. In the shadows below the curved canopy a barrier of stone slabs, corroded metal poles and battered containers had been built across a wide entrance. Dead lizards lay in heaps before it and their blood spattered the stones.

Forms moved in the gloom beyond. Dervla watched with rapt attention, both eager and wary at what might await Pyke and the others. Suddenly a dark humanoid hand gripping a slender-barrelled pistol jabbed out through a gap in the barricade, pointing at Pyke. The hand's dark hue, Dervla saw, was due to some kind of tight-fitting glove, while the weapon was levelled unwaveringly at the captain's head.

A voice spoke a brief string of harsh syllables, impatient and commanding. Pyke holstered his own sidearms and raised one hand.

'My name is Captain Pyke, we come in peace to rescue you, blah blah blah – Scar, please tell me that you've cracked this language, otherwise this might turn ugly, I'm thinking.'

'I have incorporated those new words, Bran, but I am no closer to certainty—'

'Well, if we don't come up with some way to communicate I might as well sing all ten verses of "A Donegal Lass There Was" and see if that gets us any further forward. Y'know, that or just turn round and go back to the fracking shuttle!'

On the bridge, Mojag uttered a low whistle. Dervla grinned and shook her head. 'I've heard worse, trust me.'

Then she leaned forward, attention caught by some exchange of raised voices taking place behind the barricade. The argument swiftly abated, however, and was followed by the sound of a throat being cleared.

'Spik yau nim!'

Over the feed Win said, 'What was that? What did he say?'

Another quarrelsome babble came from the hidden shadows, then the voice spoke again.

'Speyk yar nerm!'

'That was Anglic,' Pyke said over the feed. 'Did that sound like Anglic?'

'Sounded like he was asking you to speak your name,' said Dervla. 'That might be preferable to ten verses of "A Donegal Lass There Was", eh?'

'Thank you for that,' Pyke said, ignoring the sound of Win stifling her laughter as he turned back to the barricade. 'Greetings – my name is Captain Brannan Pyke, and we followed your distress beacon with the aim of helping you off this wreck of a world.'

There was no response and on Win's cam Pyke turned and shrugged. Before he could say a word the voice spoke again.

'Moar.'

'Eh? You want me to keep gabbing . . .'

'Moar!'

'Okay, keep the head – right. So, as I said, I am captain of the good ship *Scarabus* whose expert and courteous crew ensure the smooth and efficient operation of all shipboard activities . . .'

On the bridge, Ancil and Mojag were standing to attention and making mock salutes to the holoscreen and each other. Dervla had to struggle to keep from laughing out loud.

' . . . and as you see we're all quite well armed; in fact, certainly well enough to take care of your local vermin problem – and to tell you the truth I don't know how much longer I can keep up this bloody jabbering . . .'

Someone behind the barricade shouted. Other voices answered, some in querying tones. The weapon aimed at Pyke was withdrawn and a moment later a section of the barricade was dragged aside, metal edges dragging on concrete. A figure came out, a very human-looking sentient wearing battered body armour seemingly collected from several differing sources. He was brawnily built and slightly shorter than Pyke, had a thick head of black hair and a neatly clipped black beard. One hand held the pistol from before, steadily couched at waist level, covering Pyke and the others. A second and a third humanoid stepped out of the shadows, both of a similar physique and likewise attired, with pistols similarly deployed. Overall they reminded Dervla of Khorr and his men, with their brute, low-tech air.

Then something like a wheelchair emerged from the gap, only it was more like a large inclined cradle in which a strange figure lay. Dervla adjusted the holodisplay, sharpening the picture quality as the reclining figure was steered over towards Pyke by a fourth bearded humanoid. Unlike the first three, this one's hair and beard were decorated with bright red streaks.

Although the cradled figure was bundled up in grey and dark green robes Dervla could tell that this was a much shorter creature than the others, a metre and a half tall at most. Its face was narrow and shrivelled and the skin appeared sallow and unwell. Drooping eyelids made it – possibly he – seem only partially awake but as the wheeled cradle stopped before Pyke they opened fully and sharp eyes stared up. Dervla frowned – not only was the stretcher case a different species from its bearded companions, it had also been subject to radical augmentation. Arms stirred beneath the crumpled robes and folds slipped aside to reveal its hands, resting atop its midriff. But instead of hands they were clusters of finely engineered rods and intricate instruments, some clad in glass or sections of a black material, others etched with circuitry or bearing slender, parallel branchings, or wound with tiny wires that trailed back up into voluminous sleeves. Gently restless motions gave an impression of fingers, adding to the unsettling sight.

'English is … the language,' said the small, reclining figure in a deep voice marred by laboured wheezing. 'Your language, Captain. Am I correct?'

'It is, after a fashion.'

The wheelchair's passenger turned his head and muttered a few words to the man who had pushed him out from the redoubt. The man with the red-streaked beard listened and gave only a nod while giving the three Humans a dark assessing gaze.

'This is G'Brozen Mav,' the small figure said. 'He leads us. I am Toolbearer Hechec, Captain. May I ask how you come to be here on this ravaged world?'

Watching from the bridge, Dervla said, 'Who calls it English any more? Bit old-fashioned, eh?'

Pyke, though, ignored her comments.

'We were following the trail of a scumbag who killed one of my crew and cheated us out of our property, and the trail led us to more closely examine this planet ...' He gave a dry laugh. 'Which is an odd place, to put it mildly.'

'Who was this murderer, if I might ask?'

'He called himself Khorr, a big muscly bastard ...'

At the mention of the name, G'Brozen Mav straightened, his expression suddenly alert and grim. He spoke briefly to Toolbearer Hechec who gave a wordless nod then addressed Pyke again.

'Khorr is known to us,' Hechec said. 'We have much cause to hate him. His purposes and loyalties have been revealed to us and we would be able to lead you to him. In return we would humbly ask for transport to a suitable world in this locale, and perhaps some medical attention for one of our number.'

Dervla nodded, muttering, 'Yes, we must.'

Pyke also nodded. 'We would be more than happy to get you off this mudball,' he said. 'And is it yourself that needs the doctoring?'

Hechec smiled. 'In the course of our adversities I acquired a wound to my leg.' He tapped the cradling frame with one of those bizarre instrument fingers. 'We were forced to improvise.'

'He must be valuable to Gibrozy whatshisname, then,' said Dervla.

'We have a few handy devices aboard the *Scarabus*,' Pyke said. 'I'm sure we can do something for you.'

'We are grateful. Is your vessel nearby?'

'The *Scarabus* is in orbit,' Pyke said. 'Our shuttle is waiting further down that road. By the time we return to the ship the rest of my crew will have quarters ready for you.'

'We are in your hands, Captain, and in your debt.'

The combined groups moved out from under the canopy's shadow with weapons ready and eyes scanning the shattered buildings to either side. Back on the bridge, Dervla turned to Mojag and Ancil.

'Well, now, looks like we've got new passengers coming aboard. And I don't think they're the paying kind.'

CHAPTER THREE

With an upgraded Tesla pistol in one hand and a frost grenade in the other, Sam Brock barrelled through the rusty hatch and caught the four Drakomandos by surprise. The grenade caught the furthest-away pair perfectly, slowing their charge to a slow, crunching, fume-wreathed trudge. The nearer pair she nailed with a volley-spread from the Tesla pistol. Webs of deadly electrical discharge crackled and lit up the anteroom's corroded bulkheads with actinic flickers.

The slo-mo Drakomandos were thawing out and getting closer so Sam switched to the haarpoon, a long-barrelled weapon that launched barbed spines of ice. She fired, caught one in its shoulder with a force that threw it backwards and impaled it to the bulkhead, dangling and dead. But the Tesla-stunned pair were coming round so she hit them with a second frost nade, haarpooned the fourth Drak as it bellow-charged, and delegged a pair of Hieroknights as they entered from the other hatch. The razor-lariat zipped back into its wrist-pod as she stepped smartly past the prone armoured bodies and exited the anteroom. Weapons reloaded, she turned to see a short, low-roofed passage leading to a platform at the edge of an immense cavernous area lit by floating clusters of polychromatic globes. From the edge of the platform an opulent antique staircase sloped down out of sight while a string of letters hung in the air before her:

DEFEAT THE HEKATON AND HIS HUNDRED GENERALS

This was it. This was the climax of *Death Colossus*, the senses-shattering grand finale in which all of the solo player's victories and patiently gathered alliances would be brought to bear. The Hekaton was the controlling intelligence, a huge biomechanical planetoid leading a fleet of heavily armed battle-goliaths straight towards Earth. The deranged core-mind of the Hekaton lay at the centre of the Sanctum Chamber, guarded by his hundred generals who were grouped into five-hand squads, each deploying different combinations of weapons and abilities. As she strode to the head of the stair-case, Sam could see her allies poised and waiting in similar openings spaced around the heights of the chamber's sloped, ribbed walls. There were the reptiloid scavengers, the freed prisoners, the rebellious cyberthralls, the warrior-bands of the Sensect Hivemind, and others, all awaiting her tactical plan, her deployment orders that would set the opening conditions for the final glorious battle.

And she felt ... well, not bored, exactly, more like blunted by the certainty that the narrative would resolve itself with an all-too-neat tying-up of all the loose ends. This was the thirty-fourth headspace game she had research-played according to the par-ameters of the Historical VR Combat project, to which she was the only assigned operative. It had not taken her long to notice patterns in gameplay, in cultural assumptions, and in narrative flow, which increasingly made for predictable outcomes. Not a little of that, she knew, was the result of commercial pressure to create entertainments for a wide audience.

But, depressingly, the very fact that she was here on Asuphel-Korporiata, stuck away in the dreariest corner of Knossos Base, was also part of a pattern.

Yeah, Sam thought sourly. *I'm getting good at pissing off my COs; practically got it down to a science ...*

But it was these Earther senior officers – they were supposed to be highly trained professionals, dedicated, knowledgeable and meticulous, yet almost from the moment she graduated from Melbourne Bastion she had seen sloppy, careless behaviour aplenty. Even as adjutant to a high-level ES colonel at the Banners HQ on Phandrek, she had come up against lazy planning, imprecisely worded orders, procurement and supply errors, most of which she had been able to catch and fix, thereby avoiding damaging repercussions. Except when her secret diligence had corrected a mistake in a delivery order (which hadn't been a mistake) and exposed her CO to the glare of a probity enquiry.

Sam was officially commended but shortly thereafter found herself transferred to the 11th Armour-Guard and assigned to a high-assault company. Before long the 11th was in action against Gomedran marauders who were raiding agri-worlds near the Fensahr border. They were tracked to the edge of the Qarqol deepzone, to a rubble system that was little more than a brown dwarf orbited by clouds of asteroids and minor planetoids. It was there that her attention to detail and strategic intuition prevented the ambush and capture of the *Indra*, the taskforce flagship. Once more she was praised and commended, yet somehow she wound up here at Knossos Base, playing antiquated games and going nowhere.

The deadest of dead ends, she thought. *Not exactly what Papa had in mind when we left Tygra ten years ago.*

Refocusing her attention on the finale of *Death Colossus*, she sighed, thought for a moment, then switched into the game's control menu and activated the heuristic autoplay mode. Now disembodied from the player-character, Sam floated over the Hekaton's huge chamber as battle was joined. Employing her playing style, it took the game more than ten minutes to reach the climax point, where the player-character fought past the generals to the Hekaton's metamind cores and destroyed the one containing the cognitive persona, thus ending the battle. Sam made numerous voice-notes throughout and as soon as the Hekaton was reduced to an ex-evil biomechanical menace, she froze and quit the game. Automatically, the neural interrupt ceased and she was dumped back in her own body, senses seesawing for a long moment before she adjusted to reality. The headspace tiarette had relaxed its grip around her temples and the contact stalks had retracted into the neckbrace. Removing the tiarette she hung it on a slender chrome stand nearby.

The room was small, square and spare, blues and greys that extended to the data console and the low recliner. Feeling aches in her neck and back Sam stood up and put herself through a series of stretching exercises. She drew water from a recessed dispenser, took a nutri-stick from a drawer in the console and sat back to review a transcript of her notes on the display. It was still the early afternoon so she could if she wanted make a start on Combat Archive 35. Or not, if she wanted.

She fingered a few lightkeys, calling up the next game. It was blessed with the title *Draconis Excelsior* and appeared to have a pseudo-medieval setting.

And an involved system of character creation, with added detail-tweaking of abilities and appearance which, over the last few weeks, she had found herself becoming increasingly engrossed by. She was about to reach for the headspace tiarette when a short tinkly sound came from the console, heralding an announcement from one of the base's sub-AIs.

'Lt Commander Brock,' it said in that no-nonsense, formal

masculine voice. 'Priority communication from Colonel Pulaski – please stand by.'

Sam sat up. The base commander? What had she done? What might she have done?

The console's sizeable display lit up with a head-and-shoulders view of the colonel. Grey-haired and gaunt-featured, he stared out of the screen with flinty eyes. Sam gave a quick, snappy salute.

'At ease, Lt Commander,' said Pulaski. 'I have in the last half-hour received new orders regarding your assignment, your new assignment, that is.' The colonel frowned. 'The abruptness of this is highly irregular but I have had veeline confirmation from Admiral Manning himself so it is official and immediately actionable.

'Lt Commander Brock, you are being seconded to work with an operative sent by one of Earthsphere's more exotic allies, the Construct. This agent is, I understand, a sentient combat drone which has previous experience with Humans, mainly during the Darien War.'

The Darien War? Her parents had had only the most peripheral involvement in the events that led to the ouster of the Becker faction on Tygra, while the Gideon cadre were fighting to the death in defence of Darien.

'Sir, may I ask – why me?'

'I put that very question to Admiral Manning,' said Pulaski. 'All he could tell me was that you were their choice – the Construct intermediaries asked for you by name. As for the assignment itself, well, I was not made privy to any details so it is safe to assume that it deals with matters both sensitive and crucial.'

Sam sat back a little, the hollow anxiety in her stomach warring with a sense of anticipation.

'When do I ship out, sir? Where will I rendezvous with the Construct machine?'

'The answer to your questions is on its way to sub-level two now and should be with you very shortly. The drone arrived not long after the new orders. Barring the formal courtesies and some small talk about the Gomedran scavenger problem, I learned very little apart from its insistence that you be ready to leave at short notice.' Then, like a crack in a weathered cliff face, the colonel smiled faintly. 'I believe your visitor has just arrived, Lt Commander – he will have a copy of the orders for you. We shall speak again before you depart.'

The display went dead and a brief moment later the door announcer chimed.

'Third Phalanx Drone R.E. 6891 to see Lt Commander Brock.'

'Admit,' she said, getting to her feet, straightening her simple dark green duty uniform.

Through the open door floated a dark grey drone which at first glance seemed rather boxy. On closer examination she quickly saw that the main part of it resembled a squat polyhedral about a metre across, its facet edges rounded, its dark surface bearing a dull metallic sheen. There were eight rounded conelike projections positioned as if at the corner of a cube – they all had a similar dark grey metallic look and, she realised, were flatter on their undersides.

'Your CO tells me that you've been carrying out a study of early-stage immersive combat games,' said the drone. 'Have you played *Citadel Shock*?'

Sam frowned as she thought. 'No, that title is not familiar. I have researched one called *Starshock*, though. It was quite inventive, and peculiar.'

The drone began to float around the virtuality lab.

'Ah, yes, the ancient asteroid city of Mophrekel, with the death tunnels and the psi-snakes and all that swapping bits of alien DNA in and out. Still, *Citadel Shock* was ground-breaking for the time. You should try it, once we've returned from this mission covered in glory!'

She regarded the drone with wary uncertainty as it continued its circumnavigation of the room. The Construct and its hyperspace force of sentient war-mechs had been a source of both reassurance and unease for Earthsphere since the Darien War. Many times Sam had imagined meeting one of those enigmatic machines but this wasn't quite what she had expected.

'The colonel said you were to deliver a copy of my orders, eh, sir ... R.E. 6891 – I'm sorry, how should I address you?'

'Hmm, just call me Rensik, and I shall call you Lt Commander or Brock, or both if I'm feeling especially officious. And these are your orders.'

A narrow aperture opened in the flank of the drone. A thin shiny cable snaked out to deliver a small blue cylinder into her outstretched hand then whipped back inside the slot, which sealed up. The cylinder split down the side and she slid out the messageleaf, saw the official seal of the director of Earthsphere Defence, a signature and several lines of text between them. She read the orders, reread them, then tucked the leaf back into the container and closed it.

'Rensik,' she said carefully. 'These orders say nothing about my duties or my role, except that the mission is vital to Earthsphere security and that I shall be under your direct command and supervision.'

'Is that a problem, Lt Commander?'

'No, sir. I shall cope with and adapt to whatever situation I am ordered to confront.'

'Well answered. Bit too much of the eager minion, though.' The drone glided towards her, halting to hover at head height about two feet away. 'Now I need you to stand very still for five seconds – can you do this?'

She frowned but nodded. 'Yes, sir.'

'Good, beginning ... now.'

With breath held she stood to attention, keeping stock still, yet her thoughts were a ferment of speculation. Should she be anxious about this and imagine the worst? Or just wait and gather more data? She suddenly realised that the both of them were surrounded by a gauzy, shimmering veil.

'There we are,' said the drone, Rensik. 'I have enclosed us in a hardfield projection of the pair of us – any observer will hear me talking to you in grave and serious tones about the movements of stealthed Hegemony fleets in the denser swirls of the Qarqol deepzone.'

Sam smiled faintly. 'Which would be genuinely worrying if it was genuinely true. And I have to say that I wasn't aware that base security extends to this lowly corner.'

'It's an AI-overseer system,' the drone said. 'My passive detects have been tingling from the moment I entered this place. Anyway, now that we can converse in private I can proceed. I assume that you've heard the term "exotic megastructure"?'

'You mean like the asteroid triangles explorers found around that star in the 4th Modynel?' she said. 'Or the Dyson-Bowl some church is trying to build in Metraj?'

'You're on the right lines. For some, engineering on a vast scale is its own justification. About a hundred millennia ago, over in the galaxy that you call Andromeda, a gaggle of utopian altruists drew together the resources of several civilisations and built an artificial star system complete with over two hundred planets. Some worlds volunteered to become part of the thing, others were donated and re-engineered to fit whatever function suited the builders' plans. The Great Harbour of Benevolent Harmony, they called it. Anyway, to cut a long story short, the completed megastructure turned out to be a centre of great political power which naturally attracted all manner of parasites and sycophants. After a century or two of intrigue, corruption and treachery, some worlds were expelled and others admitted in their place.

'After yet another century of this the Great Harbour was starting to become the exact opposite of what its builders had intended – but then, what else can you expect from organic sentients? After spending several tens of millennia touring the Andromeda galaxy, exacerbating conflicts and starting new ones, the Great Harbour was confronted by an alliance of the civilisations which it had victimised and otherwise abused. They hounded it across the stars and after a gigantic battle forced it to flee into the intergalactic void. That was about seventeen thousand years ago, since when there were no confirmed sightings.'

'Until now?' Sam said.

'If I had a Human face I'd be wearing a sardonic smile – thankfully, though, I don't.' The drone drifted back slightly. 'The thing is lurking in the Indroma Solidarity, not that far from the Earthsphere border, in one of those near-starless gaps the Paramount Council of Indroma so tenaciously holds on to. The unknown powers that control this megasystem are ruthless and brutal and they've left a string of wars, destabilised civilisations and plundered planets in their wake. Our job is to infiltrate, gather intel, contact anyone resisting the rulers and help them to do it a bit more effectively.'

'What does this Great Harbour look like?' she said. 'And how can a star system move around?'

'Your guess is as good as mine, Lt Commander. Most likely these worlds are connected in orbiting bracelets or some arrangement of staggered rings. As for the means of mobility, I can only speculate on giant hyperspace drives powered by part of the output of the artificial star. Perhaps. We'll know more when we get there.'

'What kind of threat potential does it present?'

'No idea. It could be bursting at the seams with heavily armed battle-fleets crewed by demented cyber-cannibals … or it could be a decrepit, burnt-out wreck too feeble to put up a fight. But we couldn't really be that lucky, could we?'

Listening to all this, Sam had found herself feeling more and more that fate was at last working in her favour. A new door had opened and on the other side was, well, unknown hazards, possibly mortal danger, or at least the risk of physical injury and disease … but also new vistas, new creatures with strange names, new worlds and the secrets that every society tries to bury. Acting as pathfinder in a hostile environment would be an invaluable experience and at last prove her worth to her superiors. And show that a Tygran colonial was the equal of any other officer in the Earthsphere navy.

During her brief thoughtful silence, the drone Rensik cancelled the hardfield projection. The shimmers of its energy mesh dissolved like misty threads.

'That pretty much explains it, Lt Commander,' the drone said.

'Thank you, Rensik, sir. How long before we depart?'

'As long as it takes you to pack your gear.'

'That would be about five minutes, sir.'

'Acceptable. My ship is parked under the roof canopy. You'll like it – the passenger compartment is fitted with circumaudio and has a comprehensive archive of mid-twenty-first-century sinosynthpop.'

She paused at the door. 'Sounds impressive, sir, but my tastes run more to boom 'n' pulse.'

'Ah, the sound of dissident youth,' the drone said. 'Ranged or auto-improv?'

'Ranged, sir – I prefer intentional genius.'

'Nice. See you on the roof.'

CHAPTER FOUR

With the shuttle safely back aboard the *Scarabus*, the crew and their five passengers disembarked into the main hold. Pyke shepherded them over to the cargo lift which served the high storage racks and allowed quick access to the gantry and the upper corridor. He explained to the wounded Toolbearer Hechec that he would have one of his crew steer his wheeled cradle to the sickbay while Dervla showed G'Brozen Mav and his followers to their quarters. But when Hechec relayed this to G'Brozen Mav, the bearded humanoid glared and gave a sharp shake of the head before responding with a few terse words. Hechec nodded and smiled up at Pyke.

'Captain, our leader insists – respectfully – that he and his suboards stay by my side while I receive treatment.'

Pyke met G'Brozen Mav's gaze and saw no give in it.

'I see. Respectfully, you say?' He gave Bland Smile No 1. 'Not a problem. In fact I'll personally guide all of you to the sickbay and oversee its operations.'

As Pyke directed the wounded Toolbearer and the stern G'Brozen Mav onto the open platform lift, he glanced at Dervla who was standing between the hold's sliding doors. He gave a half-shrug, she gave a weary nod and stepped out into the corridor, letting the doors close behind her.

A few minutes later they reached the lateral corridor leading to the sickbay. At this point Toolbearer Hechec spoke directly to Brannan Pyke.

'Captain, before I undergo the machine healing I should take precautions in the event that I do not survive its touch.'

'If I can assist in any way just say the word,' Pyke said. 'But the autodoc here is a smart device, and the ship's artificial intelligence lends its extensive faculties as required.'

The diminutive humanoid suddenly looked anxious.

'There is a machine mind controlling this vessel?' His wide eyes darted to and fro. 'Are you then its ... servants?'

'No, no,' he said. 'The ship's mind is our assistant and is under my control, as captain ...'

As he was explaining, Hechec was relaying this to his companions, who suddenly looked even more tense and on edge than before.

'The machine mind obeys your commands?' said Hechec.

'Indeed, yes,' Pyke said. 'I can demonstrate – Scar, what is our general status, where we are, any ships in the vicinity, that sort of thing?'

'The *Scarabus* is still maintaining orbit over the replacement Nadisha II, Bran,' said the ship AI. 'Sensors report no other vessels within the system. Analysis of the Khorr ship drive emissions has narrowed possible pursuit courses to less than five hundred—'

'Thanks, Scar. Is the autodoc ready to diagnose our guest's condition?'

By now they had reached the sickbay. The open sliding doors revealed a cramped, semi-circular room with an examination table jutting at the centre and treatment recesses to either side. A curved rack of articulated surgical effectors hung over the central table, interspersed with extendable sensors. Lighting was bright and diffuse, certainly brighter than out in the corridor where G'Brozen Mav's followers had to stand due to the lack of elbow room.

'The autodoc is fully apprised of our guest's non-Human nature, Bran. Field and sonic pain relief will be employed rather than biochemical methods.'

Pyke looked at Hechec. 'So, how does that suit you?'

'It appears satisfactory, Captain,' said the Toolbearer. 'But before I submit to this device it may be wise for me to give you the location of the world where Khorr has gone. Do you have star charts that I may consult?'

'Shouldn't be a problem,' Pyke said. 'Scar, can you retask a sickbay holomonitor to show the stars of the local area?'

'Yes, Bran.'

A section of the curved wall next to the head of the examination table slid open, revealing a dark recess studded with holofield emitters. A touchboard protruded below it, an array of glowing multicoloured symbols. The emitters glimmered with pinpoint ripples for a moment before a 3D star map appeared, each star a glinting mote enclosed in a small opaque sphere. When the view zoomed in closer to one of them, running text strings appeared and revealed that this was a representation of the Nadisha system.

The Toolbearer's cradle was wheeled round to bring him closer to the display. Pyke glanced at the small being's grotesque hands with their cyborged finger-tools, started to explain the viewshift controls then offered to direct it for him. Hechec smiled.

'Captain, I think I understand.'

He raised one baggy-sleeved arm with its protruding group of enigmatic probes and instruments. Two articulated digits unfolded weirdly into clusters of shiny tendrils that spread across the touchboard. The holodisplay flickered, switched abruptly through 90 degrees and back.

'You're sure I can't help you out there.'

'A slight recalibration problem, Captain. All is well.'

The holomap returned for a moment to its original setup before zooming out, a sudden shrinking of the surrounding stars into a denser cloud of points. The border between Earthsphere and the Indroma Solidarity became visible, a pearly irregular veil that wove and curved and angled between clusters and tresses of suns. Then the mapview zoomed in again, a headlong plummet past dozens of star systems, arrowing straight in on one in Indroma space, some nine light years from the border. The mapview changed to a stylised sun-and-planets graphic, showing four worlds – the second from the sun bore a handful of bright blue surface dots and a fan of radial data tags.

'That is the world where Khorr is,' Hechec said. 'It is sparsely populated and apart from a scattering of unmechanised farms it is unexploited. There are many mountain ranges rich in metal ores, as well as easily accessible fields of liquid hydrocarbons, a prize of great value to the Shuskar. I have used the marker function to show the course that you should take.'

The mapview returned to the zoomed-out state, which now showed a pale yellow dotted line leading from Nadisha to the system Hechec had tracked down. The Toolbearer's arm slipped off the touchboard and lay still across his chest. He looked weary and unwell but Pyke had to know a few things.

'Hechec, soon as we get you on the autodoc table the medical systems'll look you over and figure out how to heal you up.' He leaned in a little closer. 'But you've told me precious little about yourselves, where you're from, what your connection is with Khorr, how you came to be down on that poisoned planet, and why you're helping us.'

Before Hechec could answer, G'Brozen Mav spoke to the Toolbearer in a peremptory tone, his gaze never leaving Pyke. The Toolbearer replied in a calming voice which served to mollify the bearded leader.

'G'Brozen Mav felt that you were pressuring me,' Hechec said. 'But I told him that we need to be … trusting with those who have helped us. So, briefly, Captain, here are your answers – we five were former crew members of an immense and ancient vessel called the *Kezurdra*. Its contracted task is to steal worlds for a brutal empire far from this part of the galaxy, and Khorr is one of the deep range scouts who search for suitable worlds. If he was trading with you, it must have been on the orders of a superior.'

'Bringing a trashed planet all this way to swap for its replacement seems like a lot of wasted effort to me,' Pyke said.

'A peculiarity of the *Kezurdra*'s employers' demands.'

'And who's the Shuskar? Is that your captain?'

Hechec gave a bleak smile. 'The Shuskar are the Lords of *Kezurdra*, an arrogant, pitiless species. We managed to escape *Kezurdra*, hiding on that broken world until you found us, and we are helping you by way of repayment.'

The reclining sentient fell silent, his face drawn and wan. Pyke felt a twinge of guilt, knowing that treatment had to commence.

With Hechec translating directions, Pyke and G'Brozen Mav gingerly lifted the Toolbearer up onto the examination table. The table self-adjusted, raising his upper torso to a semi-seated angle. Smiling again, Hechec murmured to G'Brozen Mav and extended a sleeve-swathed arm. A brassy tube telescoped out and dropped a cluster of red glittering objects into the bearded man's waiting palm. He nodded and transferred them to a ragged pocket in his ragged jerkin, then gave Pyke a stony glance.

'What are those?' Pyke said.

'Survival teachers,' Hechec said. 'To help these brave Shengak if I do not survive.' He closed his eyes, then opened one to look at Pyke. 'I mean no disrespect, Captain. Life has taught us that the Gatherer is always waiting for us to make that fatal step or decision, so we always try to be prepared.' He paused. 'Should I disrobe to permit access to my wound?'

'No need, Toolbearer,' Pyke said. 'The autodoc can manage very well. Are you ready now?'

'I am. Please proceed.'

Pyke nodded. 'Scar, time to fire up the diagnostics.'

'Yes, Bran. Preliminary scans indicate that the subject has undergone extensive cyborg augmentation in the form of skeletal recoring, load-bearing substructures and several implants that function like small-scale biofabricators ... initial diagnostic scan running ... scan reveals an entry wound above the right hip angling down through soft tissues; a projectile is lodged between a bony spur and an unknown organ. Hardfield instrumentality will allow the projectile's removal and realignment bonding of broken tissues, as well as sealing the entry wound.'

'And how soon can our guest be up and about afterwards?'

'Mobility is permissible after four or five hours, Bran, but I would recommend twice that period. Certainly no strenuous activity should be undertaken.'

'And how about that world he found on the holomap? Got any data on it?'

'Yes, Bran. It leads to an Indroma world called Tigimhos whose system is set apart from busy transport routes and hubs. Population is less than forty thousand, mostly Bargalil, and the economy is wholly agrarian. Estimated journey time, four hours forty-five minutes.

Pyke nodded as he gazed down at Toolbearer Hechec who now lay still, eyes closed, breathing a quiet and steady sound. The autodoc's hardfield effectors were already at work, pale blue rods angling down from above, peeling back layers of heavy woven cloth to reveal the injury. At the same time extruded emitters projected a number of amber beams onto Hechec's forehead and neck, maintaining sedation and pain negation.

There was some movement from the sickbay entrance, where G'Brozen Mav and the other three had assumed guard positions. What had Hechec called them? The brave Shengak? Pyke couldn't know if that was their species name or their rank or whatever. But their mistrust was palpable, a background constant. G'Brozen Mav muttered to the others, handed out the small red objects he'd got from the Toolbearer and they all swallowed them at once. The bearded leader then crossed his arms, leaned against the sickbay wall and went back to watching Pyke's every move. Pyke smiled.

'Well, lads, let me tell you, this has been a blast, and as much as I want to hang around for more of your tall tales and hilarious jokes, I must tear myself away and get back to running the ship. But I'll have one of the crew check in on you every now and then, all right? Excellent!'

G'Brozen Mav frowned as Pyke went to the door, and stepped out into the corridor. Glancing back he saw the Shengak leader point at Pyke with a jabbing motion.

'Oh . . . kay!'

Pyke paused in midstep. 'Er . . . okay!' he echoed.

G'Brozen Mav gave a sharp grunting nod, as if satisfied at something, and went back to his spot at the wall.

Hechec called those red gem things survival teachers, Pyke thought as he hurried away. *Are they teaching them our language? Hmm, better let the others know . . .*

'Scar,' he said. 'Set course for that Indroma world which our guest found – what's it called again?'

'Tigimhos, Bran.'

'That's it, and depart orbit soon as you like. I'm on my way to my quarters to change out of these raggies, then I'll be on the bridge if anyone needs me.'

Less than ten minutes later, he walked onto the bridge and found nearly everyone waiting for him. At once a barrage of questions framed in a variety of tempers engulfed him (although he noticed that Dervla made her comments in a level, near-formal manner). Clearly they'd picked up some details from the suit-cam-feeds during the planetside foray but explanations were needed, especially in the light of Scar's announcement of the break from orbit a few moments ago. Pyke filled in the gaps with a condensed version of Toolbearer Hechec's own story and the news of Khorr's whereabouts.

'We're in hyperspace,' said Win Foskel, 'so the hunt must be on.'

'It most certainly is,' said Pyke. 'Flight-time to Tigimhos will be about five hours, and when we get there Scar's sensors should be able to pick up the trail of Khorr's ship and track him to wherever he's holed up.'

Ancil seemed unconvinced. 'I have to say, chief, I'm not exactly keen on crossing the Indroma border ... it's not the Indromans that worry me, it's the Earthers. Going by tiernet scuttlebutt, their intercepts have been getting sharp and fast in the last few months.'

'Thought about that,' Pyke said. 'Once we conclude our business with Khorr, we'll head into the Jatzilil CoSov and scout around for a legit milkrun job heading into Earthsphere-space. That lets us slip back in, no mess, no stress.'

There were nods of approval at this and Pyke felt a little knot of warmth on seeing Dervla's endorsement smile (which was several notches below the dazzle of her admiration smile, but you can't have everything).

Just then, she spoke up from where she lounged next to the command console.

'Bran, Mojag is following all this from Engineering and has a question for you.'

'Sure – Mojag, what's your point?'

The grey-haired tech expert appeared in a couple of displays on the bridge, and Pyke tried not to think about the dead-but-digitised Oleg that Mojag was carrying in his cranial prosthesis.

'Captain, I'm curious to know what we'll be doing with the Toolbearer and his companions.'

'I thought we'd take them with us to the CoSov – bound to be someone on Parimel III or Kanipha Station that they can find a berth with.'

Mojag shrugged. 'You may be right in that regard.'

'I'm sure I am,' Pyke said with a chuckle. 'Right, five hours – that should be enough time to run diagnostics on the weapon systems, don't you think? Not saying that I'm expecting to run into serious trouble but we should be prepared.'

'In case we run into this cronking big planet-jacker ship, you mean,' said Win, eyebrows arched.

Pyke grinned. 'I got the impression that the planet-jacking is done by a pack of smaller ships.'

'Oh, that's okay, then.'

There was low laughter at that, with Pyke joining in.

'Don't forget that we're carrying hi-spec stealth gear,' he said. 'If we need to merge into the background, it's there. So, if that's everything ...'

'We haven't mentioned burials for Oleg and Hammadi yet,' said Ancil.

Pyke glanced involuntarily at Dervla, found his gaze locking with hers, and abruptly looked away. On the screens Mojag appeared unchanged, composed and relaxed. *But you've got Oleg's ghost in your head!* Pyke's thought ran. *What's it going to say about this notion?*

'We've had burials before, Cap'n,' said Krefom the Henkayan from where he sat on the deck with his back to the command console. 'Remember the one we had for the Ruboyek triplets ... well, two of them.'

The Ruboyeks were a gen-empath trio of Gulkranis, a species of small wiry bipeds. Pyke had hired them as general tech hands, and for their clandestine skills which were considerable.

They had lasted over a year until a lethal part of their own past caught up with them on Firlong's World, leaving two of them dead and the third missing a hand. When it came to the burial in interstellar space the surviving Ruboyek had to be physically restrained to prevent him jumping into the polycrate along with his dead, plastic-wrapped siblings. Once the improvised casket had been sent off into the icy black by the trash ejector, the third Ruboyek calmed down enough for treatment at the sickbay. Not long after that, at his request, he left the *Scarabus* during a stopover on some world in the 4th Modynel which had a small Gulkrani enclave.

'Yes, true, we have had the sad duty of consigning less fortunate crew members to the void,' Pyke said. 'I'm just wondering if we can come back to this subject after dealing with the crisis at hand.'

'But Hammadi was a 3rd Ka'abaist Muslim,' said Win. 'And a strict one. They require their dead to be given the last rites within twenty-four hours of death.'

Pyke nodded, while wanting to shake his head.

'Scar, any info on 3rd Ka'abaist burial customs, especially anything on burial in space?'

'I do, Bran. Third Ka'abaists are strongly in favour of burial in space since it lacks air, moisture or bacteria, or carrion creatures to corrupt or consume the body.'

'Right, that sounds good. Mojag, d'ya know if Oleg had any preferences as to how he wanted his mortal remains disposed of?'

For what felt like a very long moment, Mojag's face stared out of the holodisplays, eyes intensely wide, and Pyke began to wonder if there was some kind of argument going on inside that augmented brain.

Then Mojag blinked, frowned slightly, gaze darting from side to side. Pyke almost felt like praying.

'Erm . . . I think I recall Oleg saying something about writing a will but I've never seen it.' His mouth twitched into a half-smile. 'I could sort through his belongings and his files, Captain, but it might take a while.'

That wouldn't surprise me in the least, Pyke thought.

'Right, that's settled then. Oleg's body will have to be stored in one of the stasis cabinets till we conclude our business, and we can hold a ceremony for Hammadi in the main hold in, say, two and a half hours. Win, can you and Scar work up some appropriate words for the ceremony? Brief but respectful.'

'See what I can do, Captain.'

'That's what I like to hear. Ancil – nip round to the sickbay and see how our guests are doing. After that I want to get into the combat system diagnostics.'

'On my way, sir.'

As Ancil and Win left the bridge, Dervla came over, but before she could begin, Krefom spoke up.

'Captain, I was checking over the lockered weapons before this,' he said in his steady basso voice. 'You want I should carry on?'

'You do that, Kref. Let me know what you find when you're done.'

Krefom nodded, got to his large feet and headed for the other hatch. Watching him leave, Pyke noticed that Punzho Bex was sitting at one of the display stations, hunched over something on the console. So Pyke beckoned Dervla out into the corridor.

'What was Mojag talking about?' she said, suddenly anxious. 'Oleg never made a will . . .'

'I have no idea,' Pyke said. 'My best guess is that old Mojag is getting a touch of grief from his passenger so came up with the will angle to put off having to deal with the real dead body of his real friend.'

Dervla clapped one hand over her eyes and brow and shook her head. 'This is idiocy. We – you! – should have told the others after you found out, because eventually they're going to figure it out!' Her hand fell away. 'Have you spoken to him?'

'You mean … eh, no, not yet. Have you?'

'I thought I'd let Mojag tell me when Oleg wanted a chat.'

'Not much of an excuse,' Pyke said. 'I thought you were the Official Second-Best-Friend.'

'And you're the captain! What's your excuse?'

'Being captain – I'm a busy man. Shortly I will have to find out from Ancil what the latest is from sickbay, then I have to see what Win's come up with for Hammadi's ceremony, then I'll be having a conference with Scar about our tactical options when we reach our destination.'

'Really,' she said, regarding him with narrowed eyes.

'Yes, really, so what I'd like you to do, dearest Dervla, is skip over to Engineering and find out from our Mojag if Mr O feels like a bit of a gab.'

She sighed. 'Okay, Bran, I'll do it. Better to find out what he actually wants rather than second-guessing.' She gave a desultory wave of her hand and hurried away aftwards.

Pyke felt a certain satisfaction. *Everyone's busy and the* Scarabus *is hurtling along on its mission …* Then he stepped back inside the bridge and saw Punzho Bex still sitting at the workstation. He was now leaning back, his tall frame scarcely accommodated by the worn couch, his long legs splayed either side of the console. His narrow features were sombre and his eyes were fixed on the small objects grouped on a flat section of the console.

Pyke recognised the Nine Novices, the figurines that Punzho employed as a focus for Weave meditation.

'You're looking a bit anxious there, Punzho,' he said. 'Don't tell me the future's that bleak.'

The tall Egetsi looked round, anxiety turning into a knowing, expectant smile. Pyke chuckled.

'I know, I know – the Nine Novices aren't for fortune-telling is, I believe, what you're about to say.'

'Quite so, Captain. Each of the Novices represents one of the Cardinal Principles and it is the intermeshing of Hvlozen and their influences which reveals the Explication.'

'Hmm, Explication, you say?' Pyke leaned against the side of the workstation and stared down at the cluster of tiny statuettes.

'It's a kind of summary of all the interweaving bonds,' Punzho said. 'For example, I laid the Novices out in the hub-and-wheel formation, all selected blind from the pouch. This formation, however, is full of contradictions. Gst is the hub – which I usually find a little pleasing since Gst is the serene, skilled one who works hard in the background, a bit like myself I sometimes think. So as you can see, Gst can form a pure triad with eight adjacent pairs around the wheel—'

'A pure triad?'

'Yes, where the pair on the wheel are adjacent. The hub can also form eight triads with pairs that are separated by one spoke – these are the Lesser Triads . . .'

Pyke held up a hand. 'No offence, Punzho, but I've got a low tolerance for jargon, I'm afraid. I get the general idea of the figures, and you said something about contradictions so let's take it from there, eh?'

The Egetsi smiled. 'I am not offended, Captain. Well, simply put, Gst has a strengthening or enabling effect on the hub positions, and in this pattern the most potential belongs to Vrn.' He reached out and laid the tip of one long finger on the head of a small dark figurine. 'Vrn gains with Gst at the hub, but here Vrn is flanked by Kld and Dgw, sometimes known as the Scions of Dusk. Together with Gst they form a Lesser Triad, and either of the adjacent Pure Triads pits Vrn against one or other of the Scions, with Gst's loyalty a matter of debate.'

Punzho paused and they regarded each other for a curious

moment, Human and Egetsi, dumbfoundedness on one side, abstruse interpretation on the other.

'So what do you get out of this?' Pyke said. 'It's not really a story or a morality play so you can't get a lesson in morals from it ... can you?'

Punzho looked thoughtful as he carefully gathered the little figures back into their pouch.

'It makes me think about the relationships between things, sometimes people, sometimes things in nature, sometimes ideas or the effects of ideas.'

Pyke frowned. 'So that could have been me on the wheel with Khorr and his thugs on either side – and was that really you in the middle?'

'Or Dervla, Captain,' Punzho said. 'Or even the ship's AI, if you look at it in terms of personalities. But we are taught that this is the least accurate use of the Weave augury.'

'Maybe it's telling me that Khorr is more dangerous than I realise,' Pyke said. 'Could be it's warning me to be very careful. Thanks, Punzho.'

The Egetsi smiled and inclined his head as Pyke patted him on the shoulder and headed for the hatchway.

Well, that'll teach me not to ask about other people's mysticism, he thought. *It's like trying to see shapes in smoke.*

He consulted Scar on Ancil's whereabouts and a few minutes later stepped into Sub-Storage 4, aft of the main hold entrance. It was a four-by-four-metre room lined with safety racking where sensitive and expensive equipment was kept, along with most of the ammunition which Kref and Ancil were cross-checking against the issue logs. The black racks with their mesh containers were protected by a monomol layer of diamek which gave it all a glossy sheen. When Pyke asked Ancil about his visit to sickbay, he shrugged.

'Checked the autodoc, all the readings were stable and the

little fellow is still under sedation. One of his friends, the one called Brozen or something, said he was muttering as he slept. I mentioned it to Scar and he said it was nothing to worry about.'

'G'Brozen Mav spoke to you?' Pyke said. 'Whole sentences, that sorta thing?'

Ancil shrugged. 'Must be those pills you saw them take. I've heard of scripted nanobots that target language centres in the brain with vocab recodes. The words and the grammar are there but it needs practise to be any use.'

'Crafty,' Pyke said. 'Maybe Toolbearer Hechec can show us how to cook them up for ourselves. Oh, and it's not long till we say goodbye to Hammadi – keep an eye on the time, both of you.'

Leaving the storage compartment he headed for Engineering, but as he drew near the open doorway he could make out the voices of Mojag and Dervla engaged in hushed conversation.

Was she talking with Mojag's passenger, the digital copy of the dead Oleg? He decided not to risk interrupting the possibly useful chitchat and retraced his steps to his own quarters where he spun out the time by flicking through his wardrobe for something suitably sombre. In the event he turned up at the hold in his usual sleeveless black commander's jacket and dark blue trousers and boots, except that he'd put on a formal, high-collared shirt.

The ceremony was stately and quiet, as directed by Win Foskel. All the crew were there, apart from Mojag. Hammadi's remains had been wrapped in white polyplas, which they had rolls of, and placed in an old sealable crate once used for storing pipe sections. The crate was loaded into the main trash launcher, set into the deck of the shuttle bay, and visible through the force-field partition.

As the crew stood in a silent line, heads bowed, Scar piped into the hold an audio recording of the Salat Al-Janazah, the Islamic funeral prayer. The Arabic prayer had several parts and after the fourth or fifth something made Pyke glance over his shoulder to glimpse G'Brozen Mav looking down from the upper gantry. The bearded man made a sharp sideways motion with his head; Pyke nodded gravely but pointed at the waiting crate, as if to say be patient.

When the final words of the prayer were spoken, leaving a soft sadness in the air, he moved back from the line of crew members and took the cargo riser up the gantry. G'Brozen Mav was waiting out in the passageway.

'So, what can I be doing for you?' Pyke said, not sure what to expect.

'Toolbearer Hechec asks for you – he will speak and you must listen.'

Pyke gave him a judicious look. 'Well, that was a very fine pill he gave you – if I ask nicely will he make up one to help me become a great zeroball player, d'ye think?'

G'Brozen Mav only gave him a dark and wordless look and strode off, as if expecting to be followed. Pyke grinned, shrugged and did so.

Toolbearer Hechec was sitting up, sipping a cloudy liquid from a tube that snaked up from a squat bottle resting on a low tray before him. The diminutive humanoid, still clad in his rough robes, smiled as Pyke entered the sickbay.

'You're looking better, Toolbearer,' he said, glancing at the examination table's monitor panel. 'Not so close to death's door, at least.'

'Yes, Captain. The Gatherer had to leave empty-handed.'

'This time,' G'Brozen Mav said. 'He waits still.'

The bearded warrior held Hechec's gaze for a long stern moment, which made Pyke realise just who was top dog among these strange passengers. Hechec broke the gaze first, his expression submissive. G'Brozen Mav glanced at Pyke then back at Hechec.

'Say your words, Toolbearer.'

Hechec nodded and he moved away.

'Captain,' he began, 'our destination is another foundling world, another innocent planet singled out to be wrested away by the thieves of the Shuskar. The brute Khorr will be on the surface, near one of the four shroud-pillars – your ship's instruments will lead you to the correct one. But the thieves' own vessels have detection devices so you will have to find a way to get there unseen.'

'Ah, we've got that covered,' Pyke said. 'Had some stealth systems installed a couple of years ago, and not long afterwards a rich and grateful client gave us some milgrade enhancements which allow the *Scarabus* to be almost invisible, if that's what we need.'

'Is your shuttle fitted with these devices?'

'No, only the *Scarabus*, but she is planet-capable.' Pyke chuckled. 'Not only can she fly in atmo, she can ghost right into a planetary sensor-matrix, slip past the detection layers and land soft and quiet as a feather. After that, there's just the matter of tracking down that ripoff gobshite, Khorr.'

'Khorr is a veteran of the Shatterground, which makes him a lethal adversary. Be sure of your preparations, Captain, before beginning the hunt.'

'Thanks for the advice, Hechec,' said Pyke. 'I'll pass that on to Win and Kref – they'll make sure that we are completely ready.'

'They must! Khorr is not to be taken lightly.' The Toolbearer closed his eyes and sank back against the inclined backrest, seemingly exhausted. Pyke frowned and looked closely at the biomonitor readouts.

'Scar,' he said. 'What's our patient's prognosis?'

'Quiet rest for several more hours, Bran.'

'I thought you said that he would be up and about sooner.'

'The patient's energy levels have been more severely suppressed than originally anticipated, Bran. Even this aided recovery period may have to be extended.'

'Right, I see.'

Hechec now appeared to be sleeping, while G'Brozen Mav stood nearby, arms crossed and regarding Pyke with apparent distrust.

As Pyke turned to leave, the bearded warrior cleared his throat and spoke.

'Thank you for your help.'

He looked back. The dark gaze now seemed tempered by something like grudging respect. 'Thank you for all you have given us.'

'Well, we both benefit from this,' Pyke said. 'Mutual aid, sharing information, a bit of medical treatment, and we're back in the game, eh?'

A wintry smile creased the warrior's mouth. 'Back ... in the game. Yes, this is so.'

G'Brozen Mav said no more, just gazed down at the Tool-bearer. Pyke nodded, said something about being about his duties and left the sickbay.

As he hurried off in the direction of the bridge he sighed. Embarrassment always stuck home whenever people started being grateful to him, whether he deserved it or not. He was a hard-bitten, border-defying, sanctions-busting smuggler who laughed in the face of boundary police – gratitude just didn't seem appropriate somehow.

When he reached the hatch to the bridge he took one step over the threshold and froze – only Ancil and Win were there and they were wrapped in each other's arms. Pyke carefully, soundlessly retreated, moving back several paces, then with a heavy tread resumed his approach, adding a cough to the performance. When he entered for the second time Ancil and Win were settling into their respective workstation couches.

'Did you get a chance to run those diagnostics?' Pyke said while dropping into his own chair.

'Mojag was good enough to set them up for me, while I was helping Kref,' Ancil said. 'I've been going over the results and so far I'm only seeing minor calibration issues – other than that the defences are at optimum readiness should we need to kick some arse.'

Pyke laughed. 'And arse-kicking could well be on the menu! Scar, what's our ETA?'

'ETA has been updated, Bran. Due to unexpected hyperspace energy conditions we shall reach the edge of the target star system in less than thirty minutes.'

Pyke shrugged. 'Sooner we're in, sooner we're out. Have you dug up any more info on the oddly named Tigimhos?'

'It is within the average planetary diameter for E-type worlds, and has three large landmasses, two of which are spread across the equator. Indroma records state it to be a class D colonial holding, since current macro-policies are focused on upgrading existent industrial base worlds. However, since it lies in the twenty-light-year strategic buffer zone it qualifies as a third-rank tactical asset and was assigned a Guardian Station, which is essentially a manned outpost capable of deploying interceptors and drones. However, a five-year-old secret Earthsphere intel report which I acquired some time ago reveals that most third-rank systems instead received an AI drone retasked for monitoring and oversight.'

'Which makes it an attractive proposition if you're a gang of planet-jackers looking for some real estate that's desirable and lightly defended.'

'Exactly so, Bran. However, we can be sure that the planet-jackers' sensornet will be on high alert.'

Dervla entered the bridge during the exchange and Pyke met her gaze as he continued.

'Then we have our stealth systems ready so that we hit the ground running when we come out of hyperspace.'

'No problems, chief,' said Ancil as he exchanged a grin and a wink with Win. 'We'll be like a shadow in the blackout, and if the worse comes to the worst we can always throw them a squawker.'

'Sounds like just the thing,' Pyke said. 'What kind of frightener are you thinking of?'

'I thought I could configure the emission profile to look like a Lion-class Earthsphere assault corvette.'

Pyke laughed. They had a small battery of missiles adapted to serve as decoys, their payloads replaced with multiband emitters capable of projecting a complex energy signature to match almost any kind of vessel. More than once a squawker had led pursuing hostiles on a merry chase while the *Scarabus* had made good its escape.

'I definitely approve,' Pyke said. 'Musical accompaniment?'

'Hmm, Wagner's "Ride of the Valkyries", or Godfog's "Hole in the Universe"?'

'Go with the Godfog – should scare the guts out of 'em!'

After that, Pyke went over the equipment manifest for the mission, the field packs and weaponry needed by himself, Dervla, Krefom, Ancil and Win. Then he moved on to the defence diagnostics and saw that Ancil had been as sharp-eyed and thorough as ever. Which still left over ten minutes till the drop from hyperspace. On the holoconsole he went into the shared crew files, opened the folder where Win occasionally left short stories and poems for the others to enjoy, chose something short and began to read. He was halfway through a curious tale about a tree whose fruit were tiny books when Scar announced a twenty-second countdown.

The all-too-familiar vertigo-squeeze came and went and the *Scarabus* was back in real-space, stealth systems running, masking the ship as it curved away from the exit point on a decelerating trajectory.

'Lots of activity around the planet Tigimhos,' muttered Win. 'No sign of any Indroman monitoring post though.'

'Anything on the jacker ships?' said Pyke. 'What kind of sensor web are they putting out?'

Dervla uttered a low whistle from where she sat. 'There's a cluster of small ships in surface-synch orbit, five all told, but there's this bigger one which is enclosed by a strange field of some kind, and it's giving off bizarre surges and bursts of energy.' She shook her head. 'Details still hazy – getting in closer would be better, if certifiably crazy.'

'Scar,' Pyke said. 'Any signs of long-range sensor scans?'

'Nothing recognisable as such, Bran, but as we reached the dehyper point I detected intermittent patterns in the pattern flows near this system.'

'No way to assess threat levels?'

'Sorry, Bran – insufficient data.'

'Then we do what Dervla suggested, get in there, close and personal, eh? Set us up for a microjump, aiming for high-orbit distance, with the planet between us and them. Ancil – better fire up every one of your stealth gambits. We're about to walk in the front door!'

The hyperspace microjump went perfectly, taking the *Scarabus* from seven million miles away to fifteen thousand miles above the surface of Tigimhos in little more than an extended instant.

'Jacker vessels still holding position,' Ancil said. 'No change in ship-to-ship comm traffic. Hah hah, they don't know we're here!'

'Scar,' Pyke said. 'Any more on those hyperspace patterns, and what about the strange field surrounding the big jacker vessel?'

'Only that some eddies in the patterns seemed to correspond to the planet. As for that field, it is more a proximity effect shed by some kind of generated force. It appears to be a transboundary conduit carrying a torrent of energy into hyperspace, into Tier 2. There's something vast there—'

'Chief, they're onto us!' said Ancil. 'Two of those five ships have broken orbit and launched several missiles, all heading our way.'

'Time for a crazy, noisy squawker, I'm thinking.'

Ancil laughed, fingers dancing across the touchboard. 'Oh yeah, a squawking, screeching delight – and it's away.'

'Bran,' said the AI, Scar. 'I've picked up drive emissions exactly matching those of Khorr's vessel – it is down on the planet's surface.'

Pyke felt a surge of exhilaration. 'Do you have precise coordinates?'

'Yes.'

'Then get us down there,' he said. 'Full burn!'

CHAPTER FIVE

'... this kind of thorough, disestablishing destruction can be found across every city and nearly every town of significant size. Only a few hinterland villages seemed to escape the bombardments and ground assaults but according to your sampler probes they didn't escape the chemical and biological weapons. Toxic residual readings for most rural settlements are similar to those found in urban zones.'

Sitting in the passenger recess, Brock paused in her recitation from the datapane projected before her, made a few notes on an archaic leafed-paper pad balanced on her knee, then nodded.

'Is there more?' said the drone, Rensik Estemil.

'Yes indeed, sir. Your clever probes have uncovered a rough timeline of planetside events from analysis of the various macroweapon residues,' Brock said. 'Incorporating dating results from organic remains, it appears that the initial attack on this Nadisha II took place over a century ago, a devastating nuclear bombardment of all main cities. Over the following decades there was a series of lesser conflicts centred on the ruins of the cities and the towns scattered all across the largest continent.'

'How many of these lesser conflicts have there been?' said Rensik.

'This is where the conclusions get hazy – your smart probes

can only offer an estimate ranging between 150 and 280. They say that most of these battles took place repeatedly in the same locations, such that the destruction of one conflict could partially obliterate the evidence from a previous one ... erm, may I ask if you're displeased with my performance, sir?'

'Why do you ask, Lt Commander?'

'Since our arrival in-system you have been nestled in your niche and your responses to me have been somewhat terse.'

'If I was unhappy with your abilities you would know about it, trust me. Don't worry, I am listening to every word you say and devoting all necessary attention to their consideration.'

Which came to roughly 4.8 per cent of his core processing power. The rest of his attention was intertwined with his ship's Construct-designed sensor arrays, overseeing the streams of incoming raw data, directing or modifying the analytic sub-cognitives and piece by piece assembling a story that explained what happened to Nadisha II. Or whatever name this ravaged world once bore.

'I see, sir. Shall I continue?'

'Please do.'

'Good, because this is the interesting bit ...'

She then went on to tell him that the probes had found skeletal remains from a number of species – at least nine, perhaps as many as fifteen – clustered around the battle sites. Which he had already figured out: this poisonous, irradiated world had clearly been used as an arena for savage, staged clashes between opposing armies. But according to the Construct's archived abstract the Great Harbour had last been sighted two and a half centuries ago in one of the galaxy's minor peripheral stellar clusters where, true to form, it left a trail of havoc and destruction. Which implied that there had been another stopping-off point prior to its arrival here.

As Brock continued her recitation of the probes' findings, the drone Rensik deepened its focus on the data flowing in from the sensors. Immense structured forces had been deployed in the second tier of hyperspace and vestiges, impressions almost, still remained, fading but perceptible. That was where this world had been parked, its vectors matched with the real Nadisha II until the time came for the in-orbit substitution. And after that ...

The analysis results at this point were reduced to a thin skein of conjecture stretched across too few verifiable event pivots. The sensors were still gathering data though, and luckily a further scatter of coherent additionals gave the picture more clarity. After the planetary switcharound, a cluster of drive emissions had then moved away a few tier-hours – the hyperspace equivalent of light years – before splitting, a single dense emission trail continuing along the initial course while a group of lesser trails veered off in another direction. This told Rensik a number of things: that the hijacked Nadisha II was on its way to a rendezvous with the Great Harbour, and that the rest of the planet-jacker flotilla was heading for its next target. Which implied that a second toxic, war-burnt world was also in transit to the same destination.

Uncovering the second course was something of a relief. The drone had already requested trans-tier scan records from the nearest Construct overwatch station (down on Tier 18) to track down non-standard drive activity in this area. It would be humiliating to have to send another begging message.

'... a thirty-eight-character alphabet and a fondness for adorning all their important civil buildings with quotes and sayings. All the important structures were pounded to rubble, of course, but the probes still managed to extrapolate a few things, including what they looked like ...'

A 3D image popped up. The original Nadishans had been bipedal, with squat physiques and a distinctly saurian appearance. They reminded Rensik of the Jegiska, an offshoot of the Kiskashin.

'Excellent work,' the drone said.

'Thank you, sir, but all I did was present the summary.'

'I know but I'd rather have you in a positive frame of mind, given the nature of what we're seeing.'

The Human paused, but only for a second.

'Sir, I would describe my frame of mind as resolute. Those responsible for ... *this* should be held accountable.'

'History is full of murderers who should have been punished, Brock. Our job, just to refresh your memory, is to track down the Great Harbour, find out what level of threat they present or intend, and spike their guns. So I'm sure that you'll be pleased to know that the ship sensors have uncovered the course they took away from the Nadisha system. We'll be ready to depart as soon as the last probes are aboard.'

'That's good news, sir. Is there time for me to finish the findings summary?'

'Ah – you have numbers.'

'Yes, sir. Population estimate for the original inhabitants comes in at 1.4 billion, plus or minus 150 million. The estimate for total subsequent combat deaths is much more problematic – between 5 and 15 million, the probes reckon. In effect, the entire planet is a graveyard.'

The drone Rensik Estemil did not have to remind itself of Brock's Tygran background. While hidden from Earth's authorities for over a century, Tygra's Human settlers had carried out massacres of the low-tech sentient natives. After the Darien War, when Tygran history came to light, the Tygran leadership had instituted an Office for Remorse and Contrition to demonstrate their stricken collective conscience. However, some Tygrans emigrated, claiming that official declarations of regret were insincere, and among them were Brock's parents.

And here you are, carrying the burden of their remorse, with your own thoughts finely attuned to any evidence of injustice and malice, even as we head towards a virulent nexus of it. I can only assume that the Construct knew what it was doing when it chose you for this mission.

'You haven't mentioned where this course might lead, sir,' Brock said. 'Will we end up at the Great Harbour?'

'It's more likely that we'll find another planet like this one, Lt Commander.'

She nodded, glancing at a nearby datapane. 'All probes now aboard, sir.'

And with that, the Construct ship broke orbit from that brutalised, contaminated world and sped off into clear space before making the jump to hyperspace.

CHAPTER SIX

From the bridge viewport Pyke was staring at the wide blue and white immensity of the planet Tigimhos, just as the *Scarabus*'s auxiliary thrusters kicked in, accelerating their plunge into the atmosphere. A new subharmonic became perceptible at the edge of audibility, made clearer by the tense silence.

'Ancil,' he said. 'How's our squawker doing back there?'

'Shouting out loud and clear, chief. Missiles seem to be taking the bait.'

Pyke nodded, biting his lip as he glanced from holoscreen to viewport and back while his fingers worked the touchboard. It was just under three minutes since those missiles were launched and hopes now lay with the AI-controlled forward shielding, which had been configured to maximise heat channelling and dissipation. Meanwhile, the centre section fields had been reshaped into aerofoil-forms to augment the ship's flight capabilities.

But in entering a planetary atmosphere at this angle and rate of descent, the *Scarabus* essentially had all the aerodynamics of a falling brick.

One part of Pyke's holoscreen showed an isometric map of the area around the location of Khorr's ship. It was a rudimentary representation but details were being added all the time as the sensors fed through the updates. Pyke's attention, though, was thoroughly focused on the possibility of imminent catastrophe.

'Any other sign that we're being tracked?' he said.

Ancil shrugged. 'I was certain that we were invisible back there yet they detected something ... wait a second ... yes, you little charmer! The squawker has snared the lot – all the missiles are on its tail.'

'And looks like those other jacker ships are moving out on intercept courses, too,' said Pyke, grinning as he watched the trails on another holopane. 'Ah, y'see what happens when ye mess around with the *Scarabus* crew, eh?'

'Shall I engage deceleration mode, Bran?' said the ship AI.

'Go ahead, Scar. Time we got down to the business that we came here for.'

The ship's inertial dampening shielded the crew from the effects of momentum shift but in his imagination Pyke still felt it as the *Scarabus*'s braking jets howled against the dive, forcing it into a curved trajectory that grew shallower by the second. At the same time the ship banked to port, its forcefield wings flexing with the fierce airflow and carrying it into a spiral descent which tightened as the airspeed fell.

'Nicely done, Scar,' Pyke said. 'Ancil, what's the latest?'

'Squawker's squawking, heading for open space with the missiles still chasing. No other activity from the jacker ships. Stealth systems are maxed out – we are just ghosting in!'

Pyke gave a smiling nod. 'Time to pay Khorr a visit, I reckon.'

The isometric overview of Khorr's location was now well detailed. Khorr's ship was sitting at one end of a wide, wooded valley in a hilly inland region of the largest continent on Tigimhos. And it wasn't alone. In a scrubby clearing a second vessel sat about a hundred yards away from Khorr's, going by the scale of the picture, and some kind of slender structure was positioned roughly midway between them.

'What is that?' said Ancil.

'Hechec said something about shroud-pillars,' Pyke said. 'Kinda implied they were something to do with the planet-jacking process. Scar, what do you think?'

'It seems very likely, Bran – in total there are four of these structures placed equidistantly around the planet, all giving off an interesting spectrum of energies.'

'The thing is, chief, who knows when their plan swings into action,' said Ancil.

'And I don't want to be down there when it starts to happen,' Win said sharply.

Pyke nodded. 'I thought about using the grav loaders to head in there along these defiles, but they give off a very definite energy signature so we'll need to get in as close as we can, and use all of our sneaky skills.'

'If I shut down some of the onboard systems,' Ancil said, 'we could really cut back on the energy profile. Probably have to rely solely on the suspensors for ground-level mobility.'

'Bran, there is actually a direct route,' said Scar. 'Our descent will bring us down south of the foothills of a range of steeper rocky hills; several deep river gullies cut through them to the northern uplands where the target vessel is located.'

'Good news, Scar – didn't much fancy a cross-country hike with nightfall moving in.' On Pyke's display the isometric had pulled back to show the greater locale, and a red dotted line that wove between the hills before doglegging into a high rocky pass. The pass led to wooded slopes overlooking the jacker ships and the structure. 'Now that's a sweet path for the cunning. So what's the timing on this – how long before we can be knocking on their door?'

'Planetside, my stealth systems still give us an advantage,' said Scar. 'We'll be at the start point in twenty minutes and the rocky hills will conceal our approach from there on suspensors.

It may take between sixty-five to seventy-five minutes to reach the entrance to the ravine, and the last section on foot might last up to forty-five minutes.'

'Sounds like a plan,' said Ancil. 'But is it a plan that we like?'

'The only other option is to charge in from the air, make an attack landing, then engage in a frontal assault on Khorr's vessel,' Pyke said. 'Which I'm pretty sure would get a swift and unfriendly reaction from the other ship – oh, and lose the element of surprise!'

'Hmm, I think I like Scar's plan more than that one,' said Ancil.

'Well, it *is* a good plan.'

'It's a very good plan.' Ancil paused to glance at Dervla. 'Don't you think?'

Dervla's amused composure was unchanged. 'It sounds like a decently cautious scheme. I'm sure that Scar has considered all the risks.'

Pyke nodded and smiled. 'Unlike our captain' was the unspoken zinger there but he decided to pretend that there was nothing out of the ordinary.

'Okay, Scar, set the course. Ancil, remember what you said about us being like a shadow in the night?'

'It's all under control, my captain,' Ancil said. 'And as soon as our velocity goes subsonic I'll start using inverted fields to mask our profile.'

Pyke leaned back in his couch. 'Work your magic, laddie.'

The final stretch of the descent took almost exactly twenty minutes. Dusk was spreading its grey gloom through the gulleys and valleys as the *Scarabus* followed the planned river route, gliding along on countergrav energy helices, a vaporous trail of fine spray whirling in its wake. Trees lined the river, their trunks sprouting strange tentacular branches that swayed in the ship's wake, while small creatures on pale ragged wings fluttered in the encroaching dark. Dervla was capturing data from the main sensor sweep and assembling a basic biosphere flora and fauna list while Ancil and Mojag were discussing the possible config of another squawker missile. But all that Pyke could think about was Khorr and the military scanner and the money and the deaths of Hammadi and Oleg, and how it felt like a deadly personal insult . . .

'So is that you starting to realise how mad this is?'

Dervla's voice was low as she perched on the edge of his console. Pyke gave her his best innocent-charm smile.

'Whatever makes you say that?'

She leaned in closer and a faint flowery fragrance teased his nose.

'That far-away look you had,' she said.

'Just imagining punishments for the thieving scum who played us for suckers,' he said. 'It's a macho payback kind of deal.'

She frowned. 'Don't think I've seen the vindictive Brannan Pyke before.'

'You make it sound like a bad thing! Look, he lied to us, killed two of our shipmates, and stole our gear and payment, so as far as I'm concerned he deserves what's coming to him.'

Dervla regarded him sadly. 'It's still mad, Bran, but we're here so no point in wailing about it, eh?'

'This is going to work out diamond fine,' he said as she returned to her station. 'We're going to dance in there sharp and sly as you like, even the score, get what we're due, then slip out and away . . . Scar, how's our time doing?'

'We are ahead of schedule, Bran. ETA is now twenty-one-point-eight minutes.'

'Great.' He switched his comm channel to shipwide. 'Attention – we'll be arriving at the debarkation point in twenty and then it's going to be the full encounter team – but one short, obviously. Everyone be at the load-out store in ten minutes.'

The full encounter team comprised Pyke, Dervla, Krefom, Ancil and Win – and had included Hammadi, whose aim with the hexbow had been deadly. Previously, that would have left Punzho, Mojag and Oleg in charge of the ship, a combination which, Pyke realised wryly, was technically unchanged.

After his shipwide address, the remaining minutes seemed to fly by. Even so, his impatience got the better of him so he told Dervla and the others that he needed to get something from his quarters then left the bridge, heading for the load-out store.

Dervla waited until Bran had descended the companionway, putting him out of earshot, then turned to Ancil.

'Leaving aside the overall craziness of this plan,' she said, 'what're our chances of getting through it alive?'

Ancil shrugged. 'It's not such a bad plan – the only real flaw is the lack of info on what kind of opposition is waiting for us—'

'Yeah,' Dervla said. 'Just a teeny, tiny flaw that one!'

'. . . which is why I'm bringing along an amped-up multi-sensor I've been working on. Looks like a regular factab but it's full of surprises.'

'Don't forget that surprise and momentum are on our side,' said Win. 'And Kref, of course.'

She had to admit – the Henkayan was invaluable. Despite his bulk he was well versed in battlecraft and fast on his feet. Former Phalanx Sergeant Krefom Graxmer in full-on combat mode was a scary thing. More than once she had thanked the gods of infinite space that he was on their side.

'Attention! All encounter team members to the load-out! Encounter team to the load-out!'

'Time to gear up,' Ancil said. 'Chief sounds just a bit cranky.'

Dervla was the last to drag herself out of her couch and follow. Aft of the hatch they trooped down the narrow companionway, and before losing sight of the low passage she caught a glimpse of one of the bearded humanoids watching from the corner of the sickbay corridor. She had intended to ask Pyke for the latest on the sick alien but when they reached the load-out storage he was clearly in no mood for anything resembling a civilised exchange. Instead he distributed body armour, weapons, ammo and the harnessed field contingency packs with a terseness that she and Ancil found impossible to ignore, responding with parade-ground sirs and yes-sirs and snappy salutes. Eventually, Pyke could not keep it up, cracked a grin but still poked her and Ancil's shoulders with his forefingers.

'Any chance you people could start taking this seriously?'

'If someone's shooting at me, my captain,' Ancil said. 'I can guarantee maximum seriousness.'

'Hey,' said Win. 'What if they're shooting at me?'

Ancil shook his head. 'Not when they've got bigger targets to aim at.'

'Hah, he's talking about me,' said Krefom. 'It's always me!'

Dervla smiled even as she found herself shifting into that half-relaxed/half-keyed-up mind-state that was her now accustomed method of preparing for a mission. Banter and crackery was part of that buildup, and even Bran seemed less of a self-important chump as they headed along the corridors to the main hold. By now the *Scarabus* had reached its destination, as helpfully seen on the wall monitor in the hold's control recess. As the main bay doors and fields were macroed into their activation sequence, they looked at the outside scenes on the monitor. They were parked on an area of level ground halfway up a woody slope, right next to a gulley that led between two craggy hills. The hullcams showed a carpet of split and broken bushes and trees by the light of down-angled external spots, with shadowy shapes in the night beyond.

'Right, shots first, then night-sights,' said Pyke.

There was a chorus of groans, which turned into curses and

teeth-gritting expressions as the dermal injector was passed around, delivering booster shots for their immu-rez. Most of the crew were overdue anyway, Pyke explained, not bothering to conceal his glee. While everyone was rubbing itchy patches on their arms (apart from Kref whose skin was tough as deck carpeting) Pyke strapped on his wrist-comm and muttered into it. The port-side bay doors cracked open and slid apart, allowing in a wave of cold air. Bright spots lit up the ground outside and the ramp, which extruded smoothly level with the hold deck. As they descended, Ancil sniffed and made approving noises as he unpacked his modified sensor-factab.

'Smells like . . . that liqueur they serve on that planetoid in the Kagashir system.'

'Planetoid T-Grej,' said Win. 'The booze was called Revelateur.'

'Could be the sap from all the trees that the suspensors smashed up,' said Dervla, noticing that an exclusion field had snapped into place across the open shuttle bay.

'Okay, my shadow warriors,' Pyke said. 'We'll use the harness lamps till we're clear of the gulley on the other side when we'll switch to the night goggles.'

The chest-height lamps had unidirectional heads. Five pale beams winked on and were angled towards the ground. Ancil was about to show round his factab, which was displaying a local physical map, when he paused and pointed over at the ship.

'What's Mojag doing here?'

Dervla looked round. Sure enough, there was Mojag hurrying down the ramp and across the layer of broken foliage to where they had gathered.

'What is it?' said Pyke. 'What's up?'

'I don't know,' Mojag said. 'Scar said that you wanted me outside immediately so I safetied my screens and came running—'

'I never . . .' Pyke began, then raised his wrist-comm. 'Scar, what the hell . . .'

'This doesn't sound good,' Dervla said.

Win suddenly shouted. 'Hey, stop! What are you doing . . . ?'

At the top of the ramp three figures stood in the open shuttle-bay entrance. G'Brozen Mav and his three followers were carrying a long-limbed form, which they quickly placed at the head of the ramp before stepping back into the bay. Most of the encounter team had already leaped forward in a mad dash but again the exclusion field reappeared. The motionless form was that of the Egetsi Punzho Bex and some of the crew went to his side to check on his well-being. Pyke, though, leaped over him and slammed his fists against the energy barrier.

'Open this frakking field, ya scum-sucking raker!'

G'Brozen Mav stepped forward, came right up to the shimmering field and stood about a foot away from the infuriated Pyke, his bearded expression grim and unyielding. One hand came up holding a wrist-comm and when he spoke his voice sounded clearly outside the *Scarabus*.

'Your ship is mine,' he said. 'Toolbearer Hechec has altered its governing intelligence and it now obeys only me.'

'Damn your eyes,' Pyke growled. 'We rescued you, and now you stab us in the back—'

'We did not escape to the ruin-world where you found us,' G'Brozen Mav said. 'We were abandoned there, tricked by one that I called brother. With this vessel I can return to the Chains, to the Warcage, and undo the damage. If we're not too late.'

'Look,' Pyke said, voice hoarse and trembling. 'If you let us back on board we'll help you get to wherever it is you need to go – hell, we'll even fight for you.'

'My companions would never agree,' G'Brozen Mav said. 'I was advised to assume control of the ship and dispose of you all before even reaching this place, but that would have been an act of shameful dishonour. I wanted you to have a chance, even if it is only a meagre one.'

For a moment Pyke said nothing, just stood with his splayed-out hands pressed against the exclusion field. Dervla knew from personal experience what that felt like; the field was a sub-molecular energy weave which at first felt tough and spongy to the touch, but it also projected ultrasonic vibrations which could become intensely uncomfortable.

'I don't give a rancid rat's bowel-scraping about your justifications and excuses.' Pyke's voice was low and raw and angry. 'The ship is mine – give it back!'

G'Brozen Mav's gaze was unwavering. 'My need is greater than yours. Thousands of lives hang in the balance and I have to do whatever is necessary to save them.' The bearded warrior stepped back. 'Khorr's vessel is still there, near the shroud-pillar – if you hurry, you may reach him before the pillars cast the great net.'

The shuttle-bay doors began to close and the ramp too was retracting, which forced Pyke to jump down onto the ground. Dervla and the others had carried Punzho Bex several yards away and as she crouched next to the semi-conscious Egetsi she saw Pyke haul out his heavy-calibre sidearm and blaze off a couple of rounds. The exclusion field in front of G'Brozen Mav flashed but he didn't even flinch. Even as the doors closed and sealed, his voice still came through.

'I instructed Toolbearer Hechec to make language teachers for you – if you fail to seize Khorr's vessel your survival may depend on understanding the Omnilect, the tongue of the Warcage. The teachers are in a small pouch secreted in the tall man's inside pocket.

'We must depart now. I urge you to waste no time in your pursuit of Khorr, but I will not lie to you – if the great net is cast and you are trapped on this world your chances of survival are low.'

Countergrav helices were building beneath the *Scarabus*, tugging at the grassy undergrowth, making a rushing tearing noise. Grassy leaves, pieces of foliage and splinters of wood were whipped up, highlighted by the spot-beams into bright swirling cones of debris. Pyke was standing too close, clothes flapping, hair streaming. Dervla yelled at him to get back but he gave no sign of hearing her, standing there, a mute still figure. She glanced at the others, saw faces full of stunned disbelief, panic and the first signs of fear. Win Foskel, though, was rifling through Punzho's pockets and produced a small transparent medical pouch which she passed to Dervla. Inside it were a number of what looked like pale ovoid tablets – she stashed it away in a sealable jerkin pocket just as another shot rang out.

Pyke had fired on the *Scarabus* again as it moved away down the valley. In the sudden darkness, harness lamps were hastily switched on and by their combined luminance Dervla could see Pyke raising the handgun again, sighting along it at the receding ship, a pose he held for a long drawn-out moment. Then the arm fell limply to his side, hand still holding the weapon. The ship, unaffected, flew away, the halo of its external lights fading, then gone. Despite the cluster of harness lamp glows, the surrounding darkness seemed to deepen, and Pyke was swallowed by it. Suddenly Dervla couldn't see him at all and was about to call out to him when the small bright beam of a harness lamp winked on and there he was.

'Ancil,' he said. 'That sensor o' yours working? Do you have a fix on Khorr's ship?'

'Within a hundred metres,' said Ancil. 'When we get to the other side I'll be able to narrow it down.'

'Good – encounter team goes with me now. We're gonna double-time it through the gulley, creep up on that scumpot and his goons and hit them hard. Mojag, you and Punzho'll have to follow as best you can.'

The Egetsi struggled to his feet, aided by Mojag who was now wearing Win's harness.

'I will not hold you back, Captain,' Punzho said. 'Nor will I be left behind.'

'Couldn't ask for more,' Pyke said. 'Right, let's move.'

Dervla frowned as he called out a marching order, then led the way at a jog, closely followed by Ancil who was consulting his sensor-factab as he ran. Then came Kref and Win with Dervla bringing up the rear. Minutes later they had left Mojag and the limping Punzho behind, and were trudging up a slope of brittle, shin-high bushes to the gulley that cut through the hilly ridge. Amid the dark their wavering lamp beams revealed trees and outcrops but also attracted odd insects that made a stuttering whine as they circled and darted about.

As they all hurried through the shadows, Dervla pondered Pyke's behaviour. She was aware, far more than the others, that the gabby, confident exterior masked a few deep insecurities. There was always that aura of unshakeable conviction in the rightness of his course, while the rest of the crew tried not to disappoint him. Which didn't help when his flawed reasoning amplified the flaws of his plans.

But now he's lost his ship and here we are stuck on a planet that's about to be snatched away, she thought. *I've just about had it – when we get out of this and back to something like civilisation I'm chucking it ...*

Everyone was breathing heavily by the time the team reached the other end of the gulley. Carrying weapons and ammo-heavy harnesses they had splashed through a couple of winding, rocky streamlets which left most of them with sodden feet. Harness lamps went off and night goggles were donned as the team skirted across the hillside behind masses of abundant foliage. The slope was heavily wooded and it didn't take long to find a gap in the greenery which provided a view of the planet-jacker camp. After adjusting her goggle filters, the first thing Dervla saw was a tall spire-like structure; it was invisible in the darkness but the goggles revealed the faintly amber energy ripples that were rising from the base to the tapered tip, which had to be about a hundred metres high. As the ripples ascended, pale blue points pulsed in spiral patterns.

And there were the two ships, located as Ancil said they would be. The large hulking one sat on formidable landing gear with four huge thrusters angled groundwards while a dozen or so biped crew members rushed in and out of a gaping stern bay. A smaller, sleeker vessel sat across the rough clearing with a couple of humanoid figures moving or sitting close by.

'Small ship is Khorr's,' muttered Ancil. 'Not getting any signs of active sensor sweeps.'

'Perimeter trips?' said Pyke, still peering through his goggles.

'No energy signatures that I can pick up.'

Pyke gave a low laugh. 'Bastard's wide open. We'll skirt round to attack from the cover furthest from the big ship. We rush them, close quarters, try to take them down quick and quiet. Let's go.'

With Pyke in the lead they headed off under cover of dense bushes but had taken barely a dozen paces when Ancil spoke up urgently.

'Wait ... stop! Chief, they're pulling out!'

Ancil was gripping his factab in both hands, staring at the detailed glows on its oval display. Dervla cursed under her breath, rushed back to where they'd paused before and was in time to see Khorr's ship, its ports sealed and the heat signatures of countergrav fields building beneath its hull.

'No, they're not,' Pyke muttered, his voice climbing. 'No, no, NO! ... Thieving scum! ...'

Before anyone could react he leaped into the chest-high weave of bush and winding grasses, tore his way through and charged off down the slope. Everyone seemed frozen with astonishment until Dervla shouted at them.

'We have to stop him – he'll get himself killed! Kref, Ancil, go after him, bottle him up and bring him back here. Oh and switch on your wrist-comms.'

Kref gave a sharp nod and moved off in pursuit. Ancil was still studying the factab sensor readout. 'Other ship is buttoned up too, ready to leave.' He glanced up. 'That's Khorr away.'

Above them a cluster of hull glows driven by a pair of stern thrusters – bright orange dots and smears in the night goggles – rose on a tight curve that turned into a steep climb skywards. When she looked back Ancil was gone, and Win was frowning at Dervla.

'Why'd you keep me back?'

'Someone has to hurry back to meet Mojag and Punzho,' she said. 'When you find them, let me know then steer them back to the gulley and wait for us.'

Win took several steps, paused and glanced back.

'Are we going to get off this planet, Dervie?' she said.

'I wish I could say yes or no for definite,' Dervla said. 'But right now it's all looking a bit shaky.'

Win let out a low, dry laugh. 'Shaky ... that's good.'

And she was gone.

Dervla turned to gaze downslope once more, crossed her arms and leaned against one of the native trees, feeling the pebbly surface of its bark through the hardweave of her body armour. Had Pyke truly lost it, and were the rest now looking to her to be captain? The thought made her shake her head. *Captain of what, exactly?*

Win had been gone just a couple of minutes when a shot rang out in the darkness, from the direction of Pyke's mad flight. Immediately she spoke into her wrist-comm.

'Kref! Ancil! Are you okay?'

Nothing, only the rustling quiet of the night-sunken trees all around her. She repeated the message, in a low, hoarse voice. Again there was no reply. She was about to try a third call-out when red light flared up into the sky. A bright scarlet spear that rushed straight up from the planet-jackers' spire, impaling the overhead layer of broken cloud. Then the wrist-comm clicked.

'... got him, Dervla.' It was Ancil. 'On our way.'

'Copy that,' she replied in relief. Still staring at the glowing red beam, she frowned when strange roseate ripples began rippling across the sky above, behind and within the clouds. The ripples pulsed faster till they became a mesh of criss-crossed rosy lines stretching in all directions. Right then, G'Brozen Mav's words came back to her: *If the great net is cast and you are trapped on this world your chances of survival are low.*

Footfalls drew near, heavy thuds and the rustle of foliage. Moments later Ancil came into view, followed by Kref carrying a limp form over one broad shoulder.

'That shot was the chief,' Ancil said. 'Must have taken it into his head that shooting at that generator spire thing would maybe make a ship come back and land. Then Kref threw a stone and brained him, helluva lucky shot.'

'Lucky?' said Kref, frowning.

'Well, it is dark.'

'Listen, I sent Win back to find Punzho and Mojag,' Dervla said. 'We'll be meeting them back at the gulley.'

But Win had not yet reported back, so as she led the way back uphill Dervla spoke casually into her wrist-comm. 'Win, we've got Pyke and we're heading back. What's your situation?'

It was a long moment before a breathless Win responded.

'Sorry ... sorry, Dervla ... still looking for them.'

Teeth gritted, Dervla kept her voice calm.

'Could be that they were spooked when the sky went mad,' she said. 'Keep searching – let me know soon as you see them.'

'Shall do – say, any ideas about these ripples and lines in the sky? Shook me when that started ... ah, hell, what's happening now?'

Dervla had become aware of the change, too, a faint glow that spread from the roseate lines, forming a shimmering, unbroken veil that stretched all across the sky. Ancil and Kref with his burden had slowed, their attention likewise caught. Dervla was about to urge them to resume when a pulse of brightness flared like a swift wave from horizon to horizon. The shimmering veil quivered like a membrane struck. There was an awful sense of premonition, while at the other end of the comm-link Win was asking, demanding, what was happening.

'Win, stay where you are,' Dervla said. 'Wait till this calms down.'

But no amount of reassurance could have prepared any of them for what happened next. The sky had steadily cleared of clouds and the glittering patterns and clusters of the stars were visible through the artificial mysterious veil. Low in the sky to the east, a piercing blue point grew and began to put out bizarre tendrils which themselves bifurcated until there was an ominous blue web hanging out there in space an unguessable distance away.

Then the radiating tendril tips began to splay and merge. Strange distortions wavered outwards from the bright, azure hub and for a moment it seemed that space itself was distending ... then came the fastest, flickering flash ... and in the next instant an entire planet appeared in the sky, its curved vastness looming overhead, so close that Dervla could look straight up and see the details of coastlines and mountain ranges and the snaking meanders of rivers.

Win Foskel was practically babbling away at the other end of the comm-link while Kref and Ancil, after the expected outbursts of cursing, had regained their composure. Kref had placed Pyke down against a smooth boulder and the erstwhile captain of the *Scarabus* was gazing skywards, open-mouthed.

Ancil took out his factab, pointed its onboard sensor nubs upwards to study the unknown world for a moment or two before lowering it.

'It's the same as that planet back in the Nadisha system,' he said. 'Wastelands of destruction, bombed-out population centres, forests reduced to pockets of vegetation.' He pointed. 'See that black smear? That's a city burning.'

'What do they do that causes all that?' Win said, privately hoping that she never found out.

Ancil was studying the factab's display again. 'That world is enclosed in the same gridded field as this one – can't be long till the switch.'

'How will that affect us?'

He gave a slow uncertain shrug. 'I'm pretty sure they don't want their purloined planets half wrecked by earthquakes and tidal waves so I'm guessing that these gridded fields dampen their inertia.' His eyes widened and he laughed briefly. 'Man, the technology required to do all that is astonishing ... well, that's my theory anyway.'

Dervla had been opening the comm-link to Win, and when Ancil finished she spoke. 'Did ya get that, Win? I'm not panicking and neither should—'

'Got it, Dervla! But I found Mojag and Punzho! That's what I was yelling about.'

'Right, I see, fine. Are you anywhere near the gulley?'

'We're minutes away from it.'

Dervla glanced over at Pyke. He was now sitting there with his head resting on arms that were crossed over raised knees.

'It might take us a little longer,' she said. 'When you get there—'

'This is it!' Ancil said excitedly. 'The night's about to go into reverse ...'

He was right. Staring up at the roseate-tinted sky she could see the stars starting to slide eastwards with calm purpose. There was a brightening to the west, casting the middle-distant mountain range into black silhouettes and steadily darkening the successive shadowy outlines of the nearer foothills, until the sun rose with a sudden, unfiltered blaze of light that made her flinch and slightly avert her gaze. She looked on in appalled fascination as the retrograde sun climbed with unseeming haste into the sky, an hours-long transit compressed into a few tens of seconds. At the same time, the newly appeared planet was moving in the opposite direction, its ruined immensity held in its own mesh of roseate fields and forces. Off to the side, Win Foskel staggered backwards and fell on her backside and then sat there, staring up. And in her mind Dervla thought she could almost picture what was happening, two worlds pivoting around some unshifting point, one swinging out of its aeons-old orbit, the other swinging in to take its place. The gargantuan audacity of it was breathtaking to her, even as she recognised the grim peril that they were all in.

From this height on the hillside she could see a landscape revealed, hills and unmarred forests rolling away into the hazy distance. Ancil, one hand shielding his eyes, pointed eastwards.

'That's the terminus,' he said.

Dervla nodded, seeing the wall of inky shadow now racing westwards. The other planet was moving between them and the sun and the nightfall of an eclipse was sweeping relentlessly in their direction. Then suddenly it was upon them, the sun sliding behind the ruined planet's obscuring edge, the curtain of darkness, the plunge into gloom. Someone moaned, Pyke perhaps, and harness lamps were switched on again. Dervla realised that she had been holding her breath and let it out in a shaky sigh.

'How long?' she said.

'A minute at the most,' said Ancil.

'They've moved this planet out of its orbit, haven't they?'

'Without a doubt.'

'When the other's taken its place,' she said, 'what happens next?'

Ancil laughed nervously. 'Well, G'Brozen Mav told the chief a neat little story about newly stolen worlds being taken to some far-off empire but who knows how much of that is true. If I had to guess I'd say that the next step is where we get whisked off into hyperspace ... my god, it's staggering, this! Flipping whole planets in and out of hyperspace! ... Ah, dawn rises once again.'

As the eclipse drew to a close, the gloomy dark was swept away by an onrush of daylight as the vast ravaged planet sailed along its inexorable course.

But we can't just wait here in the open like dumb prey, she thought. *No way of knowing what happens to these hijacked worlds, so we should act as if the worst is heading our way.*

It didn't take much to persuade Kref and Ancil to get moving again – Pyke refused Kref's offer of being carried, hardly saying a word as he forced himself to his feet and began trudging upslope. Progress was slow and, as they climbed, Dervla began to realise that the sun, now a thumb's width above the eastern horizon, had not moved for several minutes. She was about to mention it to Ancil when there was a shout from further uphill – it was Win, waving at her from between large clumps of prickly bushes, and Mojag and Punzho at her back.

'Did I not tell you to wait for us at the gulley?' Dervla said.

Win glanced at Mojag and Punzho then shrugged. 'We were getting back from where I found them, spotted you through the bushes – and here we are.' She gave a bleak smile. 'Bit of a hellish stew that we're in, eh?'

'Dervla,' Ancil said sharply.

She had seen the change already in the way shadows were moving too quickly across the ground. Turning she saw the sun climbing into the sky again, getting close to its noon high-point before curving southwards. Its progress seemed to accelerate as it rushed overhead and fell beyond the horizon, plunging all into funereal darkness.

There was a muttered cursing as lamps were fumbled on. Someone coughed, someone muttered angrily in a language Dervla didn't know and someone hushed them. She wished she knew how to calm fears with easy words and a chuckle, something Pyke was adept at. All she could do was urge them to stay together and carry on up the hill so, stumbling in the dark, they did so. The fear that still made her chest feel hollow spiked a few minutes later when the roseate sky above quivered suddenly. The bright starry points started to blur against the inkiness of space, gleams and clusters smearing into trails that faded as a maelstrom of steel greys and razor-silverness swirled out to span the sky.

'That ... that's hyperspace!' Mojag cried out. 'How is that possible?'

And Dervla recalled what Pyke said he was told by the alien Toolbearer Hechec, about the Shuskar and their huge ship, *Kezurdra*. If it was true that they were bound for some distant, savage star empire then this planet could be in transit for days. When she relayed this conclusion to the rest of the crew their consternation was undisguised.

'We only have rations for two days,' Win said. 'Three at a push ... hey, what about checking the landing site near that spire structure? Maybe the jackers left some supplies behind ...'

'What about attacking – firing at the spire?' said Mojag, whose drawn features gleamed with sweat while nervous fingers pawed at his scalp. 'Knocking out that energy field would bring rescuers running—'

Ancil was looking at him as if he was mad. 'Yeah, and then the entire planet drops out of hyperspace and we freeze to death in the black emptiness of interstellar space! Is that what you had in mind?'

Mojag bowed his head and covered his face with his hand. 'No, you're right, you're right ... don't you see?'

'Look,' Dervla said, 'we have to keep our cool. If we are going to be trapped under this sky for a while we either stay put or head for the nearest settlement.'

'That's a good fifteen klicks east and north of here,' said Ancil.

She shrugged. 'Anyone feel like sitting down and just hoping for the best? ... Nah, didn't think so.'

Moments later packs were reclipped to harnesses and the crew resumed hiking up the bushy slope. Pyke was stumbling along, flanked by Win and Ancil and shaking off helping hands whenever they were offered. Kref led the way and Dervla brought up the rear, walking in Mojag and Punzho's footsteps. It now seemed that the Egetsi had gone from being the recipient of assistance to its donor as he tried to calm or reassure the increasingly fretful Mojag.

This situation is crazy, she thought. *Pyke's turned into a lethargic basketcase and Mojag's having a gradual meltdown, no doubt caused by the copy of Oleg that he has in his head. And everyone's looking to me for leadership! Damnation, we are in trouble!*

'Something new is happening!'

Ancil had slowed and was looking up. The sky was changing again. The churning greys and silver stria of hyperspace were melting into each other, the vast eddies and swirls flattening, the entire convulsive embrace of it darkening, deeper and darker – and suddenly the wide blackness of space snapped back in, scatters of stars clearly visible through the rosy veil.

'How long was that?' Dervla said. 'Twenty minutes? Twenty-five?'

Ancil was checking his factab. 'Twenty-three and four seconds.'

'That's only long enough for a jump of about fifteen light years,' she said. 'Can this be the destination ... ?'

The stars began to slide sideways, as if the planet was being turned. At the same time something swung smoothly up from the horizon to loom vastly into view. At first glance Dervla thought she was seeing at an angle a widely separated formation of ships, huge ships, set out in a perfect grid array that curved oddly away. Then a bright radiance bloomed on the western horizon and the array of distant objects shone as its relative position began to change. Dervla gazed from array to horizon and back, trying to take it all in. The planet was being steered towards the curved array of bright, round objects, moved level with it, positioned, and realisation struck.

'Those are worlds,' she said. 'Oh, that's amazing ... '

Everybody else was staring too.

'There must be ... scores,' said Win.

'And we're being fitted into an empty slot,' Dervla said.

Surveying the incredible sight, she counted nine rows in the array, then made a rough estimate of the worlds visible along one of them, then tried to reckon how many were strung along each encircling chain, then added them up ...

'About 250?' she said.

'More like 290, actually,' said Pyke. 'Maybe 300.'

At the sound of his voice she whirled to see him standing next to Ancil, switching between glancing down at the factab's oval display and peering up at the grid of worlds now half filling the sky.

'You sound okay,' she said, suspicion fuelling a growing irritation. 'Got over that little tantrum, did we? Have you been faking it all this time? I'll bet you have you—'

'Faking? I'll have you know that I was distraught, beside myself with sheer unmitigated anguish at the way they stole my ship ... well, not so much anguish as a right steaming fury. Yes, I did kinda lose it, really felt like I was blowing my top after seeing all our plans fall apart, so I went off on a wee rampage and was gonna hand over my guns until Kref decked me.'

'So you've been back to your normal egomaniacal self since you came round,' Dervla said. 'Back down there? And did you enjoy seeing us worrying ourselves sick over you?'

Pyke sighed. 'Everyone did their job, Dervla, and that was in no small part due to yourself. I've always wanted to see how you'd manage under pressure and then this opportunity presented itself – it was too good to pass up. So now that you've had a taste of command you have an idea of what it's about, y'know, if another job offer comes yer way, like.'

'You let me think you were having a . . . a breakdown or something.' She paused as Pyke arched an eyebrow and glanced over at Mojag who was standing off to one side, hands linked behind his head as he muttered to himself. Mojag was a friend and crewmate, and it was disturbing to see him in this state, but it didn't lessen Dervla's resentment at Pyke's fakery. Then she stopped and wondered . . . was this the fakery? Was this just a desperate piece of face-saving, something to avoid the embarrassment of admitting that he lost it?

She inhaled deeply, exhaled, and forced herself into something like composure.

'In the circumstances, *Captain*,' she said, 'we had better get focused on survival. Could be that the new owners will be along shortly to check out their new property.'

Pyke nodded, glancing once more at Ancil's factab. 'Some big damn pretty thing, this artificial solar system, eh? I mean, what kind of tech would you need to hold all these worlds in place?'

Ancil lightly prodded several display emblems. 'Well, chief, they're capable of taking one of these planets, bundling it up in an inertia-dampening field, flying it through hyperspace, swapping it for a fresh one and bringing it back. My guess is they're pretty far up the pecking order.' He gave Pyke a sidelong look and grin. 'Good to see you back in the game, by the way.'

Yes, Dervla thought. *The boy's game!*

Above and outwith, one final gentle gyring motion seemed to lock the world in place and left their surroundings in darkness once more. Overhead, the roseate veil abruptly vanished, even as the early grey fingers of another daybreak spread slowly from the west. It was dawn on an unknown world, and all the other worlds that Dervla could see curving away in perfect regimentation.

Right now, just give me one without Pyke on it and I'll be the happiest girl alive.

CHAPTER SEVEN

The skies of the affray-world, Brayl, were troubled, threatening. Dark rain-clouds loomed low over the ruined canyon city, filtering the light to a brassy gloom. Out on the severed remnant of what had once been a cross-canyon bridge, Second Blade Akreen and his Shuroga scout awaited the Treneval leader, Livakaw. The dreg-bout had not gone well for the Treneval task-army: in the face of the Zavri onslaught it had fallen back to this final redoubt where, depleted and hemmed in, their leader had requested a truce-parley. When recordings of this clash were replayed all across the Warcage it would amply demonstrate the enduring might and irrevocable judgement of the Shuskar Gun-Lords.

'He delays, invincible one,' the Shuroga scout said in her sibilant voice. 'He insults you by making you wait, which is an affront—'

'He knows that an ordained death decree hangs over him,' Akreen said. 'For one so condemned, the import of lesser censures is minor at best. Besides, skulker, the insults of traitors mean nothing to me, pointless noises from a worthless source.'

'We know how to deal with betrayers on Kuloz,' the Shuroga muttered, hunching her skinny shoulders beneath battered hide armour. 'An arm, a leg and an eye, to begin with …'

'Enough,' Akreen said, pointing with one silvery, emblem-adorned hand. 'He comes.'

Livakaw was taller and burlier than most Trenevali and wore an impressive cloak of shiny black *chol* fur across his wide shoulders. He was bareheaded and otherwise clad in the rough grey leathers of a Treneval ranker, apart from the segmented metal gauntlets on his large hands.

Akreen had pondered briefly on how to configure his body-frame, swiftly settling on the symbols of punishment. His arms, chest and legs bore their usual archaic battle-armour skinforms but they were now covered in the emblems and glyphs of the Shuskar Lords, the Redeemed Order of Steel, the Grand Escalade and the Chamber of Judgement, as well as the sigils of the holdworld viceroys and the banner-badges of those task-armies whose loyalty to the Lords was unblemished and unquestioned. In addition he had lengthened his legs and adapted his shoulders to resemble the formal robes of the Chamber Judges, which included the crossed hilts of execution swords jutting up at the back. Akreen wanted to be the embodiment of the Warcage in all its dutiful and honourable glory, the personification of the inexorable fate which had come for Livakaw. Brayl would be his tomb.

And as Livakaw approached with a steady, heavy tread, one of Akreen's precursors chose that moment to bestow an utterance.

[*To the cooking pot the yosig-bird came, self-plucked and trussed!* – Zi]

Maintaining his outward composure took some effort. It was Zivolin, of course. If any one of his seven precursors was likely to violate the in-combat silence vow it would be Zivolin. As some of the others offered up remonstrances, Akreen closed them all off by focusing on the traitor Livakaw who came to a halt several paces away.

'Thank you, Second Blade, for agreeing to this truce,' said the Treneval leader, his voice guttural and hoarse. 'Our collective gratitude for allowing an exchange is—'

Akreen cut him off. 'The bouts of the Grand Escalade, even the dreg-bouts, have clearly set-out rules. My acknowledgement of their primacy here has no bearing on emotive issues. Gratitude has no place here, only the matters under discussion. What are they?'

Livakaw gave him a heavy-lidded look, dark eyes sunken beneath a furrowed brow. 'Clemency,' he said. 'Not for myself, obviously—'

'In accordance with the dreg-bout ordinances, all who take the field are considered combat effectives. The Chamber judgement also provides the following rules of engagement: if you are killed or captured within the first ten minutes of the final bout stage, then one quarter of Trenevali effectives selected by lot will face execution; if you are killed or captured after the lapse of ten minutes then one half of Trenevali effectives selected by lot will face execution; if in either case, after your death or capture, the Trenevali task-army continues to fight then all will face execution without exception.' Akreen paused, glanced back along the canyon wall to where the shiny ranks of his half-battalion of Zavri veterans awaited. 'Or you could immediately surrender yourself to my custody and only a tenth of the Trenevali would face execution. What say you?'

Livakaw nodded thoughtfully. 'Correct me if I am wrong, Second Blade Akreen, but I do not believe that the Trenevali and the Zavri have ever faced each other across the battlefield, not in all the many millennia of the Grand Escalade. Or am I wrong?'

Akreen pondered this, sent a query-scrute scurrying through his siloed memories and found confirmation of the Treneval leader's comment, along with a strange then-mote.

'Your observation is correct,' Akreen said. 'The Treneval task-army never rose above the 32nd grade while the Zavri have never fallen below 19th. Treneval, however, has always been loyal to the Shuskar Lords, unwavering in their duty across the centuries.

Records also show that the Treneval holdworld sent several task-armies to fight for the Shuskar Lords during the Beshephis Insurrection, acquitting themselves with great honour.'

'We still sing songs in their memory,' said Livakaw. 'Their valour lives on.'

'Yet by your actions you have sullied their name,' Akreen said. 'The Trenevali honour was unmarred until just days ago when undeniable proof came to light that you, their general, had conspired with the rebellious Chainer vermin. Just in the last hour, the Treneval viceroy has repudiated your actions and stripped you of all titles, subsequent to the Iron Chiefs proclaiming the Sever Shun against you. Actions like yours seem insane, yet to my eyes you do not look like one deranged.'

'Insanity comes in many colours, Second Blade,' said Livakaw. 'Like consigning millions of thinking, feeling beings to short lives of brute drudgery and planned ignorance. Or like channelling untutored youngers into the triumph camps which indoctrinate them for combat, for the bouts, to die on some affray-world far from their kin for no good reason—'

'Underworkers are by nature fitted to their labour,' said Akreen. 'I was wrong – you now begin to sound like one gone insane, not unlike the Chainer vermin to whom you passed on vital secrets.'

Livakaw shrugged. 'I do not expect you to understand these things. Your eyes show you only the things that they've been taught to see.' He gave Akreen a narrow look. 'Indeed, I have heard that the Zavri enjoy a peculiar form of immortality, that the spirits of your ancestors live on within that gleaming metal flesh of yours and that your own spirit will live on after you cease to be – is this so?'

Akreen heard the stirrings at the back of his thoughts, irritation from Drolm, indignation from Iphan, the grand outrage of Casx, Togul's self-important disdain, Zivolin's seditious glee, the cold malice of Rajeg. As usual from Gredaz, eldest and most elusive, there was nothing.

And for a single moment Akreen felt a strange urge to confide in this criminal, to explain how the process of scission created the next generation of Zavri and how only one in a brood would end up carrying the self-patterns of the precursors, the lineal ancestors. How that responsibility conferred the advantage of having all those life experiences to draw on, and how this could cause resentment in his brood divisiblings ...

Suddenly appalled to find himself thinking these thoughts, he quickly erased them from awareness and addressed the traitor with the appropriate level of scorn.

'My forebears oversee my every decision and act,' Akreen said. 'Their guidance safeguards the honour of my line. Clearly, you hold your ancestors in scant regard.'

'The holy walkers say that the souls of dead Trenevali are sent to be tasted in the mouths of the Night Gods – the balance of purity and taint in our essence determines our fate in the Shroudlife. When I meet my ancestors I shall at least know if my truth is the same as theirs.'

[*Tribal primitives!* – To][*A heroic insolence!* – Zi][*Have him flayed* – Ra]

Ignoring these backbrain mutters, Akreen considered the Treneval leader's response and felt a slight echo of the envy that picked at him whenever he encountered one of his divisiblings. None of them, after all, had to share their minds with the dead.

'Your replies are not relevant to the matter under discussion,' he said. 'I have made clear the adjudged outcomes – what say you?'

Smiling, Livakaw glanced thoughtfully up at the decrepit ruins of the canyon city. 'Originally, our dreg-bout adversaries were to be the Tephoy, against whom we judged we would have a better-than-even chance. But not long after gating here a day ago an Escalade official brought word of the verdict from the Chamber, and then the decision to allow the dreg-bout to be played out – with the Tephoy replaced by the more formidable Zavri. My rankers were a little surprised but their resolve was unshaken and they looked forward to pitting themselves against your shining legion. That has not changed. We will see the bout through . . . and we will try to make you remember us.'

'Then there is nothing more to say.'

The Treneval leader nodded, turned away and retraced his steps back to where the remnants of his task-army were positioned by crumbling walls and sagging floors. Akreen's Shuroga scout chuckled as the burly figure receded.

'Hah – perhaps a vestige of honour yet remains in his putrid mind,' said the scout.

'The judges of the Chamber have spoken,' Akreen said. 'A traitor shall die this day.'

'Amid bloody slaughter,' the Shuroga scout said with relish.

And the scout was right. On his return to the canyonside territory held by his Zavri half-battalion, Akreen ordered the maul platoons to advance. This was a close-quarters dreg-bout, no energy or projectile weapons permitted, so the maul platoons were armed with pulverhammers to break down walls and sawglaives for hand-to-hand combat. The hammers pounded, the floors shook underfoot, and the Zavri crashed through, heralded by clouds of dust.

Battle was joined. The Trenevali were valiant and showed no fear, only their blood and viscera. They were skilled with light to medium weapons and armour but they could not stand against the superior speed and strength of the variable Zavri physique. They were not without a certain tactical cunning, however – twice, solitary Zavri were cut off and doused with viscous flammable mixtures that clung and burnt at a high temperature. At the same time the Trenevali ambushers wound lengths of wire around the burning Zavri's midsection, arms and legs, obviously thinking that they would be weakened by the heat. But the flaming mixture did not burn hot enough and the ambushers died.

Akreen led the assault from the centre of his forces, monitoring the progress of the forward platoons, and examining the bodies of the enemy to see if Livakaw had fallen. Once, as they passed through a gallery lined with heavy pillars, masking covers fell away from two columns and a pair of Trenevali leaped out, hurling spears. One was snatched in mid-air by one of Akreen's guards, the other was deflected by the arm-shield of another guard. The two attackers were cut to pieces without hesitation. And through it all Akreen's precursors sang battle fugues in joyful chorus – they revelled in these moments, the chance to live through him and taste even the meagre shadow of glory.

After the first ten minutes of combat operation, no evidence of Livakaw's death had emerged. By the twentieth minute the Zavri progress along the canyonside corridors had slowed due to the defender tactic of shoring up entrances and walls with mounds of rubble and masonry. Faced with this, the assault platoons simply threw together ramps from the plentiful debris and broke through to the upper floors. The Trenevali had already laid some spring-loaded traps up there, along the likely approaches, but they caused only brief, annoying delays.

After nearly thirty minutes of bloody, one-sided slaughter Akreen's Shuroga scout came to him with news.

'The end is near, invincible one,' she said. 'The last of them and their timid leader have barricaded themselves into some ancient blasphemous shrine at the end of this level. There are no more stairs beyond it, no tunnels and no escape.'

'How many still live?'

'A handful, perhaps as many as ten. There are two entrances, both blocked with rubble and smashed furniture.' The scout twitched her nose. 'I could smell oil, so they are planning a warm welcome.'

Akreen shook his head. 'The same failed tactic. Tell the maul platoons to get to work – bring that wall down, move in and crush them. Say that I want Livakaw taken alive if possible.'

The scout chuckled and scurried off with the new orders.

The pulverhammers were creating a thunderous, non-stop cacophony by the time Akreen and his command officers reached the shrine. Wide steps led up to a towering facade covered in an ornate frieze of coiling creatures arranged around three huge faces which time had ravaged and rendered unrecognisable. It was a venerable remnant from the canyon city's lost past, its every carven glyph and creature carrying a message out of antiquity. Akreen took it all in with understanding and appreciation for a brief moment before ordering more platoons forward. The barricades at the entrances burst into flames just then but the besieging Zavri ignored them. As the pulverhammers battered down the entrance pillars, widening the gaps, others moved in to attack the burning debris and drag some of it out of the way.

Then success – joyful cries rang out as a section of the ornate facade came down with a loud rumble. One of the immense corroded faces shifted then toppled backwards to land with a resounding crash. All around the ragged gap flames flickered, ruddy glows veiled by clouds of old dust sent aswirl as the silvery forms of Zavri troopers rushed in, heedless of the fires. Flanked by his guards, Akreen followed the main body of his troops into the shrine from which a rhythmic banging racket was now emanating. In the grey gloom rotted rags of banners and tapestries hung along the left-hand wall while to the right were two flights of steps – one led down the far wall past banks of seating to the pillared floor of the shrine, while the other led down the middle. More huge faces looked down to where a handful of Trenevali stood in a line before a lamp-lit altar, beating the pillars with clubs, staffs and blade hilts. Behind the altar, Livakaw sat in a canopied throne.

At Akreen's gesture the Zavri rushed down the stairways to close with the last defenders. Even as the charge began, Livakaw threw back his head and roared with laughter. Akreen was moving towards the middle stairs to begin his own descent when someone plucked at his arm. Whipping round in annoyance he saw that it was his Shuroga scout.

'Incomparable one, I can hear hammering!'

'Yes, from those doomed fools below.'

'No, from beneath, from the underpinnings!'

A deep muffled thud, loud enough to be heard right across the shrine, came from under the steps. Akreen felt the floor tremble, and knew that they had been led into a gigantic trap. The scout was tugging on his arm, begging him to move back, as were his precursors, wailing in unison from the confines of his mind. The scout hauled him back towards the ragged gap between the shrine's entrances. It was ten or fifteen paces away, which now seemed like a great distance as terrible screeches and structural groans came up from below as dust began falling from above. The floor suddenly lurched and slumped noticeably, sloping away from the exits. Down on the shrine floor, Zavri attackers and Trenevali defenders alike had abandoned the fight and were scrambling up the banks of seating. Dust and grit was coming down in trickles and curtains along with chips and pieces of masonry.

Akreen was just a few paces away from safety when there was a deep grinding noise and a gap tore open right across the floor directly ahead. A sudden jolt knocked Akreen off his feet and the section of floor he was on sank and tipped back still further. As he regained his feet, fear filled his limbs with energy and he drove himself forward in a leap towards the receding stable edge.

Self-preservation instincts had already forced his limbs into their strongest elongation pattern, giving him just enough reach. His splayed hands slammed onto the jagged floor brink, grabbed for solid purchase, hung there for a second before he was seized and pulled up to safety.

Held there, Akreen had enough time for a single glance back over the precipice – and saw the whole of the shrine break away and fall, saw sunlight spear through the splintering walls, saw the silver forms of Zavri troopers caught in the chaos ... then the ceiling itself cracked and fell, a roaring cascade of shattered masonry. One monstrous shard struck the uneven floor edge a few paces along, shearing off a large area and narrowly missing one Zavri who gave a disdainful sneer before retreating a step or two.

Quickly, Akreen directed everyone back to the corridor outside the shrine then further back to safer passageways and chambers. Once there, he ordered his Shuroga scout and his command staff securitor to head down one of the lower floors to find a spot from which they could use their scopes to study the floor of the canyon, more than a thousand *yiten* down.

While they were away, Akreen went from platoon to platoon, compiling an index of the missing. He was mulling over the disturbingly long list when his securitor and the Shuroga returned unexpectedly.

'We had just reached a good observation point a couple of floors below when the Grand Escalade inspection barge arrived,' said the securitor officer, whose name was Tesnik. 'Moments later, however, three fliers bearing Chamber of Judgement sigils swooped in and took up positions around the Escalade craft. About a minute later the barge rose back up and flew over this side of the canyon.'

Akreen nodded. *Back to Kamax Base, the bout encampment.* He looked at the scout. 'What did you see?'

'Death and wreckage, illustrious one,' the scout said thoughtfully. 'At a thousand *yiten* these scopes do not reveal many details, but I could see a few of our troops moving around the impact area. No sign of Trenevali survivors. The Chamber's judgement has been accomplished.'

'At a heavy cost, Second Blade,' said the securitor, Denesk. 'Multiple involuntary scissions may well have taken place already.'

'I am aware of this, Securitor Denesk,' said Akreen. 'When the Chamber of Judgement assigned this duty to the Zavri they did not promise that the Trenevali would meekly offer no resistance. Was that what you were expecting from this dreg-bout?'

'Why, no, Second Blade, I ...'

'Perhaps you seek to undermine my status and the legitimacy of my orders – is that your purpose?'

'Second Blade ... I ... spoke in error. My thoughts were flawed.'

'That is a great shame, Securitor,' Akreen said. 'Then I suggest that you reconsider your fitness for this post on my staff. In the meantime, ascertain from the pathfinders if they have yet determined the most direct route to the extraction camp.'

'At once, Second Blade.'

As Denesk hurried, the scout gave a grunt and a grin.

'His comments reached no audience, masterful one,' she said. 'Was he more stupid than ambitious?'

'Denesk is a lineager with two precursors,' Akreen said. 'One of them, Dijal, I met early on in my latter-youth stage and his feral manner made a lasting impression upon me. My harsh words were meant as much for him as for Denesk.'

[*Denesk's other precursor is that black-souled meaning-twister, Tashor, who I warned you about, boy. And still you advanced their lineager to your staff. Fool* – Ip]

Iphan, his most immediate precursor, had never risen above

Overplatoon Leader, despite his ambition. Akreen's contrasting success in rising to the rank of Second Blade provoked only a tireless fault-finding which Akreen had grown adept at blanking out. Most of the time.

The Shuroga scout uttered a dry chuckle. 'Yes, keep the ambitious ones on a leash – a wise arrangement. There will be concern about our losses, however.'

'Yes, which is why we must move out,' Akreen said. 'Go tell the platoon leaders to be ready for imminent departure. Tell them that I expect to hear news of casualties by the time we reach Kamax Base.'

'As you will it.'

The Zavri half-battalion – being half of the Blackshield Battalion – took only a short while to repack and form up. The path out of the canyonside city followed a zigzag of stairs, flights of pale stone steps, worn, cracked and rounded that climbed through a dozen decrepit floors. The machined edges and surfaces of a technological civilisation were still visible on all sides but the firefights of innumerable Escalade bouts combined with climatic weathering over a century or more had left their mark.

The extraction camp – Kamax Base – was actually a complex of buildings located not far from the canyon passage exit. The Zavri emerged into bright sunlight, marching three abreast. Silver limbs and torsos were coated in dust as fine as the swirls kicked up by the warm moist wind now blowing in from the wastelands. The previous dark cloud had dissipated to thin tails strung out across a bleached sky. At this latitude, it afforded a magnificent view of the nearby Warcage worlds, lines of pale, hazy planets that faded into the distance. Only the oceans and landmasses of the nearest were properly visible.

An Escalade bout officially ended when the victors crossed the camp threshold under their own efforts. Outside the gates, shackled lines of brownclad underworkers sat in the shade of the walls, possibly a lull between labour periods. Just inside, grey-robed Escalade arbiters were waiting as Akreen led the Blackshield half-battalion through. The victor's bell began to clang, nine harsh peals, and he was surprised to see the red-cowled and blue-masked form of the Arbiter-General himself descend the steps of the Afterbout Hall. Normally, victors were welcomed by the camp's Overarbiter, so perhaps it was the significance of Livakaw's betrayal and subsequent death sentence which had earned the personal attention of the Arbiter-General of the Grand Escalade, Shuskar Lord Veshen.

Akreen came to a halt two paces from the foot of the hall steps where the Arbiter-General now stood. Behind him, the Zavri column likewise stopped, several hundred feet slamming down into the ready stance in perfect gleaming unison.

'Second Blade Akreen, say what must be said.'

The Shuskar were tall, broad-shouldered bipeds who always wore elaborate attire and those serene, pale blue masks. The Arbiter-General's regalia consisted of layers of exotic, finely made garments, rich reds and yellows fringed with amber, the whole assemblage offset by the bulky, dark grey iron gauntlet that Lord Veshen wore on his right hand. From within his red cowl the pale blue mask gazed at Akreen, its frozen features sculpted to convey strength, wisdom and benevolence. The bare left hand was pallid and wrinkled, long trembling fingers absent-mindedly stroking the edge of a brocaded pocket.

'Lord Arbiter-General,' Akreen said. 'The strong have triumphed and the weak have been vanquished.' The traditional words felt both reassuring and charged with meaning. 'Death has eaten its fill and we hunger for honour.'

'The honour of the Zavri remains bright and undimmed, Second Blade,' said the Arbiter-General. 'You have carried out your duties in an exemplary fashion. I am gratified to confirm that the Zavri are welcome in Afterbout Hall!'

That was the cue for the Blackshield troopers to shout as one the word 'Shyur!', meaning loyalty, and to shout it four times – after which Akreen nodded to his command staff who then led the platoons up the broad steps. But foremost in his mind were his concerns for those who had been caught in the collapsing shrine. It was customary at this juncture for the Overarbiter to hand to the victorious general a preliminary bodycount assessment but the Arbiter-General, flanked by flashlance guards, was drawing off to one side. Before he could take a step in pursuit, though, he was forestalled by the approach of an Escalade official, a gangling Tephoy in the black and dun robes of an Adviziar, normally an Overarbiter's deputy.

[*Hrrm, the Tephoy. Indifferent battle skills* – Ra][*Petty bureaucrats well suited to their masters' purposes* – Zi]

'Second Blade, I am Adviziar Padkel,' said the Tephoy in an officious monotone. One gold-gloved, four-fingered hand came up and held out an erasable missiver. Wordlessly, Akreen accepted it, flipped back the cover and read the casualty report, committed the figures to memory, then closed the missiver and passed it back. Akreen saw him surreptitiously activate the erasure mode just before it was slipped away into an inside pocket.

'My congratulations to you and the Blackshields for achieving victory without losses,' said the Adviziar.

[*How charmingly corrupt* – Zi][*Burnishing the likeness of invincibility* – Dr]

Akreen ignored his precursors.

'Honour and hard-won prowess told in the end, Adviziar,' he said. 'That and the blessings of the Shuskar Lords.'

[*A fitting response* – Ca][*The response of a worm!* – To][*Just another step in the dance of the burnishers* – Zi]

'Their blessings illuminate our lives,' intoned the Adviziar. 'Also, at the behest of the Chamber of Judgement I am to give you a new set of interim orders. You are to make whatever command delegations you deem appropriate then go straight to the primary launch platform where a ship awaits you. Once aboard, you will receive additional orders.' He shrugged. 'There is little else to say, Second Blade, except that these orders came directly from one of the Judge-Eminents, Shuskar Lord Zahnar himself.'

'An interesting elucidation,' said Akreen. 'It is appreciated.'

'All in service to the Warcage.'

With that, Adviziar Padkel gave a small bow and moved on.

Akreen watched him stroll away, feeling slightly puzzled. *All in service to the Warcage?* It sounded almost like a formal axiom but Akreen had never heard it before. But he put that aside while he absorbed the main morsel of information, that Judge-Eminent the Lord Zahnar was present and taking a personal interest in the last moments of Livakaw's treacherous existence.

Two Shuskar Lords overseeing a dreg-bout, and in person! Clear evidence, perhaps, that the Shuskar were determined and committed to crushing the Chainers and their allies and supporters.

Akreen's command staff – the Securitor, Tacticor and Irruptor officers – were waiting at the top of the stairway, outside the entrance to Afterbout Hall, a pair of tall and clearly old ragiron doors. He instructed them to keep the platoons under strict observance until everyone was gated back to the Zavri hold-world, Drevaul. When he explained that his own return would be delayed due to 'command obligations', no one queried further. On asking after the whereabouts of his Shuroga scout he was told that the scout had followed the rest of the battalion into the Hall. Gauging that he had little time to see her out, Akreen bade farewell to his officers, descended the steps and headed for the launch platforms.

The blazing sunshine fell upon the sloped grey buildings of Camp Kamax, revealing every stain, every crack, every vein-like spread of rust trails from rusty pipes and fittings. Akreen had previously participated in several pinnacle-bouts on this world but this was the first time he had fought through that curious canyonside city. Apart from that cunning suicide trap, the Trenevali had presented no challenge to the Zavri. But if they had faced the Avang, or even the Sujalka, ah, what a test of body and spirit that would have been!

Also, this bout had been comparatively restrictive in terms of both troop numbers and combat area. This was reflected in the dusty quiet that hung over much of the camp – barracks, infirmaries and mealhouses that could accommodate opposing hosts four or five times that which the Zavri and the Trenevali had fielded lay empty and closed up. And a few hours from now, after the Zavri Blackshields had gated back to Drevaul, and the Shuskar Lords and the senior Chamber and Escalade officials had likewise departed, the camp personnel would commence clear-up operations in advance of the next bout.

[*Battle, blood and strife are the hallmarks of normality; stillness and repose are anomalies* – Ra]

Tall blast shielding walled off the primary launch platform from the rest of Kamax Base. Akreen's bout-token gave him access at the guarded entrance from where a dozen strides took him to the foot of a three-flight gantry. Above, the rim of the blast basin occluded much of the sky, plunging the ground beneath into shadow, along with the sixty or more heavy supports built to withstand the basin's weight and the force of thrust engines. Climbing the last few steps he reached a covered landing at the top and allowed a rare smile to crease his silvery face when he saw who was waiting for him.

'New orders, illustrious one?' said the Shuroga scout.

Akreen regarded her with a kind of stern amusement. 'How did you know I would be here?'

The scout arched a pair of bushy eyebrows. 'Some of these bases huddle close to the ground, like docile leafeaters, but

Kamax has a tower and a mast which I climbed to get a better view of the Escalade wagons bringing the bodies up from the canyon. I also saw you talking with the Arbiter-General, then one of those Tephoy puppet-faces. And when you left the Hall and headed towards this part of the camp I knew where you had to be going, knew that it would be needful and fated.'

'Sometimes you presume too much for your own good!'

The scout nodded. 'It is true, perceptive one, I do. I cannot think why you keep me in your service . . .'

Giving the Shuroga a mock serious glare, Akreen stepped across the covered landing to a doorway opening onto the primary launch platform. And when he saw the ship a certain understanding dawned.

[*The Master descends, his ordination to bestow* – Dr]

It was the *Urtesh*, command cruiser of the Zavri battle array, which meant that First Blade Tevashir was here and had sent for him. But did that mean that he knew about how the dreg-bout ended, about the collapse of the shrine? And the apparent ease with which Zavri casualties had been erased from the record?

[*A scolding, a reprimand, or a demotion? Oh, the harsh fruits of disgrace!* – Zi] [*Punishment for such insignificance? Your babble grows ever more inane* – To]

Although Akreen had at times engaged his precursors in dialogue, most of the time he had learned to maintain a taciturn distance, a strategy which conferred some peace of mind. He had even stopped obsessing over the speechless, grim presence of Gredaz who in all of Akreen's years had spoken only three times with a grand total of eleven words, consisting of three *Nos*, two *Not acceptables*, and his longest ever comment, *It does not matter.*

'First Blade awaits, fearless one,' said the scout. 'Do you wish me to attend?'

[*Fearless, hah!* – Ca]

Akreen nodded. 'Follow.'

As he descended to the basin, he erased from his bodyframe the last vestiges of the Chamber judge appearance that he had adopted earlier, along with all the symbols and emblems. In their place he raised the standard officer armourform, formal and plain. Tevashir deplored the current fad for elaborate exteriors and fanciful decorations, favouring instead a more traditional austerity which was in keeping with the stern discipline that accompanied his command over the Zavri battle array.

With the Shuroga scout in his wake, Akreen strode down towards the slope-hulled shape of the *Urtesh*. It was a storm-grey and blood-red ship with raked, predatory lines, crouching on six heavy jointed legs, thick armour sections matching the open recesses in the hull. As they approached, one of the cargo lifts descended from the underside, bathed in light. Akreen and the scout climbed on, the lift began to rise and moments later they were stepping off it within the crate-crowded confines of one of the *Urtesh*'s secondary holds. A low, long console divided it from the cargo-controller room where Tevashir and some others were waiting. Akreen strode through, halted before his superior, and raised both fists to his chest in the officers' salute.

'This is later than I wished, Second.'

'Deepest contrition, First. I came as soon as I received the interim order.'

Tevashir, Pre-Eminent Combatant and First Blade of the Zavri, nodded, cold silver eyes studying him intently.

'I've seen a preliminary report on the dreg-bout,' he said. 'Officials from the Chamber were keen to let us know the high value they place on good relations with the Zavri, thus the document came to us by way of a consideration courtesy.' Tevashir's composure could not mask the contempt in his voice. 'So I know about Livakaw's last desperate stroke, an unexpectedly drastic attempt to take you with him, yet clearly your luck held.

'But that is not why I wanted you here. There has been a development of some significance – G'Brozen Mav has escaped from the Warcage.'

Akreen felt a part of him grow still, even as angry outbursts raged back and forth in that gallery where his precursors came and went. Akreen's thoughts whittled down the possibilities, cross-referenced with any notable Warcage events, anything that might provide an avenue of egress.

'First Blade, could the Harvest Flotilla have played a part?' he said suddenly. 'The flotilla recently departed with two burnoff worlds – perhaps he found a way onto one of them, stowing away ...'

Tevashir had turned to a nearby console and was flicking through screens of pale blue data, then paused and pointed. 'There was a report from a source on Sastok stating that G'Brozen Mav and several companions were seen entering an illegally displaced monogate. Timeframe comparison shows that would have happened less than an hour before the Harvest Flotilla excised the second burnoff from the Warcage.' He offered a sharp smile. 'Well deduced, Second. Know that our Shuskar masters have assigned to me the task of bringing that vermin to justice, and that I want you to accompany me to wherever that task takes us. I am sure that your own interest will add sharp eagerness to the hunt.'

Akreen nodded. Four years ago he had been a lowly 3rd Claw leading a long squad on wilderland patrol during the Interdiction of Palotreg City – G'Brozen Mav and a mob of four-armed Hvlozen had attacked, using freezer weapons that completely routed the Zavri, with only Akreen and a handful and his Shuroga scout escaping. Later it was found that the Hvlozen had piled the frozen bodies into an industrial ore crusher then fed the result into an arc furnace. In later actions the Hvlozen suffered greatly but the freeze weapons were never again seen in action.

Akreen bowed his head a little, glanced at his Shuroga scout, saw an eager gleam in those eyes while his precursors crooned a fervent assent.

'To the utmost limits of gratitude, I am honoured, First Blade,' he said. 'I await your orders.'

'Good. Find quarters for yourself and your underling,' said Tevashir. 'In only minutes from now the *Urtesh* shall depart this world.'

CHAPTER EIGHT

'Interesting,' Rensik said. 'Definitely interesting.'

The Human, Brock, looked up from her lapscreen.

'Really, sir? Ruthless intruders are on the point of abducting their second planet in less than twenty-four hours and you think it's just interesting?'

'Compared to some of the sights I have encountered during my time in the Construct's employ,' said Rensik, 'yes, Brock, interesting. By which I mean grotesque, ambiguous, and even enigmatic.'

Brock frowned. 'I see. So if it was exceptional it really would be something, then ...'

Just so, thought Rensik, as Sam Brock went back to monitoring the data flows from his ship's sensor array. *The cosmos creates an endless supply of marvels and hazards and I've seen my fair share of them – well, mine and someone else's too. But that doesn't lessen the quality of the enigmas emerging from this situation.*

Take intership communications, for example. As in most advanced civilisations, all seven vessels in this fleet from the Great Harbour (including the big armoured one carrying all those generators) used the subspace boundary as the transfer medium for data streams, except that the flow of their data was compressed and far more destination-specific. It wasn't encrypted as such but since current comm technology was essentially blind to their messaging it presented no risk.

Except that this kind of subspace data compression is well known to the Construct's developers and the possibility of unknown observers listening into their low-brow, self-aggrandising drivel clearly hasn't occurred to them. Or, as seems more likely, they just don't know how to encrypt their own comms.

An alert popped up on the edge of the drone's analyticore, and the merest glance revealed the nature of the event. As he returned his attention to the interior of his small craft, the Human was just flagging it up on her lapscreen.

'They've activated a global shell field of some kind,' she said. 'Running state-model scrutiny on the field's energy components.'

'You'll find that it's mainly an inertial cut-out,' Rensik said. 'I theorised extensively on this after leaving the Nadisha system, you may recall, Lieutenant.'

'I do recall, sir. I merely wanted to gather some empirical evidence on the properties of the field itself.'

'And you'll find that it isolates objects – worlds in this case – from the mass-energy bonds of the cosmos. A second world, doubtless another pitiful war-trashed planet, will soon emerge from hyperspace, similarly field-trapped, and the substitution will take place ...'

Not so dissimilar to that gravity amplifier field developed by the engineers of Fophathir the Paramount, Tyrant Designate of the 2nd Modynel. That bloodthirsty butcher used it to destroy nine populous planets and triggered two novae before we caught up with him. Ninety thousand years later here we are, face to face with another psychotic gang armed with world-hurling tech – at least this lot seem to be working to a different plan, as well as being amateur users of a fabulously advanced and powerful technology.

'Well, that's ... unusual,' said Brock.

'Summarise,' Rensik said.

'A small-medium ship – profiling as an armed-trader – has just punched through that shell field and is heading for open space.' Brock peered closer at her lapscreen. 'Some of the Great Harbour vessels are targeting it with beam weapons but to little effect. The big ship isn't firing anything—'

'All its generators are powering the inertial shell fields and managing the planet substitution phase, which shouldn't be far off—'

'That's our mystery ship made the jump to hyperspace,' said Brock.

'I've just retasked one of the hyperspace probes to scan its drive emission and track its course ...' The drone broke off as the probe's data feed started to come through. Oddly, the ship was still running in partial stealth mode, a countermeasure useless in hyperspace and which actually left a vestigial trace.

Well, well, thought the drone. *This situation has a bit more mystery and surprise than I expected.*

The intermittent traces left by the drive emissions and the stealth countermeasures were merged, resulting in a definite, consistent direction. Cross-referencing with location estimates from the Construct's meagre background data, he was able to narrow the possibilities down to a twenty-seven cubic light-year volume of space in the Hakulatu Khasma, a huge starless zone not far from the Earthsphere border.

Got you.

'Okay, Lieutenant, you can dispense with those scans and prep for a hyperjump.'

Sam Brock looked up, blinked in surprise then cleared her lapscreen with a touch.

'Are we heading off in pursuit of that ship, sir?'

'Indeed we are, Brock. My analyses have laid bare its

destination, which is the same as that first abducted planet. Oddly, that ship's tech and construction is nothing like those of the Great Harbour vessels – hmm, a question to be answered as and when.'

'So it is a mystery ship,' Brock said. 'Possibly carrying mysterious passengers.'

'And possibly deliberately leaving a trail in its wake. Yes, Lieutenant Brock, I am officially promoting this mission to the "very interesting" category.'

The Human female nodded. 'I see, sir. So, as well as grotesque, ambiguous and enigmatic, could we add ominous and maybe even perilous?'

'Oh, at the very least, Lieutenant.'

CHAPTER NINE

After departing Kamax Base and the canyon city, Akreen spent an hour wandering around the *Urtesh*, reacquainting himself with its passages and decks, chambers and drop-holds, berth carrels and equipping stations. The austere dark blue bulkheads of the soldier quarters and the subtler moss greens of the command section, the gloom of Tevashir's bridge and the pale glows from the hooded operator screens, the brassy gleam of ornamental fittings, console controls, and the relief profiles of heroic Zavri ancestors decorating the walls.

Although the movement of task-armies around the Warcage from holdworlds to affray-worlds usually took place via the gates, the *Urtesh* had the capacity to transport a full company of Zavri, mechanised if necessary. The berth carrels could accommodate 150 fighters while the main drop-hold was big enough for six heavy vehicles or ten light, or whatever combination was called for. The generals of the senior task-armies were assigned small interplanetary craft in recognition of their position and prestige, but only the Loyal Seven were accorded the honour of a craft like the *Urtesh*.

As he strolled up the inclined passage leading to the bridge, Akreen ticked them off in his mind – the Avang, the Yniich, the Sujalka, the Cregrin, the Lorzavel, the Muranzyr, and the Zavri...

[*Ah, the Cregrin! – never was a gang of uncivilised marauders promoted so far beyond their talents* – To] [*The Muranzyr were once the epitome of combat perfection but the recent generations are lesser breeds* – Ca]

The arguments were so well-worn that for Akreen they were like background murmurs, empty of meaning or content. Some of his precursors' commentaries had become so rote that they were like recordings, word-for-word repetitions that sometimes rambled on for long periods. Akreen used to think that the patterns of his precursors were fixed and limited, no matter how elaborate they were occasionally. But with the passing years he had realised that there had to be more to them than that, going by the pointed and specific remarks which sporadically shook him out of his easy disregard. And whenever those remarks came from Gredaz, rare as they were, they had proved to be significant.

The sloping walkway led through an arch and onto the bridge of the *Urtesh*. Zavri operators sat at hooded screens, faces bright from the displays, contrasting with the subdued lighting. Few heads turned, a bridge guard, one of the three short, hunched Toolbearers standing at the wide master console, and Tevashir, First Blade.

'Your appearance is timely, Second. I was about to comm you to attend me.' Tevashir beckoned Akreen over to a recessed wall display behind the master console. 'We have been in contact with the Harvest Flotilla. The planet Grelcq has already been exchanged for a newly harvested world. That was nearly twenty hours ago and the flotilla is in the closing stages of the second reciprocation. However, they have reported some unusual activity on the surface of the second harvested world so I want you to take the *Urtesh*'s scoutcraft, fly to the flotilla location and investigate. The intercept course is already set in its crystals so you will be leaving immediately. While you are pursuing that, I shall take the *Urtesh* to Grelcq and track down that murderous vermin, G'Brozen Mav.'

Tevashir wore a grim smile and Akreen could only nod.

'May I take my Shuroga scout?' he said. 'She has proved useful in unusual situations.'

'Only yourself, Second. Such crucial matters are for our consideration only. We are engaged in vital tasks blessed by the Shuskar Lords – now go.'

'With all alacrity, First. Eternal loyalty!'

'Loyalty eternal, Second.'

With that, Akreen hurried from the bridge. While it would have been deeply satisfying to have joined the First Blade in the hunt for G'Brozen Mav, being assigned a ship mission outwith the Warcage was still a considerable privilege. He tried to look upon it in that context but he could not avoid feeling a thin trickle of disappointment.

With a vigorous pace he made his way down through two decks, from subdued greens to dark blues then the ash-grey of maintenance as he turned along a linking passage that led past storage cabinets, a well-remembered short cut to Holds. It was shadowy, proximity lighting winking on at his approach, blooming from the ceiling domes, and they were slow and blurry ...

Onward the smoky figures shuffled. Akreen shuffled with them, unable to make out their faces but aware that they were all following another who led them through a murky, high-walled maze ...

Suddenly he was in bright light, in the main Holds corridor, standing not far from the automatic doors to the launch bay. His sense of balance felt distorted, and he swayed on the spot. Something like panic shivered through him, something cold and sharp. What had just happened?

He made himself move forward. The doors parted and he

stepped through into the comparative gloom of the anteroom to the launch bay.

'Ah, Second Blade, you're here. Bridge was concerned.'

On his right, the techniciar, a cowled Toolbearer, regarded him from just inside the narrow control cabin that overlooked the bay.

'I was delayed,' Akreen said. 'A small matter, no significance.'

The Toolbearer nodded. 'Are you ready to embark, Second Blade?'

'I am. Proceed.'

But am I ready? The big pressure doors rolled apart and the boarding cupola's low gate swung open. The cupola carried him over to the scout ship's gaping main airlock into which he stepped. As the lock thudded shut behind him he glanced at the timer embedded in his lower arm then shook his head, realising that there was no way to discover how long the nullout had lasted ...

Nullout.

No Zavri remained truly unmoved when the subject of nullouts was broached. They were the first signs of perception instability, intermittent frailties of the mind which could then lead to decrentia, the irreversible loss of intrinsic traits and persona disintegration. It was a rare condition but only because it afflicted the very old, and very few Zavri lived to very great ages. None of Akreen's precursors had lived past 417, reputedly the age at which Rajeg had opted for voluntary seccision, prompted by a decrentia diagnosis.

A narrow passage led forward to the pilot booth, a rounded compartment full of ReBuild control panels, graceless boards moulded in a standard blue-green resin. ReBuild replacements could be made on the spot by Order of Steel techniciars, usually Toolbearers, temporary substitutes which invariably became permanent.

As Akreen settled into the pilot couch, a row of oval displays came to life. Most showed odd graphical shapes that twisted or pulsed while lines of raw data periodically fanned into the display from the edges. Then First Blade Tevashir appeared in one and stared at him.

'May the luck of the Lords be with you, Second. Eternal Loyalty!'

'Loyalty eternal!' he said automatically as a multiplicity of unseen systems and subsystems awoke throughout the craft. The deck, the couch and the whole pilot booth quivered, then there was a lurch as the bay's handler frames moved the vessel into the launch position. The booth had forward-facing viewports but the safety shields were locked down – one of the console displays showed what was happening. The outer bay doors unsealed and slid up, releasing a cloud of tiny ice crystals. Moments later the scout ship was speeding away from the *Urtesh*, with Akreen pressed back into his couch by the acceleration, feeling curiously frozen, both physically and mentally.

Perhaps the nullout was an atypical event, he thought. *Some kind of anomaly triggered by stress and continual vigilance and with no connection to decrentia. It has been nine days since my last reposal, after all.*

Patterns on the display changed and he heard a shift in the ship's power librations which he knew heralded the imminent leap into hyperspace. Akreen laid his head back against the padded rest and closed his eyes ...

The smoky figures shuffled along in dimness, knee-deep in a pearly mist. They had a strange luminous aura which flickered and melted into threads and wisps of drifting vapour. When he reached out to the nearest figure, he saw that his arm was the same ...

And opened his eyes. And immediately realised that there had been another nullout. He was still in the pilot couch. Before him the instruments said that the scout ship was now travelling in hyperspace but he had not experienced the transit, an unmistakable effect. Then he glanced at the timer on the communication display and saw undeniable proof, a lapse of nearly eleven u-minutes which he could not account for. He gripped the sides of the couch, feeling the onset of a new kind of fear ...

[*Space is no place for a warrior of the Zavri. We brace ourselves against the solid ground of worlds, we rush onto the field of battle, we seize the enemy's territory and bury him in it* – To]

It was Togul, his fifth precursor, offspring of Drolm, parent to Casx. The relief he felt on hearing the crusty old bore was absurd.

Togul, he said in his thoughts. *What was I doing since we left the* Urtesh?

This would be hard for any of his precursors to answer. To them, time was an abstract notion, fragmentary and subjective at best.

[*You were leading your troops against the traitor, I believe. Splendid battle, boy, although nothing like the bouts of my day* – To]

I mean after that. We all came back to the camp and I got aboard the First Blade's ship.

[*Ah, the* Urtesh, *a fine vessel – Kalmer was First Blade in my time, you know* – To] [*What nonsense is this? Why are you disturbing my contemplations? –* Dr] [*Young Akreen's having trouble with his memories since arriving on this craft – my own memories are, of course, faultless and extensive* – To] [*Hmm, memory flaw, nullouts, decrentia, and a wandering mind –* Dr] [*I will not stand for such insults! –* To] [*Not you ... the boy Akreen! –* Dr]

Drolm, the third of his precursors, was descended from the malign Rajeg and was parent to the insolent Zivolin. His character was petty and irritable, qualities well suited to the low-level Chamber of Judgement functionary that he was in life. But right now Akreen needed him to use what wits he still had, just to find out a few facts.

Esteemed Drolm, forebear of shining repute, I seek your guidance in this matter, specifically your observations of my activity since I came aboard this vessel.

[*Ah, young Akreen, your courtesy does you credit but it would appear that the activities you speak of escaped my attention as my thoughts were occupied by weightier concerns – Dr*]
[*Of course, you could just be going mad! – Zi*] [*Begone, you worm – Dr*] [*Insufferable imbecile – Ca*]

Akreen shook his head. Now Zivolin and Casx were joining in, which usually heralded a spiral of bitterness and invective.

Peerless precursors, I beseech you to lend me your invaluable counsel in this troubling situation!

[*Scion Akreen, if this is a truly grave predicament then prudence dictates that you abort this mission and return to the Warcage – Ip*]

Iphan, former Raidmaster of the 2nd Battalion and Akreen's direct progenitor. The unanswerable truth of his words struck home. Akreen would have to alter course back to the Warcage then inform the *Urtesh* and First Blade Tevashir – there was no other course open to him. He swivelled his couch to face the helm controls, reached out and . . .

Onward they shuffled, vaporous, faceless forms. Matching them, step by trudging step, he realised that they were now journeying along the foot of a vast wall, steel blue, towering, featureless, limitless . . .

Then he was back in the scoutship, as abrupt as a flicked switch. But now he was in the passenger compartment, perched on the edge of one of the low bucket chairs, arms extended, silvery hands holding the broken pieces of a yellow disposable beaker. Akreen let the pieces fall, clicking, clattering on the deck, and sat back. The fear was like a high, tight whine thrumming at the edge of perception, a pervasive undertone that made his earlier panic seem like mere discomfort.

He glanced at the timer on his arm – nearly seven hours had passed since that exchange with Iphan, while seated up in the pilot booth. What had happened in all that time? He looked down at the broken beaker, the seven yellow pieces. And who had been in command of his body?

[*Leaving a ship in the hands of an autopilot is like trusting a box of numbers to write poetry* – Zi]

Zivolin's voice broke through his transfixed frame of mind. Clenching his fists, he made himself stand.

Shrewd and artful Zivolin, he began, *have you noticed that I am no longer in the pilot's couch and that some hours have passed since we last spoke?*

[*Of course I have. I'm dead, not stupid* – Zi]

Did you witness my actions during that period?

[*You misunderstand – I am aware of the gap in time but have no memory of it. You should be asking which of us is conspicuous by his absence ... Ah, I knew that our disciplinarian would eventually put in an appearance!* – Zi] [*What a waste and an irritation you are – you should have died with someone's boot on your throat* – Ra] [*And yet I lived to a corroded old age and died nowhere near a battlefield* – Zi] [*Your ignoble life concerns me not – I have spoken forth to discover when our irresolute host intends to return to the Warcage and to war* – Ra]

Most fervent Rajeg, Akreen said in the field of his thoughts. *Despite my seniority I am bound by the commands of the First Blade. Further, I am constrained by the unique predicament in which I am caught.*

[*What is the nature of this predicament?* – Ra]

Since coming aboard the Urtesh *there have been several*

intervals of which I have no memory, yet I have still been carrying out actions of some kind.

[*Nullouts. Decrentia* – Ra] [*Too young for it and he does not appear to be drooling or giggling* – Zi] [*Such an impressive show of medical acumen. I stand by my judgement* – Ra]

By now Akreen was on his feet and heading forward to the pilot booth. There, he paused to lean on the back of the couch as he studied the instruments. Then he pointed.

Ah, see! We are in hyperspace but the course is leading us back to the Warcage! And since I know that I did not carry out these actions I must unfortunately conclude that my body is being hijacked by one of my precursors.

[*An infamous accusation!* – Ra] [*Slanderous upstart!* – Ca] [*A shameful imputation* – Dr] [*What proof do you have?* – To]

Plentiful, abundant proof! Akreen retorted. *Which you seem incapable of recognising* . . .

And the gravity of it all suddenly struck him. If he could not convince his precursors that some malign presence was using him for unknown purposes, how hard would it be to convince someone like First Blade Tevashir?

His precursors were still declaring their innocence with varying degrees of outrage and contempt, a strident uproar that Akreen knew would eventually subside. He could, of course, leap at the controls with the goal of altering course, but such an action would doubtless provoke an intervention by his shadowy overseer. Who, if Zivolin was correct, was Gredaz, first precursor, the enigmatic presence who had almost entirely shunned Akreen throughout his life. The others had been a rambling, echoing blend of dusty memories not his own, and his inner self rebelled at the idea of any of them seizing control and blotting him out in the process.

But what could he do? He had heard several stories about ill-fated Zavri whose minds became battlegrounds where their precursors vied for dominance – such tales usually ended with the victim succumbing to a kind of mind-death, leading inexorably to physical torpidity and subscission. He wanted desperately to fight it but beyond those stories his knowledge was a blank. Perhaps, while the other six precursors were engaged and aware, he actually should pounce at the controls in the hope that some recollection would remain with them. Yet the last nullout was like having a switch in his brain turned off ...

Then Akreen heard a chiming sound and saw symbols blinking on the communications panel. All of a sudden he heard Zivolin shouting in his thoughts, urging him to answer it, even as he was already pushing past the couch to lunge at the comm panel. But cloudy grey surged at the edge of his vision, and his legs gave way. In desperation he levered himself up to the control board with his arms only to find that his fingers and hands were now useless and shaking. He could see details on the comm panel, see that the incoming signal was from the *Urtesh*, from the First Blade's own secure line ...

The faceless, smoky figures plodded along, stooped in their gait as if from some heavy burden. The glowing mist rippled and flowed around trudging feet. Some minor compulsion made him count his marching companions, and he found they numbered six ...

Before him the pilot's control board, dull green moulding with openings for panels, instruments and displays. Timers revealed another gap less than four hours long. Beneath him, the pilot's couch into which he was strapped. In his mind, the crawling vermin of fear, and the hard-bitten resolve to master it. On the displays, readings showed that the scout was back in normal space and heading along a high-velocity trajectory ...

Akreen sat back in surprise – the scout was on a course that would soon intercept with the *Urtesh*. His shadowy overseer had altered the destination ... and that comm signal which came through before the nullout had been from the *Urtesh*. He leaned forward and thumbed the comm display but all it would show was the 'Unavailable' message.

[*Communications disabled while the ship hurries towards the Zavri banner-vessel? What perils await us? – Zi*]

Whatever we must face, Akreen said inwardly, *one thing is very clear – I am no longer fit to carry out my duties.*

[*Without a doubt – Ip*] [*A correct appraisal – To*] [*A harsh outlook in my view – Zi*]

There is no way to discover what Gredaz has been doing during the nullouts, and that makes me a security risk. As soon as we dock with the Urtesh *I must ask the First Blade to confine me to quarters with an armed guard.*

[*You assume that Gredaz will allow you to even begin such action. But we will shortly find out – Zi*]

It was a sharp observation. One of the scout ship's hull sensors was tracking the *Urtesh* while a pilot monitor showed the approach. As the minutes passed, the command ship drew nearer and the quiet was reflected in Akreen's head where all his precursors were uncharacteristically silent.

Under autopilot the scout manoeuvred smoothly back into the open launch bay. Akreen felt the knocks and lurches as the positioner guided the small craft into parking lockdown. Standing by the main airlock he went over practised lines of resignation and surrender in his thoughts while keeping his real intentions low key. The plan was to say nothing until he came face to face with Tevashir, then launch a physical attack upon him. Getting himself chained and locked in a cage would ensure that his shadowy overseer could do no further harm.

Muffled thuds and clangs came through from the brightly lit launch bay as it was repressurised. At the ready light he opened the lock, cycled through to the outer hatch where he stepped onto the embarkation platform. It deposited him before the double doors, which then parted ... He had barely taken a step towards the gloomy corridor when several pairs of dark hands seized him by the arms and thrust him face down on the corridor floor.

As his exterior skinform was roughly searched for personal weapons, he realised that these were not troops from any Zavri order. Instead his glimpses revealed that they were in fact Avang sceptre-carls! Here, aboard the banner-vessel of the Zavri! What upheaval of insanity had convinced the barons and counts of their Ebony Council that attacking the Zavri was advisable?

Having relieved him of his barb-dagger, the Avang hauled him to his feet and without a word rushed him along the passageway. Dark-armoured, goggle-helmed, they were heedless of the bumps and knocks Akreen suffered as they dragged him up companionways and down narrow passages. Minutes later they arrived at the *Urtesh*'s bridge. Avang sceptre-carls stood over Zavri operators, still seated at their stations with hands on their heads, but it was the figure seated in the command chair that drew Akreen's attention. Someone had turned up the overhead lightsource and the still form of First Blade Tevashir shone in the illumination. Akreen's escort brought him up close to the command chair and forced him down onto his knees.

At first he was certain that Tevashir was dead, and that some grotesque spectacle had been arranged for his benefit – then his gaze settled upon the First Blade's rigid face from which the living eyes quiveringly stared. Akreen felt cold horror pierce him. Tevashir's body seemed frozen, his skinform garment looking pitted and dull, like a shell. A dim and distant memory stirred, some half-forgotten child's fable ...

'Do you recognise this punishment, Second Blade?'

The voice came from behind and had a vaguely slurred,

machine-processed quality. Not knowing who had spoken, Akreen just shook his head.

'It is the inexorably terminal condition caused by a weapon designed specifically for use against the Zavri. A single round penetrates that metalloid skin, delivering a range of para-virals which alter the molecular structure of the outer layer while others eat at the inner tissues and skeletal frame, reducing them to corroded detritus—'

He could not help himself. 'But the Zavri are loyal!'

'In recent times, yes, but it was not always so. During the Great Unshackling War sizeable factions of your people fought on the side of the Apparatarch. Even then, 25,000 years ago, the military prowess of the Zavri was formidable, thus a suitably lethal weapon was required.'

A short figure emerged from the shadows, a cowled Toolbearer carrying a bulky, shoulder-slung, long-barrelled weapon. One of the Toolbearer's instrument-hands was embedded in a bulging socket in the midsection while the other was clamped around the thick, asymmetrical barrel. It looked old, its surface tarnished, dented and scratched, but status lights glowed around that rounded socket and Akreen understood the message that was being sent. Here it is, the weapon that brought your race to its knees thousands of years ago, and look, it's still in working order.

But although Akreen knew of the Great Unshackling, the accompanying commentary sounded like Chainer lies ...

'Forgive me,' he said, 'but the histories I was taught said that our precursors ... '

[*Among whom would have been the enigmatic Gredaz! –* Zi]

The revelation made him pause only for a moment.

' ... they fought alongside all the other liberated species to overthrow the Apparatarch.'

'They had to be persuaded,' said the unseen speaker.

'Captured, treated, rehabilitated, given new purpose then given new weaponry. Eventually we crushed that demon-ghost's forces, threw down its orbitals, laid waste to its fleet-armies, tore open its citadels and melted its datacores down to slag. Since then the Zavri's loyalty to we Shuskar has been gratifyingly resolute and undimmed. Until now.'

Kneeling before the wide-eyed, slowly dying form of Tevashir, First Blade, Akreen forced himself into a state of composure. The realisation was stark – only a Shuskar Lord could command the Ebony Council of the Avang to lend their soldiers in a punitive action against one of the Loyal Seven. All that remained was to discover if he was to share Tevashir's fate.

Heavy footsteps approached from behind as the voice continued.

'The testimonials of clandestine agents have proved beyond any shadow of doubt that your superior, First Blade Tevashir, has been collaborating with the Chainers. While you were travelling in that scoutcraft, it was his intention to rendezvous with the Harvest Flotilla, board the hubship and turn it all over to a crew of malcontents and seditioners who were smuggled aboard in a backup fuel tank. However, we stole a march on Tevashir's treason, intercepted the flotilla, exposed and executed the stowaways, then despatched the flotilla back to the Warcage on a deviated course. After which we waited for the arrival of the *Urtesh* – and here we are.'

The speaker came into view with a lurching gait, the tall, red-clad figure of a Shuskar Lord but then Akreen saw what curled from the side of that strong-featured face, under the jaw, round the back of the neck, a ribbed thing like a tentacle or a tail, following the line of the right shoulder and down the arm, engulfing it below the elbow. Instead of a lower arm and hand there was a bizarre organic weapon, a long-barrelled artefact thick-muzzled enough to be a beam cannon of some kind. But it had bony ridges, leathery membrane stretched over bulbous chambers, webs of thready veins, scars and lumps. It was a waxy, pale brown colour, and as Akreen stared a large bump halfway along the barrel split open and an eye gazed at him.

Not just a Shuskar Lord, but one of the five Paramount Gun-Lords! The teacher-cubes that educated every Zavri child provided only basic grounding in the history of the Warcage but the Gun-Lords featured prominently throughout. They were the Shuskar researchers who, during the early stages of the struggle against the Apparatarch, found the ancient symbioweapons buried on a harvest-acquired world. Study led to dialogue, then a merging that created the five Gun-Lords who were able to turn a desperate rebellion into the Great Unshackling. There could be no denying their power and their right to rule all the worlds of the Warcage, or the unqualified irreducible loyalty which was their due. Or the fear and awe that they inspired.

'I am Xra-Huld,' said the Gun-Lord softly. 'Do you know of me?'

Akreen nodded. 'The defence of Mt Krallen, the flight to Ajibhur, the Lothata ambuscade . . .'

'Millennia have passed yet the memories are as fresh as they were in the days that followed,' the Shuskar said.

'And Beshephis, Lord?'

'Beshephis, too, I recall in every glittering detail.' The Gun-Lord Xra-Huld wore a high, encircling collar fashioned to resemble crenellations, but his grin was still visible, revealing pointed teeth stained yellow. 'An insurrection driven by a traitorous faction of the Order of Steel, colluding with Maklun's sect of demagogues and saboteurs, rousing to revolution the underworkers of half a dozen worlds.' Xra-Huld had been standing behind the high-backed command chair – in which Tevashir was slumped and slowly dying – and now he leaned forward to rest that disconcerting weapon-arm on the raised back. 'These were enemies that the Shuskar faced with unity and resolve. Now it is the Retrocessionists – a secret coterie within our own number! – against whom we must strive. Distrust is degrading the chain of command and suspicion spreads like a disease.

'Which brings me to you.'

Akreen averted his gaze, inadvertently letting it settle upon the mute figure of the Toolbearer, still standing there with the Zavri-killer gun hanging at a slant, muzzle down.

[*Put iron in your spine. Accept whatever judgement is laid upon you* – Dr]

'Most paramount Lord,' he said with a relaxed calm which was wholly fabricated. 'I cannot understand why the First Blade would break his vows, nor why he would carry out actions designed to harm the Warcage—'

[*Really? I can come up with one good reason without trying* – Zi]

Zivolin's interjection almost made him stumble but he made it look like a natural pause and carried on.

'As for myself, I can only point to my record of service, and the numerous assaults upon the Chainers and others in which I played notable roles.'

The Gun-Lord gave a one-sided shrug. 'Tevashir's record was – ah, is – more extensive and illustrious than yours by far so it seemingly counts for little in matters of loyalty. However, it is worth noting that he is the bearer of two precursors, neither of whom accounted for much, whereas your own precursor lineage possesses a greater distinction and goes back to the Great Unshackling itself.' The Shuskar's smile was equal parts savage humour, anger and calculation. 'In short we need an experienced officer to take Tevashir's place and you appear to be well qualified. So be upstanding, Akreen, scion of Iphan, and the new First Blade of the Zavri.'

'Lord, I am honoured,' Akreen said as he got to his feet. Any intention he'd had of resigning his post now seemed ludicrous, not to say suicidal. 'Honoured and humbled. My vow remains that of the Zavri – eternal loyalty.'

'Pleasing words, First Blade, but keep in mind that there is a provision set upon your new station, as you might expect. Any sign of treachery on your part will result in punitive action being carried out against the Zavri holdworld, Drevaul. As you can see, the anti-Zavri weaponry is satisfyingly effective. Ah, finally!'

In the command chair, Tevashir's head wavered slightly. His mouth opened but only dark glittering gravel spilled out. The staring eyes grew still and dull, then cloudy, then dark and gleaming. Xra-Huld, Gun-Lord of the Shuskar, smiled approvingly then glanced up at Akreen. Who kept his face composed and apparently untroubled.

'Do we have an understanding, First Blade?'

'Yes, Lord, and I repeat my vow – eternal loyalty to the Shuskar, loyalty eternal!'

Xra-Huld smiled coldly then straightened from his leaning position.

'Very well, First Blade. You shall now speedily acquaint yourself with the duties of your new status. You will also place all units of the Zavri on a war-footing, including the half-battalion you recently commanded. When you return to the Warcage, set your destination as Armag. On arrival, assume stationary orbit above the capital city and await further instructions.'

'Armag ... is that the Gruxen holdworld, Lord?'

'The same. Consult your archives and be prepared – the final chapter of the Chainers' tale is about to be written.'

With that, the Gun-Lord cradled the grotesque bioweapon arm against his midriff and left, closely followed by the Toolbearer with the Zavri-killer. The Avang sceptre-carls were the last to depart, with a leisurely swagger in their gait. Akreen could feel the relief of his precursors when the bridge was finally cleared of intruders. The need to act decisively was undeniable – he assembled the bridge officers and gave out a batch of directives which put into effect the orders of Xra-Huld. The removal of Tevashir's brittle, shell-like corpse was assigned to the lowest ranking crew member, who was told to ensure that it was ejected via the refuse lock. That should satisfy any Shuskar spies among the crew – it was only sensible to assume that there was at least one – that the former First Blade's remains were being treated with the bare minimum of respect.

On the bridge's main screen, a large vessel of severe brutalist design was firing its manoeuvring thrusters, moving away from the *Urtesh*. It was one of the Shuskar's belligerator ships, now clearly the seat of command for Gun-Lord Xra-Huld. Akreen instructed the helm officer to wait for ten u-minutes after the belligerator's departure to hyperspace before following on. Then he decided to retire to the commander's abeyance chamber and quiz the archives on the subject of Armag. As he descended the narrow companionway at the rear of the bridge, his precursors broke their silence.

[*Such vile deceit! It will find you out* – To] [*What monstrous creatures are our overlords. Yet Tevashir deserved his fate* – Dr] [*All things that live can be killed* – Ra] [*Be ready for a pretty festival of ruin where every brute has its own death-dance!* – Zi] [*Restraint is key, bide your time* – Ca] [*Those half-beasts, degenerates and brigands must never be allowed to set foot on Drevaul – never!* – Ip]

As the door of the abeyance chamber – so recently Tevashir's – slid open, Akreen tried to think of something to add to the babble of declarations. But as the door closed behind him, the babble faded away to just one voice which only laughed quietly for a moment before …

Again, he was in the misty gloom, in the lee of that vast featureless wall, with a single smoky figure standing nearby. The stranger turned and approached, his face a real face, silvery and craggy, and vaguely familiar from the lineage archives.

'Hello Akreen,' he said. 'I am Gredaz. I thought it was time we had a little chat.'

CHAPTER TEN

Pyke woke to the sound of shouts and thudding Bargalil hooves. And Ancil saying his name over and over while shaking his shoulder with unmistakable urgency.

'...yeah, right...okay! – what's happening?'

'I think our hosts are under attack from other Bargs,' said Ancil. 'Can't see much from the window, just some big shapes dashing around beyond that fire pit. What's really worrying is the comms – tried calling the others and got nothing but static.'

That made Pyke sit up. 'Jamming?'

The only light in the hut came from a small iron brazier, the dull orange glow of embers. Ancil's vague form nodded in the gloom.

'Seems likely, which means someone out there has much better tech than these Bargalil farmers.'

'Someone like the new owners of this planet, you mean,' Pyke said, swinging his legs out of the big padded cradle that was the Bargalil equivalent of a bed. Tugging on his field jacket he went over to the small, slit-like window and peered out at the forest clearing just as Kref came into view, leading Punzho and Mojag around the fire pit. Even as Pyke whispered sharply to Ancil, a battlestripe-daubed Bargalil warrior burst through a bushy wall of vegetation, brandishing a spear in either hand. In the next instant it saw the three offworlders, let out a blaring roar and charged. This was a very different Bargalil to the ones they had encountered last night, peaceful villagers who were friendly and welcoming to footsore travellers, despite the upheaval that was afflicting their world.

Like Punzho and Mojag, Kref was armed but as the Bargalil warrior bore down on them the Henkayan knocked the extended spear-arm aside and launched a devastating punch at the creature's head. It had the desired effect – the Bargalil's legs gave way and it crashed to the ground, limbs akimbo. Ancil was already at the open door as the others dashed across the remaining distance, closing and barring it after they were safely inside.

'Captain, what is going on?' gasped Mojag.

'Huh, even I know that one,' Kref said. 'Somebody's trying to kill us!'

'Where are the others?' said Pyke. 'Dervla and Win's hut wasn't far from yours – did you see them?'

'We tried calling them and you on the comm,' Mojag said, 'but all we heard was hissing.'

'The window of our hut faced away from theirs,' said Punzho. 'But the walls are only made of rushes and mud so I made a hole to get a view. I saw several Bargalil bodies lying on the ground and someone firing from the hut window.'

'Weapon discharges,' said Pyke, looking at Ancil. 'Could that be detected?'

'Could be,' Ancil said. 'Chief, we've got to go get them ...'

'Picking up anything on your factab?'

'It's not been on,' Ancil said, digging into his backpack. 'Trying to conserve the battery ... right, passive detection is showing a comm frequency jammer about twenty klicks to the northwest. And several telemetry sources, airborne, moving south in overlapping search patterns.'

'Heading our way?' said Pyke.

'Be here in about seven minutes.'

The two men shared a grim look for a moment, and Pyke gave a sharp nod before turning to the others. 'You three be ready to leave when we return,' he said. 'If we're not back in five, no, six minutes, make a run for the forest and keep moving south for half an hour.'

'I wish we'd never asked the Bargalil for shelter,' Mojag muttered.

'And if wishes made a difference I'd be carrying a phased plasma rifle right now!' He crossed to the door and glanced at Ancil. 'Ready?'

'I better be.'

Pyke yanked open the door and dashed out with Ancil hot on his heels. But they were just skirting the fire pit when he heard a shout from Ancil and felt a hand grab his upper arm.

'Wait, they're already here!'

Ancil had slowed and was staring at data on his factab. Pyke dragged him into the lee of a low firewood shelter. 'I thought they were minutes away,' he said.

Ancil shook his head. 'Another craft, a bigger one, swept in from the west, and it's practically sitting on top of their hut.' He gave a wordless snarl and prodded the factab display. 'They must have tracked the energy-weapon discharges – perhaps if we charge in, surprise them ...'

Pyke felt the same impulse but his responsibilities forced caution and survival upon him. 'Can't do it, Ancil – if we end up dead, how can that help Win and Dervla?'

'So, we just leave them behind, Bran, is that what you're saying?'

Pyke grabbed a handful of Ancil's jacket shoulder and pulled him closer.

'I'm not about to go up against whatever's over there in the darkness, but if you want to run on in and get yerself shot, fried or disintegrated or all three be my guest. I'm going back to collect the others and head for the forest. Then maybe we can figure out what to do next.'

He let go of Ancil, turned and ran lightly back the way he'd come. The hut's door was already open, revealing Mojag's puzzled features. Pausing only to give a summary of the new danger, he got all three of them outside and dashing towards the shadowy forest. Ancil was there too, clutching his factab to his chest as he stumbled after them.

Away from the clearing, night closed in. Their harness lamps sent wavering beams into the dank gloom, angled down at the forest floor. The ground was damp and uneven, the undergrowth tangly and often home to peculiar insects that made tiny warbling sounds; when disturbed their emissions resembled quiet, eerie choirs.

The ground also sloped upwards as they moved south. After about twenty minutes they reached a clearing with a cluster of mossy rocks and boulders where Pyke decided to call a halt. As they settled down to rest, Pyke got them to dim their lamps to conserve power cells and the anxiety on every face grew indistinct. Harness rations were produced, sampled, swapped, chewed, and water pouches were sparingly sipped from.

'Ancil,' Pyke said eventually. 'Those survey units still in the area?'

'They switched their sweep away to the west,' said Ancil, features pale grey in the muted radiance of the factab. 'That other big craft has dropped off the scanner as well ...' Not meeting Pyke's gaze, he bowed his head. 'If I went to active scanning I could get more detail but then those hunters might detect the factab's signal – and it would drain the cells too.'

Pyke nodded sombrely as he got to his feet. 'Right, then – see if I can't find out some facts,' he said. 'Me and Kref will head back to the Barg village for a scout around—'

'I'm going too,' Ancil said as he stood up.

'You most certainly are not – you get to stay with the others and keep an eye on that screen. Any sign of bandits nearby you up-sticks and go deeper into the forest.'

Ancil glared at him but sat down heavily. 'Find Win for me, chief. Find something – I have to know …'

And from the inky shadows outside the halo of their clustered harness lamps, a voice spoke.

'I believe that I can tell you all you need to know.'

Hands reached for holstered weapons as eyes turned in the direction of the voice, just as a couple of soft-glowing points winked on a short distance away. One was fixed to the shoulder of a tall figure approaching through the trees, the other to the same-side wrist. Even before the face resolved itself out of the gloom Pyke knew that it was the thief and murderer, Khorr. And an awful certainty took hold when he saw a confident smile on that hated visage.

Several weapons were levelled at Khorr by the time he came to a halt at the edge of the clearing, empty hands held out.

'I'll come to the point, Captain – I have the two females.'

Pyke's grin was cold. 'And I should believe you … because … ?'

Khorr nodded. 'Proof, then.' He touched something in his ear and muttered a few indistinct words.

There was only the breeze-stirred silence of the forest for several seconds, then a faint hum grew in the air and when Pyke looked up he saw a craft, some kind of open-top antigrav lighter, descending to the clearing. It slowed and stopped just above head height. Aboard it, several dim forms shifted about – then a light came on, revealing Dervla and Win, hands bound, both looking dishevelled and harassed with three of Khorr's goons holding on to them.

'How are ye doing up there, Dervla?' Pyke said.

'Fine, Captain, fine. Wind's a little bracing and our dance

partners are a bit short on technique. Can't wait to teach 'em a few new moves.'

'You just hold tight, darlin'.' He looked back at Khorr. 'Well?'

'Captain, it comes down to this – there is a vital task to be undertaken and you and your crew are perfect for the job.'

Pyke allowed himself a bleak smile. 'Now, there's a thing, 'cos we've already carried out a contract for you. Didn't work out too well for us, you might recall.'

'Circumstances change, Captain. For example, you are all now fugitives, trapped here among the shackled worlds of the Warcage – and you've lost your ship ... oh, I know that you rescued G'Brozen Mav and I would guess that his Toolbearer was the one who seized control of your vessel.'

'Well, we know about you,' Pyke countered. 'Mav told us who you take orders from—'

'*Mav* told you?' Khorr let out a rasping laugh. 'The man who stole your ship suddenly becomes a reliable source! ... Look, I could try to explain that, unlike him, I want to actually defeat the Shuskar, which means no half measures. I could try and persuade you to understand why we had to remove the indecisive Mav from the situation by marooning him on that ruined planet. But really, all that matters, all that you need to keep in mind, is that I have your crew females and that their lives depend on your cooperation.'

Pyke rubbed his jaw thoughtfully and glanced at the others – only Ancil met his gaze, giving a resigned shrug.

Damsels in distress, he thought. *Ah, the joys of command.*

'All right,' he said. 'Let's hear it.'

Khorr gave a wide smile.

'Wise decision. Now attend closely – the rule of the Shuskar—'

'Who?' said Pyke.

Khorr gave a soundless snarl. 'The Shuskar, those who give the orders. Their rule lies heavily upon the worlds of the

Warcage but only the holdworlds enjoy the permanent presence of a Shuskar Lord-Governor. One such is the planet Armag, a key industrial centre with its capital in Armag City. The native Gruxen are hierarchic, caste-conscious, and while their Dynarch Houses run Armag society on behalf of Lord Gyr-Matu, the Shuskar Governor, the underworkers tend to be less compliant.

'Your task is to infiltrate the manse-tower, ascend its garden-galleries and clerk chambers, get into the Pendatoria then find Lord Gyr-Matu and kill him, with gun or knife, it matters not.'

'Assassination, eh?' Pyke folded his arms. 'Serious business to entrust to a gang of smugglers from outside this Warcage of yours.'

'Your escape from the doom we arranged for you and your crew proves your resourcefulness. But you need not worry about being cast adrift on an enigmatic world – we put our trust in the Gruxen rebels of the Armag subdistricts. They are working closely with the new Chainer leadership, and the addition of your crew will make the overthrow of the Lord-Governor all the more certain.'

Pyke was regarding Khorr closely, imagining whereabouts on that thick neck he would have to apply his hands, and how much force he would have to apply. 'Must say I like a good strong dose of sedition now and then but I'm wondering about how our appearance might fit in, or not, and then there's ...'

'The language barrier, Captain?' Khorr reached inside his bulky armoured jacket and brought out a transparent square wallet containing a cluster of small pale objects. 'These were retrieved from one of my "guests", your deputy, the Human female – language teachers, fabricated of course by G'Brozen Mav's Toolbearer – cunning devices to impress the patterns of the Omnilect upon the brain. I'm disappointed that you didn't make use of them earlier, but you will all take one before departing for Armag. As for your appearance – although Armag is a Gruxen world, the movement of workers around the Warcage means that you will see a scattering of other races among the underworkers, and you will not be as eye-catching as you might think. You will be presented to the Gruxen rebels as new allies from the replacement worlds, while to anyone else you are merely draftee apprentices from the same.'

'That's some amount of planning,' Pyke said. 'All for us.'

Khorr shook his head. 'You and your crew are taking the place of another team which has been ... unavoidably delayed. But I have every confidence in you and your talents.'

'Compliments, now.'

'No, Captain. Ultimately it comes down to a matter of incentive.'

Khorr glanced up at the hovering lighter and gave a signal. One of the three captors raised a snub-nosed handgun and pressed it against Dervla's neck before she could react. There was a faint, sharp sound, Dervla let out a muffled cry, then the process was repeated with Win, who glared and made no sound.

'Idler rounds,' said Khorr. 'They are tiny but sophisticated pellets that travel through the body, homing in on the main valves of the heart. In two and a half days, by your reckoning, the idlers will reach their targets and your friends will die. Luckily, the operation is scheduled for completion in less than two days and as soon as confirmation of the death of the Lord-Governor reaches us the idlers will be removed and your crew members will be safely returned to you.'

Still staring up at the lighter, Pyke could feel a maddened rage warring with caution, but the certainty of consequences was unavoidable. *Idler rounds ... that travel through the body ...* He reined in the anger as mutters and curses reached his ears. Turning, he saw similar emotions darkening the faces of the others, and Ancil slowly reaching for his sidearm. Pyke gave a wordless shake of the head, and after a moment the murderous look in Ancil's eyes faded a little and his hand fell limply to his side.

Pyke faced Khorr.

'So, just taking hostages wasn't enough.'

'I want to be certain that your every thought and action is focused on carrying out the mission to the end, to the final blow.'

'Oh, we're focused, all right. You can be sure of that.' Pyke's thoughts were full of violent imaginings, smashing an elbow into that throat, a fist into that face. Instead he spread his hands. 'Let's waste no more time – let us get on with this black business.'

Khorr had then muttered into a cuff communicator and less than a minute later a second lighter swept into the gloomy clearing. Small leaves were swept up in its a-grav helices as it descended, access ramp already extended. Khorr was first to hop up and inside and before long Pyke and his crew were aboard and aloft, speeding off into the darkness, closely followed by Dervla and Win in the first lighter. They were in the air for only a matter of minutes, during which Khorr failed to order the pilot to deploy the canopy so all had to endure the chilly buffeting of the slipstream. Pyke felt the cold biting through his skin but was resolute in maintaining a matter-of-fact demeanour in the face of this icy blast, especially whenever Khorr glanced back at his passengers. To which Pyke would flash a grin and a wink, just for the hell of it.

But his private assessment of the situation was stark – in taking Win and Dervla hostage, Khorr had cut his crew's combat effectiveness in half; Kref and Ancil were thoroughly at home with a variety of mayhem-dealing weapons but Mojag and Punzho's skills lay elsewhere. He had considered asking that skagbucket Khorr to swap Mojag and Punzho for the women, but not only might Mojag and Punzho be less than appreciative at such a deal, they would almost certainly be less able to cope with captivity than Dervla and Win. So, what with it being just a right crappy deal all round, Pyke decided to stick with the hand he was dealt.

Khorr's ship was parked on a level barren ridge overlooking dark, unbroken forest. Bay doors parted as they drew near, a broad fan of light in the murk. The leading lighter, with Dervla and Win, swung smoothly down towards the bright entrance and glided inside but by the time the second had slowed and manoeuvred in beside the first there was no sign of its occupants. As the lighter came to a halt Pyke got to his feet, ready to raise a protest but was forestalled by Khorr.

'They are safe,' he said. 'Merely being confined to suitable quarters. For their own protection.'

'And in the meantime?'

'You and your people can resume your seats.' Khorr made a small gesture. 'In a few moments we shall be under way, a short journey to the nearest monoportal, no more than a couple of hours.'

'Monoportal?' said Pyke.

Khorr let out a dry chuckle. 'How to explain ... simply put, most of the worlds of the Warcage are linked together by a network of instant transfer portals. Most have one or two that still function, while worlds newly integrated with the Warcage start off with the full complement of four. The bridging point for one is not far from here ...' He shook his head. 'On new worlds like this, the portals are only partially anchored so we need to stabilise it before sending you on your journey.'

Pyke's mind raced on hearing this. 'So we step through one of these portals and we're on Armag ...'

'Not so simple. Unauthorised portal travel is a capital offence so portal snaggers are a cautious bunch, jealously guarding all their tiny secrets. Once we've stabilised the portal's anchorpoint we can send a coded message through to the snaggergang on the other side, on a world called Kothahil. They'll be expecting our contact and once you're through they'll set up the next stage taking you to Armag.'

Pyke, still standing, glanced at his crew and saw edgy mistrust in their faces.

'And when we've danced your little dance and done what you want,' he said with undisguised bitterness, 'how do we get our people back? Where do we meet? Not back here, I'm guessing . . . '

'No, not here – modulator teams will have secured the portal bridge by then. More likely somewhere on Kothahil, or on Armag if we can be sure of our safety. And we'll do what we can to recover your ship.'

Pyke nodded as he regarded Khorr, almost feeling as if he were seeing him for the first time. Apart from the details about the journey to Armag and what they had to do there, everything else he said felt like a lie. Everything.

So Pyke sat down on one of the aisle-facing seats, rested his left leg across his right knee and gave an easy smile.

'In a way this reminds me of that time we had to collect a package from an antiquarian on Nightlantern on behalf of an anonymous client. Oh, the trust issues we had, and the never-ending ganshing over it all! But it all worked out in the end. So we'll just settle down and take our rest, get some of our energies back. I'm sure we'll be busying around soon enough.'

As he made a show of relaxing, the others did too, reassuring evidence that they'd got his message – any mention of Night-lantern was code for 'life or death situation, play it very cool'.

'How reasonable of you, Captain. I approve . . . ' Khorr paused as the bay doors closed to a chorus of machine-actuations, followed by a series of muffled thuds. 'Seals are secure so we shall be under way in a few moments. I leave you under the attentive custody of two of my most trusted guards. There is a food dispenser and a waste stall in the corner over there – my guards can demonstrate any operations as required.'

With that he clambered out of the lighter and strode along a narrow walkway to a hatch that slid shut behind him. Pyke waited three seconds before sitting up and turning to face the others.

'What's the plan, chief?' said Ancil. 'Please tell me that you've got a plan.'

Pyke raised a finger to his lips as he regarded the others. Punzho the Egetsi was hunched into his seat, tall bony frame almost crammed in on itself. He held his pouch of Weave figurines in one hand, long fingers tracing their shapes through the material. Mojag sat in a seat towards the rear, tensely watching Pyke, his features a mask of weariness yet there was something sharp in his gaze, an echo of Oleg, perhaps? Pyke knew that he had to find time for a private gab with Mojag, just to find out the state of his mind. Or minds.

Kref the Henkayan occupied a whole double seat, a stolid formidable bulk, sitting there with arms folded, craggy features seemingly composed, but there was a perceptible furrow on that wide brow and he wasn't saying much. Come to think of it, he hadn't said anything for hours.

And here was Ancil, his face an open map to all the thoughts and feelings currently bouncing inside his head. Pyke recognised them all in himself, the anger, the frustration, the hate, self-recrimination, all funnelling into a burning need to act. But Pyke was the captain, and he could not afford the luxury of acting on instinct ...

This is my crew, mine, and I'll keep them alive no matter what ...

'Sure, I gotta plan,' he said. 'We endure. We lost the ship and these gouging scumsuckers have our weapons, so we endure, we survive, and we wait for our moment.'

Ancil looked at him. 'And this isn't it? Our moment doesn't happen before we and Dervla and Win end up worlds apart?'

Pyke locked gazes with him, leaned forward, raised a finger then pointed off to the side. 'If you cast your gaze forward to the ceiling above the walkway where our custodial goons are parked, you'll see what appears to be a pair of circular housings jutting slightly proud of the ceiling, which is probably semi-hollow, strutted plastone. Remind you of anything?'

Ancil gave a sideways glance, angry eyes taking in the details. Then his shoulders slumped. 'Armoured turret recesses. Tell you, chief, this Khorr—'

'Is a lying, thieving murderer, oh yes, I can practically smell the kills he's made.' He gave them all a hooded look. 'So when I say we must endure it is for a reason, trust me. We'll survive, we'll watch each other's back, and we'll wait ...'

And as he regarded Khorr's brawny, slope-browed, body-armoured guards he suddenly remembered the language teachers, those pills made by Hechec, G'Brozen Mav's Toolbearer. He took the little transparent pouch from his chest pocket, tipped one out onto his palm, and stared at it for a moment. *We mustn't be the ignorant playthings of others.* Then, taking a deep breath, he swallowed it back. Ancil and the others were wide-eyed as he smiled, and licked his lips. 'Tastes of absolutely nothing, lads, so here, share them around. I'm pretty sure they're not poisonous but you can keep an eye on me just in case. Or just take the damn things now – up to you.'

Hesitantly, suspiciously, one by one they followed suit, with only Punzho taking it with a little water from his waist bottle. After that everyone tried to get comfortable enough to rest, if not actually drift off into sleep. At some point Pyke found himself fuzzily awake, muttering something in an unknown language, before lying back with eyes closed, dozing on and off until a sharp tapping jolted him into full awareness. One of the guards, a scar-faced, bull-necked humanoid blessed with what looked like an ingrowing nose, grunted a few words that sounded like 'hey, butt-scum, boss is here', and gestured over his shoulder.

Khorr was standing on the dockside walkway, prodding and tapping a thin, triangular datapad of some kind. Seconds later the bay doors parted and began to open, admitting a grey, watery light. Khorr then glanced down at Pyke, lips halfway between sneer and smirk.

'So, how is your facility with the Omnilect, Captain?'

Khorr had started the sentence in Anglic and halfway through switched to the alien language. Pyke felt an odd delay in hearing the words and understanding them. He levered himself upright and caught sight of the dull grey of an overcast dawn beyond the bay doors. He scratched his head, combed back his hair.

'Not too sure, yet – I'll have to see how some traditional limericks come across in it.'

'I'm certain you will find out in due course,' Khorr said as he clambered down into the lighter, followed by three of his over-brawny guards. 'It is time for you to leave this world.'

Minutes later, Khorr was guiding the craft out of the bay. On this occasion the canopy was activated, unfolding in sections over the seating, its opacity shimmering into hard transparency. It shielded the interior from the squalls of gusting rain that battered the lighter from all directions as it swept away from the parked ship and out over a dense forest.

Beyond the trees, Khorr brought the craft down near the bank of a wide river. By now he was taking readings from a blue hemispherical device sitting neatly in the palm of one hand. With the lighter now at rest on a pebbly strand, Khorr rose and looked at Pyke.

'Not long now, Captain.'

Part of the canopy concertinaed open and Khorr stepped out, followed by one of his pet goons carrying a large hiking pack of some kind. Pyke gave a sideways glance at Ancil, who was leaning on the seat in front of him, his expression morose. A few minutes later the two remaining guards stirred, gnarled hands raised to their earpieces before beckoning the crew to disembark. Pyke was first out, clambering down onto the strand, pebbles crunching underfoot as he shivered and drew his jerkin tighter against the cold breeze.

Khorr waved at him from over near the water's edge, about a dozen yards away. With the others at his back, and the armed goons flanking them, Pyke strolled over with as much swagger as he could muster.

The bulky pack now sat splayed out on the pebbles and Khorr was standing over a tripoded device whose glowing panel he was poking with a thin stylo. There were also a couple of silvery poles sticking up from the water several paces out. As Pyke drew near, faint pencil-thin beams sprang out from the device, stuttering in a seemingly random fashion, but then blue outlines emerged from this activity, growing from the tops of the poles, curving over into an archway. As they watched, the view through the arch darkened and dissolved into blurry waves that pulsed towards its centre.

'Quickly, Captain,' said Khorr. 'We can only maintain portal stability for another minute or so. Step through and the Kothahil snaggercrew will be waiting to take you to the next stage in your journey.'

'I really hope that proves to be true,' Pyke muttered as he splashed past Khorr and out into the shallows.

Up close, the portal had no edges as such, instead a fuzzy outer boundary that circumscribed the murky nothingness. Pyke glanced back at his crew, saw their nervous faces, gave his best devil-take-the-hindmost grin and stepped into the pulsating gloom ...

And stumbled as his foot landed on a hard stone surface

somewhat higher than the pebbly shore he'd just left. First impression was that he had emerged amid a cone of pearly radiance surrounded by inky shadows and an atmosphere that was cold and damp ... Before he could turn to see who was following someone grabbed his arm and pulled him back from the quivering face of the portal.

'Out of the way! The incoming margin has to be vacant!'

Pyke's manhandler was short and bundled up in tawny furs topped by a hairy, bearded face with intense eyes. In the background a handful of similar fur-clad beings – who had to be the snaggercrew Khorr mentioned – busied themselves with handheld devices with which they were scanning the portal, and Pyke suddenly realised that he was in a cave with an uneven ceiling. He was about to utter a hearty greeting to all and sundry when his snagger guide stepped smartly around and was just in time to catch Ancil as he emerged from the portal and tripped on the exact same spot.

Mojag made it through without mishap, as did Punzho although he had to duck under the arch. Kref also ducked and while his large leading foot found safe purchase his trailing foot caught on something, causing him to swivel round, fall backwards, and land with a hefty thud that drove a wordless snarl of exasperation from his lips. Yet when Pyke helped him to his feet the Henkayan gave forth only a grunt and his craggy face looked dark and surly.

Straightening, Pyke turned to the fur-clad snagger he'd spoken to first, and said, 'Profoundest apologies to you – we're usually a bit more coordinated than that. So, this is Kothahil, then—'

'This is a cave, a stinking damp cave riddled with gegishi nests ...' The diminutive snagger let out a curse-sounding word and lashed out with his foot to stamp on something in the shadows. 'Hate the verminous infesters. My name's Feskavoy – are you Pyke?'

'That's me, all right, and that over there is—'

'Don't want to know names, don't care, no time for it anyway. We're in a hurry to get out of here before any of the Governor's padfangs come sniffing around.'

Sure enough, the rest of the snaggers were hastily breaking down several wall-mounted, U-shaped sensors along with the tripod device and stowing them away in blue leathery sacks which were slung over shoulders.

'Padfangs?' said Ancil.

'That's right,' Feskavoy said with a wicked leer. 'Four-footed death-machines, all lean muscle, gleaming talons and rabid snouts that can't wait to bite your face off! So – less jabbering, more speed. Here ...'

Pyke suddenly found himself holding armfuls of musty-smelling fur cloaks.

'Get these on, all of you, and be quick about it. We have to leave now.'

Minutes later the crew were lining up after the Kothahil snaggers, all enfolded in odour-heavy furs, even Kref who had one that was clearly two stitched together. A narrow passage-way led out of the cave, its air growing colder with every step as they shuffled along in single file. A couple of their guides carried lamps but these were dimmed as the passage widened out. Frost glittered on all rock surfaces, freezing gusts brought in swirls of fine snow to be caught on cloak fur. Pyke was first out, his throat chilled by the air. They were on a high moun-tain track, that much was certain, but heavy snow mixed with mist made it impossible to tell if there was a gentle slope just feet away or a plummeting drop into some abyss. Without pause or explanation the snaggers strode vigorously onwards, descending the path which at times was no wider than an arm's-length. After a few minutes, though, the path led to a slope scattered with heaps of ice-bearded boulders half buried in the wind-driven snow. Peering beyond the boulders, Pyke got an impression of murky emptiness, a void. Then came a point when a greater blast of wind tore a fissure in the even greyness and for a second Pyke was staring out across an immense gulf at a sheer black peak crowned by a dark citadel speckled with tiny window lights.

Then a great curtain of snow swept in, the gap was gone, and freezing mist closed in, cutting visibility to only a few yards. The freezing wind rushed and moaned around them. Snow gathered on shoulders, stuck to bare faces and hands, leaching a deadly chill into the bone. No one felt like talking in the cold, muffling deadness.

By now their path was following the line of a ridge and had just begun to slope upwards when a high wavering howl rose out of the unseen depths off to the side. Footsteps slowed and widening eyes stared into the greyness as mouths puffed white clouds.

'Was that . . . ?' Pyke began.

'Padfangs,' Feskavoy said as he came back along the single file to speak with the rearmost snagger. 'Brekin, that sounded as if it might have come from Fulcrum Three – when did you last check the intrusion readings?'

Brekin, who was shorter even than Feskavoy, dug madly through his cloak pockets. 'Not since we left the cave . . . here it is.' He yanked out a thing like a knuckle-duster with an opaque flattened oval attached to its underside, nestling in his palm as he studied it. 'Yes, right, it's . . . they've . . . '

Feskavoy silenced him with an upraised hand. 'What about Fulcrum Seven?'

Brekin stared at the device while thumbing several dimples along its edge. Pyke peered over his shoulder, saw coilesque symbols flicker and change.

'Secure, unchanged,' was the verdict.

'Good, then we have a change of plan,' said Feskavoy.

'That'll be plan B, then,' said Pyke. 'To get us where we're going.'

Feskavoy gave him a sharp look. 'Yes, after a fashion.'

Before Pyke could quiz him further, the snagger leader started barking out orders and moments later they were turned about and heading back along the snow-choked pathway. Feskavoy led them to a sidetrack Pyke had missed seeing and soon they were descending a steep path consisting of cracked and worn sections of stairway interspersed with stretches of gravel and loose scree. All of it was being buried by the ceaseless snow, though, and the footing was becoming uncertain. After going to Kref's aid three times and Punzho's twice, Pyke was relieved when the slope flattened out. Under cover of the snow he sidled forward and nudged Brekin's shoulder.

'So we'll be on our way to Armag pretty soon, then, eh?'

Brekin rocked his head from side to side judiciously. 'Well, it's Fulcrum Seven so you'll have to detour via Yegutra. Course, you'll be in the hands of the Deadfire snaggers and they can be ...'

'Cranky,' said Feskavoy, who was suddenly nearby. 'You know, grumpy, short-tempered types.'

'Short-tempered, eh?' Pyke said.

'Yes, but don't worry, the Deadfire mob'll make sure you get to Armag – just don't expect polite conversation.'

The chief snagger ended with a weak smile then hurried off to resume leading them down the trail. And not long after, they reached a tall dark crack in the face of the ridge cliff and lamps were turned on as they passed from blanketing snow into stony darkness. A twisty tunnel led to a cave with a tilted floor marred with scrape marks and drilled holes. The Kothahil snaggers began setting up their equipment even before the last of Pyke's crew, Kref, trudged into the cave. The Henkayan sat down heavily on the floor and mini-avalanches of accumulated snow spilled off his fur-clad bulk.

Ancil sidled up to Pyke. 'What was Feskavoy saying about this detour? Something about them being cranky?'

'Ancil, look, they can be a squad of psycho-grandmothers for all I care, or four-footed lizardmen addicted to Daliborka wine, or troglodytes with a woolly-sock fetish – don't care just as long as we get to Armag City, do the job and get the girls back.'

By now the others were clustered close by, and Pyke could see a change in their demeanour; more resolve, less despondency. Only Kref seemed as doleful as before, which Pyke found dragged on his own mood.

'Pyke, we are ready for you and your followers.'

Feskavoy was standing once more at his tripod device and a dark, pulsing portal was starting to form. The other snaggers were taking readings with small handheld probes which they used to make remote adjustments to small fringed antennae dotted here and there.

'I've signalled the Deadfire snaggers on Yegutra,' Feskavoy went on. 'They replied. So, are you ready?'

'We are,' Pyke said, glancing at the others. Composed and unsmiling, Ancil gave a weary thumbs-up. 'I just hope they're ready for us.'

'Right, all of you line up in front of the portal!' ordered Feskavoy. 'Quickly! The pre-interlock fields are starting to harmonise.'

As the crew moved forward the arched portal darkened to an inky gap in which glimmering ripples continually swirled into the centre. Ancil was first through, followed by Punzho and a trembling, sweating Mojag. Kref stepped forward and was about to duck under the arch when he looked round at Pyke and said, 'Chief ...' He frowned, pursed his wide thin lips, and with a kind of discontented insistence said, '... I really miss my cabin!'

Then, half crouched, he pushed on through, shoulder-first, while Pyke stared at his vanishing form and shook his head.

His cabin! So that's what's been eating him all this time!

With a laugh he waved at a bemused Feskavoy and with a long stride entered the portal.

And came out in dazzling, blinding light. There was an incoherent bellowing noise nearby which he immediately knew was Kref. He was just raising his hand to shield his eyes when his arms were seized and a hood was thrust down over his head, plunging him into darkness. Panic and anger erupted in him and he began to struggle, twist and kick. Someone ordered for him to be forced to his knees and as his legs were kicked from under him his face was pressed against some kind of mesh-covered pad inside the hood. It smelled sweet, pungent, and in the instant that he realised what it was, fluid began to seep out of the pad. Caught in mid-exertion he couldn't help inhaling and the seductive narcotic sweetness filled his head in seconds.

The strength in his limbs drained away almost as quickly as the hot anger and the will to resist. His senses were swallowed up in a kind of soft numbness and he lost grasp on the passage of time. Now and then he heard a voice shout out a declaration of some kind to which several others answered with fervent cries. Lucid moments were interspersed with periods of sourceless hilarity, which usually provoked a slap on the head and led to another bout of helpless laughing.

The lucid moments grew longer as the narcotic effect gradually subsided. He dazedly realised that his wrists were before him and joined by rope to someone in front. He could also make out the footsteps of someone behind him. From the air, the small far-away sounds and the softness of the ground underfoot he was sure that they were travelling in the open. Then that changed to uneven and muddy, then to hard and gritty. A few paces along, his shoulder was grabbed as a voice told him to stop. His wrists were yanked round to the right and his captor said, 'Stairs! Climb!'

They were spiral stairs which went on and on for a while then ended abruptly when one foot encountered a flat stone surface rather than another step.

'Welcome, guests,' said a flat, monotone male voice. 'Do not speak – the speech of cinders is profane. I am Hejgol and I am the lowest and least of the Sacred Tenders of the Godflame. Visitors like yourselves are an increasingly rare occurrence, and once you have been sent on your way we shall all have to undergo the purity ritual to eliminate the profane air you have expelled. Have patience.'

Pyke grimaced beneath the hood. *How much more absurd can this get?*

'The hoods you wear,' Hejgol went on, 'prevent any instance of the worst profanity of all, the beholding of our appearance by the likes of you, the impious cinders of life. Likewise, they protect you from the transfixing beauty of our forms, a magnificence so unbearable that minds can become unhitched from their moorings, yes. Any who catch so much as a glimpse of our manifest glory are condemned to a lustral fate!'

All of which was intoned in a flat, vaguely nasal voice that Pyke had started to find amusing, then funny, then ridiculously funny. By the end it was a strain not to burst out laughing.

Then he was grabbed from either side and frog-marched across the unseen stone floor.

'May this fleeting encounter with us, the numinous and elevated ones, guide you along the shining path of enlightenment!'

Pyke's escort brought him to a halt for a moment before he was shoved roughly from behind. He could feel the air change as he staggered forward a few paces, tripped and sprawled on wet grass. Now openly laughing, he pulled off the hood with his bound hands, blinked in bright light for a moment then pushed himself into a seated position. *Hell and a half! They shoved us through another portal!*

'Nice to see that they're still sending live ones through from Yegutra,' said a voice off to the side. 'Are they still calling themselves the Divine Deadfire Congregation?'

'It seems not,' Pyke said as he got to his feet. 'Apparently our erstwhile hosts were claiming to be the Sacred Tenders of the Godflame.'

'Not their first name change, and won't be the last.' The speaker was a lanky man in brown leather armour, sitting on a boulder a few yards away, toying with a curved dagger as he studied the new arrivals.

Pyke was about to remark upon the risible element of their temporary captivity when a black-hooded figure staggered out of a familiar dark oval nearby and fell full-length on the grassy slope. A bald man in light blue fatigues hurried over to help him up, removing the hood to reveal Mojag's dazed features. The portal was sited in a clearing on a gentle hillside surrounded by tall, spiral trees with blue-green foliage. The air was cool enough for late afternoon and a low fractured sunlight twinkled through the leafy branches. Behind the sitting man, further upslope, others in a motley array of garment styles gathered around a near-dead campfire while a trio stood over by a device on a tripod while pointing handheld devices at the portal.

'They sounded mad,' Pyke said. 'Thoroughly and completely out of their minds. Any further off the map and we might not be here.'

'Their leader is a deranged Tephoyan by the name of Bexoc,' the man said. 'Every few scoredays, he has a vision from the Cosmic Oneness telling him to change the name and rituals of his pathetic little sect. The craziness seems to have been escalating recently, however.'

Pyke laughed as he shook his head. 'Feskavoy told me that we might find them a bit cranky.'

'Binding, hooding and sedating transients oversteps normal security concerns, to my mind. Anyway, thankfully they let you pass onwards. Feskavoy's message said to expect someone called Pyke. That you?'

Just then another hooded figure emerged from the portal, stumbled sideways and slumped sideways to the ground. Pyke nodded.

'Captain Pyke, actually, and this fine fellow is Ancil, my science officer!'

Aided to his feet by a couple of the bald assistants, the newcomer's hood was pulled off and Ancil blinked widely a few times, shook his head, and said, 'Yep, that's me. How did you know ...?'

'Boyo, I'd know that lithe and graceful agility anywhere.'

The lanky armoured man sheathed the dagger, straightened from his seat on the boulder and came over, hand extended. 'I am T'Loskin Rey. Khorr tells me that you and your compatriots will be the cutting edge of our rebellion.'

Pyke accepted the man's hand and they shook. Rey had a large hand yet the grasp was firm, almost matching the effort Pyke put into it without any attempt to make a dominant point.

'Funny, that. Khorr's not really told us enough,' he said, deciding not to mention Khorr's two hostages. 'But I'm sure you can help us figure out the steps of the dance, eh?'

T'Loskin Rey gave him an appraising look. 'We were told that you and your people are from outside the Warcage, from a civilisation in the local stellar region. You understand, I hope, that the rulers of the Warcage, the Shuskar, are ruthless in their tyranny and cunning in their distorting ways. They invented the Grand Escalade as a way to divert the energies of the peoples of our worlds, and to set us against each other. We are the Chainers – long ago our forebears took the symbol of our oppression and made it into the name of our community and our defiance. For generations we have been fighting the Shuskar and over that time they have grown steadily weaker, to the point where we are sure that a concerted rebellion can topple them. Here on Armag is where the first blow will be struck – and with the industrial abilities of Armag City further rebellions can be seeded all around the Warcage. Khorr has been of great help to us, so when he told us about you we decided to trust his judgement.' Rey smiled. 'We'll be leaving here soon, decamping to a waysite where we cached arms and stores ahead of this meeting.'

'Do ye have a change of clothing in yer stores, as well, do you think . . . '

'Chief,' said Ancil. 'Where's Punzho?'

By now Mojag and Kref and Ancil were clearly present, but the Egetsi was not to be seen.

'He has to be here,' Pyke said. 'Maybe he wandered off . . . '

Ancil shook his head slowly. 'Those portal techs say that only four of us came through. They insist that no one matching Punzho's height arrived . . . but I thought he might have been displaced, or dumped nearby . . . ' His voice trailed away.

Pyke ran a hand through his hair, grabbed a clump of it and clenched his teeth. The last time he saw the Egetsi was just before the departure from Kothahil, at the Fulcrum Seven portal, which meant . . .

'We have to go back,' he began.

But even as he spoke the portal arch wavered, blinked and vanished.

'I'm sorry,' said T'Loskin Rey. 'Anyone who violates Bexoc's demented rules doesn't make it – I've seen this before and trust me, no plea for mercy has ever resulted in the release of one of his captives. Threats are pointless because all they need to do is shut down the portal at their end.' Rey shook his head. 'But some day, justice will be exercised upon them.'

By now the rest of Rey's people had finished striking camp and a few were heading down towards the trees in ones and twos, hefting sacks and shoulderpacks.

'There is nothing to be done,' T'Loskin Rey went on, 'except for us to leave the place before any slaywing patrols pass overhead.'

The remaining members of the *Scarabus*'s crew looked at Pyke, who found that he had nothing to say, who knew that no words could console them. But he also knew that saying something was his job. Any lie, no matter how comforting, would be an affront to Punzho's memory so a kind of truth would have to do.

'Now listen to me, all of you,' he began. 'We're going to carry out this cursed mission, then get Dervla and Win and the *Scarabus* back, then we're going to find those mad-bastard vermin, wherever they are. And if Punzho isn't alive, I'll show them the meaning of pain.'

With that he turned and strode downhill a few paces. He stopped, half turned and looked back, face grim and unyielding. He stood there, watching them, waiting until Ancil shrugged, said something to Mojag and Kref, then all three followed. Pyke met Ancil's gaze, nodded and continued downwards.

Some fine posing, there, Bran boy, he thought. *And a stirring, manly speech – hell, I bet ye even believe some of it yerself!*

CHAPTER ELEVEN

Apart from the hum of the consoles and the small screentip sounds of their operators, the bridge of the *Urtesh* was suffused with a certain kind of quietness, the hush that comes before expectancy, before orders. But it was nothing compared to the cathedral silence that reigned within Akreen's head. Before his audience with Gredaz his thoughts had been an elaborate stage upon which his precursors had conducted a perpetual cavalcade of worn-out clichés, empty repetition and fruitless verbal clashes, but since that astounding encounter his precursors were conspicuous by their absence. There was room for relaxation and meditation, as well as hard thinking.

Earlier, the commander's chair had been cleared of Tevashir's brittle, crumbling remains then scoured with a cleaning device, while Akreen had been closeted in his abeyance chamber, conversing in his mind with Gredaz. Now it was some hours since the arrival aboard and his promotion at the behest of the Shuskar Gun-Lord Xra-Huld, and as he sat there he knew that his senior officers harboured great doubts about his fitness for the rank of First Blade. In the normal course of events, such doubts would be allayed by demonstrating his grasp of the responsibilities of command and allowing his characteristic talents to colour his decisions on strategy and tactics. The ship was just over an hour from its arrival at the planet Armag, so opportunities to prove himself would soon present themselves.

But the revelations unveiled by the precursor Gredaz made all of that look unimportant. Akreen recalled perfectly the icy shiver he felt when Gredaz had introduced himself, within the misty thoughtscape which had crept stealthily upon him. In the lee of that vast-looking wall, Akreen had found that he was incapable of saying anything while the craggy silvered features of Gredaz regarded him for a long considering moment.

'There is so much to tell you,' his most ancient precursor began. 'Perhaps the first thing you should know is that there were other precursors before me. Yes, there were other generations of Zavri, a chain going back into the past.'

Akreen's attention was unwavering. 'How many generations? How far back?'

'That ... I do not know. In some ways I am a useful, sophisticated bundle of memories and characteristics, but in others the gaps in my knowledge are echoing gulfs of nothing. I have tried to conjecture what is missing from the shape of the holes but it is difficult to arrive at conclusions of any real utility.'

'My guess is that you will have more to tell me than any of your descendants,' Akreen said.

'Like Rajeg, that simple-minded butcher? Upon my scission there were other scions more deserving of lineagerhood, of carrying the spark of our precursors – ah, but we cannot choose the vessel, only hope that it will learn something from its ancestors.' Gredaz paused. 'My generation was the first to arise after the Great Unshackling War, as the Shuskar call it. Xra-Huld spoke some truth earlier – most of our people did fight on the side of the Apparatarch and against the Shuskar and their allies, but after a time that alliance developed new weapons specifically to use against us. You saw one in the hands of the Gun-Lord's servant. And there were other more abominable devices which were designed to erase our precursors from our bodies – they wiped out our past, all our glories and achievements, to create a new blank race for them to write commands of unthinking loyalty upon, an iron, eternal loyalty. As we proved it to be during the Beshephis Insurrection, only too well.'

'You said that we fought for the Apparatarch?' said Akreen. 'How did that allegiance come about?'

'I only have scattered fragments but the picture they suggest is this: the Apparatarch was an amalgamation of the various machine intelligences that had served the Builders of the Warcage before their political ousting many millennia ago. The leadership that took over, the Integration Council, reached an accommodation with the machine intelligences in order to maintain the smooth operation of the megasystem's myriad interlocking processes. After that, the Integration Council proved incapable of living up to its name and a succession of factions jostled for control and power while representation at grassroots level was suppressed or otherwise withdrawn.

'To cut a long story short, the Council grew corrupt and the Great Harbour of Benevolent Harmony – as the Warcage was then known – continued on its journey around the home galaxy, spreading dissension and conflict rather than peace and resolution. A league of civilisations banded together, assembled a massive armada and harried the Great Harbour to the galaxy's edge, eventually forcing it to depart. A series of journeys in dimension-space brought the Great Harbour to the fringes of this galaxy, by which time the Integration Council had become a vessel of corruption where only power and brute force were worshipped, and that is when the Apparatarch took up the arms of rebellion. The Zavri, apparently, were a minor species invited into the Harbour during one of the Council's last periods of comparatively civilised behaviour. Perhaps it was the nature of our metalloid biology, with its information-storage propensities, that attracted the Apparatarch's attention but in time we became one of its favoured collaborator species, and when the decision to overthrow the villainous Council was made, our forebears were quick to offer assistance. With us at their side the Apparatarch almost won, until the Shuskar-led alliance deployed their new weapons.'

Akreen took this in greedily, a banquet of knowledge and revelation which laid bare so much yet presented so many more questions. Especially when it came to Gredaz's purpose, and why he had waited until now to make himself known. When he voiced these queries his precursor's dull silvered features creased slightly with a bleak smile.

'Your predecessor, First Blade Tevashir,' he began. 'That was the catalyst, witnessing his ignominious death at the hands of Xra-Huld.' He gave Akreen a sombre look. 'I have always been there, you know, far back in the shadowy recesses of your thoughts. It has taken a long time for me to reach this level of awareness and ability, and it is no shame to admit that I had help. The very nature of our biology can allow us to tune in to certain parts of the electromagnetic spectrum, if we have already been taught how.'

'I was never instructed in the body-sense disciplines,' Akreen said. 'I take it that you were.'

A nod. 'Some years ago I began to notice, at the very edge of my already tenuous perceptions, a kind of whispering. Fragmentary, inconstantly fading in and out, but definitely there. I found, remembered, the capacity to respond and did so, and over time and many exchanges I learned how to define my tiny territory at the back of your mind, how to refine and strengthen my sense of self and how to relearn much that had been forgotten.'

'Who was it?' Akreen said. 'Who was talking to you?'

'By the end of the Great Unshackling War, nearly a fifth of

the worlds of the Warcage had been ruined, bombed, burnt, poisoned or wrecked, to some vile degree or other. Those which had been the Apparatarch's citadels were so comprehensively bombarded and engulfed by destruction that we now call them the Ashen Worlds.'

'Kasramyl, Gatuzna and Stoam, all quarantined from the portal network.'

'Just so. No orbits or landings permitted, on pain of death. But even though the Shuskar techniciars did all they could to sever connection to the portal network some vestigial links remained, and it was through them that thready, fitful messages were able to reach me.' Gredaz leaned in a little closer, as if confiding. 'The Shuskar fancied that their world-shattering weapons had obliterated the Apparatarch, rendering down every last piece of tech and machinery to burnt and twisted wreckage, but its constituent machine intelligences had been devised by the original Builders, thus their capacity for guile and subterfuge was considerable.'

Akreen gazed at his precursor, tempted by several threads of inquiry which beckoned from this abundance of exposed knowledge. But he kept to what seemed to be the most urgent.

'So the Apparatarch still survives,' he said. 'Does it act through you? Are you its agent?'

'I am a messenger. In the last days of the Great Unshackling War, when the last of the Apparatarch's forces were being hunted down and destroyed, and when almost all of the Zavri had been taken prisoner and neutralised, contingency plans were activated and the intelligences' cognitive cores were hidden from destruction. After the war, deeply buried microassembly seeds awoke and began to fabricate a passive sensor web through which the hidden cores could monitor events across the Warcage. They were aware of the Beshephis insurgency but were too weak and isolated to play any part, but now, after so many passing centuries, the cores of the Apparatarch have rebuilt some essential resources.'

Akreen studied Gredaz, engrossment and wonder vying now with an undercurrent of curiosity driven by a growing bushel of unanswered questions. 'What did they do with these resources?'

'Oh, these were device assemblages created to listen in on the Shuskar's communications and to monitor activity in the portal web. And to protect the cores.' He gave a secretive smile. 'And the other things that they buried out of sight – like a Zavri lineager, from the generation before me!'

Akreen was appropriately amazed, his thoughts roiled by the possibilities this presented. Lineagers were like him, the one scion from a scission group in whom the precursors of past generations were able to live on. If such a Zavri from before the Unshackling War yet survived, then it would be a precious repository of lost knowledge ...

His thoughts came to a sudden halt. 'Are you saying that this is a still-living ancestor? Is that possible? Thousands of years old ...'

'Neither living nor dead,' said Gredaz. 'Changeless and sealed in what the cores call a terminal-shift field, shielded in an armoured chamber sequestered deep within one of the worlds, one of the Ashen Worlds. And at this very moment ancient machinery is gradually bringing it to the surface.'

Akreen and Gredaz stared at each other for a moment.

'You can regain the history of our people,' Gredaz said. 'You will be able to see their memories of all these worlds before conflict and insanity wrecked them.'

'Why?' Akreen found himself saying in spite of himself. 'Why would the Apparatarch go to such lengths to preserve one of our ancestors?'

Gredaz shrugged slightly. 'Foresight? A gamble? Perhaps they knew that even if our people were suborned into allegiance to the

Shuskar, our intrinsic nature and integrity would maintain itself, a pure thread passing unbroken from generation to generation.'

'Does it ... do they hope that we will switch sides, go back to serving them?'

Gredaz shook his head. 'They have neither the strength nor the followers and allies to mount the kind of open rebellion in which that scenario would make sense. But the Chainers do have the backing and the skills and the will to mount just such a challenge, sufficient at least to distract the attention of the Shuskar Gun-Lords and tie down their ships and troops. It is the cores' hope that, if you join them, you will be able to use your position and influence to bring some of the Zavri over, enough to form a strike force that can be used like an assassin's blade to attack them where they are most vulnerable. But first you must get to the Ashen World Gatuzna and meet our long-lost ancestor.'

Akreen thought for a second. 'There's no point in using my ship since the Ashen Worlds are interdicted, and they've all been isolated from the portal network ... apart from these vestigial links you mentioned.'

'Correct. You are headed for Armag, and Armag has two functioning portal gates,' Gredaz said. 'Can you come up with a plausible excuse for visiting one?'

Akreen offered a sly smile. 'Hot pursuit of dangerous Chainer operatives seeking to sabotage vital installations – that should be enough.'

'I believe it would.'

'Good,' Akreen said. 'Then we have a plan. Do I need to worry about how my precursors might react?'

Gredaz looked amused. 'Zivolin might hear you out but, like the others, his instincts are still informed by Shuskar allegiances. Don't worry about them – they are still in there, muttering and ranting and recycling old arguments. All I've done is deny them access to the particular pathway clusters which allow them to intrude on your thoughts. The peace and quiet should give you plenty of room for consideration of tactical matters.'

Now, as he sat in the command chair on the bridge of the *Urtesh*, that inner peace and quiet felt so deep and encompassing that a ripple of unease passed through his mind. As if at some level he had grown accustomed to that non-stop carnival of aged small talk and archaic self-importance and its cessation was depriving him of some indeterminate element of . . .

Akreen frowned, straightened his posture and resolutely put that shade of unease out of mind.

Tactical matters, he thought. And his thoughts were like musical droplets echoing in a vast glowing cavern.

CHAPTER TWELVE

The grey-purple storm-skeins of hyperspace streamed past the Construct shimmership as it hurtled onwards in pursuit. The quarry – now identified as a Type-38 Ombilan transport called the *Scarabus* – was on course for a location in Indroma space, with its hyperdrive pushing near the design limits. The stealthed shimmership had managed to cut the transport's lead to a mere hundred klicks-subjective and now a fist-sized silver-white probe was gliding out ahead of it, heading straight for the transport.

In control of the probe was Lt Sam Brock. She was strapped into a recess in the shimmership's compartment, knees drawn up, arms crossed and eyes closed as the interface tiarette cued her sensorium into the probe's function set. She could see the *Scarabus* directly ahead and growing larger as the intervening distance shrank.

'Four minutes and twelve seconds until clusterbulb launch, Lieutenant,' said the drone, Rensik Estemil. 'This stealth-hunt tactic of yours is beginning to look promising.'

Brock smiled tolerantly (or was she just imagining herself smiling?). She was sure that the drone had expected her to be so disorientated and nonplussed that she would have asked to relinquish control to the shimmership's own AI, or even to

Rensik. Which would have turned her surveillance idea into the drone's – but that wasn't going to happen.

'All systems are optimal, sir,' she said. 'Launch-prep is complete.'

'Versatile efficiency in a Human! My probabilistics partition may never fully recover.'

On through the roiling, mad-cyclone chaos of raw hyperspace the ships flew, pursuer and pursued, with the small probe sitting at the tip of a forcefield array braided in a spear configuration. That spear of structured energies now projected thirty kilometres in front of the shimmership and was still extending.

The seconds ticked away and the probe steadily moved closer. With ten seconds to go, the intervening distance was not quite the five klicks Brock had presented in her simulation but was still within the clusterbulb's range. The countdown reached finality and the probe/Brock's awareness experienced a slight kick as the clusterbulb was launched. It was about the size and shape of a small egg and a cross-shaped aperture in its rear was emitting a blue-white flame, the output of a tiny reaction drive burning some propellant of the drone's own devising. It shot away from the probe, steep acceleration sending it across the last few klicks in less than a minute. Two hundred metres from the transport an inner mechanism triggered the dispersion stage and the bulb broke apart into an expanding cloud of nano-assembled sensor mites.

'Impact in five seconds,' Brock said, although to be more accurate the leading edge of the mite cloud would land on the transport's stern first with the rest touching down all across the upper hull from aft to prow. 'First scans coming in – compiling initial list of accessible hull ports and devices—'

'How good of you to keep me informed,' said the drone. 'Notify me when we have any data that's of any use.'

It did not take long. Every sensor mite was equipped with

a squad of nanobots capable of breaking into hull devices and conduits and using the ship's own cables and substrates to build their own surveillance network. In one layer of the tiarette interface Brock could see the clandestine connections spreading and multiplying, reaching out to encompass the shipboard commweb, node by node. Data began to stream, audio feeds coming from two areas of the ship, voice conversing. The shimmership's linguistics AI was ready with a battery of cognitisers to deal with vocabulary and syntax based on – but not limited to – the intel gathered at the last planet. Heuristic conversion yielded dialogue strings that were subjected to response logic analysis. After entire minutes both Brock and the drone were taking in the content of two discussions, one from the vicinity of the main cargo hold, the other from the ship's bridge.

The former involved two bodyguards pledged to one G'Brozen Mav, also on board: they discussed which clans they came from, any possible family connections, favourite sidearms and melee weapons, and the incomprehensible strangeness of the ship's previous crew, going by the enigmatic things they kept in their cabins.

The other conversation was between G'Brozen Mav himself and another follower called Hechec, also referred to as 'Toolbearer'. As they talked about their situation it quickly became clear that some catastrophic trap or ambush was due to happen at a place called Armag City and that it would lead to the death or capture of several important resistance leaders.

Other pieces of background and recent events cropped up here and there: the ship's original crew and its captain, a Human called Pyke, how G'Brozen Mav and his followers had been marooned shortly after his discovery that the trusted Khorr was a traitor. And there was mention of the rulers of the megasystem, a species or authority called the Shuskar against whom they were rebelling, and a small group of senior Shuskar called the Gun-Lords. There was also speculation as to whether the Shuskar would deploy the Zavri or the Avang against the unsuspecting resistance forces – both options were framed in overtones of dread.

'Well, at least now we know who the Big Bad is, or are,' said the drone, Rensik. 'The Shuskar – not heard of them before but cultural data from the Andromeda galaxy has never been comprehensive by any means. Preliminary cultural analysis indicated that they have been in control for several centuries, though, so these tournament battles clearly serve a purpose of value.'

'Like pitching possible allies against one another?' Brock said. 'Divide and conquer, foster tribal rivalries to fever pitch to ensure the minions never unite against their rulers.'

'Point being?'

'Sir, if this ambush succeeds it could seriously affect the outcome of our mission.'

'You're suggesting that we ride to the rescue, Lieutenant? This is a spy ship, not a planet-burning super-dreadnought.'

Sam smiled, sure that she had the drone's measure. 'I think we can, sir, but subtly. Throwing spanners in the works when they're looking the other way, that kind of thing.'

'Nice use of action-based metaphor, there. Must admit that I almost wish we were flying a battleship, one of those big jobs the Ufan-Gir used to make, multicycle shields and an insane number of gun batteries … but this is a clandestine mission, nominally anyway, so subtlety is our middle name and we're not at home to Mr Frontal Assault. What do you have in mind?'

Sam glanced at the status updates. 'Well, sir, we need a lot more intel and we won't get it from the *Scarabus* memory banks, therefore we need to shadow G'Brozen Mav all the way to the Great Harbour system. When we reach this Armag City hopefully there will be some kind of datanet that we can infiltrate and cajole into giving up its secrets.'

'That's refreshingly practical of you, Lieutenant. You can decouple from the probe now – my monitors indicate that our quarry is about to drop out of hyperspace.'

The probe was already being pulled back to its little recess in the shimmership's hull as Sam took off the tiarette.

'Sir,' she said. 'Would this be a good time for me to learn the basics of the ship's weaponry?'

'Weaponry? I think you may have misconstrued the shimmership's design philosophy, Lieutenant. Essentially, it's built for sneaking, not for skirmishing. It has no attack capability, but its stealth systems are second to none.'

'I see. May I ask if you have a decent-sized nanofac onboard?'

'I do. Why?'

'I was not permitted to leave the base with standard-issue weapons but I did bring along some templates for useful handweapons. Sir, if mission progress requires actual boots-on-the-ground intervention at some point I would like to be able to defend myself.'

'I already have a selection of small arms designs drawn from the Construct's archives, but feel free to load your own if you prefer ... there, you now have access to the builder systems. You'll see that there are dimensional limits so portable pulse cannons are sadly off the menu.'

Sam smiled brightly. 'Thank you, sir. I am sure that I can come up with something ... practical.'

CHAPTER THIRTEEN

When the lighter slid into the bay in Khorr's ship and was docked and locked, Dervla and Win were hustled along the walkway at gunpoint and through a sliding hatch. The passageways were narrow, the lighting was muted, and the few other crew members they passed on the way looked just as barbarous and feral as Khorr and his guards and, seemingly, of the same brawny humanoid species. And when they arrived at a brighter chamber and were pushed back into recesses that suddenly held them immobile, she knew with a dark, bitter certainty that she would never see Pyke again.

Win flung a string of florid curses in Anglic at their burly, over-armoured guards, eventually falling as silent as Dervla when her verbal stamina ran low. Moments later the guards stiffened and hoisted their weapons as Khorr entered, gave the Human women a single appraising look and said, 'Are you able to understand me when I speak in the Omnilect?'

Dervla glowered at him. It was several hours ago that a couple of his skagsniffing underlings force-fed them small crystalline capsules, washed down with a spurt of brackish water.

'Sure I can understand you,' she said. 'All we need to do now is learn how to swear in it.'

'Not advisable since new lives begin for you today, so forget your pasts and forget any notions of defiance. Those I obey have determined that you shall serve the needs of one of our supreme leaders. In time, you will understand what a great honour this is.'

There was a sick feeling in Dervla's stomach.

'So you're *not* with the rebels ... but Pyke and the others ...'

'They have key parts to play in the grand drama about to unfold, and their inevitable deaths will ultimately serve the ends of my masters. But as I have said, your fates lie along a different course.'

Khorr nodded to one of his guards, who stepped forward and sprayed something in Dervla's face before turning to do the same to Win.

'I will be greatly occupied for the next hour or two, so this sedative will help to allay any anxiety you may be feeling.'

Dervla had caught the spray in her mouth and eyes, and the effects were coming on strong, a floating sensation and a numbness on the tongue while her surroundings began to undulate and distort. As her mood lifted, Khorr's face became a swollen cartoonish monstrosity adorned with a single immense eye. Dervla was sure that she could see tiny, toothy-jawed fish swimming around inside it. She started to giggle and was on the verge of a mad outburst of laughing when a wave of narcotic nothingness swept over her.

When she came to it was in response to a harsh tickling in her throat, which led to a vicious and extended bout of coughing.

'My god, Derv – y'okay?'

She cleared her throat, grimacing at the rawness.

'I think I'll live, though I may never sing opera classics again ...' There was a knot of discomfort low down in her midriff, which quickly made its presence known. 'Win, how long were we out? I've got an urgent need to deal with!'

'My optic timer says about five hours,' said Win. 'And you're not the only one. I woke about ten minutes ago and got a guard to understand that if he didn't provide a bucket or something soon he'd have some explaining to do when his boss came round.' She paused at the sound of rattling from the door. 'This might be him ...'

One of the guards entered, flat-snouted auto-weapon over one shoulder, his other hand gripping a blue triangular tub. He put the container on the floor near Win's binding recess then stepped back and pressed a button on a small wall panel. Released from the restraint field, Win staggered forward a pace then bent slightly, leaning on her knees.

'My companion needs to make water too,' she said. 'Please release her as well.'

For a moment the guard just glared, then he grunted, thumbed the wall button again and moved to the door. It slid aside, he stepped back, gun now aimed at them, then it slid shut. Dervla sagged, rubbed her aching wrists, then exchanged a look with Win. The two women began laughing.

'I better go first,' Win said. 'I really wasn't kidding about an imminent disaster ...'

The blue triangular tub had a circular twist-off lid and while Win went first, Dervla took a closer look at the restraint field controls. But all she saw was a metal panel set flush with the poly-composite wall and two round buttons likewise flush with the panel surface. Without some decent tools the anti-tamper controls were effectively invulnerable.

Then it was her turn and where Win had uttered only a long sigh Dervla let out a groan that turned into a low giggle.

'Derv, I swear you've got the dirtiest laugh sometimes.'

She was fastening her camo-leggings when the door slid open again. It was Khorr, flanked by his guards. The battered frontier-merc leathers were gone, replaced by a close-fitting uniform in a fabric so profoundly black that no seams or details of any kind could be discerned. At the neck was an odd high collar in a dark grey material, its sides extending to either shoulder where metallic badges sat. Matching gloves completed the ensemble.

Recalling Khorr's predictions as to the fate of Pyke and the others, Dervla met the merc leader's gaze, quickly glanced at the guards as if gauging tactics, then tensed her shoulders and made a sharp forward motion. Khorr immediately stepped back while barking an order and raising one arm. The guards brought their weapons to bear on Dervla, and Khorr's outstretched grey-gloved hand blurred ... and was suddenly holding a long thin blade.

Dervla just laughed, relaxed her stance and leaned back, folding her arms. She had not even taken so much as a step forward.

Khorr regarded her with restrained anger. 'You seek to test me, yet I am no longer the one who controls your fate.' The slender dagger blurred in his hand, vanishing as he closed the gloved fingers in a fist. 'Now, hold out your wrists – both of you!'

Opaque plastic bands were snapped into place and Dervla could feel the fetters moulding themselves to the shape of her wrists as she and Win were marched out of the cell and along a narrow passage. *Survive*, she told herself. *Where there's life, there's vengeance.*

After a couple of turns along short dim corridors they passed through a wide hatch and down a gantry leading outside the ship. They were, Dervla realised, in the docking bay of a much larger vessel, perhaps even an orbital of some kind. Despite the poor illumination, she straight away got a sense of the bay's size, which was respectably roomy. Ducts and piping latticed corroded bulkheads half lit by glowspikes scattered across a ceiling that bore the scars of old cables and conduits long since ripped down.

And there was an armed welcoming party, a line of tall humanoids in shiny black goggle helmets and dark blue body armour over which a purplish, asymmetrical cloak was draped. All carried long weapons that looked as if they were moulded from night-blue glass: the barrels ended in curved, beak-like muzzles. Dervla gazed enviously at the beautiful weapons, imagining pressing the cold smoothness of one against her chin as she sighted along the barrel.

Two tall figures stepped into view, taller than either Khorr's mercs or the armed guards. They wore grey and white robes split from the waist, with armless jerkins over their torso, their ochre-quilted chests dotted with a variety of metallic sigils and emblems. Their scalps were enclosed by close-fitting caps, the front of which extended down like a mask over the eyes, which were hidden behind dark, impenetrable lenses.

As they approached, Khorr crossed his arms across his upper chest and gave a stiff bow.

'Luxator Khorr, be welcome aboard the *Deliverance of Judgement*,' said the shorter of the pair. 'I am Lord-Mediary Gezath, this is Lord-Mediary Mendar. The Master is discussing the Armag operation with the new Zavri First Blade but has asked that you be brought straight to the command chamber without delay. He is keen to assess your offerings.'

Dervla glanced at Win, who met her gaze with a dark and worried expression.

Flanked by the dark-armoured troops, Khorr's party set off, led by the Lords-Mediary who headed for a tall exit in the corner of the bay. Khorr walked between them but even though they were only a few metres ahead Dervla could barely make out the occasional word above the noise of tramping feet.

Offerings, she thought bleakly. *Sounds like another word for 'bribe'*.

The route led along corridors, up oddly springy stairs and through lobbies, all fairly spacious. While the *Deliverance of Judgement* was undoubtedly a capital ship, its interior design was turning out to be yet another variant of Iron-Fisted Gothic. The architecture was half temple, half monumental, and all about the worship of power. A single symbol was repeated over and over, in wall mouldings, on decorative hangings and on floor patterns, a hand holding a dagger with an eye in its blade. The warlike symbolism was obvious but the eye staring out from the blade was unusual, even unsettling when used as an omnipresent decorative element.

At last they came to a double-door entrance which parted in sections from top to bottom. It made a quiet rhythmic hiss, like a series of blades being drawn forth. Inside, the ceiling sloped up towards the far wall of a buttress-walled chamber of a fair size, although slightly less imperious than Dervla had been expecting.

Narrow spot-beams speared down upon tall silvery figures standing in motionless, glittering ranks, facing forward. As the Lords-Mediary led them into the chamber, Dervla noticed that their armed escort were remaining outside and taking up sentry positions along the corridor. Dervla and Win were made to stand in the shadows at the rear, flanked by Khorr's guards, while the gathering of shining forms continued. In the tense hush, a deep rasping voice was speaking.

'... be sealed, trapping the outworlders within Gyr-Matu's tower. The tower guard is under orders to convey the Lord-Governor to the inner refuge and pull all their squads back to protect it. You, First Blade, and your Zavri will enter at the base of the tower and scour it from bottom to top, leaving no avenues of escape. Keep in mind that I wish the outworlders taken alive so that they may be displayed and seen all across the Warcage – Zavri combat skills should be equal to such a task.'

'It shall be as you command, High One,' said a second voice. 'These interlopers will be no match for battle-hardened Zavri veterans.'

'An excellent declaration, Akreen! It pleases me that you have adapted to your new rank with such zeal. Leave now – when we next meet it will be to celebrate the new heights of glory attained by the Zavri!'

Typical, Dervla thought. *As usual I can't see what's happening on-stage because of all the Tall People blocking the way!*

They were flippant thoughts but the best she could do in an attempt to keep her worst fears at bay.

'Eternal loyalty to the Shuskar!' said the voice of Akreen.

'Loyalty eternal!' the ranks of silver Zavri warriors replied in unison.

As Dervla watched, the ranks drew aside to form an aisle down the centre. There were heavy footsteps and another tall silver figure, presumably the recently promoted Akreen, strode into view. These Zavri were tall and broad-shouldered with shiny, smooth forms that were seemingly sexless. Akreen, on the other hand, was decked out in ceremonial garb, bulky archaic armour abundantly provided with symbols and emblems, a glittering regalia.

Looking neither left nor right, the Zavri leader marched from the chamber, followed by a double column of his troops. As they filed out, the other side of the chamber was revealed: a low curved dais with a large chair in which there sat a Shuskar. Unlike the two Lords-Mediary, this one wore no headgear and the dominant colour of its attire was a deep red, a long plain coat-like affair with another of those high collars. It also seemed to be holding the stock-grip of a long-barrelled weapon, the bulk of which was resting on a spidery stand, angled to point at the ceiling. The array of spot-beams speared the deck before the dais like a square cage of glowing columns, yet the enthroned Shuskar leader was not well illuminated. Neither were the half-dozen shorter figures who were stationed around the edge of the dais. One of them beckoned to the Lords-Mediary, who looked round at Khorr and muttered, 'Follow.'

The procession crossed the floor. Nearing the dais they passed through the bright beams and Dervla was dazzled, twice, three times, and after her vision adjusted, the dais and all it held took on more detail and clarity. As Pyke's second-in-command she had travelled to a good number of exotic, out-of-the-way locales and clapped eyes on some conceptually and viscerally challenging sights. But few had struck as deep into the core of her fears as the creature that watched her approach.

'Ah, my offerings! A new species, new DNA to taste!'

This close, Dervla noticed the other humanoid figures spaced around the dais; gaunt, listless and androgynous in appearance, they were swathed in grubby windings of thin, pale blue material against which the waxy pallor of their skin scarcely contrasted. Bony hands held chunky-looking autopistols of an unusual design. Red-rimmed eyes stared out from folds of the same stained sheeting. When they regarded Khorr, his guards and captives, it was with a pitiless disdain; when they gazed at the seated Shuskar leader it was with adoration.

'Most paramount Xra-Huld,' began Lord-Mediary Gezath. 'Your servant, Luxator Khorr, seized these two Humans in order to coerce the remainder of the outworlder party into carrying out their parts in your insurpassable drama. Shortly thereafter, he realised that these captives should be gifted to you as a tribute to your supreme greatness!'

Boot-licking barf-monger, Dervla thought.

From his throne, the Shuskar known as Xra-Huld surveyed them all thoughtfully. There was a curious atmosphere in the room, a subdued watchfulness, an ambience of something cold at rest yet with an edge of anticipation. Then her attention settled on the long-barrelled weapon, dull brown with a thick muzzle, still resting on its stand – only now she could see that it was actually an extension of the Shuskar's arm. Then she saw where a protrusion emerged from the side of the weapon, lengthening into a flattened tentacle which coiled around the arm and up to the shoulder, looping around the back of the neck to curl under the jaw and further up to merge into the skin at the temple. Tentacle and weapon were one, a biomechanical whole, adorned with bony ridges, membranes stretched over glowing nodules, even scars and traceries of veins.

Dervla felt oddly light-headed as her deep reflexive dread transmuted into a surging, clawing terror, a terror which she was resolved not to show. Win wasn't faring as well – when Xra-Huld leisurely got to his feet she closed her eyes and started praying.

The Shuskar lifted its gun-arm, cradled it in the other with an odd gentleness, then descended from the dais. The scrawny sheet-garbed acolytes tracked him with their revering eyes, the Lords-Mediary looked on from behind their strange dark lenses, and Khorr just grinned. Xra-Huld loomed over Win, studying her with a piercing gaze, nostrils flaring as he inhaled deeply. Dervla's attention, though, was drawn to the grotesque semi-organic weapon – it was clearly a biomech implant designed in accordance with some anomalous combat paradigm. Indicators glowed and pulsed beneath its blemished epidermis, so energy had to be coming from somewhere, body heat, perhaps. Also, going by the round muzzle she was pretty sure that the weapon fired a heavy slug or projectile, which would allow for a wide range of possible ammunition ...

And just then, as she was studying the biomech weapon, a lump halfway along the barrel opened and an eye stared out at her. Her intake of breath was involuntary. Xra-Huld's gaze swung round and with a single stride he was standing before her, his very presence bearing down like a weight.

Can't cave in, she thought. *Maybe we are dead, but damn them all if I go out like a whipped dog!*

By sheer force of will she made herself look up into that alien gaze and crack a devil-dodging grin.

'Mornin', yer majesty – nice ship ye got here.'

There was a palpable increase in tension and a long moment of stillness. Xra-Huld bent his head while staring down at her, as if he was scrutinising a nasty stain on the floor and wanted a closer look. Then that thin-lipped mouth widened into a horrible smile full of splintered teeth.

'A species with spirit,' the Shuskar leader said to the Lords-Mediary and Khorr. 'And doubtless a world worth the harvesting. I find your offerings most acceptable, Luxator Khorr – they suit my requirements.' Xra-Huld glanced over his shoulder at one of his wan acolytes. 'Prepare them.'

Khorr's guards stepped back as four of the sheet-garbed acolytes seized Dervla and Win and pushed them away from the dais and all those gathered there. Like Win, Dervla had one heavy pistol aimed at her from the side and another pressed in the nape of her neck as they were both steered towards a concealed entrance in a side wall. A sliding door led into a small chamber smelling of something vaguely ammonia-like. There were four tall transparent cylinders, one in each corner, all empty and sitting open. From their bases cables snaked over to wall sockets, while carts like large grey bowls on wheels were parked next to them. The sight did not inspire confidence.

One of the acolytes waved her pistol in Dervla's face and plucked at her clothing. 'Outsides! Take off!'

Win was getting the same treatment and a minute or so later, barefoot and down to their underkit, each was being shoved into a big cylinder. A curved section slid shut with a faint hiss and its edges seemed to dissolve, leaving the cylinder a seamless whole. The pistol-packing acolytes then picked up the discarded garments and without a backward glance left the way they came in. Dervla watched them go, then leaned against the inside of her cylinder and gave it a shove, then again, then slammed both hands against the cold surface, finally kicking as hard as bare flesh could stand. Nothing. Not a crack, not a rattle, not the slightest movement. Not only was it made from tough, impact-resistant materials, it was also solidly anchored to the deck.

Across the room, Win was holding her shoulder as she gave her prison an irritable if feeble kick. Then she waved at Dervla and said something. Hearing nothing, Dervla pointed at her ears and shook her head.

'Can't hear a thing!' she shouted, even though it was pointless.

For a few moments they stood there, looking silently and dolefully out at each other. Then Win held out her hands towards Dervla with a 'Now what?' look on her face but all Dervla could do was shrug. Win glowered and leaned back against the inside of her cylinder, arms crossed. They were isolated and vulnerable, the prerequisite to either interrogation or brainwashing, and since neither of them knew anything about the Chainer resistance they might be in for a bit of both.

But what did the Shuskar leader mean when he said 'a new species, a new DNA to taste'?

Such speculative brooding ended a few minutes later when the red-coated Shuskar leader entered the white room and strode over to Dervla's cylinder. Three of the sheet-wound acolytes trailed in after him, mesmeric devotion in their faces.

There they are, she thought. *The brides of Frankenstein.*

Xra-Huld smiled at them as they gathered around him, glancing at Dervla as if gauging her reaction. That grotesque gun-arm was now supported in a webby sling carefully positioned to allow the creepy eye a view of its surroundings. She tried to ignore it as the Shuskar turned his attention towards her, passing a gnarly hand across a point on the outside of the glassy surface. A glowing tracery of symbol-strings and odd flickering emblems appeared for a moment then melted away.

'I assume that you can hear me,' came the Shuskar's rich yet gravelly voice.

The base of the cylinder was a couple of inches higher than

the deck so, although the Shuskar was still the taller, Dervla felt slightly less shrunken and dominated. But only slightly.

She nodded. 'Guess that means you can hear me too,' she said.

'Understanding each other is important, of course.' Xra-Huld raised his gun-arm and tapped its muzzle on the outside of the cylinder, quite soundlessly. The gun's eye gazed unwinkingly at Dervla. 'Your companion seemed to find my appearance frightening – what do you behold?'

Dervla leaned forward to stare at the eye – its pupil was large and dark, unfathomable.

'Do you see what your gun sees?' she said.

'What the Tokaw sees I see also. Do you experience no fear? The monitor web tells a very different story.'

'O' course I've got the fear!' she burst out, slamming her open hand against the cold inner surface. 'I'm scared of being turned into whatever you are ... of being joined to a festering chunk of biomech, feeling my mind being infected by it ...'

The Shuskar Xra-Huld's laugh was deep, throaty and unpleasant.

'None can become as we are! Only five of the Tokaw were ever found, and the Gun-Lords number five, as they have for many centuries. You and your companion are fated to become more than you are, to take up service to the Gun-Lords, to guard the manifest supremacy with your new lives!'

A dread suspicion crept over Dervla as she glanced at the sheet-clad acolytes.

'Never!' she cried. 'I'll never serve you!'

Laughing, Xra-Huld went over to Win's cylinder. She was sitting on the small circular floor, clasping her knees, and drew away as the Shuskar tapped some symbols on the glassy exterior. As Dervla watched, the Shuskar then brought its gun-arm round and pressed its muzzle against the cylinder. Win was on her feet and coughing as grey vapour swirled around her. Xra-Huld glanced round at Dervla, grinning as he retracted the gun-muzzle and sauntered back across the room. He stood before her, angling the gun-arm so that the eye could see her, then glowing symbols were tapped and Dervla saw how a circular aperture opened in the glassy curve. As the gun-muzzle came up, she lunged forward to press her hands against the hole. But it was no good – grey vapour still managed to seep in, oozing between her fingers, spreading fine smoky threads through the air around her. She could smell it, taste it, a cold, vaguely coppery taint which, once savoured, did not fade.

'You will be changed,' came the Shuskar's voice as she hunched down, trying not to sob as hot tears slid down her cheeks. 'We subjugate you, we remake you then we command you. We have always done this, and always will.'

She could not answer. Terror choked her throat and strange, miniscule things like translucent glyphs were swimming across her vision, across her eyes.

CHAPTER FOURTEEN

The way to Armag City led through a stretch of colossal, half-buried ruins. A humid jungle haze hung over vegetation-shrouded buildings leaning drunkenly against each other. The chitter of small creatures emanated from empty windows, and occasionally flocks of bird-things trailing odd, coiling tentacles burst out from hiding and swept across to lose themselves in leafy shadows. The ground here had swallowed the lower levels of some buildings and more than once T'Loskin Rey altered course when his pathfinders picked up instabilities on their hand scanners.

The planet, too, was named Armag and when Pyke asked if the ruins were some earlier, abandoned Armag City T'Loskin Rey laughed.

'Armag is a Gruxen word meaning haven. The Shuskar mass-relocated them to this planet when their own finally became too toxic to support life without the construction of costly habitats. The original name of these ruins and even this world is a mystery, just like the former inhabitants.'

Climbing a rocky outcrop smothered in a shiny, dark blue ivy, Pyke gazed up at the buildings with their oval windows.

'When was that? When the Gruxen got dumped here?'

'Historymen say it was not long after the Beshephis Uprising so that would be roughly 230 full-axials ago.' The resistance leader shrugged. 'I don't know how long that would be in your reckoning.' He pointed to a tilted staircase which jutted from a mass of undergrowth near their level and curved up to a higher vantage point where one huge tree had over the years grown up the side of a large, crumbling edifice, its trunk and major branches curved around and through the windows and other ruptures in the masonry.

'From there we'll get a good view of Armag City,' he said, 'and the estates of the aristarchs.'

As T'Loskin Rey's company started up the ancient cracked steps, Pyke found himself joined by Ancil, Kref and Mojag.

'Finally got tired of loitering at the rear, eh?' he said.

Ancil gave a sly grin. 'Ah, but chief, this is all too good to just hurry on through without taking a good look around. Most of these buildings have been reduced to weather-beaten shells full of collapsed floors – the only things holding up some of them are all those roots and vines . . . '

'We found a big room,' said Kref. 'Lots of wall carvings and pictures of skinny ant-people . . . '

'You're spoiling my story,' Ancil said, giving the Henkayan a look.

Kref shrugged. 'Just left out the boring bits.'

'Context isn't boring,' said Ancil. 'Facts don't exist in a void, unconnected to other knowledge. This place has a history just waiting to be uncovered – I wonder if anyone's ever made a study of all these worlds.'

'It strikes me that only the Shuskar and their minions have the means to do that,' Pyke said. 'But what do they do instead? Strongarm all these worlds to send armies to compete in their death and destruction league. Looks like they'd rather blow up or poison the past than examine it.'

T'Loskin Rey had been listening to the exchange. 'There are

a few scholars among the upper ranks of the eminent,' he said. 'And I've heard rumours of a group of nomad sages who wander from world to world by mysterious means. But you are correct, Captain – this is the Warcage and war is all we know.'

The resistance leader shrugged and turned away as he continued to lead the way on through. Pyke, despite his habitual outward cynicism, had been quite enjoying all the talk of historical mysteries and felt a certain deflation creeping in, mirroring the frown Ancil now wore. Not until they reached a bushy ridge between two cliff-like, creeper-swathed buildings did his spirits rise again. From this vantage they could see clear along a green, cultivated valley to a blue and white city whose clusters of domes and towers rose in stages to cling to a steep mountainside at the valley's end. The highest structure was a stepped, four-spired tower that flashed like crystal in the sun.

'Armag City,' said T'Loskin Rey. 'A beautiful sight, at this distance. And laid out before it like a carpet of rotting greed, the estates of the aristarchs.'

The valley was perhaps two kiloms across, and was divided into a regular pattern of triangular parcels of land. Each estate was centred on a large structure, some blocky and functional, others rising up several levels with towers and spires flying crest-adorned banners. T'Loskin Rey pointed out the different crops, orchards and paddocks, the processing and packing sheds, the tanneries, brewhouses and wineries.

'What about the labourers?' Pyke said. 'Do they travel here from outer villages or reside in dorms or the like?'

T'Loskin Rey gave him a considering look. 'The aristarchs enjoy using their power, Captain, even though it derives from the Lord-Governor and his garrison. All their workers live on the estates and sleep underground, and many of them seldom see the sun since they also work underground.' He surveyed Pyke and the others. 'Maybe now you begin to see, and to understand. For every warrior that takes the field, another eight or ten or twelve must labour in chains or the dark to support his participation in the battle-games that please our rulers so. Millions must sweat in servitude so that a pointless slaughter can continue unhindered. Across the worlds of the. Warcage, Chainer insurrectioners rebel against the Shuskar because of their cruelties – slight or monstrous, they are beyond counting but few are as cruel as condemning powerless people to live out their lives underground, like worms in the dark! The Shuskar and the loathsome Gun-Lords must die, every last one of them!'

By the end of his tirade, T'Loskin Rey was quivering with emotion. It had transformed him, adding a cold glitter to eyes that stared while a faint sheen of perspiration covered his features, and his fists clenched and unclenched. With a visible effort he calmed himself, relaxed his hands and wiped one across his face.

'We must move on,' he said, voice low. 'Too exposed here. Local Chainer contacts will be waiting for us at the edge of these ruins and they'll guide us to the staging point. Let's go.'

As the Chainer rebels followed their leader down the other side of the overgrown ridge, Pyke and Ancil exchanged a look.

'As we used to say back on Cruachan,' Pyke said, 'the man's been grinding his axe that long ye could slice fog with it.'

'Wouldn't like to see that temper cut loose,' said Ancil. 'Maybe explains what happened to G'Brozen Mav – perhaps he wasn't keen on the kill-'em-all policy.'

Pyke shrugged. 'Further in we get, the more we'll learn. Get the others – we better keep together.'

From the ridge a foot-worn path led down the creeper-smothered slope. Steps made from odd-sized stone blocks descended to a dank tunnel through compacted rubble. A few handheld torches lit the passage, revealing the protruding masonry chunks and broken pipes that needed avoiding. Pyke felt a certain resentment gnawing at his thoughts. Ever since rescuing G'Brozen Mav and his band, nearly every stage of their journey had been undertaken to fulfil the aims of someone else, and usually with only the sketchiest of explanation. But now they were getting close to the focus of the action, or at least their part in it, and if Pyke was going to have to lead the others into combat he would need real detail and lots of it. Because the reason for all this remained unwaveringly stark – Dervla and Win would die if they failed.

The tunnel opened out at a steep slope of old, bush-entwined debris. A pathway curved down past tall charcoal-black trees fluted with strange bright green channels, down to where a rough bridge crossed a thin stream. And on the other side T'Loskin Rey called a halt then took two of his Chainer fighters and went off to scout the immediate vicinity. Ten minutes later they were back, accompanied by a skinny elderly native in baggy green garments. Rey brought him straight over to talk with Pyke.

'Captain, there is a problem,' T'Loskin Rey said. 'This is Vralko – he was sent by the Gruxen Chainers running the hop-on part of the operation. The plan was to get you and your crew into a tunnel that passes through the lower massif which forms the southern flank of the Great Valley. A supply convoy from the camp farms runs through it every day and it's not far from Armag City's main roadway entrance ...'

'Let me guess,' Pyke said. 'Once the convoy reached a certain point in the tunnel your people would engineer a temporary obstruction, allowing us to hitch a lift.'

The elderly Vralko spoke up. 'The hauliers have their own guards, heh, so – always some risk but we usually get our berth. But today? Today, they have units from the Stonehead garrison along for the ride.' Vralko spat on the ground. 'Too much risk with those crawlers.'

Pyke regarded the Chainer leader. 'Looks like we need a backup plan – if ye have one.'

T'Loskin Rey said nothing for a moment, just stared off into the middle distance, eyes grim beneath a dark frown. Then nostrils flared and he inhaled and exhaled noisily.

'Yes, Captain, there is another way, secret crawlways that shadow the power network's service tunnels. That's one way of getting you into the city.'

Vralko grunted. 'It also means getting down into the under-districts and finding a way through the Iron Theatre.'

T'Loskin Rey faced the older man. 'Gyr-Matu must die but time and chance are against us – if you can lend us any help we'll take it and gladly. Otherwise ...'

The elderly Gruxen gave a sly smile and nodded. 'I know people in the Favassy underfactory. They might be able to get your skulkers to the crawlways.'

'Are there any evasion ditches left in that area?' said T'Loskin Rey.

'Enough to get us into Favassy and right up to a hidden access tunnel I've used in the past.'

'Are you sure, now?' Pyke said, casting a meaningful glance in Kref's direction. 'Some of us aren't quite built for the narrow places of the world. No offence, Kref.'

'No offence taken, chief. Was wondering about it, m'self.'

Vralko gave a dismissive gesture. 'Not a problem – I've smuggled things you wouldn't believe in and out of Armag City before now.'

Pyke looked at the Chainer leader. 'Right, so ... we have a plan, then.'

T'Loskin Rey remained serious. 'Then it's agreed. I won't be going with you – I have to be elsewhere to make sure the insurgency's first phase goes smoothly just after dusk. I'll send three of my best fighters with you but first let us get you into clothes more suited to the netherstreets of the under-districts.'

Garment bundles were dug up out of some supplies cache

secreted within the nearby overgrown ruins. After a hectic sorting for low-grade labour coats, cloaks and breeches, T'Loskin Rey guided the party downslope and to the edge of the forested hillside.

'You'll be in Vralko's hands now,' he said. 'Despite his age he has a reputation for getting the job done so heed his words—'

'And my gestures,' interjected Vralko. 'Not all of which will be polite.'

T'Loskin Rey gave a wry smile. 'My scouts will be with you up to the edge of the Favassy estate – after that, may the Infinite light your path.' He paused. 'Oh, and Khorr was adamant that I remind you of your goal – Gyr-Matu must die. Without that, the insurgency will most likely fail.'

Pyke's own smile was bleak. 'We know, Rey, we know – not something that's likely to slip our minds.'

The Chainer leader nodded, as if in understanding, then turned and retraced his steps back up the hill. Pyke and the others shared dark, grim looks, then followed Vralko along the valley.

By the time they reached the boundary of the Favassy estate it was dusk. The fence was a barrier of criss-crossed wooden piles across which barbed wire was strung. The foot of the rocky valley side levelled out quite close to the fence in places, some of which was masked by clumps of bushes and creeper-wound clusters of boulders that looked like they'd rolled down from above. It was not long before dusk darkened into night, at which point Vralko led them to a bare grassy spot near the fence, between two bushes. He poked and kicked at several small rocks before pouncing on one in particular, and when he pulled it Pyke could see that it was attached to a cable feeding down into the dirt. And a couple of feet away a section of ground hinged down like a trapdoor, making a faint thud. Vralko grinned over his shoulder at the rest, then scuttled forward and dived into the hole.

'Now what?' whispered Ancil.

Pyke was about to say something devastatingly witty when another couple of grassy patches flapped down, widening the gap in the ground. A skinny hand poked up and beckoned frantically. Chuckling, Pyke said, 'Okay Kref, you first.'

The Henkayan led the way, performing an incongruous crawl across to the hole into which his bulky form toppled out of sight, accompanied by a muffled wooden crack and a curse. Pyke sighed and waved Ancil on next, then Mojag, with Pyke bringing up the rear. Drawing near to the hole, Mojag – who had seemed much calmer since arriving on Armag – half turned to speak in a hoarse whisper.

'Captain – we need to talk!'

Pyke stared at him. 'You couldn't pick a worse time – get in there before I give ye a helping push!'

Down hastily stacked crates they descended into earthy gloom, which became an inky darkness after Vralko resealed the entrance. A moment later a bright narrow beam winked on, a torch held by Vralko, resembling some kind of wooden handle in which a small lensed emitter had been embedded. It revealed shored walls and a packed dirt floor strewn with rubbish, smashed debris of a wooden crate, a mud-caked unidentifiable garment, and a couple of bent, worn shoes. The elderly Gruxen rebel snorted and shook his head.

'Luck has been with us so far,' he said. 'The outer boundary is usually closely watched but I do know from past glories just where the weak points are, like back there where four estate boundary fences meet. Some of these petty Lords are diligent and jealously guard every square *trul* of their holdings, but fortunately the noble Favassy family is as lazy as they are rich and have cut back on the guard patrols.'

'Their folly is our luck,' said Pyke.

'Just so,' said Vralko. 'But from here on we must act as if heavily armed Stonehands are waiting around every corner. One mistake is all that's needed to bring calamity down on our heads.'

For the next hour or more they sneaked from one evasion trench to another in a route that wound halfway across the Favassy estate. The Favassy dynasty, according to Vralko, supplied garments to most of Armag City's mid-caste, officials, techs and other vocationals. So the Favassy estate was nearly full of sheds for weaving, treating, cutting and stitching, and staggered shifts of workers were moving in and out hourly. They witnessed just such a changeover just after reaching a deeper trench; from an under-shed hatch propped open a finger's width, Pyke saw scores of shadowy figures stumbling and shuffling wearily into view, some falling to their knees, some so exhausted they had to be carried to the small, angled huts where stairs led underground.

Suddenly the view was cut off as Vralko pulled the hatch shut, barring and sealing it.

'There is more for you to see,' he told Pyke and the others. 'Much more. Come – this way.'

After a dozen paces several misshapen stone steps led down, turning left into a short stretch that ended at what looked like a circular, grate-covered pipe.

'Gets a bit hazardous from here,' said Vralko. 'This pipe leads down to an unused service passage for a sewage treatment tank that was never built. The Favassy stampers don't patrol there but a locked door still links it to the main underground accessway. What it does have is a hidden entrance to the Favassy netherstreets, where workers and their families live ... after a fashion.'

The elderly Chainer rebel then reached behind the pipe's grate cover, grunted as he twisted something, then did the same at another two points around the cover. Dusting off his hands, he then grabbed the grating and hauled on it but to no avail. He paused to give the others a meaningful look, and Pyke and Ancil leaped forward to join in. The three of them pulled in unison, and there was a soft cracking sound and a grinding as the grating swung open.

'It slopes downwards but not too steeply,' Vralko said. 'Make up your minds who is to go first, but I'll have to be last to seal up the pipe. And be careful at the other end – the concealed exit is a hanging cover made to look like part of the wall.'

It was a generously proportioned pipe so Pyke led the way, then Kref, Mojag and Ancil. He wrinkled his nose at an acrid sewage odour and ignored whatever was squelching underfoot as he reached the camouflaged flap and cautiously pushed it open. Vralko had given him a cunning little torch embedded in a wooden peg and after surveying the vicinity of the opening he decided all was clear and climbed down. Kref was next and after a minute or two everyone was out of the pipe and standing in an oasis of torchlight in the pitch-dark tunnel.

'This passage is just one long stretch with a short branch tunnel not far from here,' said Vralko, pointing in one direction, 'and a second back along at the other end. They were put in as spurs for tunnel extension but the plans were shelved and they didn't go anywhere until the Chainers figured out how to ...'

'Chief,' Kref muttered. 'We ain't alone in here.'

Someone off in the darkness coughed theatrically and a sneering voice spoke.

'Heh, looks like a hulking brute but has good tunnel ears. What is he, Vralko? One of those Treneval fur-chewers?'

Pyke and Vralko both pointed torches towards the voice, and a strange figure was revealed. It was a short muscular Gruxen, wearing a long, ripped and ragged robe over nondescript labourer gear, and a helmet with a visor that only came down to the nose. Below that was a mouth full of discoloured teeth widening into a grin while one gloved hand brought a short heavy weapon down from its resting place at the shoulder. The other hand caught its undergrip, steadying the aim, and Pyke found himself staring into the business end of a triple-barrelled shotgun.

'Nice piece ye got there,' Pyke said. 'Must be weighty, though, eh?'

The helmeted intruder gave a chuckle which turned into a grating cough.

'Hello Relch,' said Vralko. 'Still scavenging for some badge-wearing arm-twister? Who is it now – Jorf?'

Relch spat. 'Shows how long you been away, you old turd. Vixo's dead and Jorf got sold. No, I'm getting orders from higher up these days.'

While the exchange took place, Pyke was studying Relch's headgear, which had to be some kind of visi-augmenter set to auto, providing nightsight and balanced filtering. Vralko's old chum might be the target of their torchbeams but his lack of anxiety suggested that he could see perfectly behind that visor.

'Stampers, is it?' Vralko's contempt was open. 'So after growing up with their boots on your neck you wanted to find out how it feels to wear the boot. Must be lonely, though, being a betrayer.'

'He's not alone,' came another voice from the tunnel darkness behind them.

Relch laughed. 'There, see? So let's have some answers, y'old wrinkler – who're yer friends and what's your business down here? What are you smuggling?'

Vralko's shoulders and head sagged, and he sighed. 'Syntha-rush, golden syntharush.'

Suddenly there was a tension in Relch's stance. He reached out a greedy hand. 'Show!'

A puzzled Pyke watched Vralko produce from his coat pocket a large black button-like disc with a yellow line around its edge.

Despite the poor light he saw the old Chainer surreptitiously press one of the faces before tossing the disc to Relch. And as he did so, Pyke saw that Vralko had palmed a second thick black button ...

Must be charges, something anti-personnel, Pyke thought madly. *The mad old bugger is going to try to take them both down ...*

'It's in powder form,' Vralko said as Relch neatly caught the disc. 'Careful not to open it by mistake.'

'Not seen it come in flasks like this afore,' Relch said, holding it up to his visor.

'High-quality merchandise, that is,' Vralko said, suddenly looking at Pyke. 'Down a spoon of that in yer wyne and it'll show you something amazing ...'

That was when it went off with a sharp pop sound, and a burst of vision-devouring, dazzling light.

Damn, a flashbang! thought Pyke, now unable to see anything more than shadowy blurs. Yet he ran forward, arms outstretched, towards where he last saw Relch standing. Pyke's last sight had been of Vralko turning to lob the second flashbang at Relch's companion. Shouts and curses had accompanied the first flash and Pyke was vaguely aware of another outburst as he charged forward, determined to deal with Relch. Instead he collided with a wall, cold grimy stone against which he crouched, backing away from the bright flare of torches.

Sounds of struggle, a strangled cry. Pyke cursed and rubbed at his stinging eyes, and shapes grew clearer and less bleary. In the beam of fallen torches forms came into focus. Vralko and Kref were drawing near, carrying a struggling captive while several paces further along the tunnel Relch lay immobile in the iron choke hold of ... Mojag?

Pyke got up from his crouched position and peered into the shadows. 'Mojag, is that you?'

Mojag, features drawn with effort, glanced up at Pyke then gave a slight shake of the head. Pyke stared back, confused, but only for a moment. As realisation struck it felt like having all his senses spun around for a second before lurching back into normality. *Oleg? Really? So the digital copy of Oleg which Mojag was carrying around is now in charge? What the hell's normal any more?*

Ancil, now carrying both torches, joined him. When the beams settled on Mojag and his prisoner, Ancil was startled.

'Mojag, you've got ... I had no idea you knew moves like that ...'

'I've been tutoring him on the sly,' Pyke said quickly. 'Thought it was long past time that he learned a grip or two.'

Ancil looked puzzled and was about to respond when Vralko and Kref arrived with the now-limp form of Relch's companion.

'You'll need to give Relch a blackout,' Vralko said. 'Press the soft area beneath his ears and he'll become as agreeable as his ally here.'

Pyke and Ancil obliged and a moment or two later Relch's struggles ceased.

'Good,' said Vralko. 'Let's get these two mudmouths along to the spur passage at the end of the tunnel. The Favassy Night-finders will know what to do with them.'

The tunnel sloped gently down into inky darkness. Pools of water had gathered near the end, adding to the already dank atmosphere. Vralko led them along to the end of the spur passage where he made a section of the wall swing up on creaking hinges. Torch beams probed the dusty space within, revealing wooden steps leading down.

'Into the depths,' Vralko said with relish as he waved the others on. 'Quickly now.'

Kref was carrying Relch's mate under one big arm while Ancil and Mojag were managing Relch between them. Pyke followed behind Kref, carrying the ambushers' heavy shotguns. Vralko closed up the secret entrance before hurrying to catch up.

'So, Vralko,' said Pyke. 'Who are these Nightfinders you mentioned?'

'They are the rare ones, Captain, the artisans of shadow, the dismal pilgrims.' The old Chainer chuckled. 'Down here in the sunless Favassy netherstreets, it seems almost natural for people to form small closed circles for protection, sadly, even against neighbours and other groups. The darkness can hide much, including spying eyes. Yet higher aspirations persist along with an angry need for a life in the sun. The Nightfinders know all the footpaths, old and new, trodden and abandoned – if there is a way to the city that bypasses the underfactory they will know of it.'

'Someone is waiting up ahead,' Kref said suddenly.

Everybody came to a halt. The passage they were traversing was low and narrow, cramped with crude supports that elbow or feet could easily catch on in the gloom. Pyke peered over Kref's brawny shoulder and saw a wavering pocket of dull light and a silhouette standing still. Then Vralko shuffled up, ducking to squeeze past Kref and his insensible burden. Reaching the front he raised his torch and flicked it on and off in some sequence only he knew. Finished, he angled the torchbeam down at the ground and a moment later the distant glow winked out. A grinning Vralko turned to Pyke and the others.

'And so we wait – one of the Nightfinders will be here soon to guide us—'

'Only if we don't decide to drop your bodies into a dregpit!' came a voice from very close by in the dark.

'Who is this?' Vralko said, sounding rankled. 'Someone who fails to recognise Vralko Dusktreader, obviously, some untutored novice—'

'Vralko, eh? If so, why bring these unknowns down into the netherstreets? A veteran would surely know better.'

'Has your life below ground blinded you to the onrush of events? I am here by order of T'Loskin Rey, general of Chainers, and my companions are the point of the spear that will bring down Lord Gyr-Matu!'

For a moment the silence was broken only by breathing and the shuffling of feet. Then there was the glow of an opening door in the right-hand wall a few paces further on.

Another secret door, Pyke thought. *Hell's teeth, this valley must be riddled with tunnels!*

'We do know about the uprisings, Vralko, so perhaps your claims deserve closer scrutiny. Pass within and take the first turning.'

Some minutes later Pyke and his crew were lounging on several crates at one end of a long, low lamp-lit room while Vralko was engaged in heated discussion with a tall, stooped Gruxen dressed in a rumpled dark green outfit. On their arrival they had been met by the owner of the distrustful voice, one of the Nightfinders, a Gruxen in an ankle-length coat and a mask that covered his nose and mouth. Introducing himself as Mokle, he whistled up four brawny helpers to relieve Pyke's crew of Relch and his companion who, still insensible, were then lugged off down a shadowy passage, along with their weapons. Now the Nightfinder was leaning against one of the stout wooden supports holding up the braced ceiling, languid eyes flicking between the newcomers and the argument going on at the far end. Whenever that distrustful gaze settled on Pyke he made sure to greet it with as rascally a grin as he could muster.

When Vralko at last came over to join them, his face was pensive.

'Sorry to be the grim teller,' he said. 'But the most direct tunnels into the city's subculverts are either caved-in or being watched by the likes of Relch. The only sure way in now left to us is through the Favassy underfactory.'

'The Iron Theatre,' Ancil murmured.

The elderly Chainer gave a sombre nod. 'An unpleasant name you will come to understand.' He glanced over his shoulder at the Nightfinder Mokle, who was now conversing with the taller, green-garbed Gruxen. 'We'll get you all armed-up before we go, because there will be dangers and Fate favours a well-aimed bullet – or so I've been told.'

Kref brightened at the mention of weaponry and even Pyke felt more upbeat as they were led through to a small armoury. One wall held a few racks of blunderbuss-like shotguns, as toted by the now-absent Relch, and large-calibre clumsy-looking rifles, while the other had about a dozen chunky-bodied, short-barrelled handguns hanging from nails and hooks. A few boxes of parts were stacked along the back wall. And when Pyke reached for one of the shotguns, Mokle shook his head.

'We must insist on keeping the damage to a minimum,' he said, indicating the handguns.

A stinging riposte immediately came to mind, begging to be verbalised, but before Pyke could reply Kref shouldered his way past, grabbed one of the big rifles from the end of the rack and started giving it the once-over. Nightfinder Mokle tried to get him to put it back but the big Henkayan just gave him looks of irritated puzzlement between working the action and crack-and-slamming the magazine.

'Er, Kref?' Pyke said eventually. 'Best if we take our hosts' advice, or we'll not get to where we need to be, get me?'

Kref grunted and reluctantly returned the rifle to its rack. ''S got a decent action as well, Captain. Better than those little peashooters.'

'They're more powerful than they look,' said Ancil, who was behind Pyke, leaning in close to scrutinise one of the handguns. 'Rifled barrels and high-capacity magazines.'

Mokle took one of the guns from the wall and offered it

to Pyke. It had a satisfying weight and the action was indeed smooth, more finely machined than the unfussy casing would suggest. He looked up at Ancil and the others and nodded.

'These'll do.'

Once they were kitted out with Gruxen guns, ammo clips and waist holsters, Vralko and the Nightfinder Mokle steered them out of the armoury and along a narrow passage, torchbeams wavering jerkily before them. After turning along a couple of side tunnels they arrived at a small round room with a trapdoor. It was hauled open to reveal the top of a ladder, and Mokle was first in.

It was a long descent, taking nearly ten minutes to reach another small room with a heavy black door. The room was so small that Kref had to ascend the ladder again a few rungs so everyone was gathered close enough to hear Vralko speak in low serious tones.

'Through this door is the Favassy estate underfactory. I will not try to describe it – you must see it for yourselves. Be as quiet as you can in there, be stealthy.'

The black door was angled back slightly and when Vralko pushed it open trails of dust and grit fell from the lintel. As they followed in single file Pyke heard the sound of machinery, a blend of motors, hammering, clanks, rhythmic clatters and the whine and shriek of power tools. Then he caught the odours, metal and burnt oil with the sharp flavour of chemicals and wood and ... something more pungent, acrid.

From the door, whose outside was camouflaged to merge with hard-packed stony dirt, a short tunnel soon opened out to a shadowy ceiling criss-crossed with girdering. Their pathway sloped up to the brink of a drop, hung with dark ragged mesh curtains, meant to blur the shapes of any who paused here to observe.

'Part the curtains carefully,' said Vralko. 'Try to keep your faces back in the shadows.'

Crouching before the ragged veil Pyke reached out and pushed the frayed layers aside to get a decent view. At first all he saw were production lines with rows of workers labouring on either side of conveyor belts, half-clothed forms sweating in the noise and the heat …

That was it, the other odour he had noticed, the sweat of never-ending toil, a desperate taint.

Then he began to notice details, like the thin cables that hung from overhead housings in clusters of six, each cluster plugged into a worker's neck, spine, upper arms, and thighs. Pyke suddenly realised what he was seeing but Ancil spoke its name.

'Neural slavery,' he said. 'Everyone on those lines – they're all remote instruments for some low-grade central machine intelligence, am I right?'

Vralko nodded. 'We call it the Stage-Master. It grips the players in its rigging, decides what work is to be done, directs their every step and motion.'

'The Iron Theatre,' Pyke said.

'So it's known to some,' Vralko said. 'Others less poetic call it the Meatgrinder.' He pointed leftwards. 'The underfactory is a linked series of large chambers, each containing twelve assemblage tracks, and our way out of this place of torment is in the third chamber along, a forgotten duct which leads to a service tunnel.'

'I expect that there's a few guards patrolling the area,' Pyke said.

'Just one guard for each chamber,' Vralko said. 'Each sits in a small windowed cockpit overlooking the main track. The Stage-Master watches everything on the assembly ways and the manipulators that it uses to handle materials and finished items are also used against intruders and any workers who disobey orders. One of the guards is a Chainer sympathiser so he at least will not raise the alarm when we pass by, although the aim is to remain unseen at all times!'

'Friends on the inside,' said Kref. 'This is good!'

'How many are there down here?' Pyke said, still staring at the nearby assembly line.

Vralko frowned. 'Guards, do you mean?'

'No, how many are working down here?'

The old Chainer shrugged. 'Varies from day to day. Each assemblage track could have between twenty and forty labouring at it – averages out at thirty – and there are twelve tracks per chamber and thirty chambers which makes ... roughly ten thousand.'

Pyke shook his head. *Ten thousand.*

'Are they awake while they work?' he said. 'Do they know what they're being made to do?'

'At the start of their shift they drink something called the sleepkey. Supposed to turn off the mind but leave the body ready for the rigging instructions.' Vralko snorted. 'The truth is that it's not sleep you fall into but a kind of hole in your mind, a grave for something half dead that gets stabbed and choked by shadows.'

All eyes were on Vralko. Hunched down next to them, his features revealed a look of far-away dread, memories of horror.

'You survived,' said Mokle.

Vralko eyed the Nightfinder. 'They had me rigged up in the Krenza estate underfactory for five years until the rasp crept into my joints, then I was put in a garment hut for two years, off to the farms to pick for a year, then barn sweeping for two. Back when I was on the lines, me and two others were caught trying to escape to the north so when we got back to the underfactory they put us on punishment pacing.' He poked Mokle's shoulder. 'You youngers'll have heard bloody tales about what the Stage-Master's rigs can do to the body but I've seen it and felt it! Spines damaged, organs ruptured, cracked bones bursting through the skin, limbs half torn off but the exposed muscles still spasming as the rig keeps making the body do the work! And you think

I survived.' The old Chainer gritted his teeth. 'Only part of me survived.'

Pyke had watched the forms labouring out there in the glare of angled lamps, and listened to all that Vralko said. And a certain type of resolve stirred at the core of his spirit, something quite different from the hot glittering hate he felt – still felt – towards Dervla's captor, Khorr. It was cold resolve, patient and ruthless.

'So, tell me,' he said. 'When we reach the tunnels on the other side of this, are there any power couplings we can sabotage that would shut it all down?'

'The main supply for all the estates runs through here,' Mokle said. 'But that's an armoured conduit which shields the cable all the way out to the distribution blockhouse – we would need upper-tech weapons to crack it.'

Vralko's grin was dark. 'That conduit runs up to a switching station that sits by the city's lower boundary wall – sabotage that and you'll also cripple some of Armag's outer defences.'

Pyke chuckled. 'Now that sounds like our kind of uproar.'

'Good,' said Vralko, standing. 'All we have to do now is creep through this place of deadly devices. The safest route is to stay in the shadows all the way round the walls of the underfactory – however, a lot of debris and discards end up there so we may have to go over or around at certain points.'

'Lead on,' Pyke said. 'We've had experience with garbage before this.'

Only a few hitches hampered their progress during that stealthy voyage across the underfactory, like a series of heaps of armoured panels, twisted frames, wheel rims, stanchions, engine components and weapon parts, all cracked, split, bent or sheared off, always smeared with oil and tangled up with wire and cabling into the kind of obstacle that only Kref could haul aside. Of course, no one heard the scraping, grinding sound that this made since the machinery noise levels were ear-shattering.

But still they had to conduct their infiltration as clandestinely as possible. While the sentries in their booths had vidcam views of the production lines and adjacent areas, it was the overhead rig-eyes which had wider observation arcs. Shepherded by Vralko and Mokle, they made uneven progress, via darkened corners and pitch-black slants of shadow. Everything seemed to be going without a hitch until they reached the junk-strewn shadows along the wall-edge of the fourth factory chamber. Vralko had just nipped across an illuminated gap when a high-pitched beeping began to sound. There was a mad scramble for cover. Pyke dived behind a rusty heap of debris and saw a startled Mojag trip over a jutting piston and fall flat on his face. Lamps were flickering in time with the alarm and a narrow bright beam suddenly lanced out from the overhead gantry – for one horrible moment Mojag's struggling form was perfectly illuminated, then Vralko popped up and sprayed a cloud of something dark grey and seething with glittering motes into the beam. The diffused light made the cloud glow and the motes flash like miniscule stars. Under the temporary veil of vapour Vralko grabbed Mojag's arm and dragged him to safety.

By now the assembly line had ground to a halt, idling engines providing a low, background rumble. Separated by several metres, Pyke was trying to ask Vralko what was going on with hand gestures and facial expressions (provoking only looks of bafflement from the Chainer) when, without warning, the docile line workers started rising into the air, drawn by tethers attached to an overhead catenary. Not having really noticed it before, Pyke now saw the catenary system which shadowed the assembly lines, curving, branching out across the factory chamber. As he watched, the limp, narcotised forms were swept off into the gloom, spreading along this or that track to their destinations.

The nearby production track seemed to be shutting down. The idling engines slowed to a stop while the lamps and spot-beams faded to a battery of dull pulsing glows. In the ensuing hot-oil darkness Vralko and Mojag sneaked over to join Pyke behind the compacted junk heap.

'Let me guess,' Pyke said. 'Those poor bastards are not being taken away for a rest and a snack in pleasant surroundings.'

Vralko gave a bleak nod. 'The Stage-Master is always seeking ways to increase the underfactory's output – at any time any worker can be decoupled from one station, moved to another and recoupled. Stronger, fresher workers replace the tiring or slightly injured ones, who are relocated to less demanding tracks.'

Pyke peered at the now-still and silent assembly line. 'So the aristos literally work your people to death.'

'On this and every other inhabited world in the Warcage,' said Vralko. 'The machine of war is a hungering beast – it eats people whole, makes weapons for other people to use and eats them too in the end. This circle of blood has ground on and on for centuries while the Shuskar preside over lavish ceremonies of slaughter.' Vralko paused, regarding Pyke and the others. 'Perhaps now you are beginning to understand.'

Pyke inhaled noisily through his nose and grimaced, a soundless half-snarl. That other smell wasn't sweat after all, but death.

'Get us out of this place,' he said.

From there it was a comparatively short distance to the chamber in the far corner of the underfactory. The assembly lines here were turning out small armoured vehicles and were therefore wider and heavier, as were the component bins and the handler grabs. To accommodate the bulk of likely offcasts and breakages a large recess had been scooped out of the nearby chamber wall. Predictably it was filled with mounds of useless parts, shells and sub-assemblies and it was up one of these jagged heaps that

Vralko led them. Hidden in the upper gloom was a small ledge and another camouflaged entrance. Vralko brightened his torch, angling the beam to find the door release.

'There is a secure hatchway from the chamber to the power-cable passage,' he said. 'Only senior Favassy officers have the open codes, so expect no more than one or two guards. This passage joins up with the cable passage which is usually unoccupied.'

Pyke nodded as he followed the old Chainer through the now-open door, pushing through dark curtains. The tunnel was a section of forgotten pipe which sloped down and curved along for about twenty paces before ending at an oval concrete barrier. Mokle pressed a switch hidden in a slot then pushed on one edge of the barrier and with a quiet gritty sound it swung open. Mokle and Vralko shared a satisfied smile, and the latter leaned out to survey the passage, which Pyke realised was below them. The older Gruxen glanced around, nodded, then clambered through and disappeared.

Making sure his Gruxen pistol was safely stowed in one of his ragged gown's deep pockets, Pyke winked at Ancil before following the Nightfinder, who had already gone after Vralko. The wall of the corridor was surprisingly high and a few hand- and footholds let him descend halfway, after which he had to drop onto his feet. Last down was Kref who, hanging from the edge of the secret exit, stretched out one hefty leg towards a lower foothold, then seemed to have a change of mind, opted for a nearer jutting projection ... then he looked over his shoulder at the ground, shook his head and muttered as he turned round to face outwards before leaping down the full height, landing with a thud that resounded along the walls. Pyke and the others turned appalled looks on the Henkayan but before anyone could speak voices called out from the passageway up ahead.

About twenty paces further on, a steep flight of steps rose to the next section of corridor. From up there a not-so-far-off voice was demanding anyone down there to come up and show themselves.

Pyke grinned. 'Well, now, boy, let's not disappoint the man.'

Weapons drawn, the six advanced to the stairs and began a stealthy crouching climb.

'This is not wise,' said Mokle. 'City guards are armed with more accurate flashguns.'

'And we have surprise,' said Pyke. 'When we get near the top, Vralko, Ancil and me will dive forward on our stomachs, firing as we go, while the rest of you aim over our heads at the nearest target, which is the nearest guy with a gun, okay? Let's go!'

But they were only halfway up when a solitary figure sauntered into view at the top. When he saw what was creeping up towards him he grabbed at his slung rifle while drawing a desperate intake of breath, clearly intending to bellow a warning. However, six handguns of various calibre targeted the guard and, with a cacophony of firing, a fusillade of bullets tore into him and knocked him off his feet. At once a second voice cried out a name, twice, three times, before the sound of running feet reached Pyke and the others, along with fearful shouts of 'Invaders!'

'Out ... of my way!' said the Nightfinder Mokle as he tried to get past the others. 'Need to stop him!'

Then he was gone, feet pounding the stone floor as he gave chase.

'And now we have a problem,' said Vralko, dusting himself off.

Pyke knew what he meant straight away. 'The guard back down there at the locked door?'

The older Gruxen nodded. 'He couldn't have missed all the gunfire, so right now he will be running off to tell a senior overseer who will have a squad at his back when he comes to unlock the door.' Vralko shrugged. 'You and your crew should hurry after Mokle – he knows how to get into the city, and which contacts to take you to. I'll stay here and hold them off for you.'

'Or,' Ancil said suddenly, producing a couple of blue-grey, palm-sized pyramids from a pocket, 'we could blow the ceiling, block the tunnel and be off into the city before they even get here.'

Vralko chuckled. 'Timer charges – you lifted them from the Nightfinders' armoury!'

'Kref ran interference for me.'

Pyke snapped his fingers. 'That whole waving-the-rifle-around business! Gave you the chance to grab some contraband, eh? Incorrigible, that's what you are.'

Ancil theatrically held one hand to his chest. 'My mother despaired of me, chief.'

'I'll despair of ye too, if that's all you got.'

Grinning, Ancil brought out his other hand to show another four charges. Pyke smiled approvingly.

'That's my boy!'

Vralko reached over to take three of them. 'With these I can block the passage and sever the power conduit. The best place is back along at the first stretch leading to the underfactory door – ceiling is at its lowest there. So all of you hurry on your way – now! Tell Mokle that I'll get out through the tunnel and see him in a day or two.'

'Sure you won't come with us?' said Pyke.

'Armag City is much more Mokle's territory. Besides, there will be more than enough excitement happening across all the estates to keep an old pilgrim busy. Now please – will you go!'

Following the maintenance passage Pyke and the others were five flights up and ascending the sixth when a muffled boom reached their ears. Ancil looked at Pyke and was about to say something when the sound of hurrying footsteps came from up ahead. With silent gestures Pyke stopped everyone in their tracks.

Has to be Mokle, he thought, staring up at the head of the stairway, readying his handgun. *Has to be*.

The footsteps slowed. And four outstretched pistols had the Nightfinder squarely in their sights when he came into view. Still masked about his lower face, his eyes told all as he glared unflinchingly down at them. Pyke coughed and gave an embarrassed smile.

'Sorry, just a bit edgy, there.'

'What was that noise?' Mokle said.

'Vralko took three charges and went back to blow the power conduit and block the corridor,' Pyke said, going on to explain that Vralko was heading back to the Favassy estate. Mokle nodded, unperturbed.

'He has a veteran's sense of strategy – the Nightfinders will need to know exactly what has happened here.'

'Did you deal with the guard?'

Mokle nodded. 'And now we must run – if Vralko managed to cut the power then alarms will surely be going off in the city as well as the estates. So we have to get outside before the retaliation squads arrive.'

'Lead on,' said Pyke.

As they set off, Ancil said, 'This is no way for a band of daring interstellar smugglers to have to get around.'

'Things could be worse,' Pyke said. 'In numerous different ways.'

'Okay, chief, that is true ... ah, dammit, he's picking up the pace!'

It could be as bad as being held prisoner on Khorr's ship, Pyke thought. *I look forward to making him pay for that.*

CHAPTER FIFTEEN

The night sky over Armag was clear, a sable canopy strewn with glitter and frost, like a thousand jewelled hoards carelessly stirred together.

'You are absolutely clear about the purpose of this assignment?'

'Yes sir, thoroughly – meet with G'Brozen Mav, introduce myself as an operative from an unnamed starfaring polity, persuade him that we share his goal of overthrowing the Shuskar, and assure him of our assistance.' Sam paused. 'Which sadly does not extend to shipments of arms.'

During their clandestine pursuit of G'Brozen Mav's stolen vessel, Rensik had listened in on communications between them and several other rebel groups, including T'Loskin Rey. When it became clear that Mav and Rey were agreeing to meet each other, with little trust on either side, Rensik proposed a low-key intervention.

'Sidebar dissent aside, you appear to be properly briefed,' said the drone. 'Stress our wide-ranging and unhindered access to all Shuskar communications and point out that we can provide the Chainer leadership with accurate advance notice of all enemy troop and vessel movements. That should sweeten the deal.' Lieutenant Sam Brock, resigned to Rensik's strategy, nodded gravely. 'What of the flotilla of troop transports now on their way here? Is it permissible to mention them, sir?'

'Leave them to me. Just focus on brokering cooperation between G'Brozen Mav and T'Loskin Rey; stress the importance of being seen as allies while their Armag revolt is getting under way, rather than carving lumps out of each other.'

'And you will make sure that the flotilla never makes planetfall?'

'Hacking into their stone-age navigationals will be child's play,' Rensik said. 'Once I've got them locked into looped manoeuvre patterns I shall hurry back here and find out how your negotiations are progressing.'

Brock nodded and went over to sit on a mossy boulder near the cliff edge. Rensik's shimmership was a grey bulbous shape half hidden by the bushy fringe of a stand of stunted trees, their foliage too meagre to block the soft pearly glow emanating from the open hatch. Other similar straggly copses were dotted back along the high, dark mountain valley which stretched off behind them. From the cliff edge they could see, beyond a long jagged ridge, the blazing radiance of Armag City. Bright tapered towers rose amid clusters of square, blue-faceted buildings from whose roofs sprouted numerous pillars of light. Flying craft hovered and swooped through the city, gathering mainly near an asymmetrical structure that was engulfed in fire and gouting spark-laden smoke into the night sky.

There were other, lesser fires on the city's periphery and several scattered throughout the noble estates to the east. Rensik had expected more, going by some of the comm traffic being intercepted by the shimmership's sensors. What was certain was that the Gruxen rebellion had taken hold in a number of strategically important areas and had a real chance of success – so long as the Chainer insurgents kept the Governor's troops trapped in their garrison twenty miles away on the coast. And that the Shuskar flotilla was halted.

'Time I was leaving,' said the drone. 'It's still less than an hour before your meeting with G'Brozen Mav – shall I transport you down to the riverbank?'

'I'd prefer to arrive when they do,' Sam said. 'It's a good view from here and the breeze is very light so when they put in an appearance I'll just deploy the wingpack, glide down and walk into view.'

'Is the translation pill working? If you are having problems, I can have one of the fabricators stamp out another variant, perhaps a different vocabulary–syntax balance in the RNA-analogue.'

'It seems to be working,' Sam said. 'I listen to the comm recordings you provided and I can understand nearly everything now.'

'Good. And the personal shield I gave you should keep you safe – well, short of cannon-calibre plasma rounds.'

'Comforting to know, sir,' she said.

'Sounds like you're ready, but if a dire situation develops don't forget ...'

'... about the panic button on my handcom,' Brock said. 'I think I'm fully prepared, sir.'

'Good. Explaining your demise would be awkward and tedious.'

The drone Rensik rose from the very lip of the cliff's edge where it had anchored itself. 'If all goes according to plan I shall return to collect you in about six hours. But since the cosmos laughs at plans and those who make them, perhaps we should treat that as a flexible aspiration!'

'Ah, the realist approach.'

The bright-cornered cuboid glided over to the shimmership. 'Good luck, Lieutenant,' the drone said. 'And try not to scare the locals.'

'I shall be the epitome of benevolence, sir.'

*

Once back inside his vessel, Rensik resynced his analytic cores with the onboard sensor hub while the autonav took care of the repulsor liftoff, a steady ascent into the atmosphere. For the last two hours the long-range detectors had been tracking that four-ship flotilla since its launch from a world called Venstak, about a third of the way round the Warcage's encircling grid of planets. Three of them were transports, each carrying a thousand battle-hardened troops of a species called the Avang. The fourth ship was the flagship, heavily armed and – unlike the others – capable of hyperspace travel. That was where the command nodes would be found, so that was his primary target.

The flotilla was burning up the distance to Armag with very powerful reaction drives, giving them an ETA of less than three and a half hours. Rensik decided to make a micro-hyperjump, thereby intercepting the flotilla after a flight-time of roughly seven minutes, ample time in which to take stock of their mission.

The shimmership's hyperdrive was engaged a moment or two after departing the upper atmospheric boundary. Transition took several seconds and the sensor hub cognitives switched to its hyperspace presets as a matter of course. Rensik had seen scan data of the Warcage's hyperspatial substructures during the stealth pursuit of G'Brozen Mav's vessel on its approach to Armag. But now here he was, travelling into its convoluted interior. Chains of worlds, over three hundred of them, orbited the Warcage's sun, all held in place by forcefield frameworks of astounding sophistication, powered by massive energy convertors feeding off the sun's fusion reaction. In hyperspace the frameworks manifested as a vast interconnecting web of field lines, a mazy obstacle of huge rods and stalks of energy through which the ship's autonav was able to neatly manoeuvre.

While part of his awareness was overseeing the route, he devoted his greater thought range to the strategic overview. And his earlier assessment concerning the disparity between the technological level of the Warcage and the technical abilities of the dominant Shuskar authority was now deeper and undeniable. From what the shimmership had gleaned from the few archives linked to Armag's rudimentary dataweb, the Shuskar homeworld had been a later addition, brought into the Great Harbour of Benevolent Harmony, as the Warcage was then known.

They played only a small part in the schisms and clashes of those times but over the following centuries and millennia their stature grew. As the Great Harbour journeyed among the civilisations of the Andromeda galaxy, fostering tyrannies and chaos along the way, the rivalries and enmities between its own worlds provided a stairway of strife which the Shuskar eagerly took advantage of. Eventually they ascended to the leadership of a fractious alliance large and strong enough to compel those worlds still ruled by the Builders' descendants to surrender or face obliteration. Other crises came along in the centuries that ensued, the most significant being the struggle against some kind of machine intelligence called the Apparatarch, and a comparatively more recent one called the Beshephis Uprising, a workers' rebellion which spread across several worlds until it was put down with ruthless brutality.

Then, as now, the Shuskar's battlefield strength was derived from militarised cadres that drew their members from the underclasses on almost all the occupied worlds of the Warcage. The Grand Escalade tournament was an early development, with considerable resources devoted to fostering and popularising a competitive culture, even to the point of concocting grudges and feuds based on minor or imagined slights and insults. The bouts themselves were shown all across a network of community screens, either as livecasts of real-time battle bouts or as repeats of past encounters.

And it was abundantly clear that the Shuskar, by now long accustomed to their position of supreme dominance, had allowed their command hierarchy to ossify into habit and tradition. Outweighing that, however, was the adaptive tactical edge of the bout armies, battle-hardened by centuries of competition against a range of opponents in a wide variety of locales. Combine this with the high tech-level of Warcage ships, many possessing self-repair systems devised by the original Builders, and the result was a fearsome assault force capable of breaking through the defences of almost any planet in this part of the galaxy.

Three worlds in the Warcage were key to the Shuskar military pre-eminence: Dushkel, Venstak and Nagolger – the fleetworlds. In addition to huge repair yards and semi-automated component factories, there were also vast underground ship arsenals, thousands of vessels stored and ready to be woken to battle by specific codes. Unfortunately, due to the rudimentary nature of onboard smart systems, these ships required sizeable, well-trained crews, something that the underpopulated Warcage worlds, hamstrung by low levels of education, were unable to provide.

The drone Rensik was musing on the three fleetworlds and speculating on how forces of Chainer insurgents could overcome their large garrisons when an exterior problem wrenched his attention away. The autonav was steering the shimmership along a laboured, more tortuous route in response to the fine, multilayered forcefield barriers that were being generated directly ahead.

And behind, the succession of huge mesh barricades springing up all along the ship's course put paid to any notion of deceleration. Yet the current dodging and twisting was becoming increasingly hazardous.

Very cunning. A counter-ingress system designed to trap and capture any intruder sneaking in from hyperspace, perhaps even crush and destroy them. I could slip down to a lower level of hyperspace but that would hamper my plans. Back to normal space, then, and resume on reaction drive ...

The shimmership's hyperdrive disengaged its field matrix and the enclosing forcefield meshes melted into the inky black of space within the Warcage. All the worlds bound to that encircling grid gleamed like shiny beads in the harsh light of its sun. Long-range sensors had located the Shuskar flotilla and the drone's ship was under way, intercept course laid in, reaction drive output ramping up. Stealth counterdetects were running and drive-emission masking agents were being released. In a matter of six minutes the shimmership would be matching course and velocity with that command vessel, then Rensik could commence hacking.

An alarm spiked across Rensik's extended awareness. The autonav took evasive actions even as the sensor feed showed the drone the kilometres-long meshed forcefield structure that scythed through the patch of space through which the shimmership had been passing the briefest of moments ago. Its shape was part wing, part stretched-out scoop, with a fringe of spikes and tentacles. It seemed to protrude from what the sensors identified as an unstable hyperspace aperture and indeed, having failed to ensnare the shimmership, it suddenly shrank back into the aperture, which then vanished.

Then more apertures began appearing directly ahead, scattered all along Rensik's intercept course.

How annoyingly persistent, the drone thought. *And effective.*

Rensik had to divert considerable cognitive-processing resources to the autonav, now switching to combat evasion imperatives. The shimmership threw itself into tight dodging coils, series of sharp turns, sideslips and jinks as massive forcefield wings proliferated and closed in. And steadily, with every lurch in this crazed, whirling, hurtling pursuit, the shimmership's intercept course slipped behind the flotilla's true position. A swift appraisal made it clear that only a daring ploy could counteract the mazy trap that was drawing in closer and tighter. So the drone Rensik took direct control of the shimmership and sent it spiralling down the thirty-kilometre length of one immense, snaring forcefield wing, streaking towards the unstable aperture at its root. At the same time Rensik fed the parameters of a hyperspace microjump into the navigationals, triggering it a mere 1.8 seconds before impact. The unleashed transboundary forces shattered the aperture and caused a radiating burst of variable-state energy which disrupted the welter of forcefield structures cluttering the vicinity of hyperspace on the other side of the aperture.

Two-point-seven seconds later, he once again emerged from hyperspace. This time the shimmership was a mere ninety-three kilometres away from the Shuskar flagship. The Construct drone swerved his little vessel round and on a tail of blue plasma energy it leaped forward ... even as more twisting apertures began to appear, leaking silver-grey radiance for a moment before pale forcefield stalks began to protrude and unfurl.

Rensik studied the scans of the flagship, still sketchy as details were gleaned instant by instant. The rest of the flotilla were now too far away so the safest place to be was either inside or right up close to the flagship, and that was his goal. Seconds passed in a blizzard of data flux and flow, the fine detail of micro-balanced power manoeuvring, and infopackets from the sensors as they probed the Shuskar flagship's interior.

And exterior, narrowing down unmonitored locations safe enough for a makeshift mooring and close to possible entry points. In microseconds alternatives were considered and discarded and an optimal selection made, instantly followed by course corrections and finely assessed thrust curves. The flagship's crude vicinity sensors were sidestepped and 14.7 seconds later the shimmership was settling into position on the vessel's midsection underhull, between a pair of bulky fulcral housings. Even though the original Builders' designs were sophisticated, in some respects there were curious gaps in their knowledge, like ship shielding. There were rudimentary anti-energy shields which seemed to rely on some complex and obsessively clumsy method of rechargeable banks, thus it was the physical structure of the hull on which the crew depended for protection. Layers of heavy alloys and fibre-crystal analogues which were designed to absorb weaponry punishment, and it was the inevitable gaps and holes which Rensik knew would allow him access to the ship's interior.

A paraprobe had already been prepared and deep-scans had found a suitable point of entry on the hull. Rensik was syncing his awareness with the paraprobe even as it was nudged forth from its finger-sized recess – tiny beads swivelled and expelled thready jets which pushed it towards the buckled edge of a hull plate. The drone's awareness was a multilayered data flow, the visual feed from the probe overlaid with basic schemata drawn from the scans, and further overlaid with a powergrid map highlighting problematic areas. The probe burrowed through the hull, using tiny cutters to penetrate seals or gain access to pipes. The deeper in it went, the larger the gaps and channels, the faster the progress and before long Rensik's probe was weaving along subsupply conduits between the command deck and what seemed to be estate cabins, heading swiftly towards the bridge. All the control systems on the flagship were hardwired so it wasn't long until the probe discovered a high-level data routing hub which opened the door to all the bridge systems.

A growing familiarity with Builder design allowed Rensik quickly to shuffle through the operational arrays. Finding out how to program the autopilots of the entire flotilla, he then set the directives with an encrypted lockout but kept them prepped to engage only on his command, once his business aboard the Shuskar vessel was complete.

As he winnowed down the streams of Shuskar data he came across reference to prisoners and their transfer to detention. There were also some data from crude medical tests but untranslatable terminology obscured the ultimate intention. Then he uncovered a vidfile archive subsystem and seeing them for himself heightened an already piqued curiosity. The two prisoners were clearly Human females, which prompted various questions and speculations, chief being the possibility that they were part of this Pyke's crew, or perhaps passengers that had been captured. And why would these Shuskar techs be so interested in human biology? Something enigmatic was going on here – the Humans would need to be examined and questioned. The drone quickly located the detention cells in question and calculated the quickest route by which he could wend his way through the decks, while compiling a list of all the hatches that would have to be sealed to ensure safe passage.

If I were watching some sweaty organic performing such an infiltration I would without hesitation call it an act of insane bravado, he thought as he edged out of the shimmership's hatch. *This is what happens when you spend too much time in their company ...*

A service port irised open to let him inside the hull, contracting shut behind him and cutting off the meagre light of the stars and the Warcage's array of worlds. Such a brazen intrusion could not go unnoticed by the flagship's security net and alarms began sounding throughout the decks. Via several emergency venting ducts the Construct drone was able to gain access to an interdeck maintenance shaft that took him down three levels to a rotary storage unit along the corridor from the detention cell. With a range of protective and interventioner fields at the ready, Rensik floated out into the corridor.

Light levels were subdued but his sensors still registered the decorative patterns on the bulkheads, strings of interlocking hooked symbols, some in different shades. Small nodules on the ceiling flashed while a harsh squawking reverberated along the passageways. A helmeted Shuskar appeared at a junction just up ahead, saw the drone and reached for a hand weapon but Rensik was quicker. A solid field projection slapped the guard off its feet while a finely tuned energy jolt put it to sleep. But from the thudding coming from some other junction hatches it was clear that others were working hard at forcing them open.

Rensik sped along to the detention cell, forced the electronic lock and glided inside. As he had already seen, there were two inclined couches, both enclosed by transparent shells. In one was the prone, naked figure of a sedated human female, just as the basic medical data suggested, but the Human in the other capsule had undergone some kind of drastic partition. Instead of one body there were a number of small pale forms which vaguely resembled new-born creatures, their skin waxy and gleaming, tiny clutching hands making slow random motions. One reasonable hypothesis was that these prisoners were the subjects of some kind of exotic genetic experiment, but without detailed study further speculation was pointless. Rensik unsealed the couch holding the intact Human, deployed gripping fields and left the detention cell, carrying the woman beneath him.

Updates from the paraprobe and the shimmership let him know that the attempts to break into his secure area were going poorly, but that it was only a matter of not much time before one of the hatches gave way. Rensik already knew that the way out would be different from the way in and swiftly flew along to what looked like a gathering room, hovered over a particular spot on the floor, deposited the Human nearby, then proceeded to tear up the decking with dense hardfield tools. Directly underneath was a small chamber with a single lockable door, as there was on the deck below that from which there was a short, fairly direct route via a maintenance booth to an airlock. He was just pushing aside sliced sections of the ceiling beneath when a voice came over on the crew address system.

'Who ... or what are you? You have abducted one of my personal assets, much to my irritation. I surmise that you are a stranger, some box of outlandish parts stirred in with a brute capacity for tactics and despatched to unleash villainy. Know then that you have earned the blood-sharp enmity of the Gun-Lord Xra-Huld – if ever we meet in battle, you will learn exactly what that means.'

What? That your nefarious boring powers only work at close range? Rensik thought as he lowered the human female down through the gaping hole. The room below was long and narrow, its walls covered in racks that looped from top to bottom. With the Human lying unconscious off to the side, Rensik first closed up the hole above, fast-welding what metal components were available, before starting on the deck, cutting aside plastic matting and ripping out linked tiling, digging into the underdeck cabling and meshes, chopping and widening, then punching through to the next chamber.

Minutes later he was down in a low-lit stretch of passageway, working on the lock for a maintenance booth with the human luggage hanging beneath him. The lock was proving a little more demanding than others, and he had to fake a recognition signal signifying that the scanner had received a stored and approved dermal pattern. As the heavy hatch began to open, his defensive sensors picked up an object racing towards him – it was one of the ship's lowly repair bots retasked to attack with its laser welder burning bright and hot. Rensik snatched it with a longer extensor field, exerted some focused pressure and snapped off the welding prong. But amusement turned to surprise when more repair bots started pouring out of their floor-level hutch slots. The Construct drone tossed the broken bot at the new arrivals, swung the Human through the half-open hatch, then swiftly closed it behind him.

Once in the booth he used codes extracted earlier by the probe to switch the airlock into its maintenance mode, which locked out the main inner hatch and activated the emergency access panel, a heavy section of the main lock which had to be physically opened. Rensik again deployed fields for bracing and for gripping the manual lever. A sharp banging commenced from the inner hatch, along with the whine of power tools, but he was reasonably sure that he would be back outside the ship before his pursuers made it through.

Communicating via the paraprobe, he had instructed the shimmership to engage the full range of stealth measures on its way across the flagship's uneven, protrusion-profuse hull. So when the Construct drone emerged from the service hatch with his still-insensible human passenger enclosed in an atmosphere-tasked forcefield pod, the ship was just arriving. In moments, handler fields deployed by the shimmership pulled them both inside, slid and sealed the entryway, and quickly repressurised the compartment to the human optimum.

Well, that's a relief, Rensik thought. *I've not had cause to use up that amount of cell capacity since – well, since Darien. But at least I got talked at by one of the fabled Shuskar Gun-Lords. Sounded as if he has a very high opinion of himself, but I'm sure we can do something about that.*

The Construct ordered the shimmership cognitives to lay in a mid-short hyperjump outwith the Warcage, followed by a return to the preset rendezvous coordinates on the planet Armag. Then he turned his attention to his guest, preparing his analytic nano-labs for a battery of extensive biomedical tests.

CHAPTER SIXTEEN

Even before the planet Armag grew to fill the main bridge view-screen, Akreen had been monitoring the planetside combat comm-streams. Initially there had been only a couple of weak support-satellite signals until the *Urtesh* was close enough to pick up the shorter-range ground-unit senders. By narrowing unit positions down to the vicinity of a specific set of coordinates Akreen was able to assemble a detailed summary of what was happening there. And it did not inspire confidence.

Armag Garrison is under blockade by Chainer forces, he thought inwardly. *The armour-wall has been sealed from sub-basement to flier deck. Nothing is getting in or out.*

So, no way of getting to that portal gate, said his precursor, Gredaz. *What about the other one?*

Taking time out from my duties to cross half a world would very likely arouse suspicion, Akreen pointed out. *Unless a senior Chainer leader suddenly decided to head for it in force, a some-what improbable scenario.*

Then we must find another portal gate that can take us to the Ashen World, Gatuzna, Gredaz said. *On another world, perhaps, like Drevaul! Once this operation is over, a return to the holdworld for resupply would surely be in line with military necessity.*

Akreen smiled. The main portal gate was sheltered in a semi-open facility between the capital city, Lantomar, and the nearby launch complex. It would be simplicity itself for him to get private and secure access to the gate for a limited period. He felt Gredaz's approval as he envisioned the gate facility and how he would place his guards ...

One of the bridge officers approached with the latest batch of status summaries for his perusal, and the news that they were less than twenty drel from attaining orbit around Armag.

'Good,' he said. 'Signal our position to the Shuskar command hub, then be attentive in awaiting their reply. We must be ready to respond with alacrity to our masters' orders.'

At least for the time being. The sooner this assignment is over, the sooner I can repair to Drevaul and use the portal gate there.

Unsure of how to crash the party, Sam Brock had held back in the shadowy undergrowth until the meeting between the rebel Chainer leaders was under way. Now that it was, her initial reluctance to make her presence known was looking like a smart move. Hanging back, she could listen in and make sure she was catching the sense of their conversation.

'And so we go around and around the matter, like *cherliss* yearlings pecking at the *murrif* but unable to get a firm grip,' T'Loskin Rey was saying with undisguised acrimony. 'The Shuskar have killed us, enslaved us, tortured us, humiliated us, stolen our children, twisted their blood and flesh and sent them back to us as our brutish overlords – their crimes against us and all the racelines of the Warcage are beyond the counting, are in fact piled up into mountain ranges of horror and suffering and agony. Every single Shuskar alive today carries the burden of those crimes and they must all pay down to the last drop of blood. How can we rebuild all these worlds ... how can we hope to lay down the foundations of a new sane future while any number of our former captors, our former tormentors, remain alive? Should we succeed, many millions will still have to live with the scars and the memories of what they have suffered – with the Shuskar expunged from the Warcage the future will at least be cleansed of their poisonous presence.'

Five figures sat around a burning wood fire. T'Loskin Rey was flanked by two brawny companions, all in body armour that was a patchwork of leather and fibreplate, while G'Brozen Mav seemed only to be wearing ordinary clothes with a bulky overcoat. His companion, a diminutive humanoid, was garbed head to foot in a concealing hooded robe. When T'Loskin Rey was finished speaking, he leaned back, arms crossed defiantly. G'Brozen Mav shook his head.

'What you demand is nothing more or less than the triumph of slaughter in the name of vengeance. Blood-drenched murder is *their* hallmark, *their* habitual trait, yet you would see it perpetuated in the name of the dead in all their generations. And why stop there? After all, the Shuskar could not and did not impose their savage will upon the worlds of the Chains by themselves – they needed helpers and allies and willing pawns, so from your perspective we should go from world to world, rounding up anyone who fought in a bout-army or performed a tour of duty here, there or anywhere, and slay them. And what of the bureaucrats and quartermasters and fabrication techs? The weapons had to be made, lists had to be compiled, cargos arranged, approved, stamped and shipped, so are they any less guilty?' The Chainer leader smiled bleakly. 'What would you rather be known as: liberator or executioner?'

T'Loskin Rey was dismissive. 'How many enemies are likely to die if the rebellion does succeed? I take no delight in the loss of life but we must fight or die in shackles. You spout hypocrisy if you imagine that our brute oppressors can somehow be blood-lessly overthrown.'

'And if they know that there is no possibility of mercy there is little chance of their allies and garrisons surrendering,' G'Brozen Mav shot back. 'The fighting will grind on and on and more lives will be lost than necessary. In fact, we might even find entire cities and worlds deciding to throw in their lot with the Shuskar if they know that we are resolved to carry out mass executions. I am not so naive as to think that the enemy's strongholds can be taken without a shot fired, but your merciless stance will lead to blood and madness – what kind of future can be built on those foundations?'

T'Loskin Rey laughed. 'If only you knew how foolish you sound. We are already living in an age of blood and madness! We are up to our necks in it. The Shuskar have watered the soil of scores of worlds with the blood of their inhabitants *for centuries*. It is a crime that goes beyond the simple pains and drama of ordinary life but instead encompasses, suffocates, each and every one of us. They must be expunged, removed from the horizons of all our lives if we intend to breathe clean air again.' He pointed across the campfire. 'You are the one who is out of step – this is something that is commonly accepted.'

'By whom? The local Chainer rebel groups on Pamary and Othunex? Wait, didn't they reject your attempt to replace their leaders with officers drawn from your own circle of lackeys?'

'That was a misunderstanding, as you full well know.'

G'Brozen Mav stood. 'Perhaps, but there was no misunderstanding when you had Khorr abduct me and my staff then maroon us on that poisonous ruin of a world.'

T'Loskin Rey shrugged and got to his feet. 'But you wouldn't listen. You didn't listen to me then and you're not listening now. Among the sentiments and instincts of the oppressed there is neither the room nor the patience for mercy. You were seen as weak and I was seen as strong, thus the roles were altered—'

'And how will they see you when Shuskar transports descend from the sky and disgorge thousands of Avang upon us?'

T'Loskin gave him a narrow-eyed glare. 'What desperate ploy is this? What can you hope to gain by peddling such disruptive lies?'

'They are not lies!' G'Brozen Mav said hotly. 'While we were marooned on that planet, a fortunate opportunity brought a spacegoing vessel into our possession which is how we were able to return to the Warcage and make contact with you. Its systems allowed us to overhear messages between the Shuskar Gun-Lords and their subordinates, and they have ordered a small fleet of ships laden with Avang infantry to Armag with the aim of putting down the rebellion.' He gave a dismissive wave. 'But disregard this as you like – we will depart this vicinity and pick up the pieces once the slaughter is done.'

'Lies, brazen lies, fabulous lies! Go on, walk away and take your lies with you . . .'

And this is where I come in, Sam Brock thought as she activated Rensik's personal shield and stepped forward, making the bushes rustle as she emerged into the firelight. Eyes widened and weapons were brought out and aimed in her direction. Smiling, Sam raised open, empty hands.

'Who are you?' said T'Loskin Rey.

'Please, gentlemen, I am no threat to any of you. My name is Samantha Brock, and I am an officer in the military forces of the Earthsphere Alliance—'

'What is an Urzfear?' broke in G'Brozen Mav.

'Earthsphere, a civilisation whose border is not far from here,' she said calmly. 'My superiors are very concerned about this Warcage, and I have been sent to offer help and advice. I and . . . another companion have been studying all these worlds and your rulers, the Shuskar – and I can safely say that they're probably the most vicious, depraved gang of bloodsucking psychopaths

I've ever come across. What little history we've gathered suggests that they have butchered their way through entire stellar regions, so we're here to make sure that they do not commit the same atrocities in this part of the galaxy.'

The aimed guns didn't waver, although frowns now accompanied the stares regarding her.

'You said there were two of you?' said T'Loskin Rey. 'Just two?'

'That is correct, sir.'

'What kind of help and advice?' said G'Brozen Mav. 'Ships? Guns? Troops?'

'Information,' she said. 'We can tap into all Shuskar communications and help you stay ahead of their strategies.'

G'Brozen Mav exchanged a wary look with T'Loskin Rey but before either could speak, the hooded figure next to the former raised an odd, swaddled hand.

'May I ask – are you wearing an armourveil?'

She regarded the diminutive figure with curiosity. 'I am wearing a personal defence shield, if that's what you mean. And who are you?'

'I am Toolbearer Hechec,' the small hooded person said. 'Forgive me if my query was lacking in courtesy – it is just that we have only heard of such things in our oldest historical records, which themselves are scarce and incomplete. Your civilisation must be very advanced.'

'Earthsphere has collaborated with some very innovative allies,' she said, trying to sound neither pompous nor opaque. 'My companion and I are operating under certain restrictions, which curtail the kind of aid we can offer—'

'So what kind of information do you have to offer?' T'Loskin Rey said impatiently, still standing with his slug weapon aimed at her midsection. 'I should warn you that it will have to be exceptional to overcome even the least of my suspicions.'

Sam nodded. 'You are right to demand assurances. Well, to begin with, I happen to know the identity of the outsiders from whom G'Brozen Mav acquired his new ship.' She turned to the other Chainer leader. 'The bold Captain Pyke and his subordinates were the original crew, I believe.'

G'Brozen Mav was staring at her with a mixture of astonishment and irritation but before he could speak T'Loskin Rey laughed out loud.

'So that's why Pyke was on that harvested world,' he said, unable to keep from grinning at G'Brozen Mav. 'He was abandoned there ... by you!'

The bearded Chainer leader gritted his teeth. 'Because I had to get back here to stop you from leading my men into a disaster!'

'What? The disaster to be delivered by your imaginary enemy ships?'

'I'm afraid that G'Brozen Mav is quite correct, sir,' Sam told T'Loskin Rey. 'Less than nine hours ago the Shuskar high command ordered three troopships to launch from a world called Venstak and head for Armag. However, my companion left here over six hours ago on a mission to sabotage those ships' navigation systems and delay their arrival.' She glanced up at the night sky. 'Which he seems to have achieved so far, buying us some time.'

'How much time?' said T'Loskin Rey.

She turned to regard him. 'Hard to say. I'm curious to know how you intended your rebellion to progress in the face of the ships that the Shuskar would inevitably send against you ... but there is another mystery I'd like to solve first. You said "that's why Pyke was on that harvested world", which implies that you have encountered this man Pyke very recently. If so, do you know where he is now?'

'What is your interest in him? Are you allied to him in some way?'

'Not at all,' she said. 'My concern is that clumsy actions on his part may jeopardise our joint endeavours.'

T'Loskin Rey was silent for a moment then shrugged. 'I have a spy among the senior ranks of the enemy – he sent Pyke to me, explaining that this Human and his crew were skilled at sabotage and shadow operations, making them ideal for an infiltration assault on the Lord-Governor's tower. I guided them through the outskirts of one of the dead cities and passed them on to Vralko, a local Chainer veteran who said he could get them past the security boundaries, into Armag City then inside the tower. I took it for granted that they would know how to turn the tower's interior to their advantage while hunting down the noble Lord Gyr-Matu.'

'And who is your spy?' said G'Brozen Mav. 'It's Khorr, is it not? The two-faced snake you paid to trick us into the portal and leave us on that toxic slagheap of a planet! He also happens to be spying on us for the Shuskar, you imbecile!'

T'Loskin Rey looked about to leap into angry denial, but Sam got there first.

'Wait, wait!' said Sam. 'You mean, Pyke and his crew are inside Armag City as we speak, carrying out this mission?'

Still glaring at G'Brozen Mav, T'Loskin Rey nodded. 'They should be at the tower by now – Vralko still has many contacts in the city so keeping them out of sight wouldn't be a problem.'

'I'm afraid that may not be the case, honoured Rey,' said Toolbearer Hechec, his hooded features inclined towards a half-visible device held in a cloth-swathed grip. 'I am receiving updates from our shipboard sensor arrays, one of which is focused on collecting messages between the Shuskar and their subordinate units and commanders. This latest is an acknowledgement sent to Xra-Huld, one of the Gun-Lords, from the *Urtesh*, a Zavri ship. It reads – "On Armag approach, landing at tower in ten drel, pursuit immediate – Eternal loyalty – Akreen."'

Hechec tapped the device with something hard and unseen. 'In your human scale, ten drel corresponds to approximately sixteen minutes, and this communication was gathered just a minute or two ago. Akreen is the First Blade of the Zavri Battalion.'

'What does that mean?' Sam said.

G'Brozen Mav looked sombre. 'The Zavri are a race of supreme warriors, and their loyalty to the Shuskar is unquestioned. Pyke and his crew will be outnumbered and greatly outskilled, but I suspect that Khorr, and the Gun-Lord Xra-Huld, want them captured alive – Xra-Huld would then parade them on screens all across the Warcage, accuse the Chainers of colluding with vile outsiders bent on enslaving every inhabitant of every world. Yes, despite the systematic slavery we already suffer, you can be certain that the Shuskar would cast up a wave of fabulous lies.'

'Such a froth of speculation,' said T'Loskin Rey. 'We should keep our minds tied to real situations.'

'Like this assault force being sent after Pyke and his people?' said Sam, unable to dampen her irritation at the Chainer leader. 'It is conceivable that your agent, this Khorr, passed on to his Shuskar superiors information about Pyke's mission ... and why would he assent to taking part in such a risky venture in the first place? He's actually a border smuggler, from data we've gathered—'

Suddenly G'Brozen Mav, who had all this time been keeping his handgun aimed at Sam's midriff, suddenly swung the weapon round to point at T'Loskin Rey.

'Khorr is the enemy's spy in *your* ranks,' he said. '*Your* negligence, and *your* incompetence has put all the Chainers on Armag at risk! The original insurgency plan included Chainer cadres travelling by portal from Demaal and Orasha, so if they are here the potential losses could be catastrophic.'

T'Loskin Rey had likewise brought his gun round to aim at G'Brozen Mav, but something in his eyes shrank from the accusations. 'This cannot be true – I am certain that Khorr is working for our side—'

'Oh, it's "our" side now—'

'With respect, gentlemen, we don't have time for this,' Sam said. 'This man Pyke and his companions are about to be caught in a trap then used as anti-outsider propaganda. Is there anything that can be done?'

G'Brozen Mav shrugged. 'We do have a ship. If I can contact one of our field commanders I might be able to persuade them to let us have a squad or two of raiders, then I can head for the Lord-Governor's tower and pray I'm not too late. I owe Pyke that much.'

Sam nodded. 'I should like to accompany you, if that's acceptable. First-hand experience of this situation is exactly what my mission requires.'

'You are quite welcome to join us.'

Just then, T'Loskin Rey holstered his sidearm, and without a word turned and began to walk away, followed by his subordinates.

'And you are going where, exactly?' said G'Brozen Mav.

'To ensure my Chainers do not die in vain,' was the flat reply.

As the other Chainer leader departed, Sam felt deep misgivings and a panicky sense of failure, as if she'd let the encounter deteriorate beyond repair. *The whole point of this was to get the two of them working together*, she thought. *Now look*.

But in the light of all that had come to the surface, any kind of collaboration now seemed very remote. Swiftly, she took out her comm device and keyed in a short message to Rensik, explaining what had transpired and what she was about to do.

'Not a surprise,' G'Brozen Mav said. 'Rey is a very skilled field commander but wider strategy eludes him. And Khorr made a most convincing rebel.' He regarded Sam. 'Am I right in thinking that your companion is actually your commanding officer?'

'That is so.'

'I look forward to meeting him – it should be instructive.'

You have no idea, Sam thought as she followed the Chainer and the hooded Toolbearer away from the camp and uphill towards a wooded vale.

CHAPTER SEVENTEEN

Pyke looked Kref up and down, struggling all the time not to guffaw out loud.

'Y'know, Kref, old son – this whole adventure has been one long costume catwalk for ye, ain't it?'

The big Henkayan was covered from head to foot in a heavy brown robe with thick, ribbed seams. Baggy sleeves almost concealed Kref's big gloved hands while a pair of boots poked out from beneath the robe's ground-sweeping edge, a noticeable amount of which trailed behind him. The hood's appearance seemed to mimic the rest of the bulky outfit, with an upper edge that drooped down like a lip, tapering lappets that dangled on either side and a rear flap that hung down to the middle of his back.

'S'right, chief,' said Kref, voice slightly muffled by the half-mask which covered his mouth and nose. 'This one's pretty comfy, though. Smells better than the last one, too.'

'Sure about that?' said Ancil. 'What does it actually smell of?'

The big robed shape gave a brief shrug. 'Sort of like baked nuts, maybe.'

Ancil, biting his bottom lip, shot a glance at Pyke who was throttling the urge to grin.

'I guess it must be pretty warm under all that,' Ancil said. 'Bet everything's getting baked.'

At this Kref tilted his head back to glare at Ancil. 'Ah, funny, you're dead funny, Ans. I can't wait till we get to do a job on a planet full of big people, then I can say that you're all my nephews from the mountains!' He chuckled deep in his chest, a throaty rumbling sound.

Pyke and his crew were sitting or standing around in a poorly lit basement half full of crates, boxes and curious hourglass-shaped storage canisters. One large box lay open, spilling brown and grey garments onto the tiled floor. Even though Kref's choice of attire provoked amusement, mused Pyke, the droopy, baggy tunics, overalls and breeches that he and the others were wearing, along with enclosing headgear of various kinds, wasn't far behind his. The smell of Pyke's own getup reminded him strongly of the worst bout of trench foot he'd ever had, but he wasn't about to tell the others all about that.

Before the exchange of banter could pick up steam, the basement door opened and Mokle, the Gruxen Nightfinder who had led them into Armag City, slipped smoothly in, closing the door behind him. He was wearing an ankle-length, dull-yellow cloak with the hood pulled back. There was a hush as he looked the crew over one by one, ending with a reluctant nod.

'A lot of city guards are busy defending some of the approaches to the estates, or patrolling the garths around the city, making sure no insurgents get in or out. Some headed up to the Stone-hands garrison, thinking they could mount a surprise attack on the Chainer forces surrounding it. No one came back.'

Pyke arched an eyebrow. 'So, do we have a clear run from here up the tower, then?'

'Not quite. Some of the dignitari families flew their own vow-guards in from plantations and breeder demesnes to the north, so that complicates matters. Also, members of Lord Gyr-Matu's bodyguard are stationed before the main and only entrance, so you will need another way in.' He gave them all a final sweeping gaze. 'You look the part, and the cargo you'll be carrying should convince any onlookers.'

'Cargo?' Pyke said.

Mokle led them to the rear of the basement, through another door to a shadowy stairwell where half a dozen large baskets with shoulder straps sat in a line on a trestle table. Strained gasps came forth as Mokle and Pyke helped baskets onto backs. Kref, bearing his burden with ease, let out another rumble of chuckling.

'Your handweapons are in the false bottoms,' Mokle said. 'When you need them, upend the baskets and rip them open.'

Pyke's own basket, like the others, was full of cloth bolts and bundles of animal hides, and was staggeringly heavy. But when Mokle came to speak with him he just gritted his teeth and gave one of his devil-may-care grins.

'Ready when you are,' he said.

Mokle nodded. 'I've told the others to keep to one-word answers if anyone says anything to them, as should you. It's very unlikely that any member of a dignitari coterie would even approach an underworker but we should be prepared.' He paused to doff the cloak, twisted it into a ball and lobbed it into a corner. Beneath, he wore a blue-grey semi-militaristic uniform, similar to the ones Pyke had seen on the various Armag guards. From a pocket the Nightfinder took a blue cap which he unfolded and tugged onto his head. 'I, on the other hand, am a squad overseer, an official with whom limited exchanges are permissible. But again, that rarely happens – the dignitari, after all, think very highly of themselves.'

He produced a folded piece of paper which he spread out against the wall close to a dull lamp. It showed the precincts of the Lord-Governor's official residence, an eight-sided outer wall beyond which lay Armag City's network of streets; inside the wall were unexplained radial layouts and what appeared to be a courtyard surrounding the Lord-Governor's tower.

'There are several entrances to the outer yards,' Mokle said. 'But getting into the courtyard would be next to impossible – normally. We will be going underground ...'

'Not again,' Ancil groaned.

'... and under the wall through what is essentially a food delivery system for the main ovenhouse.'

There were puzzled looks all round except for Pyke, who had got the measure of this society.

'What you're saying is, no one cooks up the feasts inside the courtyard,' he said. 'Might disrupt their highborn sensibilities, I'm thinking.'

Mokle smiled. 'Yes, that is exactly right. Servants work and serve – they do not share the exalted ambience of their masters' playgrounds.'

'Will it work?' said Mojag all of a sudden. 'And what do we do if that way is blocked to us?'

Pyke felt a chill go down his spine. It was Mojag's voice but Oleg's speech pattern and assertive querying style.

'It should work,' said Mokle. 'A lot of workers have failed to turn up, for obvious reasons – the shooting, the fighting and so on – so there are fewer eyes taking notice of their surroundings. But if something gets in the way, I do have an alternative, slightly riskier way to get you all to the objective.'

'Right, then let's not waste any more time,' Pyke said.

The dark stairwell went up to an arched door that led out to a small square. By now night had fallen and the air smelled of ash while minor alarms were ringing several streets away. With Mokle leading at the front, the crew lined up behind Pyke, then Kref, then Mojag, then Ancil, and trudged off towards a main road. The Nightfinder led them across the thoroughfare to a side street which curved round towards the outer yards of the Governor's residence. Plodding through the darkness, Pyke recalled the city as he'd seen it in the fading light of day, remembering the richness of the architecture, the jutting window bays, the well-formed stonework and the plentiful blue and gold trim, all of which bore evidence of decades of wear and tear; scores and cracks, themselves rounded by the elements, as well as the cracked pavements, and roads originally cobbled with hexagonal stones which now were worn near-smooth and half buried in accumulated dirt and gravel. There had been more inhabitants around earlier, although the occasional side glance revealed street-level bars and cafes doing a busy trade.

After turning another couple of corners they came to one of the entrances to the outer yards, the artisans' zone. The guards wore mauve uniforms and carried double-barrelled pistols in bulky holsters strapped to the leg. Mokle insisted on showing them several pages of documentation, which quickly provoked glazed eyes and a useful amount of tedium. They took a look inside one of the baskets then shrugged and waved the party on through.

The buildings here were taller and better maintained while the roads were narrower and surfaced with some kind of artificial, rubbery red material laid out in large square sections. Some of the tall buildings were grouped together with covered walkways linking them at different heights. There were enclosures where rows of handcarts were parked, and stone outbuildings with flat roofs and the kind of venting machinery which was a sign of temperature-regulated storage, perhaps for food.

Mokle steered them along a curved pathway running parallel with the outer wall, before turning onto a wider street which ran straight and unbroken to a high wall which enclosed the inner courtyard. Gyr-Matu's tower was visible in its entirety, with its spacious balconies and its clusters of oval windows all shuttered and dark under the security lockdown. This close, Pyke realised that it wasn't a proper free-standing tower after all, since Armag City was built at the foot of a sheer cliff-sided promontory and the rear of the lower sections of the Lord-Governor's tower extended back to the rock face, so clearly the interior floors spread back into the promontory itself. Higher up, a single arched bridge joined the penultimate floor, which lay beneath the landing pad, to the cliffside. Against the night sky it looked imposing, regal, a manifestation of authority with a heavy dash of impregnability.

We'll see about that, Pyke thought with a smile in the shadows.

Following Mokle's lead they turned a corner in time to see two large carts carrying big bright yellow canisters go past at the next junction, their hauliers straining at their yokes with a fevered urgency. Mokle held up a hand to stop the crew and then gestured them into the shadows of an alleyway.

'Wait here for a moment,' he said and was gone.

Everyone was hushed and tense for a few seconds, then Ancil spoke in a stage whisper.

'Does this mean we don't have to go crawling through tunnels again, chief?'

'If there's any justice in the cosmos,' Pyke said just as Mokle reappeared.

'The ovenhouse is belching smoke,' he said, 'and court sentries are all over the place, cordoning off part of the street and questioning anyone in sight. They seem to think that Chainer sympathisers are responsible.'

Pyke gave him a sympathetic pat on the shoulder. 'Well, me old sweat, time for plan B, I reckon.'

Mokle regarded him in a measuring kind of way for a second. 'You may not be so keen when you hear what it is, Captain.'

'Let me be the judge of that,' Pyke said. 'If I think yer talking a complete crock you'll know soon enough, so let's hear it.'

Mokle breathed in deeply. 'Kitchens and artisan workshops are not the only things which the dignitari prefer to keep beyond the courtyard wall. The sons and daughters from some of the dignitari families favour pastimes that require a certain amount of technical support but which the seniors have relegated to the outer yards. In short, the more daring of their offspring like to manually fly lightwings, small propeller-driven craft – there are four of them hangared in the top floor of a workshop block back round the other side.'

Pyke smiled. 'So, we'd just hop into these little fliers, buzz right over there and get ourselves onto one of those pretty balconies.'

'Each of the lightwings has a built-in suspensor so that the precious progeny of the wealthy don't face too much risk. With those activated, getting everyone airborne and safely across shouldn't be a problem. Of course, to get inside the tower you'll need to break into one of those armoured balcony shutters.'

Pyke nodded then muttered over his shoulder, 'Ancil, you got any of those tasty charges left?'

'Still got half a handful, chief. Get us through anything short of a blast door.'

'Good,' said Mokle, straightening and pulling his cap tight. 'It's not too far but we'll still need the baskets.'

About ten minutes later, after a gruelling trudge through half-lit side streets, Mokle led them into some kind of loading cloister at the rear of an eight-storey building showing no lights above the ground floor.

'The dignitari's rising generation insist on round-the-clock protection for their toys,' the Nightfinder said as the crew doffed disguises and retrieved weapons from their baskets' false bottoms. 'I was told that there are at least three guards inside, and we need to bring them down fast and silent, before they can trigger any alarms.'

'So how'm I gonna get over to the tower?' said Kref. 'I'm not a skinny midget like Ancil and I don't know if I can fly a little plane.'

'You'll be with me,' Pyke said. 'And I'll be flying – don't eat yerself up about it. I'll have the suspensor running on full and we'll be fine.' He turned to Mokle. 'Right, how are we going to play this?'

'I'll start a diversion at the main door while you and the others creep in from the goods entrance over there, rush and drop them.'

Pyke chuckled. 'Sneaky and underhand – I like it! Is that back door visible from the front door?'

The Nightfinder shook his head. 'Through there is a storage room and a ramp down to the basement. Another door leads out to the hallway.'

'Okay, let's get to it.'

Everything seemed to go quite smoothly. Mokle picked the lock on the rear entrance before heading round to the front of the building. Pyke ushered the others inside one by one, ensuring that footfalls were careful and quiet. Then came the sound of someone banging a fist on the front door, shortly followed by Mokle's mock-drunken voice insisting that he had been sent by one of the aristo lightwing owners to collect some essential personal effects. This exchange led to raised voices and developed into an argument of increasingly angry loudness.

Pyke nodded to the rest, then gingerly opened the door to the hallway. From a tiptoe start they leaped forward and took the three guards completely by surprise. Mokle closed the front door as the guards were variously buffeted or choke-holded into insensibility. All according to plan ... until a fourth guard appeared at the back of the hallway and made a panicky dash for the main stairway.

'Stop him!' yelled Mokle. 'Quick ...'

Pyke whirled away from one of the motionless guards and lunged back down the hall towards the foot of the stairs. But Kref, betraying an unexpected presence of mind, simply smashed aside a couple of the stairway banister supports, grabbed the fleeing guard by the ankles and dragged him screaming back through the splintered gap. One punch from the Henkayan and all was suddenly silent. Apart from the thud of the unconscious guard falling to the floor.

'Nice interception, there,' Pyke told Kref.

'I like the direct approach, Captain,' said Kref. 'It's direct.'

Mokle straightened from searching one of the guards, holding up a set of keys. 'I'll lock the doors then we can head upstairs.'

Minutes later the five of them emerged onto a long dark rooftop. Coin-sized guidance lamps embedded in the flat roof traced out a landing strip barely twenty metres long, a double line of glowing pale green dots. Mokle was already over at the small hangar, tugging open the concertina shutters.

'We should leave the main lights off,' the Nightfinder said. 'If we rely on the lightwings' own panel lights it will minimise being spotted from out there.'

Pyke followed the brief gesture, which encompassed the outer yards, the buildings, the main wall and the rest of Armag City. Smoke was rising from several locations like strange, pitch-black fountains billowing and bleeding into the night sky. Sounds of gunfire came from every direction and just occasionally Pyke heard the crump of grenades.

A series of clicks, hums and rustling sounds made him turn. Mokle and the others were wheeling a couple of odd-looking craft out of the hangar. Tiny lights glowed in their open-work cockpits and their opaque wings were unfolding and stiffening into flight configurations. Then Pyke noticed that both cockpits could only hold two, pilot and passenger sitting back to back.

'Not coming with us?' he said.

Mokle gave a regretful smile. 'It has been quite an invigorating task getting you and your crew to this point, Captain, but from here you must steer your own fates.' He looked out at the city. 'I need to be down there, helping my people free themselves.'

'Yes, I know what that feels like,' Pyke said. 'Mokle, it's been a bit of a mad hooley with yourself and Vralko – tell him to keep his head down next time you see him.'

'I shall, I promise.' Mokle indicated the nearest lightwing. 'Time to board your flying machine, Captain.'

Ancil and Mojag were already climbing into their craft. A frowning Kref, however, was staring at their lightwing with suspicion.

'Don't see how I can get into it . . .'

'The passenger seat and its framework are adjustable,' Mokle said. 'I've already prepared it for you, look.'

Grumbling, Kref let the Nightfinder guide him into the passenger seat then help him get belted in. Over in the other craft Ancil was watching the entire process with a kind of wondering gaze. Pyke pointed at him and made a shh-gesture; Ancil grinned and shrugged.

'Well, now, this is cosy,' Pyke said as he strapped into the pilot seat, grabbed the basic-looking control column and peered over it at the small dashboard. Mokle leaned in to show him the button that started the twin propellers and, more importantly, the suspensor on–off knob which could also turn the antigrav up to maximum. He thumbed the engine start, listened to the low hum of the motors climb in pitch, then turned on the suspensor and nodded to Mokle.

'You'll have to judge it finely when you get near the tower balcony,' the Nightfinder said. 'Keep the suspensor up full, turn off the motors and glide to a slow landing would be my advice.'

Ancil and Mojag were already taxiing onto the tiny runway and Pyke heard one of them let out a whoop as the lightwing leaped forward in a sudden surge of acceleration. A curved incline had been added to the runway, at the edge of the roof, and the lightwing zoomed off the end and into the air.

Then dived in a sickening sideslip which took them out of view.

'Holy mother of god,' Pyke said through gritted teeth – then let out a gasp of relief when the small craft reappeared on a climbing course that curved back round towards the rooftop. They waved to Ancil and Mojag but then saw Ancil pointing back and to the ground.

'... guards are coming!' he shouted as he skimmed past overhead.

Mokle turned to Pyke. 'Get going!'

Pyke cranked up the engine speed and steered onto the runway.

'Now you coming with us?' he yelled at Mokle.

He shook his head and waved farewell. 'They'll find me hard to track down,' he replied, and dashed off back to the hangar.

Pyke turned the engines and the suspensor up full and let the craft hurtle down the roof. Kref was bellowing something but the vibration was making it hard to understand and Pyke started to yell back that he shouldn't worry, when the lightwing leaped off the edge of the building ... and they were in flight. Suddenly Pyke had to grasp the control column and keep them on course for the tower, keep the lightwing's nose up but not too far. Part of him wanted to look back at the landing strip, or down at the ground, but instead he stared ahead, glancing at the tower. And for one clear cold moment as they coasted through the air Pyke looked up at a cloudless night sky and saw the nearby worlds of the Warcage, that vast megasystem with its hundreds of planets, silvery crescents of worlds hanging in that artificial array like jewels in a lattice, serene and beautiful.

Dervla, darling, he thought. *This better work, and Khorr had better be keeping you and Win safe ...*

Then he turned his attention back to his goal, the Lord-Governor's tower. But more immediately, where were Ancil and Mojag? He gave their surroundings a quick scan as he leaned forward to adjust the suspensor controls, allowing him to decrease altitude while swooping towards the tower in a gentle curve.

'Captain,' Kref said loudly. 'We might have a problem!'

Just as the Henkayan spoke Pyke heard the faint crack of small-arms fire and the high-pitched insect whine of rounds.

'Evil gougin' maggots!' Pyke roared as he wrenched the light-wing into a tight bank.

The tower swung across their path, looming hugely as Pyke's manoeuvre brought the craft in close. He had to reduce the sus-pensor field a notch again so that he could dive and try to locate Ancil and Mojag ... and there they were, already on one of the lower balconies. He cheered and pointed them out to Kref.

'But how we gonna land on that little shelf, Captain?'

'By virtue of me amazing talents and piloting skill, of course!' *And our handy onboard antigrav generator!*

Coming around and gaining a little height Pyke managed to get a better view of the balcony in question. As he caught sight of it again he was in time to see two figures go into crouching positions at either end of the balcony a moment before there was a flash, a gout of smoke and the muffled bang of a detonation. Pyke grinned – Ancil wasn't wasting time with those charges!

'Ancil's just blown open the shutters!' he yelled over his shoulder. 'I'm gonna try to get us down on that balcony, nice and gently.'

'Wha—?'

Pyke laughed and shrugged in the icy slipstream. He now had to bring their altitude down, level with the balcony, simul-taneously increasing the suspensor field strength while cutting the lightwing's airspeed enough to result in a soft landing. Pyke thought it was an excellent plan but the guards on the ground had other ideas. A volley of shots, including bright energy-weapon barbs, whined and buzzed past, with accompanying cracks and rips as rounds struck the lightwing. Hanging on to the control column he felt the craft lurch to the side even as Kref let out a wordless yell of panic.

'Hold on, Kref!' Pyke roared.

The suspensor unit, mounted directly beneath their back-to-back seats, was giving off a high-pitched wavering rasp sound. The lightwing was jerking in time with it and as more shots cracked past, Pyke knew that he wouldn't get another chance at this.

'Brace yerself, Kref – this'll make yer teeth rattle!'

The tower rushed towards them. Snarling and cursing, Pyke fought to keep the craft level as it swooped towards the balcony. Ancil and Mojag were crouching either side of the now-gaping window – it looked as if they had pulled the broken shutters aside or away because Pyke could actually see into the shadowy interior. And for a second he locked gazes with a wide-eyed Ancil when the lightwing was just yards away ...

There was a cracking sound as the lightwing's landing struts sheared off, then Pyke and Kref and their flying machine plunged through the open window into shadowy darkness. The wings were ripped away in an instant. Pyke tasted dust and grit and he held grimly on to the control column as they struck the floor of some large chamber, scraped and slid across it and eventually slewed to a halt next to a wall. Dizziness assailed him for a moment then he began tugging at the safety belt, just as Ancil came rushing over.

'Dammit, chief, ya made it!'

'Well, o' course! I got too many axes to grind to peg out this early ... How's Kref doing?'

'Lost my boots, Captain – something knocked them off.'

Coughing, Pyke stood, brushed dust off his jacket then stepped out of the lightwing's wreckage and headed back towards the balcony.

'Hang on, chief,' Ancil said. 'Shouldn't we set about heading up this damn tower?'

'Yes, laddy, just as soon as I bid farewell to our good friends.'
Pyke went out onto the balcony, leaned over the balustrade and
bellowed at the guards milling about below:

'Pog mo thoin, ya gang of pukes!'

Grinning, he pushed away from the stone coping and went
back inside. Mojag was leaning on a large piece of furniture like
a gargantuan desk, arms folded as he watched Pyke haul out
the big chunky Gruxen pistol and check it. Mojag's smile was
languid, thoughtful and distinctly un-Mojaglike as he glanced
over at Ancil, who was still helping Kref out of the destroyed
lightwing.

'When?' he said. 'I can't go on pretending like this, so if you
don't tell them, I will.'

In a low voice Pyke said, 'Not the time, Oleg, and not the
place. Let's just get this devil-damned mission settled and try to
get Dervla and Win back, then we'll get everyone together and
lay it all out, right?'

Frowning, Oleg-Mojag nodded.

'Okay, my crafty brigands,' Pyke said loudly. 'Get yer guns
at the ready 'cos we're off to find the aristothug who runs this
shack, and send him to his maker. Then maybe we can get out
of this madhouse.'

Ancil raised his gun, a heavy fat-barrelled revolver, and spun
the cylinder. 'Lead the way, chief – let's give 'em a thrashing.'

Kref looked unhappy. 'But I got no boots . . .'

Pyke pointed a thumb upwards. 'I'm sure we'll find a guard
in this place who'll be only too happy to lend you his. As long
as you ask nicely.'

The big Henkayan gave a wide grin. 'I'm good at that,
Captain.'

CHAPTER EIGHTEEN

It was dark and cramped inside the Zavri troop lander, with only shipboard system indicators providing the meagrest of glows to brighten the gloom. The lander engines moaned high and loud as the craft swooped into the heart of Armag City, braking strongly for touchdown. The impact gave everyone a jolt, then the pitch of the engines slowed and dropped. Akreen nodded to Temek, the strike squad-leader, and the main boarding hatch unsealed, hinging down to become the disembarkation ramp.

At the head of twelve shining Zavri fighters, First Blade Akreen walked out into the smoke-hazy air of Armag City. The Lord-Governor's tower loomed imposingly nearby and moments later they were approached by an officer in the sheer black uniform of the Governor's compound guard.

'First Blade, it is a great honour to welcome you to our city. I am Pro-Captain Yorez – how can we—?'

'Pro-Captain, we are in pursuit of dangerous extremists reported to be operating in this part of the city. Have you heard any reports of intruders that might match this description?'

'Indeed, yes! A group of armed terrorists gained access to the tower through a second-floor balcony – I saw it with my own eyes.'

'I assume that you have sent your men in after them.'

An agonised look came over the pro-captain's face. 'Sir, earlier today the Lord-Governor ordered us to seal the tower and admit no one, including ourselves, whatever the reason.'

'And what if I wish to enter the Lord-Governor's tower to continue my pursuit?'

'Honoured First Blade, I was given the strictest of instructions ...'

'Pro-Captain Yorez, I am conducting the operation under the express authority of the Shuskar Gun-Lord Xra-Huld himself. I strongly advise you to order that the tower entrance be unsealed.'

The pro-captain's face went pale at the mention of Xra-Huld; he swallowed hard, then gave a swift, sharp salute.

'First Blade, by your command.'

Minutes later the line of tall silvery figures had reached the head of the wide ornamental stairs that led up to the tower's majestic entrance, triple doors of masterforge steel inlaid with fireglass. Once all the squad were inside, Akreen ordered Temek to close up the doors and seal them from the inside. He was intent on completing this mission as swiftly and efficiently as possible – Gredaz's advice to proceed to the Zavri holdworld, Drevaul, and its portal gate, was constantly in his thoughts.

The grand entrance hall was dark, with only a handful of muted maintainer lights indicating the location of doors to ancillary chambers and the main curving staircase. Once he had all twelve Zavri gathered around him, Akreen paused to take in the encompassing grandeur but only for a moment.

'You have been told that we are in pursuit of armed and dangerous terrorists,' he said. 'I can now tell you that the ones we hunt are no ordinary extremists, fostered in some diseased slum on one of the agri-worlds. They are in fact advance scouts sent here by one of the civilisations that border on the territory where the Warcage is currently at rest.

'Intruders such as these will carry invaluable information which is why Gun-Lord Xra-Huld has authorised us to carry out this operation, because they are to be taken alive. That is his express command and we possess certain attributes which make us ideally suited. This task will present us with difficulties but I have every confidence in your matchless skills and unvarying courage. Eternal loyalty!'

'Loyalty eternal!' came the massed reply in voices pitched low.

He then turned to Temek.

'Squad-leader, I reiterate the Gun-Lord's orders – the intruders are to be taken alive, whatever the sacrifice. Is that clear?'

'We will fulfil our duty, invincible one, to the very limits of our being.'

'Good – despatch your scouts.'

Temek nodded and hurried off, rapping out a string of orders.

The very model of the efficient Zavri warrior, said Gredaz within Akreen's thoughts. *Does he brood over Zavri history in his private moments, do you think?*

I cannot picture him doing so, Akreen replied. *Temek focuses mainly on maintaining his combat effectiveness.*

Which is admirable, if somewhat austere. Our distant ancestors counted composers, writers, musicians and all kinds of artists among their number. Once we had a culture, rather than just a parade ground.

Akreen frowned. *You've been very quiet up until now. Is something wrong?*

I decided not to disturb your thoughts while you were busy with this assignment, but something new has come to my attention since we landed, something quite crucial.

Squad-leader Temek, having sent his scouts off to make a slow, careful ascent, had also readied the rest of the squad and was now waiting at the foot of the stairs for Akreen. The First Blade nodded to him and began to follow.

I assume that you are about to reveal your discovery before my patience runs out.

You may have to reassess the tactics of this ongoing assignment, Gredaz said.

And my store of patience continues to run down.

Then listen – through the medium of your physique, and the singular Zavri biology, I have detected a weak energy emission with a very specific pattern, namely the cyclic signal of a portal gate in standby mode!

Akreen almost stumbled on his way across the darkened grand hallway.

Are you certain? he said.

Yes. This is not the kind of thing that can be mistaken for something else.

Akreen gestured Temek to ascend the stairs ahead of him while he followed at a steady pace.

And where?

Up high, near the tower's apex. It appears that the exalted Lord-Governor Gyr-Matu has his own private escape hatch.

A sardonic smile passed across Akreen's features.

In that case there is no need to concern ourselves with the Lord-Governor's safety.

You think that he has already departed?

The very moment that the intruders broke into his tower, Akreen said. *But you are correct – I will have to rethink this operation as I now need to be leading from the front, not the rear.*

Perhaps Temek's scouts could benefit from the First Blade's incomparable expertise in clandestine techniques.

Perhaps they could.

By the time they reached the fifteenth floor they had already encountered and dealt with three two-man guard posts, each protected by a barricade of furniture and fittings. Ancil's charges had smashed apart the improvised defences and a barrage of gunfire through billowing clouds of dust and smoke had settled matters with brutal finality. But this one was somewhat different.

The fifteenth floor was similar to the ground floor hallway, at least in scale – it had high walls with shining pillars, seating balconies, a profusion of decorative plants, and an elaborate central atrium with a pulpit-like platform fringed with glittering bushes. Little waterfalls trickled down stepped channels on either side of the atrium to a wide ornamental pool, filling the air with a constant liquid whisper. Raised stone flags led across the water to a recessed elevator, but Pyke felt sure that couldn't be the only way to the upper floors.

Crouching with the others behind a wide, low stone barrier out on the lobby-landing, he peered over it at the lie of the land, indicating the balconies and the pulpit.

'Sentries at three points,' he said. 'Filthy gougers have set up a nasty crossfire. Could be tricky.'

Ancil frowned as he peeked over the barrier. 'You sure they're up there, chief? I can't see ...'

There was a stuttering flash as a cluster of blaster bolts struck the edge of the stone barrier. Splinters flew amid puffs of pulverised dust and Ancil cursed floridly while dabbing at several cuts on his forehead. Pyke smiled.

'Believe me now? Question is, have you got any of them charges left?'

'All out, chief.'

'No throwables at all?'

'Nah, not unless yer counting Kref's socks.'

'I heard that,' came Kref's basso voice from further down the steps where there was sufficient cover for his bulk. 'My feets is still getting a good airing – all those guards had titchy little boots.'

'We could try sniping at them from back here,' said Mojag. 'But then they could break out the suppressing fire and one of us might get hit!'

Pyke caught the emphasis in the last few words and conceded that Oleg-via-Mojag had a point. Kref was usually target No. 1 in these situations.

'So this is basically a bottleneck with limited options,' he said. 'Not the kind of situation where we can set up a diversion, either ...' He shook his head, feeling stumped but letting his gaze roam around the sumptuously ornamented landing, the friezes, the statues, the vidframes showing odd writhing abstract patterns, the gauzy drapes, the cornices ...

Suddenly, he chuckled quietly and took out the bulky Gruxen revolver. He aimed its hefty barrel up at one of a line of bulb-like protrusions dotted along the stairwell ceiling, and fired off a couple of rounds. The bulb object disappeared in a scattering of sparks and fragments. He gazed at the others in the line, waited for a few seconds, then a few seconds more just to be sure.

'Chief, I think that was one of the fire sprinklers,' Ancil said.

'Well spotted! Which is why we're going back down a floor to start collecting furniture, curtains, rugs, anything that'll burn. Then we haul it up here, stick it all in a grand old heap ...'

'And get a blaze going!'

'... but not before we shoot out all the sprinklers near this landing, get me?' Pyke grinned. 'Yeah, get a good bonfire going, then start throwing some plants on it. That should get it nice and smoky in there, eh?'

'A smokescreen,' said Ancil. 'Good cover for all manner of skulduggery!'

'Right enough, so let's head down and start scavenging.'

The internal structure of the tower was similar to that of the chambered shells created by certain sea creatures. Each floor was made up of pleasure bowers, plunge pools, party rooms and picture galleries, almost a self-contained unit linked to other floors by stairs and elevators of one kind or another. As the crew raked through the fourteenth floor for burnable (and carriable) items, Kref was sent down to the thirteenth to tear down the curtains from a series of high windows that they'd passed earlier.

After about half an hour they had gathered a growing stack of divans, chairs, stands and strange frameworks hung with paintings, thick jewelled cords made from braided hair, and what looked like groups of small toy dolls, all with open mouths. But no curtains. Pyke was about to wonder aloud where Kref had got to when he spotted a mound of tangled drapes ascending the stairs, one heavy footstep after another. On reaching the landing, the mass of patterned cloth was dumped unceremoniously at their feet, revealing a red-faced, gasping Kref.

''s hot!' he said. 'Smells like flowers, too.'

A frowning Mojag lifted up a fold of gauzy material, sniffed and nodded. 'Perfumed.'

'Bet they have servants for that,' said Ancil. 'An official curtain-scent technician – or Lord High Pongmaster to his friends!'

'Did you see the moving statues?' Kref asked Ancil.

'Moving what?'

'Yeah, I seen one when I ripped down one of the big curtains – weird-looking silver thing, really lifelike. Saw it turn its head, like a robot, then it froze.'

A dubious Ancil eyed Kref. 'Creepy.'

Pyke picked over the drapes, tugging them out one by one. 'This is good – wind 'em over and around, set fire to the gauzy ones first, that'll get the heavy ones going and pretty soon we'll have a monster holy show!'

A smiling Ancil held up one finger and, wordlessly, reached down behind a nearby padded chair and came up with a cloth bag, which clinked. He delved in with his free hand and brought out a squat triangular bottle half full of something with a rich red-brown hue. He unscrewed the stopper and held the bottle up for Pyke to take a sniff. The pungency of it made his eyes water.

'That's some powerful rocket fuel, Ans, me old blagger,' he said. 'Are you by any chance thinking "Molotov"?'

Ancil jiggled his bag to a chorus of clinks. 'In the plural, chief!'

'Nice bit of rummaging. Okay, boys, light 'er up!'

The bonfire had been piled up next to the entrance to the atrium, its base spread nearly halfway along the threshold. Flames were quick to take hold in the curtains, which were interwoven through the furniture as well as around it. Then seat padding caught fire while melting paints and lacquers added inflammable fumes and it wasn't long before the wood started to burn. The growing heat drew in air from the stairwell and thickening clouds of smoke billowed out into the atrium.

Pyke grinned at his crew and gestured for them to start adding the plants and bushes which had been pillaged from the floor below. And at last the guards hidden on the balconies opened fire. Bright barbs flickered through the haze, hammering burning holes in the furniture, in the floor, in the walls.

'Got the mollies ready, chief,' said Ancil.

'Wait till we've got a bit more smoke ...'

Suddenly, an urgent high-pitched beeping cut through the roar of the bonfire, and water began to spray from the atrium's high ceiling. Out on the landing only steady dribbles fell from the wrecked sprinklers.

The air was now getting warm and thick with smoke, and difficult to breathe. Coughing on the charred soot, Pyke tapped Ancil on the shoulder. 'Now's the time – you and Kref take out the sentries to either side.'

Rather than provide a static target, Kref and Ancil one by one dodged into the gap beside the bonfire, tossed a flaming missile and spun away into cover, all in one swift movement. Ancil's was bang on target, a neat lob right over the balcony plants to smash against stonework and splash fiery liquid over every surface. Kref's Molotov shattered against the metal balustrade but the result was the same, a wave of burning alcohol engulfing both balconies. There were cries of panic and fear from one, screams of pain from the other, and through the haze of smoke and water spray Pyke saw from his position one figure coughing harshly as he scrambled away from the flames towards a doorway. The screams from the other balcony had faded to a horrible choking sound, then silence.

'Ancil,' Pyke said. 'Think you can land a molly on the atrium platform from behind that trough?' He pointed at a greenery-smothered stone trough half inside the atrium, slightly left of the ornamental pool.

'Is the Cyberpope a quantumystic catholic?' came the reply.

Pyke laughed and beckoned Mojag and Kref over.

'Okay, we'll be plastering 'em with a few volleys to make 'em keep their heads down while you dash in. Ready?'

'Well, I suppose I better be, chief.'

By now, everyone had a strip of torn-off fabric covering their mouths, although the smoke from the fire showed signs of diminishing. Ancil was crouched and ready near the atrium entrance. Kref and Mojag stood near Pyke as he counted down from three – then they brought weapons to bear on the upper atrium platform and unleashed a barrage of gunfire. A second later Ancil darted into the great chamber, heading for the big plant trough ... and halfway there slipped on the water-slick floor tiles.

Pyke yelled at Ancil to get to cover, even as his revolver ran out of shells. Kref was dragging him away from the atrium entrance while Mojag finished emptying his own weapon.

Staggering back behind the wall, Pyke reloaded with furious haste, then dived over to the other side of the landing, peering past the slumping bonfire, and saw Ancil sprawled safely behind the stone trough. Grinning a manic, sweaty grin, Ancil gave him a thumbs-up.

'Just say the word, chief!'

Pyke glanced at Kref and Mojag, who both nodded their readiness.

'Okay,' he called out. 'The word is – banjaxed!'

The three of them swung out in unison and fired round after round up at the atrium platform. A moment later Ancil threw the Molotov, a blazing knot that arced up, smashed against a pillar and sent fiery tendrils in all directions. A figure leaped up, batting at flames on its head and shoulders and staggering off to one side until further shots caught it in the head, and it fell out of sight.

Pyke glanced at Mojag who was calmly reloading the long-barrelled pistol he was given back in the Nightfinder's underground refuge. *The old Mojag would have gone into agonies of guilt if he'd only wounded someone in a firefight,* he thought. *And even Oleg wouldn't have been quite this casual about it* ... He allowed himself a private moment of doubt. *Truth be told, I'm feeling a bit edgy about this whole deal. Sure, cooking up moves on the fly has been our* modus operandi *in many a caper, but this is on an entirely different level altogether. Feels like we're flying down a slide in the dark, with flashes of light showing up people and places as we hurtle past, and no way to get out. Bit of a scary craic ... and exciting as hell!*

'Time to take the high ground,' he said, leading the way in, joining up with Ancil.

With guns at the ready they hurried across the waterlogged atrium, careful not to slip in the numerous puddles. As Pyke had suspected, there was another way up to the next level, twin stairs that curved up to the rear of the wide platform. At the top, Pyke sidled warily out of the stairway landing, senses edgily alert as he peered left and right. One of the balcony sentries had not yet been accounted for so he whispered to Ancil to take Mojag and scout that half of the upper atrium. At the same time he and Kref scoped out the balcony and rooms on the other side and found not a living soul. Some minutes later they all rendezvoused back at the atrium platform, overlooking the lower level.

'Found the missing sentry, chief,' said Ancil. 'One of us must have hit him 'cos he was off at the rear, dead in a pool of his own blood. Checked his gun, same as the others, but we did find a doorway to a stairway leading up.'

Pyke nodded thoughtfully, eyeing the semi-transparent shaft enclosing the elevator that linked both levels of the atrium, noting that it went straight up into the ceiling. 'That lift must go up to the next floor, surely . . .'

So saying he strode around the waist-high marble coping that surrounded it, stood before its tri-segment door and prodded what looked like a call-button. A moment later the door slid open followed by a curved inner door, all smooth and silent. The lift chamber itself was cylindrical and on its control panel were ten hexagonal buttons.

'The Lord-Governor's digs are right at the top,' Pyke said. 'How many floors to go, d'ye reckon? Seven? Eight?'

Ancil gave a narrow-eyed, considering nod. 'Could be, chief. I'll take it up to the next floor, if you like.'

'I do like – save me having to volunteer ya!'

Pyke exited the lift and Ancil took his place.

'And listen, no thrilling heroics,' Pyke said. 'Head up, take a look around, then back down here, got it?'

'It's just me, chief,' Ancil said, stabbing the third button. 'I don't do solo heroics – not in my job description!'

As the door closed, a frowning Kref said, 'Hey, Captain, what's in my job description?'

Pyke smiled. 'All the good fighting stuff – what else?' He indicated the elevator. 'You two keep an eye on the lift – I'm just going to check on something.'

Leaving Kref and Mojag to lounge against the wall, he went around the lift to the banistered platform which jutted out over the atrium pool. The half-incinerated body of the sentry lay off to one side, while the decorative greenery had been reduced to a mass of intertwined blackened twigs. The air was still warm and stank of charred wet wood. Ashen water leaked from the planter containers, clouding the large puddles. The water sprinklers had either run dry or ceased after a preset period, and anyway the bonfire had burnt itself down to a low smouldering heap of embers and metal frames clumped with wads of melted plastic. Every surface in the atrium had a glaze of smoke-stained moisture and a thin haze still hung in the air. It felt like a showroom of ruination.

He was about to return to the others when a movement down by the bonfire caught his eye. Instinctively, he ducked behind the charred vegetation, peeking through the web of black stems. A tall silver form came into view, then crouched, staying close to the atrium entrance. Pyke then remembered something Kref had said after bringing the curtains for the fire, a comment about a moving silver statue ...

So as well as the Lord-Governor's bodyguard in front, now we have to worry about who knows how many big silver bastards creeping up behind us! Well, that's just brilliant.

Moving in a quiet-footed crouch he retreated from the edge of the atrium platform, straightening as he reached the area behind the lift shaft. And found Kref and Mojag still standing there. By themselves.

'Where's Ancil?'

Kref gave a large shrug. 'He's not back yet.'

Pyke gave a snarly half-smile. 'Something's up – we better head upstairs, sharpish.'

'We're not waiting here for him?' said Mojag in an Oleg fashion.

Pyke jabbed a thumb over his shoulder. 'Bad news is that we've got some mysterious uglies on our trail so we'll have to keep moving. And hope that we meet up with him soon.'

Kref actually looked upset but nodded and went along. Pyke led the way up the broad curve of steps, keeping the pace steady but not hasty, with footfalls measured enough to minimise noise. Handguns were at the ready, held at waist level and with fingers off.

Then sounds came from the floor above, sharp knocks and scrapes. There was an open doorway at the top of the flight and Pyke indicated that they slow their ascent and bring their guns up in the aiming position. The knocks sounded like footsteps that were drawing near and Pyke steeled himself, hands gripping and steadying the big Gruxen pistol as he climbed, all his attention focused along the barrel ...

A figure lurched into view and Pyke was an instant away from pulling the trigger before he recognised Ancil ... who had himself ducked, out of reflex, on seeing all the guns pointed his way.

'What ... what in the name of bloody black saints! ...' Pyke had to make himself stop, force his temper back down and concentrate on being relieved that Ancil was still alive. 'What do you think yer playing at?'

'Sorry, chief, sorry, I really am ... it was the lift!'

'Doesn't sound convincing so far, but go on.'

'Chief, I swear – got in the lift, went up to the next floor, this one, popped my head out for a look-see, then stepped back in the lift, pressed to go back down to you guys, and the fragging thing went up instead!'

'Then what?'

'Well, I panicked for a second then hit the button for the next floor up – luckily it stopped there, I got out and the lift carried on up. I knew you'd be wondering so I hurried back down.'

Pyke nodded. 'Question is, was it another guard post higher up that called the lift, or someone at the top? ... Look, we can't hang about, we've got some gang of mystery villains hot on our heels.'

'What if a squad of guards comes down in the lift looking for trouble?' said Ancil.

Pyke opened his mouth, finger ready to jab in Ancil's direction – then stopped as an illuminating thought made him smile. 'Well, now, if that happens we get to take the fast track to our destination! A guard post wouldn't send out a small team to scout around but a large detachment like the Lord-Governor's bodyguard might.'

Ancil looked at him askance. 'So we should take out their team when they get here?'

Pyke shook his head. 'What we do is head up a couple of floors and call the lift – by then it should have taken the scout team down to the atrium, so then we grab the lift and ride it to the top and finish this thing!'

Ancil nodded, his weariness showing for a moment. 'Sounds like a plan to kick down doors with – I'm in.'

Kref nodded eagerly, Mojag shrugged, then they were off, hurrying up the remaining steps and following Ancil to the next set of stairs. Even as they emerged from the stairwell Pyke spotted the shadow of the lift descending behind the frosted glass outer doors and had to physically hold back Kref's plodding bulk for a couple of seconds before the Henkayan realised what was happening. Breaths were held as the lift passed by, then Pyke pointed at the next flight of stairs.

'Double-time, let's go!'

They ran up the steps two, sometimes three, at a time. Pyke slowed at the top, exiting to the floor in a crouch, gun held ready, eyes and ears alert. But as with the rest of the evacuated tower there were no signs of life. He then rushed over to the lift and hit the call-button. He positioned Kref and Mojag on one side and Ancil and himself on the other, in case the lift had any undesirable passengers, but when it arrived it was empty. Quickly they all crammed inside but before Pyke could press the topmost button Ancil said, 'Chief, if that team is in touch with the bodyguard detail they'll be expecting us.'

Pyke gave a dry chuckle. 'Caution, Ans? At this late stage? So we jump off at the last but one, is that what yer saying?'

'It is – gives us a chance to get sneaky.'

'Sometimes sneaky is good,' said Kref.

Pyke glanced at the Henkayan. 'Ya don't say? Okay, then.'

Deliberately he punched the topmost button, then flashed his mad-as-a-bag-of-spiders grin and jabbed the button below. The doors closed and with smooth ease the lift began its ascent. After several drawn-out nerve-twitching moments the elevator stopped and opened. With his gun-butt Pyke smashed the lift control panel, then stepped warily out and scanned the vicinity with narrowed eyes. The ceiling was low here and to left and right were wide pillared areas, low lit and shadowy and cluttered with large storage crates. Curiously, between the edge of the ceiling and the outer wall there was a wide gap which curved all the way round, with pale golden light shining through from above.

'So the top floor is like a huge platform held up by those pillars,' said Ancil. 'If only I had some of those shaped charges left – just two would knock a honking great hole in the thing.'

'We get out of this in one piece, I'll buy you a super deluxe gift pack of stuff that goes boom,' Pyke said. 'But right now we need to find out how to get to the Lord-Governor without attracting attention . . .'

'Er, Captain,' said Mojag. 'Too late . . .'

Two figures in dark body armour had appeared down the far end of the low pillared area and were firing energy weapons while on the move.

'This way!' Pyke yelled, plunging off to the side in a pell-mell run, using the crates for cover. On his first sight of this huge shadowy floor he thought he had spotted an illuminated exit off to the right, in the corner. Sure enough, it was there – weapons drawn they rushed through the lit doorway and leaped up the stairs. Pyke slowed suddenly on the second flight, giving Ancil wordless hand commands to keep eyes on the entrance below.

Up the stairs, exerting concentrated effort to be as silent as possible, holding breath near the top, staring out of the door, studying what he could see of this upper floor as he sidled nearer. Peering round the corner he experienced a certain awe as he took in the surroundings.

The topmost floor of Lord-Governor Gyr-Matu's official residence was an extravagant play-palace. A broad section of booths and bars and entertainment cupolas led via curved stairs and gantries to a series of raised platforms with the highest of them joining onto a large upper section. Large overarching framework carried arrays of lights and odd networks of catenaries probably purposed to allow celebratory exhibits or opulent decorations to glide up and down and around this citadel of the elite. From all the gilded opulence Pyke was certain that the upper level was where Gyr-Matu's inner court resided; overlooking it and all the lower levels was a broad dais complete with a high, grandiloquent throne. Pyke could imagine the place thronging with thousands of courtiers, cronies, supplicants, toadies, and other creeps while music blared, the booze flowed and the stimulants stimulated, a cacophony of privilege somewhat unlike its current state of silent, echoing vacancy. Empty, that is, apart from the four dark-uniformed guards up on the courtiers' level who had spotted Pyke and the others and were scrambling to bring their energy rifles to bear.

Getting Kref – the largest moving target – out of harm's way was their first task and, after finding him a refuge in one of the small enclosed serving kiosks, Pyke was able to concentrate on dealing with the Lord-Governor's bodyguards. The next twenty minutes were a disjointed sequence of crazed dashing for cover, hearing the hiss-stutter of particle energy bolts stitching holes across the decor, smelling burnt wood and melted plastic.

With a combination of misdirection and suppressing fire, Pyke and Mojag made it possible for Ancil to dodge his way to one of the bars where, crawling on his stomach, he grabbed a clutch of bottles containing strong alcohol. When Pyke saw the thumbs-up signal he and Mojag alternated with a crossfire aimed up at the guards while Ancil ducked and dashed over to a stairway leading up to one of the intermediate platforms. When Kref then vaulted out of his kiosk – as best as a bear-sized Henkayan can vault – and rushed after him, Pyke had to confine his disbelief to some ear-scorching curses which only waned when it became clear that the desperate duo had found some solid cover.

Then came the hair-raising journey from cover behind a solid partition near the stairwell over to where Kref and Ancil were waiting. Mojag's position was close by and between them they feinted, baited and decoyed their way across the elaborate maze of raised seating, dance-pits and racks of playscreens. Pyke practically threw himself to the floor next to where Ancil was working on a handful of bottles.

'Hey, chief, welcome to the party!'

Pyke gave a half-smile. 'We're not close enough yet to use those, ye know that.'

Ancil, tamping a wad of cloth into the neck of one blood-red bottle, smiled a knowing smile. 'What about Kref?'

'Kref's throwing arm couldn't hit a barn door the size of a barn – sorry, Kref.'

'S'okay, Captain, I know I'm not the best chucker around.'

Ten minutes later Kref had his chance to show that this was not entirely true. Repeating the well-tested process of diversion, decoy and suppressing fire, Pyke was able to get his crew up as far as the last small platform before the more luxurious court level. On the way everyone picked up scratches, bruises, grazes from scrambling, diving and ducking on the rough flooring material. But just as they reached the final platform one of the guards aiming over the balustrade shot Kref in the leg. With a roar of pain the big Henkayan went down between a row of chairs and a big display unit composed of bubble-like niches. Mojag was nearest and went to help but Kref angrily brushed him off, got to his feet, his face a mask of rage, then with one hand picked up the closest padded armchair and hurled it. Pyke and the others watched in awe as the chair tumbled through the air in a perfect arc and struck one of the guards, knocking him flying.

Another chair followed, then a small carved table, by which time Ancil had a lit Molotov ready to slap into Kref's empty hand. Kref spared it only the briefest of glances before hurling it straight after the flying furniture. The bottle shattered against a raised bench and flaming fluid splattered over a wide area. A couple of figures with blazing arms and hair darted away, crying out in pain and fear, while another was helping the chair-crippled guard off to the side. By the time Pyke reached the upper floor one of the burning guards seemed to be dead on the floor and the others were cowering in surrender, weapons cast aside. A happy Ancil was quick to grab the discarded rifles but then dumped them over the side when they turned out to be DNA-locked and useless.

Pyke scanned the luxurious upper floor as best as he could,

given the number of decorative screens and gauzy canopies positioned around the clusters of sofas and divans.

'Wondering about them guards we saw downstairs?' said Mojag.

Pyke nodded. 'Plenty of sweet little hiding places for them, too.' He pointed to where a broad stairway led up to a raised section with the big glass and chrome throne and, behind it, parted indigo drapes and a set of dull golden double doors. 'That looks like a convenient bolthole, so that's where we're going. Ancil, you and me will be the bait.'

'Uh, bait?'

'Yes, indeedy, bait on legs as we run like a pair of mad dogs right around the side there, heading for the big stairs.' Pyke reached over and slapped Kref on the shoulder. 'Meanwhile Mojag and our chair-chucker supreme here will be watching for any guards sticking their heads up to take a pop at us, so that they can smack 'em with a big chunk o' furniture. Or a coupla rounds, if ye like.'

Ancil smiled and gave a weary shake of the head. 'Play moving target for thugs with energy weapons? Sure, why not?'

'That's the spirit. Right, ye ready?'

Ancil quickly fastened his throwable satchel, shortened the strap so it was tucked snugly under one arm, then spread his hands. 'Ready enough, chief!'

'Stay a coupla yards behind me,' Pyke said. 'Makes it harder to target the two of us!'

And he was off, just a light jog for the first few seconds then picking up the pace, trying not to think of the Lord-Governor's guards drawing a bead along their energy rifles. Legs pumping, he jumped over low tables, vaulted across high chair backs, heard the thud-clatter-oof-curse of Ancil not quite making it, and let out an exhilarated half-whoop, half-peal of laughter as he mounted the wide steps with wide running strides. *Still alive,* he thought, as he lunged towards the massive gleaming throne, ducking behind it. *And we did it, got here, most of us ...*

Then Ancil arrived, collapsing next to him, gasping for breath.

'Nothing, chief, not ... a shot, not a ... sign of 'em.'

'You sure?' Pyke stood and peered around the side of the glass and chrome throne, and Ancil was right, no armed hostiles to be seen. Away at the far side Mojag was waving and shouting that there was no one else around.

'So where are they?' he muttered, frowning at the big double doors behind the throne.

'Not much room behind those doors, chief,' Ancil said as he stood, pointing out how close they were to the tower's outer wall. 'Must be more stairs or another elevator up to a penthouse or the like.'

'Well, we're gonna find out,' Pyke said, hefting his heavy Gruxen revolver then checking the extent of his remaining ammunition. 'Many shells ya got left?'

Mojag and Kref arrived a moment later and a swift appraisal revealed that Ancil was down to a handful of rounds while Kref still had nearly two dozen. Pooling and dividing the stubby, weighty shells gave everyone enough for a full load and a couple spare.

As they gathered before the double doors Ancil said, 'Time for yet more bold exploits, chief?'

'You mean something crazy and daring, yet showy?'

'That's it – just as well I'm getting the hang of it.'

Pyke nodded and then waved a hand in front of a chest-high sensor aperture. The doors parted and, weapons ready, they moved warily across the threshold. Inside, more curtains enclosing either side, dark blue drapes hanging from a curved rail which carried small pinspots that shed a buttery yellow glow. There were no sounds, just a muffled silence. Pyke fingered the heavy drapes, found a gap and pushed on through – and found himself descending a few, shallow steps to a round, wood-tiled floor and there, at the back of this small chamber, was a dull grey, oval metal frame nearly three metres high. It was firmly bolted to the floor, had a number of small shiny spikes spaced evenly around its outer edge, and was easily, disturbingly recognisable.

'Chief,' said Ancil. 'That looks a lot like one of them portal gates.'

'That's what it is, all right,' Pyke muttered, as a horrible realisation began sinking in.

Ancil's face had gone pale. 'Hang on, where's this Gyr-Matu guy? If we don't send him to meet his forefathers, how do we get Win and Dervla back? He has to be here!'

'The esteemed Lord-Governor has departed,' came a deep, expressive voice from above. 'Your assassination plot has failed.'

Everyone already had their guns out and ready but Pyke only had to make a half-turn and glance sideways to spot the two guards who had stealthily emerged from the drapes on either side. Each held an energy rifle aimed unwavering at the ones closest to them, Kref and Mojag.

'Please drop your weapons,' the voice said. 'Or prepare for death.'

Pyke uttered a stifled snarl through grinding teeth and tossed his weapon off to the side with a harsh clatter. Mojag and Kref followed suit, but Ancil's angry face caught Pyke's eye and for one moment it seemed that the fury in his eyes would boil over into violence and blood. Then the fury subsided, Ancil closed his eyes, shook his head slightly, and threw his gun away.

'A wise decision. You may yet live to see out this day.'

Pyke glanced up to see a circular railed balcony empty of any presence. Then he heard descending footsteps and a moment later the drapes parted and a tall, barrel-chested silver figure stepped into view. At first sight the newcomer looked as if he was wearing a sleek suit of shiny armour but then Pyke realised that all the segments were like a kind of surface moulding. And the silverness had a dull textured, rather than a mirrored sheen.

'I am Akreen, First Blade of the Zavri Battalion,' the tall one said, clearly in command. 'You were sent on this mission by one you know as Khorr, correct?'

Pyke advanced a step or two and glared up at their captor. 'That piece of scumtrash is holding members of my crew – if we get through the day, what are our chances of seeing them again?'

'The female prisoners are no longer in Khorr's custody,' said the Zavri leader. 'They were transferred into the control of Shuskar Gun-Lord Xra-Huld and are now confined aboard his command vessel. He has instructed me to bring you all to him for questioning.'

'Forgive my impertinence, Exalted One,' said one of the guards. 'Since these savages have been detained while in pursuit of our most puissant master, Lord Gyr-Matu, they surely fall beneath the jurisdiction of the Lord-Governor's security services.'

There was a tense moment before the Zavri Akreen turned his head and gazed impassively down at the Gruxen.

'Towerguard Ruserl, it is no impertinence to make a valid statement and I thank you for it. Towerguard Vatasc.'

The other guard stiffened slightly, still aiming at Kref's head. 'Yes, First Blade?'

'I need you to leave this chamber and hurry down to the elevator – the rest of my strike squad should be arriving. Inform them of my current status and escort them here with all haste. Can you do this for me?'

'I am honoured to obey, Invincible One.'

Pyke, feeling that something was vaguely amiss, glanced at Ancil, who met his gaze with a frown and a slight shrug.

The towerguard meanwhile had put up his energy rifle, saluted sharply and hurried past the drapes to the doors. Once he was gone everyone stood still in their poses for a moment, a frozen tableau that Pyke instinctively knew could not last.

'Towerguard Ruserl,' said the Zavri leader. 'I must command you to put up your weapon.'

Before Akreen had finished speaking the guard swivelled on one foot and backed away a pace, rifle aimed squarely at the Zavri.

'Respectfully, First Blade, I must place you under . . .'

Akreen struck in a blur of motion so fast that Pyke could only analyse it in retrospect. One instant the Zavri was under the gun, in the next a large silvery hand had snatched away the guardsman's rifle while the other had broken his neck. It was an overt display of sudden, overwhelming and brutal violence. Shocked amazement made Pyke and his crew recoil and take a step backwards. The Zavri dropped the rifle and with both hands carefully, almost gently, lowered the dead guard to the floor. Straightening, he regarded Pyke and the others.

'That was regrettable but necessary. Myriads of similarly unjust deaths have befallen the maimed worlds of the Warcage throughout the centuries, and there shall be many more before the Shuskars' long voyage of tyranny and mutation reaches its conclusion.'

He stretched out to point at the oval portal gate and the spikes around its outer edge suddenly flared with bright energy. Quivering tendrils of lightning linked them all and tiny sparks buzzed and spat. The crew moved aside as First Blade Akreen approached the portal, now pulsing with a sucking darkness.

'I must pass through,' he told Pyke. 'I go in search of various truths, including the true history of my people and how they once fought against the Shuskar, not for them.' He paused, tilted his head as if at something only he could hear, then nodded.

'You and your followers are welcome to accompany me – in fact, I strongly advise that you do so.'

Pyke's frown turned into a wary smile. 'Did I hear you tell the other guard to bring the rest of your squad up here? I'm guessing that they know nothing about this truth-seeking of yours.'

'Exactly so. Were they to capture you, I can assure you that you would be brought before the Gun-Lord Xra-Huld and that would be very unfortunate.'

'Xra-Huld has our people,' Pyke said bluntly.

Akreen nodded. 'Anyone taken aboard his vessel as a prisoner can in the end only expect to become a test subject in one of his experiments. Recognise this as a near-certainty and you may avoid the trap of hope.'

There was a strained silence for a moment before Ancil spoke. 'Are you saying that they are very probably dead, or is it that you know they are?'

'Beyond knowing that two captives were transferred aboard the Gun-Lord's flagship, I have no other knowledge of their fate. I would not be permitted access to shipboard updates of that nature.'

Ancil was so tense and grim as he faced Akreen that Pyke thought he was just an impulse away from giving the tall Zavri a belligerent shove.

'And what's your trophy in all this – what's the prize? Is it something you're ready to go to war over?'

'I am still journeying towards the truth,' the Zavri said. 'But it is already too late for me to go back, therefore I must do battle whenever it stands in my way.'

Ancil tilted his head back thoughtfully, eyes narrowed, then he glanced at Pyke. 'He's all right – I say we go with him!'

Pyke gave a judicious nod and glanced at Kref and Mojag, who likewise agreed.

'Okay, First Blade, we're with you. You lead the way through the gate and we'll follow ... er, where are we going, by the way?'

'Gatuzna, one of the Ashen Worlds, situated over on the other side of the Warcage.' The Zavri paused a moment then continued. 'The realignment of the transfer continuity is a little slow over such a distance so you should wait about three seconds before stepping through.'

'Is that three seconds between each of us as well?' Pyke said.

'If you cross over in pairs, the portal machine will adjust itself accordingly. I have seen such a method used before.'

Pyke wasn't entirely convinced. That said, the rest of the Zavri's actions and words had a certain sombre authenticity and since they now urgently needed a way out of Khorr's trap alternatives were conspicuous by their absence.

'Okay, whatever you say, First Blade – lead the way!'

Akreen nodded gravely and walked up to the portal gate. He paused, glancing over his shoulder as Pyke gestured Mojag over to stand beside him and behind the tall silvery figure. Then the Zavri walked forward, his form plunging into the pulsing dark whorl of the gate, a weirdly even, undisturbed surface which swallowed him whole.

'Keep a hand on my shoulder,' Pyke told Mojag as he counted out three seconds on his fingers before moving forward.

What happened next was hair-raising. The sensation of entering the gate was as unsettling as before but this time there was a perceptible interval rather than an instantaneous crossing. Straight away he was able to see something of their destination, dark ground strewn with gravel and charred debris, the First Blade slumped in the dirt, convulsing as whips of actinic energy lashed at him, fired from a long-barrelled weapon wielded by ... Khorr!

All this he saw in that single moment, and felt a surge of primal hate untempered by caution. He would soon be thrust through onto the surface of Gatuzna and able to get his hands around the throat of a vile murderer . . .

Then the moment ended as he was pulled away from the grim scene. As if he was at the end of a long elastic rope that was contracting at a dizzying speed. Suddenly he was out of the bizarre inter-portal zone, falling in a blur of shadows and yellow glows . . . and he let out a gasp as he landed on something rounded and cloth-covered which jerked away and yelled a curse in Ancil's voice.

'Gah, get yer frackin' foot off my frackin' . . . Chief, you, you made it!'

Having rolled to the side (and noticed the dazed-looking Kref and Mojag lying sprawled nearby), Pyke strove to take in their surroundings. A dank, low-ceilinged chamber made of rough-shapen stones, constructed with columns and arches, lit by torches. Only feet away was a portal gate, flanked by racks of blank black units all linked together by a rat's nest of cables. And now a number of robed and hooded figures were hesitantly converging on them. None seemed to be armed but Pyke was getting a vague sense of familiarity with the place and casually reached for his heavy handgun.

But then the row of hooded strangers parted and a tall, slender newcomer in similar garb stepped forward. A long-fingered hand came up, palm out, and the hood fell back to reveal the happy features of the missing Punzho the Egetsi!

'Captain, all is well – they mean no harm!'

Pyke got to his feet, leaned against one of the arch columns and grinned, shaking his head. 'Hell of an entrance, there, Punzho – timed it nicely!'

'So sorry, Captain – I was on lookout duty in the Thurible Tower and was only informed of the portal readings moments ago.'

'This is Klothahil, isn't it?' Pyke said, to which Punzho

nodded. 'And question is, did you bring us back here, and are these monkish fellows those same Sacred Order of the whatever?'

'Erm, yes and yes, are your answers, Captain. Except that they are now called the Transnuminous Congregation of the Celestial Nine-Fold Way.' The Egetsi rolled his eyes for just a moment. 'The story I have to relate will amaze you!'

Pyke nodded amiably, but the sight of Khorr standing over the helpless Zavri with that lightning weapon was still bright and sharp in his mind's eye. 'I have no doubts on that score, Punzho, but can you give us the handy pocket-sized version 'cos there's someplace else that we really need to be!'

CHAPTER NINETEEN

'So you wouldn't say that Kref was a typical Henkayan, then?' said Sam Brock, frowning as she read through Pyke's sketchy notes on the big enclosed operator screen. Hechec had retasked one of the bridge workstations for her use, but the screen surface was old and the sidebar of touch controls slightly under-responsive.

'His combat and weapons specialisation is a little unusual for a Henkayan of his lower-middle status,' said the ship AI. 'What is remarkable is a Henkayan willing to work and live alongside Humans, never mind taking orders from one.'

'I see,' Sam said. 'What about the Egetsi, this Punzho ... ?' She gave the screen touchbar a firm tap, switching to another file while making notes on a slimpad. 'Does he fit in well?'

'Lt Brock, it would be safe to assume that all the crew members have learned how to coexist in one way or another.'

Sam made a few more notes, frowned, then paged the slimpad back to remind herself of earlier comments. Inevitably, however, her thoughts veered off into brooding and speculating on what was happening outside the ship. After the parting of the ways with T'Loskin Rey, Sam had elected to accompany G'Brozen Mav aboard the *Scarabus*, acquired from Brannon Pyke by devious subterfuge. The Chainer leader's efforts were now devoted to persuading rebel groups from other worlds to switch allegiance back to him. G'Brozen Mav had explained some of the background soon after the *Scarabus* landed on a high mountain shelf west of Armag City.

'Lieutenant,' he had said, 'you have to realise that months of planning and preparation led up to the Armag uprising, and not just here – another seven worlds, important production worlds, are staging their own insurgencies at this very moment. I was deeply involved in the planning and in regular contact with intermediaries, up until the day that my deputy, T'Loskin Rey, had Khorr remove me from the scene. And now I must reassert my leadership, but if I attempt such a thing in the middle of the fighting what might the outcome be?' G'Brozen Mav had frowned. 'From experience I know that Rey's sense of strategy is weak, so if I do not act, his failure may be catastrophic.'

In the end, G'Brozen Mav opted for resolve and had the Toolbearer bring the *Scarabus* down to land in a secluded, high mountain shoulder. Before leaving with his bodyguards he ordered the ship AI to allow Sam full access to the databanks. That was over two hours ago, during which time she set herself the task of putting together a file on Pyke and his crew and ship, just to satisfy her curiosity. The AI proved very helpful, offering up a range of resources, cargo manifests, fund transactions and transfers, shipwide chat logs, bridge operator reports, hull and system reports, onboard environmental analyses, crew journals, Pyke's own assessment files and others.

Sam knew that this was an attempt at discouragement by overabundance of information. She dipped into the avalanche of data, here and there, just to get a flavour, then settled down with the personnel files, both the crew's own monthlies and Pyke's assessments, and began assembling a report of sorts.

Finishing with the Henkayan, Kref, she moved on to one

crew member whose species had immediately marked him out, the Kiskashin, Oleg Qy-Kelitak. The reptiloid Kiskashin were known to be clannish and intensely conscious of tradition and hierarchy. In some regions of the greater interstellar region they were well known for their trading families and their extensive commercial interests, but in Earthsphere the Kiskashin had yet to establish a single offshoot-brokerage. Thus it was reasonable to speculate that this particular Kiskashin had either been exiled or had fled some dark shame or disgrace. But when she asked the ship AI for updated files the response was unexpected.

'It is my sad duty to report that Oleg Qy-Kelitak is deceased – he and Engineer Hammadi both suffocated when this vessel was hijacked by hostile forces.'

'How tragic.'

'Due to the state of shipboard systems I was unable to conduct detailed autopsies – Engineer Hammadi was given a swift space burial in accordance with the strictures of his faith, and Oleg's remains were hastily consigned to cryostasis storage. Since then, however, a few anomalies associated with the Kiskashin's body have come to my attention but without the captain's permission I cannot investigate them.'

Sam frowned. 'Are you able to tell me about these anomalies?'

'Certainly. Data from the stasis canister's monitor systems show a complete absence of the organic compounds that usually transpire from a dead body, even one kept in cryostasis. Also, the temperature is slightly and constantly higher than it should be. Speculation – cellular degeneration is not taking place and the body's core temperature is being maintained by some unknown autonomic agency.'

'You mean the Kiskashin could still be alive?' Sam said. 'I've heard that they can go into a hibernation state if wounded – could it be that?'

'No, the slow trance pseudo-hibernation exhibits definite, perceptible heartbeats and respiratory activity. This is an entirely different form of biophysical arrest ...'

Sam's attention was broken by footsteps and voices in the corridor outside the bridge. A moment later an anxious G'Brozen Mav entered and came over to the command console.

'Lieutenant,' he began. 'I hope you have been able to occupy your time well since I left.'

'The ship intelligence has been very helpful,' she said.

'Any communications received from your colleague?'

'No, not one,' she said. 'I admit that I am starting to be concerned about his safety. What about your mission? Any successes?'

'Two of the six cadre leaders dealing with the estates agreed to see me straight away,' he said. 'One refused my proposal outright, the other offered only qualified support, and I was on my way to meet with a third when I received some disturbing news.'

By now the hooded Toolbearer Hechec had arrived on the bridge and looked anxious on hearing Mav's words.

'When you say disturbing,' Hechec said, 'do you anticipate minor worries or a major crisis?'

G'Brozen Mav arched an eyebrow. 'I have heard from separate sources that Zavri troops have been spotted in Armag City and that a Chainer patrol was ambushed on the main highway by an Avang squad. In broad daylight.'

'So, not minor worries but not yet confirmed as something worse. Yet.'

The Chainer leader smiled thinly at this. 'We always knew that lack of airborne forces was our main weakness, which is why we need to leave here, cross the valley and investigate the ambush location. If we can use this vessel to hunt down the Avang, if indeed they turn out to be responsible, then the news would strengthen the rebels' resolve.'

'And let everyone know that you're alive and giving the Shuskar a bloody nose,' said Sam.

'Which would be helpful when it comes to persuading cadre leaders of the advantages of being in your camp,' added Hechec.

G'Brozen Mav gave an amused nod. 'Such unanimity is gratifying. Now, let us be on our way – a journey across the valley should not take very long.'

Sam sat back, doodling notes on her slimpad, while the diminutive Hechec delivered several verbal commands to the ship AI. Moments later the *Scarabus* was rising from its high mountain hiding place, a steady ascent until it reached roughly two thousand feet then moved in a descending curve whose end point was a wooded ridge overlooking the ambush site. All told, from liftoff to the new landing spot the short flight took slightly less than ten minutes. As the *Scarabus* settled onto the bushy undergrowth of the ridge, images of the ambush scene began appearing on Sam's screen. They showed a portion of the highway, a couple of overturned and smouldering vehicles, and a number of dead bodies. There were close-ups of wounds, weapon damage to the armoured cars, and marks on the ground.

'Impressive,' she said. 'Sophisticated sensors for a trader ship.'

'Actually, the bulk of the data is streaming from a probe that I despatched just after we lifted off.' Toolbearer Hechec frowned as he studied the screen before him. 'We were told that the patrol consisted of three Gruxen rebels and five Chainers from Emestra, and the probe has tallied only three bodies in the vicinity . . .'

'And they're Gruxen,' said G'Brozen Mav as he studied the data on another screen.

'Sadly, yes.'

'So it looks likely that the ambushers were Avang?'

'Both vehicles were disabled by heavy-calibre one-shots,' said Hechec. 'The Gruxen are all dead from toxinated needle rounds ...'

'And they've taken hostages,' finished G'Brozen Mav.

'Why is that significant?' Sam said.

'Avang fighters have a special brand of cruelty bred into them,' the Chainer leader said. 'Their society – if a thousand tribelets perpetually at each other's throats can be called such – is rotten with it. But then, they did learn all they know from the Shuskar, including methods of interrogation and torture and how to take pleasure in it.'

Sam nodded sombrely. 'They've learned how to feed off others' agony,' she said.

Nodding, G'Brozen Mav then leaned in closer to Hechec. 'They must have a squad carrier or similar to get their captives out of the vicinity so fast.'

'The sensors have detected emission traces consistent with pyrafuel engines, my leader,' said the Toolbearer. 'There is a trail, leading south-east ...' He stiffened, frowned. 'Wait, there is a priority connection request for you coming through on several channels.' He glanced at Mav. 'It's from T'Loskin Rey.'

The Chainer leader looked irritated for a moment, then shrugged. 'Any of these channels secure? Acknowledge it on the least insecure one and put him up on the lieutenant's screen.'

That's all right, she thought. *I can catch up with the mysterious dead-or-just-sleeping Kiskashin later.*

She pushed herself out of the workstation couch, nodded to G'Brozen Mav and retreated a pace as he slipped in to take her place. The face of T'Loskin Rey appeared as he was settling in.

'Rey,' he said tersely.

'Mav – thank you for accepting my call.'

'Is there a problem, Rey?' G'Brozen Mav maintained a composed, serious demeanour. 'How goes the garrison blockade?'

'Circumstances have changed,' said T'Loskin Rey. 'The Governor's garrison troops have managed to break out and push us back towards the city – we have taken up positions about half a mile from the garrison and are holding against further attacks.'

'How?'

'They used remounted air-defence batteries to blow holes in our blockade before we could knock them out. Also, my scouts have reported sightings of Avang hunters leading the breakout units, corroborated by frontliners who have come face to face with them.'

'Are you in need of assistance, Rey? Is that what this is about?'

'We are experiencing ... difficulties, no more, but—'

'I can bring my ship to you in a matter of minutes, Rey – its weapons can deal with the garrison units and their Avang advisors, but I want something in return.'

On screen, T'Loskin Rey had a sullen, cornered look. 'Name it.'

'Confirm me as joint leader of all Chainer forces throughout the Warcage, subject to ratification of the Chainer council and plebiscite—'

'Are you insane? How can the Council carry out a plebiscite of all ranks while hostilities are continuing?'

'Those are my terms – do you accept?'

'Accepted.' T'Loskin Rey's eyes burnt with resentment. 'Now get here with all haste.'

The screen went dead and G'Brozen Mav leaped to his feet, laughing.

'We have him, hand and tongue! Hechec, set a course for the garrison locale at maximum speed.'

The Toolbearer nodded and linked the data control spikes of one 'hand' to a nearby console. A moment later he said, 'Course laid in, my leader, thrusters engaged, and we are flying at target-sensor altitude, according to my screen.'

Sam sank back into her seat as G'Brozen Mav went over to Hechec's station. The bridge of the *Scarabus* seemed half deserted, with the pale morning light coming in through the unfiltered viewport casting some sharp shadows over the equipment and the empty hooded workstations. Memories of past experiences aboard Earthsphere ships made her imagine how this one might look with a full crew rather than just Mav and his handful of followers.

Am I actually going to survive this mission? she wondered. *Why hasn't that stupid Construct drone made contact yet?*

'Sensors have detected a small craft taking off from inside Armag City,' said Hechec. 'Launch point was close to the Lord-Governor's residence.'

'So Lord Gyr-Matu has finally realised how hopeless his position is,' said G'Brozen Mav. 'Good – farewell to another useless bloodsucking noble.'

'Interesting – the craft's profile seems overpowered for conventional civil authority forces … Ah, wait – systems have picked up a second craft, a small one- or two-seater, lifting off from wooded hills outside the city.'

Sam turned to look round and saw the Toolbearer frown as he paused, then glanced at Mav who was standing nearby. 'We have just received another priority call from T'Loskin Rey.'

Toolbearer Hechec stood aside and G'Brozen Mav took his place. A moment later Rey was looking out from the screen, features creased in a smile.

'We're still a minute or two from your location,' Mav said. 'Are you still holding?'

'Just thought to tell you that the situation is no longer urgent – only moments ago all the garrison forces abandoned their positions and retreated back into the garrison, so you can take your time, Mav!'

'I assume that our agreement still stands,' said Mav.

'Oh, I wouldn't call it an agreement,' T'Loskin Rey said. 'More like topics for further discussion. For example, I can confirm that there is an opening for a second-in-command ...'

Sam was only half listening. Her attention was focused on the broad sensor sweep of the valley now currently visible on her own screen. As she watched a bright point rose from building clusters outside Armag City – almost immediately it was tagged with a little text flag and a tiny arc of stats.

'That's another departure,' said Hechec, who had moved to another station. 'Probably Avang ...' He leaned forward. 'And a fourth ...'

These aren't random flights, Sam thought. *They're part of a pattern ... of evacuation!*

'Hechec,' she said hurriedly. 'Are the sensors registering any major ships or vessels in the area?'

'Long-range sensors are tracking one large vessel which dropped out of orbit several minutes ago.'

'What's its altitude and heading?'

'In the last few seconds it switched course to descend through the cloud layer and is about to pass directly overhead.'

'You've got to take evasive action,' Sam told Hechec, then turned to G'Brozen Mav who was still arguing with Rey. 'They're going to hit the city and nearby rebel positions! We need to get out of here!'

The Chainer leader was on the point of reacting angrily to her interruption, but then the voice of the ship AI cut in. 'Unidentified missiles launched from unidentified ship – multiple ground targets – time to first-wave impact 8.7 seconds – recommend crisis-mode evasive action ...'

'Do it!' yelled G'Brozen Mav.

On the screen a puzzled T'Loskin Rey looked away as a subordinate hurried up to whisper something. The Chainer leader only had time to bellow 'Take cover!' before there was a thunderous crashing sound. Everything on the screen blurred and there was a bright glare. Then there was a second explosion, so loud that it distorted the audio feed. Then the screen went dead, but Sam could see a red-orange light pouring in through the viewport as beneath them the valley burnt.

CHAPTER TWENTY

The immense curved grandeur of the planet Armag was spread out below, its intricate patchwork of landmasses and oceans obscured here and there by complex weather systems pushing, streaming and gyring in perpetual combinations. At that particular moment the drone Rensik's shimmership was in a stable orbit and passing directly over an island archipelago a few hundred miles east of the continent where Armag City was located. Rensik might have spared the magnificent spectacle a glance, were he not at that moment keeping his sensors on the ship's effectuator arms as they lashed and flailed at him with their grab-tool tips. He himself was hanging safely off the small ship's stern, connected by two metres of tether improvised from a spool of multipurpose cable retrieved from the materials locker.

Then the arms went limp and drifted, which told him that the four-minute cycle was now in its abeyance phase. He only had two minutes to get back inside the Construct craft, check on the Human female, run another test or two, then be back outside before the assimilation phase started up again. Letting the tether spool run he used his own manipulators to clamber swiftly around the bulbous hull to the gaping hatch. The impermeable containment forcefield was still in place so the field generation systems were still unsubverted. Sensors fixed near the hatch tracked his approach and the field deformed around the drone's casing, allowing him to enter the small compartment.

The female Human, who called herself Dervla, sat at the tiny fold-down table, legs akimbo, one arm folded against her chest, the other raised and laid flat against the system and conduit panelling, held in place by the strange ribbed tendons that had grown out of her flesh. Rensik could see that the outgrowths were working their way up the arm and would soon start protruding from her shoulder.

Her head lolled forward and some saliva drooled from her mouth. Glancing up she saw the drone approach and smiled weakly.

'Eh, 's my little robot friend . . .' Her speech came out hoarse and slurred. 'Got any ideas yet? . . . Whassat bassard done t' me? . . .'

Aware that time was running out, Rensik directed a coded light pulse at the bioscanner he had epoxied to an overhead panel rib twenty-four cycles ago, and got an encrypted lightburst of data in response.

'Still working on the problem, Dervla,' he said. 'As soon as I figure this out you'll be the first to know.'

Eight seconds left. Dervla opened her mouth as if to speak, something glinted down in her throat and her head slumped forward again. Rensik was already heading for the hatch propelled by his own microjets. He could actually feel the assimilation phase kick in, like a palpable wave of voracity rushing after him as he plunged through the containment field. The tether spool unreeled to its maximum as his inertia carried him outwards then round towards the stern. He braked with the microjets and reeled in the tether, careful to stay out of range of the effectuator arms which struck and strained towards him with eager, mindless hunger.

Mindless but not indiscriminate. During her time aboard the

Shuskar vessel, the Human had clearly been infected with some kind of highly advanced nanovirus which was in the process of rewriting her body from the nervous system out – except that the process had now reached an intermediate stage beyond which it could not progress, stuck in a holding pattern where it alternated between vigorous grasping and still dormancy. Clearly, the nanovirus was modifying the Human, converting her into a host for some kind of biomech parasite, and it seemed that Rensik's electromagnetic emissions, from the powered systems of his shell, qualified him as a viable match.

So, not indiscriminate but still wide of the mark. The steady accumulation of data, and his cogitations and reflections, sparked off waves of datasweeps in his own core memories, eventually flagging up a reference to an archived document which he had acquired a long time ago. Close study might well set more speculation in motion but there was no time for that right now – all resources had to be devoted to finding a way to neutralise the nanovirus without killing the Human. And even killing her on purpose might not work – for some of these nanoviruses, death of the host was just another minor obstacle.

Hanging off the stern of the ship – of his own ship! – Rensik went over the bioscanner data, complete with latest update, and saw what he had seen before: steady growth in complexity and connectivity. There had been none of this at the start, soon after their escape from the Shuskar ship, not until Rensik began examining the Human with a variety of probes and scanners. Initially he had speculated that one of his instruments had emitted some tiny blip of energy which had triggered the nanovirus to alter its state but he was less sure of that now.

Realising that all the data-gathering had been largely fruitless, he decided to instigate a reappraisal of the entire episode, this time taking it back to his first encounter with the woman aboard the Shuskar ship. He reran the visual record, from when he entered the detention chamber with the transparent cells to when he left, bearing the insensible Human in his gripping fields. And the answer was there, clear and plain to see – the nanovirus was not triggered by Rensik's instrumentation but by the act of removing the female Human from her confinement. She had not been connected to any wires or intravenous tubing so there must have been a localised suppression field and when he removed her from its influence the virus awoke and began proliferating.

On this basis the drone called up the bioscanner data again, searching for evidence of change in energy states or some kind of electro-synaptic wave with a fixed frequency. There was one, buried beneath other peripheral nervous system readings and yes, it had a four-minute active/inactive cycle! Now, suppressing the nanovirus would require a counter-field attuned and calibrated to precisely negate the electro-synaptic wave pattern that was carrying its preset commands. The bioscanner could be adapted, its output parameters modified to emit just such a suppressing counter-field.

When the next abeyance phase of the cycle took effect, Rensik swiftly swooped over to the gaping hatch and eased through the containment field. The female Human, Dervla, was watching as he entered, eyes glazed, her features drawn and blotchy. As the drone commenced unmounting the bioscanner he heard her mumble something.

' . . . careful of the gun . . . watch his gun watching you . . . '

'Don't worry, Dervla,' he said. 'I'll soon have that virus turned off, then you and I can have a proper chat.'

With the bioscanner in one of his effectuator grabs, he glided out of the hatch and let inertia and the tether carry him back round to the stern. He accessed the bioscanner's main function set and began recalibrating the probe fields to match the frequency of the nanovirus's synaptic wave with a mirror version that would cancel it out. It took only moments for the drone to complete the retasking but another two minutes to conduct three data-model test runs, which was far from ideal but better than nothing.

A few metres away the shimmership's external effectuator arms continued their flailing and lashing. Then suddenly they were lifeless as the abeyance phase began, and Rensik launched himself over the curve of the little ship towards the hatch. Once through the containment field he reaffixed the bioscanner to the mounting pad which he had left behind. The Human female was slumped over the tiny table, insensible while her arm remained pinned to the nearby panelling. For a brief moment he toyed with the idea of staying in the compartment to witness how the negating fields might affect her, but he thought better of it, triggered the bioscanner with a burst command, then left via the hatch. This time he let the tether unspool to its full length, without using his microjets to swing sternwards. He hung there, suspended over the planet Armag, aware of all the other worlds of the Warcage, this gigantic engineering feat which looked like so many bright jewels caught in an invisible web ...

And below, on the planet's surface, something bright bloomed. His onboard sensors had their restrictions but they were still able to pick up the presence of a large vessel hovering in the lower atmosphere, firing missile volleys at ground targets. A survey summary placed the target zone very close to where he had last seen Lt Brock – once he was back in control of the shimmership he would unlock the encrypted standbys, reactivate the comms system and quickly make contact with her.

He switched his receptor cams from the planet back to the shimmership and there, beyond it, away in the far distance, was ... something. To the naked eye of some sweaty organic it would have been no more than a speck, a distant mote, but Rensik's lenses saw further and deeper, reeling in the intervening gulf, bringing it closer, revealing its details, sharp and distinct.

Without any shadow of doubt, it was the Shuskar flagship, the vessel from which he had rescued the Human woman, and it was heading straight towards their position. Meanwhile, inside the shimmership, the Human female was sitting upright and trying to free her arm from the panelling, so he decided to see what he could learn from her while bringing the shimmership's drive back online.

He glided over to the hatch, slipped through the containment field and began issuing silent subcast commands to the initialiser systems.

'Greeting, Dervla,' he began. 'I am Rensik Estemil, senior tactical drone in the auxiliary cohorts of the Construct, ah, Empire' – *Well, when one has to improvise a background on the fly, do so with gusto!* – 'and I rescued you from a ship whose owners call themselves the Shuskar ...'

She glared at him and, with an angry tug, freed her arm from the panelling with a tearing of the grotesque fibrous tendrils. She gasped with pain, stared in horror at the blood trickling from the severed tendrils, winced and cradled the arm with her other hand.

'What did he do to me?' She glanced at Rensik. 'What about my friend, Win? There was a friend of mine in the other glass cage.'

'Sorry, but there was no other Human in that lab,' Rensik said carefully, deciding not to mention the bizarre foetus-like things he had seen clustered on the couch inside the transparent cylinder. 'You've been delirious since the rescue and you said something strange about your captor – "careful of his gun" and "watch his gun watching you". What does this mean?'

A haunted look came into the Human's eyes as she heard her own words repeated back to her. With halting words that grew steadily more fluent, she related how she and the other members of a trader crew became caught up in the intrigues of the

Warcage's conflict, how she and her friend were captured then handed over to the Shuskar, and what happened when they met the Shuskar leader, Gun-Lord Xra-Huld.

As Rensik listened, the shimmership was awakening around them. All the systems he had powered down when the nano-virus made its first move to take control through Dervla were coming online, with the sensors high up the priority rankings. Interacting with the sensor array he found that the Shuskar flagship had put on velocity and would be close enough for its low-grade beams and missiles to make hits in less than thirty-eight seconds, whereas the shimmership's thrust drive would be ready in twenty-nine ...

The Human female was still talking – and swearing – at him, her suppressed grief at what she had to know was the truth about her friend breaking out in anger. As she talked, Rensik was con-tinually cross-referencing with his deep archive, prompted by her description of the parasitic biomechanical weapon to which Xra-Huld was joined. As a technology it hinted at an entire structure of development wildly at variance with that on show across what he had thus far seen of the Warcage.

The datasweep came back with barely a handful of results, which satisfied a strict set of criteria: three myth fragments, each from a post-techno-collapse civilisation, and a short pas-sage from the Vojalin Codex, a notorious document of dubious provenance claiming to be a study of the Zarl Imperium, a vast galaxy-spanning hegemony which disintegrated over a million years ago.

Then the 'ready' alert from the thrust drive flashed up in his awareness. His preset commands took effect: the hatch closed through the containment field, which then vanished, just as the shimmership's thrusters flared into life. There was a brief inertial lurch before the dampener field cut in, then the velocity began to ramp up.

'That's us under way, Dervla,' Rensik said. 'Soon we'll be safely away and hidden from their ...'

The Human female had been tilting her head slightly, as if listening to something, then she sat bolt upright and shot a look of stark terror at the drone.

'I can hear it – it's coming for me! I can hear it in my head ...'

But the sensors were detecting nothing, no threats, no coherent signals, in fact nothing from the Shuskar vessel but a halo of white noise ...

Without warning something brutal engulfed the shimmership, sending interference screeching across every sensor and input. The Human female cried out and slumped over the table, burying her head in her arms. The feed from one surviving hull receptor showed a long wavering tentacle of dazzling electroplasmic energy which split into webs and jagged tendrils that lashed and stabbed at the ship. The safeties had activated, isolating the main systems, powering down the thrusters.

'Intruder, you musssst, y-you will face judgement ...'

The Human female, Dervla, was sitting up again, staring at the drone with eyes that blazed an effulgent blue.

Great, thought Rensik. *Some alien thugmaster has managed to bypass the ship's shields and datawalls, just so it can use this poor defenceless puppet to mouth egomaniacal threats at me.*

'You sweaty organics are all the same,' he said. 'A whiff of absolute power, some biomech scraps that escaped the slopout bins of a failed empire, and a big showy lightning machine, and you're suddenly convinced that it's all for the taking. Well, sorry to pop your colossal vanity-bubble but I think that you will find that there's always someone bigger and nastier waiting just around the next corner.'

'Such extravagant fury for one sssso impotent.' The woman Dervla's face muscles twisted, the lips drawing back to bare the teeth in an awful parody of a grin. 'Let us ensure that you remain so.'

Another surge of that electroplasmic energy washed over the shimmership, and Rensik saw it fill the air around the Human with a shimmering mesh of thread-like tendrils. Clusters of them stretched out in all directions, as did one that quivered towards the drone, extending with serpentine movements. And when they at last touched his outer casing everything stopped . . . and started again. Internal regulators told him that forty-two minutes eleven seconds had elapsed and his auto defences indicated that for the last ten minutes he had been stationary. Vidsensors showed that he was lying inside a rectangular box with transparent sides and lid. Also, his suspensor and thrust systems were unable to respond: despite their powered status and accepting commands they could not activate their functions. A very specific kind of suppression field was clearly operating nearby.

Rensik decided to examine his surroundings. A large grey crate was blocking the view on one side but from the gloom and the repetitive tile patterns on the deck he surmised that he was back on board the Shuskar flagship.

Wonderful – another chance to sample the delights of this interplanetary dungeon.

There was movement in the shadows. A cloaked, hooded figure leaned in, fixed a T-shaped handle to the top of Rensik's box then lifted it up and away. Suddenly he could see that he was in a large, gloomy hold. After being carried for a few paces Rensik was set down on a metre-high plinth, right next to a lifeless, sprawled corpse. A short distance beyond it was the low-profile Construct shimmership, sitting illuminated by an overhead spotlamp. The entry hatch was round the other side, where a couple of hooded figures stood, just visible over the small vessel.

Rensik turned his attention to the body. From previously gathered data it looked like a Shuskar, only wrinkled and skinny, especially its left arm, which looked strangely malformed and emaciated. Curious grooves in the grey flesh curved up to and around the neck, up the side of the face to a bloody hole in the temple.

The hooded attendants shifted position as a figure stepped out of the shimmership and together they skirted the vessel and strode towards Rensik. Before she came fully into view, the drone knew who it would be. The parasitic biomech was now bonded to the Human female's left arm and its spine-tail wound from shoulder to neck to head.

'Your ship defends itself,' it said with Dervla's voice.

'That is most gratifying to hear.'

A weird leer crept across the face. 'There are five of us, impotent machine. We have lived in many beings for many, many centuries, and outlived them all. We are mighty, and intend to remain so.' The Human female leaned forward, placed her hands on the transparent box, then brought her face up close. The eyes were dead. 'You will tell me everything.'

'Doubt that.'

'Yes, everything, not long after we return to the Shuskar Citadelworld. All the loot of a thousand worlds lies there, including devices capable of interrogating other devices.'

'I am not a device.'

'But we have you.' The thing controlling the Human made her grin horribly. 'And we can be very persistent.'

'Yeah, yeah, you're scary and unpredictable. What do you do when you're bored? Pull the legs off your servants for laughs?'

'Oh, we tired of that millennia ago. You know, machine, you were right – it really is all for the taking. And most glorious of all, after more than a hundred thousand years we are yet to encounter anyone bigger and nastier than us!'

CHAPTER TWENTY-ONE

Pyke had to admit – Punzho was right. The view from the top of the Thurible Tower was exceptional. The small, circular candle-lit chamber had two windows: the south-facing one looked out from its mountainside altitude and across a vast forest. It was early evening and the fading light together with the gathering mist highlighted some details and blurred others. The distant forested horizon was a soft grey outline but the closer stretches were darker and impenetrable. Winged creatures chased each other through the crepuscular light, and a few lights twinkled through the trees here and there, campfires, he guessed, with a couple or three haloed clusters that could be villages. After they had stood and gazed out for a few minutes, Punzho closed the shutters, then went over to the north window, unfastened the shutters and parted them. Pyke's first reaction was a low whistle.

Looking south allowed him to survey far-off land from a high vantage – to look north was to stare up at a range of peaks and the gargantuan structures that loomed grey and dust-wreathed. Buildings that had to be over a kilometre high, some square-cornered with vertical lines, others with convex exteriors sweeping to tapered pinnacles, others with splayed upper sections or stepped projections. Windows were dark holes, geometric in shape, triangular, square and circular, like blank eyes in dead faces. Most were still standing and all had lost some of their upper floors while a few had collapsed entirely. The nearest of these ancient, decrepit obelisks had at some time leaned out-wards from the rest and would have crashed down onto the rocky slopes, leaving a kilometres-long trail of rubble, had a medium-sized mountain not been in the way. It lay at an incline up its northern face with the topmost half-dozen floors overtopping the peak. When Pyke looked closely he could just see wind-driven tails of dust streaming out of the gaping windows on one side of the crumbling edifice.

'Klothahil was, it seems, the holdworld of a species called the Zimzin, who had wholeheartedly backed the Apparatarch against the Shuskar-led coup. Of course, they backed the losing side and when retribution arrived it came in the form of lethal poison gas seeded across the planet's atmosphere. The death toll must have been horrific.'

'History lesson, Punzho? No need to convince me how bad these bastard Shuskar are – I've seen more evidence than I can stomach, I tell ya.' Pyke regarded the tall hooded Egetsi. 'But I'm guessing that you got something to tell me that you couldn't say back downstairs ...'

'Yes, Captain, yes! I really want to come with you when the coordinates for the Ashen World Gatuzna have been recali-brated.' The hooded features looked agonised. 'But I don't think the brotherhood of the Congregation would allow it! They think that I am some kind of holy seer.'

'Tell me something,' Pyke said. 'Why do some of those broth-ers wear those gauzy masks under the hoods?'

'They cannot shake off the precepts of the previous creed of the Sacred Flame, an egotistic belief that only the Chosen are permitted to see each other's faces – the novices must only be seen by the high transcendent One. Some haven't progressed enough to become Chosen, yet. Despite this I've been trying to teach them the essential oneness of all sentience.'

'In the name of the cosmic pixie,' Pyke said. 'How did you wind up becoming their pet guru man?'

Punzho pushed back the capacious hood and stared mournfully out of the northern window. 'You recall how they drugged us when we arrived from that icy world? Well, rather than subduing me the fumes made me so panicky that I broke free of their hands and tore off that bag they put over my head. So I saw their faces.

'You saw their faces?' Pyke said. 'What do they actually look like?'

'I think I was expecting something grotesque or extreme; instead they look quite strange – their heads are a little large for the rest of their bodies, and their facial features are oddly small ... for their big faces.

Pyke gave a low laugh. 'So, not exactly awe inspiring, then. You were saying.'

'Yes, so I was face to face with the brothers, and their leader, Yustem Podjag ... '

Pyke snapped his fingers as memories came back. 'Yes, pompous, self-important pukestain who said our weak brains couldn't handle the godlike aura of his mighty countenance or some other bollocks.'

The Egetsi nodded. 'That is Podjag, without a doubt. While you and the others were being drugged and hauled through the galleries to the egress portal, they seized me and shoved me into a filthy cell. I was so fearful, so filled with dread, knowing that you and the rest of the crew were sent on without me, that I had to seek reassurance, no matter how meagre. I took out the pouch containing the Nine Companions and laid them out on the rough stone floor next to the door of iron bars. Light from the torches outside made each figurine gleam as I moved them through the meditation forms. The next thing I knew, one of the other initiates was standing at the door, staring at the Weave pattern I was contemplating – then he called some of his fellows over and by the time Podjag joined the audience I managed to ascertain, from whispered exclamations and snatches of muttered prayer, why they were so engrossed in my activity.

'It seems that the original founders of this community of portal snaggers followed a creed similar to that of the Weave, with an additional evangelising component. They came here over seventy years ago, nine seniors and eighteen subinitiates, set up the power cells and assembled the portal machinery – a gift from some Chainer leader. Every few years one of the seniors would gather his or her belongings, bid farewell and depart through the portal, off to spread the Words of Light, and a new senior would be promoted from the subinitiates.'

Pyke shook his head. 'Picturesque bit of history, there, so ... cut to the last bit of the chase, eh? The bit about being a holy seer.'

The Egetsi's shoulders slumped in an attitude of misery. 'The subinitiates and the seniors all hang on my every word, apart from Podjag. They see cryptic meaning in everything I do – I've only experienced a few days of this and already my sanity feels threatened. The only good thing was their willingness, at my request, to use the portal machinery to scan for your biophysical signatures and set up an automatic diversion command. I told them that you and the others were my followers, novices to my teaching.'

Pyke grinned. 'And hasn't that always been the way of it!'

'But Captain, what can we do?'

'Are they armed?' Pyke said. 'With real weapons, I mean.'

'They have sequestered a variety of sidearms and light arms from unfortunate travellers,' said Punzho. 'A cache of them is always to hand ... but you and the others are likewise armed, yes?'

Pyke ran a hand through his hair. 'Ran into a tight spot before

ending up here – complicated situation, fast-moving, and we were
briefly taken prisoner.' He couldn't admit that he'd left his pistol
lying on the floor of Gyr-Matu's escape room, but surely one of
the others had retrieved theirs.

Punzho gave a doleful shake of his long narrow head. 'Even
if you were all armed, there are still eleven of them and a chest
full of energy weapons.'

Just at that moment, completely unannounced, the door to the
tower chamber rattled and swung open and one of the hooded
Congregation brothers entered, carrying a heavy bundle on a
strap over one shoulder. Ignoring the two of them, the newcomer
closed the door with a back-heeled motion, then went over to a
solitary crude table lit by the chamber's candle-sconce, set the
bundle down, turned and pushed back the hood. Punzho was
taken aback.

'Brother Podjag!'

Podjag was a middle-aged, scrawny humanoid whose small
yet resentful features reminded Pyke of just about every customs
official he had ever met. Podjag directed a vindictive glare up at
the Egetsi, along with a trembling pointed finger. Pyke tried not
to laugh.

'This holy place is not for the likes of you,' he said. 'You
have besmirched our work and us and ... and me! Worse than
this, you have bedazzled and beguiled all the brothers, even the
seniors. There is no place here for you' – a withering look came
Pyke's way – 'or your followers. You must leave, begone, gather
all your accoutrements and depart!'

'But Brother Podjag ...' Punzho began, 'that's exactly—'

'Wait!' Pyke cut in abruptly. 'Now, great and wise Punzho,
perhaps you should wait and hear all that the devout brother
has to say, hmm?'

Punzho looked baffled. 'I should?'

'Indeed, because I am sure that Brother Podjag understands

how attached you have become to this sacred retreat and how leaving it would be a deep, heartfelt wrench, yes?'

Punzho's bafflement seemed to reach cosmic proportions. 'I have? It would?' Then he caught the hard gleam in Pyke's eye even as the captain continued to smile and nod. 'Ah, right, yes ... so ... Brother Podjag, I am sorry for interrupting – what were you about to say?'

Podjag gave Pyke a narrow-eyed glance before continuing. 'You are a disruptive influence, and when those followers of yours leave you must go with them. I am prepared to offer you something of great value if you agree to do this.'

And there it is! thought Pyke. *Yes, here's Podjag, jealous and resentful of being upstaged and dislodged from his lofty perch of authority so he decides to have a chat with the usurper and brings along a mysterious package. All Punzho has to do is remember how we do this kind of negotiation!*

Punzho's features were frozen in a kind of wide-eyed bemusement for a moment, then a thoughtful gleam became evident. He cleared his throat, delicately.

'Oh, Brother Podjag, but as my unworthy neophyte here has said, I have grown deeply fond of this refuge and all our Congregational fellows. To break these cherished bonds and abandon you all would be like unto a wound in my spirit ...'

Steady now, Pyke thought. *Don't overdo it!*

'... but if I were to accept your thoughtful advice, how would your generous gift aid me in my mission to spread the Words of Light?'

Podjag regarded Punzho with undisguised dislike then turned to the table and began to unwrap the bundle, pulling away the folds to reveal a wedge-shaped boxy unit with a brassy appearance, a small panel of press-button controls and a small curved display moulded into the casing. Podjag thumbed a button recessed into the lower right corner and the panel and the display came to life, the latter showing an array of dots in nine parallel rows. One of them was haloed and bright blue and was surrounded by a cluster of greens while the rest were a rosy red. The pious brother zoomed the display in on the greens and indicated the blue dot with a skinny finger.

'Our location, this is, with a surrounding field of possible destinations.'

He then prodded a four-way rocker switch which moved the halo away from the blue dot and among the greens. With a certain smug ease he set the target as one of the outlying greens and tapped a button marked with a red triangle while gesturing Punzho and Pyke to move a couple of steps to the side.

Several wire-thin beams stabbed out from the rear of the device. They flickered and strobed and a familiar dark pulsing oval appeared: a portal gate. Podjag gave a satisfied nod.

'Works as well now as it did when I first obtained it. Once created, the portal is self-sustainingly stable for some minutes, long enough to pick up the portal-maker and step through to the other side. Is this a sufficient answer for you?'

Pyke exchanged a conspiratorial glance with Punzho then turned to Podjag with as innocently amazed an expression as he could manage.

'Oh pious one, I know I speak for the devout Punzho when I say that this is a gift of surpassing quality and utility.' He shook his head. 'How could you bear to part with such a precious possession ... unless it so happens that you have another one hidden away?'

Podjag was the essence of smug satisfaction.

'I have another two,' he said. 'Did you see the great ruin lying against the mountain just north of here? Some years ago, while exploring its dusty chambers, I found an unlooted crate containing the portal-makers. The Zimzin were the supreme techniciars of their age, yet their world became a tomb.'

'Most instructive,' Pyke said. 'And more than adequate for our needs – don't you think, great Punzho?'

'Yes, er ...' Punzho said. 'Yes, most useful. Very well, I agree to your terms, brother.'

'And once you leave, you vow never to return?' Podjag said.

'Harsh but ... if that's what ... yes, as you say.'

Podjag relaxed visibly, switched off the portal device and rewrapped it in the thick cloth. The smug smile that slithered across his lips just then gave him the kind of face that Pyke would never have tired of slapping.

'This is what we shall do – I will descend to the main vaults and announce that a new vision came to me, showing you leaving with your followers. A few moments later you will appear and tell the Congregation that your Weave meditation showed you stepping out of a portal on another world somewhere across the Warcage. Are we in agreement?'

Punzho and Pyke gave nods of assent. Podjag's smile widened a notch and he went over to open the door, pausing on the threshold. 'Your resolve to travel to that wrecked Ashen world is inexplicable to me, but whatever you do afterwards I strongly counsel against any return to Armag – the Lords of the Shuskar have punished the city with skyfire.'

'How could you know this?' Pyke said sharply.

The hooded brother's expression turned sly. 'The portal-makers were not the only devices I found in the mountain ruins.'

Then he was gone.

Some moments later, after a brief discussion with Punzho on timing, Pyke was back down in the torch-lit vault with the bundled portal device tucked under his arm. Ignoring glances from the cowled acolytes, he strolled over to where the rest of the crew were sitting beneath one of the arches, not far from the alcove where the interplanetary portal gate apparatus hummed and blinked.

'Here, chief,' said Ancil. 'That boss monk just told the rest of his flock that Punzho is coming with us, and they weren't happy.'

'Well, he had to tell 'em something,' Pyke said in a low voice. 'And Punzho'll be along in a second to deliver the clincher, then we're out of here, my lucky lads.'

'What's in the package, Captain?' said Kref in his deep basso voice, which, just at that moment, found one of those mysterious dips in crowd noise, allowing his query to carry right across the stone vault. A few curious glances came their way and Pyke clenched his jaws as he crouched down out of sight.

'Aye, turn it up, why don't you?' he muttered through gritted teeth. 'There's some folk on the next planet that didn't quite hear ye!'

'Er, sorry, Captain, sorry . . .'

'Just ignore this bit of luggage, okay? Don't mention it and don't even look at it till we get off this rock, got it?'

There were subdued nods all round and Pyke allowed himself a small measure of relaxation from the tension. Then a stir of mutters passed through the waiting brothers of the Congregation as Punzho came into view, walking through the small crowd to the best-lit area, where a couple of hanging lamps added to the flickering glow of torches. Even before he reached it questions came at him from all sides, all adding up to the same thing – was Podjag's vision true? Was he leaving them? Over and over the anxious voices called, pleading, demanding, until at last Punzho made hushing gestures with his hands.

He then went on to explain how he had climbed to the top of the Thurible Tower, seeking peace for a meditation with the Weave. He told them how he took out his pouch of the Nine Companions and one by one laid them down on the chamber's cold stone floor . . . but as Punzho set his scene Pyke found his thoughts drifting back to Podjag's almost offhand comment when they were up in the tower, that the Lords of the Shuskar had punished Armag City with skyfire. And he knew that if the Shuskar had opted for a ground bombardment the city would not have been the only target. A shiver of dread went down his spine as horrible imaginings filled his mind.

Having divulged the sad truth revealed by his Weave meditation, Punzho was saying his last farewells to the distraught brotherhood. Shaking hands with Podjag – whose sorrowful expression could not conceal the glee in his eyes – Punzho then wended his way through the Congregation as they began singing a lamenting hymn. By now, Pyke and the others had shuffled over beside the gate machinery, whose operator triggered the portal when Punzho finally joined them.

'Okay, let's not waste any time,' Pyke said, turning to the portal operator. 'Is the destination set for Gatuzna?'

The reply was a wordless, anxious nod.

'Good – Kref, you're in first, then Mojag, Ancil and Punzho, and I'll be bringing up the rear.'

One by one they approached the portal gate and stepped through the slow-swirling pulse of darkness. When Ancil's turn came he looked round at the singing congregation, then kissed the fingers of one hand, which he swept out in a theatrical wave goodbye before following Mojag through. Pyke rolled his eyes heavenwards.

Punzho hurried after Ancil, despite the surge in singing and wailing from the brotherhood. When he vanished into the dark swirling oval the noise level reached a crescendo for a second or two, then swiftly subsided. Pyke tucked the cloth-wrapped portal device under his arm and marched determinedly into the gate.

The cold dank air, the flickering torchlight and the sounds of the Congregation all ceased abruptly. Unlike his last portal experience there was only an instant of no-light before his leading foot came down on hard, stony ground and the sights and sounds of Gatuzna burst upon his senses.

Such as those sights and sounds were. He was standing on the gently sloping surface of a pale grey stone slab half buried in what looked like black sand. He felt the touch of a warm gritty breeze as he looked around and saw a few more similar slabs scattered nearby, lying on or jutting out of drifts and dunes of this unnerving sand. He reached down to scoop up a handful and let it trickle through his fingers – up close, it glittered like coal or glass.

'What a dump,' he said. 'No wonder they call it an Ashen world.'

'Captain, you said we had to come here to track down the vile Khorr,' said Punzho. 'But there's no one around except us.'

'Clues, Punzho, clues,' Pyke said. 'If that brother operator of yours did his job we should be practically on top of the spot we were originally supposed to arrive at . . .'

'Got something here, Captain!' said Mojag, waving them over.

Sure enough, the sand was disturbed, some areas gouged and furrowed while a wide flattening trail started at the centre and led away in a straight line, up the shallow slope where they had arrived. In his mind's eye Pyke replayed his last glimpse of Akreen, the Zavri leader, that tall silvery form writhing on the ground, swathed in the jagged energies from Khorr's long-barrelled weapon.

'Drag marks,' said Ancil, following them. 'Leading this way.'

Keeping the tracks in view they steadily mounted the slope, which stretched ahead of them for a good hundred yards or more.

'Hey, Captain,' said Kref. 'Can we ask what's in the bundle yet?'

''Course ye can.'

It took Kref about ten seconds to realise Pyke had not given an expected answer, especially when Pyke's smile widened into a grin and a wink.

'Okay, I get it – Captain, what's in the bundle?'

'I'm very glad you asked that question, Kref, me ould son. We are, I'm frankly amazed to announce, the proud owners of one portable local portal gate generator, aquired as a nudging sort of bribe to get Punzho to leave along with the rest of us.'

'Does it actually work?' said Mojag.

'It actually does – we were given a live demonstration,' Pyke said, patting the bundle. 'It appears to be the real deal.'

'So what is the plan, chief?' said Ancil, who had slowed in his tracking of the drag marks.

'Well, that gouger G'Brozen Mav has the *Scarabus* and my bet is he's long gone.' It was a bitter thing to admit, never mind speak out loud. 'But Khorr, that scum-sucking murderer, was here less than an hour ago, along with Akreen, the Zavri general, and we know that Khorr has been working for the Shuskar all along, so ...'

By now they'd all come to a halt on the uneven slope and were listening intently.

'... so we lay hands on Khorr and ...' He shrugged. 'We persuade him to tell us how to steal a ship from one of those Shuskar fleetworlds.'

'What are they?' said Mojag.

'Planets where the Shuskar have their repair yards, as well as mothballed ships in their thousands.'

Eyes widened at this.

'And before you ask, they don't have armadas floating around for the simple reason that they don't have the crews. Something about their societies not being able to turn out smart enough personnel.'

'It's all about the dominance of pre-rational power structures,' said Mojag unexpectedly. 'Authoritarian leaders fear their subjects getting too smart, so schooling is restricted to the offspring of reliably loyal sectors of the populace, who are more interested in being part of the dominant power structure than learning how to use tools and figure out astrogation. After several centuries, all they have left here are semi-feudal societies that churn out serfs and peasants, low-level labourers fit only for their brutal factories or those tournament battles. Sure, the Shuskar can field a few ships but that's all.'

'Nice, Mojag, very nice,' Pyke said, giving him a brief hard stare. 'So long as they're hard to come by, I'll be happy. So, long way round, we grab Khorr, use the portal gate to travel to the nearest fleetworld, and steal ourselves a medium-sized transport, y'know, with indoor pool, fully stocked bar and a hi-spec holo gallery.'

'Chance would be a very fine thing,' said Ancil.

'Okay, okay, anything that we can fly would be great.' He took a deep breath. 'Then we make Khorr help us track down Dervla and Win and once we've got them back we can make ourselves scarcer than scarce.'

Ancil suddenly looked tired. 'Sounds like a tall order, chief, but thanks – I'm with you.' As he spoke, Kref and Mojag nodded.

'We'll find them, Ans, we will . . . now, what's Punzho found?'

The Egetsi had trudged on up the black sandy incline, long strides carrying him a fair distance in just a minute or two. Now he was standing straight and waving and calling to them but the warm dusty breeze was blowing towards him, carrying his words away.

'Let's find out what's got him jiggin' all about,' Pyke said, setting off. 'But let's keep an eye on them tracks, 'kay?'

Seeing the crew resuming their approach Punzho ceased waving and continued on up the slope. As they reached the spot where he had waved from, Pyke could start to make out what lay beyond the top of the slope, what he had at first thought was going to turn out to be the raised lip of the far side of a huge crater. As he strode further onwards and upwards, pace by pace, a far-away line of landscape came into view beyond Punzho's standpoint, a line that he at first thought of as the horizon. Then he saw how the horizon dipped as no horizon should, how grey clouds shifted and partially masked a yawning gulf. When he climbed the last few yards to stand beside Punzho he finally saw the grandiose, terrible, impossible devastation in its entirety.

The disconcertingly smooth precipice where they stood was part of a cracked and crumbling cliff edge that swept away to either side, with jagged promontories jutting for miles out into a vast, gloomy abyss. That void stretched away, becoming a colossal, planet-cleaving canyon which left the horizon looking as if something had taken a bite out of it.

'The Ashen Worlds were where the AI servants of the Builders made their last stand against the Shuskar and their allies,' said Punzho, who then appeared a little embarrassed. 'I learned some history from the brothers while I was with them.'

'Some piece of planetary destruction,' Ancil said, eyes wide as he drank in the sight. 'That hole is deep, chief; crazy deep. Usually the horizon is only a few miles away at sea level but this monster gap cuts right through it, goes on for hundreds of miles.'

'What the frack could do something like this?' Pyke said.

'Burrowing munitions,' said Ancil. 'Combine a thermonuke with a gravity disruptor, send a few of them a coupla hundred miles down beneath the bedrock and set them off. The merged shockwave would damn near tear a planet open to the outer core. In fact, if the attackers were hunting for AIs I bet there are a few more of these megarifts dotted around.'

Pyke nodded thoughtfully. 'Hell's gnashers, they wanted them machines badly ... but a planet as badly damaged as this would become unstable, surely.'

'It's the subspace forcefield structures of the megasystem,' said Ancil. 'They hold every single world in place, even a wrecked one like Gatuzna.' He gazed out at the hazy abyss. 'Don't know if any civilisation could have survived this.'

'Okay, astrophysics lesson over,' Pyke said. 'Do these tracks come up to the cliff edge, Ans?'

'They certainly do, chief, along a bit where there's a notch in the brink and a path that leads down to a wide ledge right under where we're standing.'

'Okay, let's keep our wits about us,' said Pyke, who then turned to Kref. 'Here, can ye hang this over yer back? It's really starting to get on my nerves!'

He handed the wrapped portal device over to the big Henkayan, who pulled the carrying strap over his head. 'No problem, Captain, carry it as long as you like.' He then lightly tossed the bundle over his shoulder where it struck his spine with a thud. Pyke winced.

'Careful, Kref – that might be our only way off this dead rock!'

Ancil led the descent. The ledge was over a yard wide and had a foot-worn path down the middle of it, which immediately put them on their guard. The pathway had been disused, littered with fallen stones and obscured here and there by black sand when it passed between rocks that sheltered it from the ever-present warm breeze. The quarry's fresh tracks continued, though, changing from drag marks partially obscuring one set of footprints to two sets of footprints. Pyke frowned when Ancil pointed this out, guessing that Akreen must have regained consciousness and was now walking along with Khorr aiming that big gun at him.

As they trudged down the path, Pyke – glancing at the huge clouds of brown and grey that hung and shifted and eddied forth in slow swirls when the occasional gust of air dipped down from above – could feel the immensity of that murky void. Once, the dismal clouds parted and he saw a far-off portion of bleak clifftop, only there was a cleft running right down the middle of it and a waterfall pouring over the edge, disappearing into the depths. Quickly he pointed it out to the others, who paused to snatch a glimpse before the clouds closed up.

'An amazing sight,' said Punzho. 'And such a beautiful waterfall.'

'Don't think that was a waterfall,' said Ancil.

Pyke gave him a puzzled look. 'You sure about that? It looked like one to me.'

Ancil shrugged. 'Sorry, chief – what you saw was tons of pulverised rock, grit and pebbles falling in a haze of stone dust. That vertical cleft is a fracture where one immense shard of the planet's surface – well, immense to us – is grinding against the rest. Which is why there were rocks and boulders falling among all the grit and dust.'

'I didn't see that,' Pyke said, turning to Mojag. 'Did you?'

'I thought that was a blurring shadowy effect.'

'Nope, trust me, boulders and rocks,' said Ancil.

'Ancil is quite correct, Captain,' said Punzho. 'It is falling debris.'

'Er, Captain,' said Kref.

'Hmm, I don't know,' said Pyke. 'It's a long way off, that cliff ...'

'Captain, er ...' Kref said, louder this time.

'What's up, Kref? Can't ye see that we're having a fine old barney about ...?'

His voice trailed off as he turned and saw what the big Henkayan was pointing at. The sheer wall on the path's left side was uneven and ridged, frequently revealing layers of sedimentary rock which weathering had eroded into shelves and strange holes in the rock face. It was on one of those shelves that a hand-sized spidery bot, or more probably a remote, sat watching him with a small cluster of shiny lenses, in the middle of which shone a blue dot.

'Welcome to Gatuzna, Captain,' it said in a tinny cheery voice.

'And welcome to your valiant crew, too, naturally. Apologies for the decrepit surroundings – they really have seen better days. We thought it only right to—'

'And you are?' Pyke said. 'Didn't catch your name, there.'

'Ah yes – we are the Inheritors.'

Pyke was caught between smiling and frowning. 'Interesting use of the word "we", eh?'

'Yes, this is one of the problems of being a distributed ultra-cognition – it's easier to adapt the collective "we" rather than concoct a taxonomy of groupings, subgroups and solitaries.'

'Well, you sound to me like a very knowledgeable kind of machine, Mr Inheritor,' Pyke said. 'So perhaps you might know where we can find an associate of ours, tall feller, silvery skin, very serious disposition.'

The spider-bot shifted position slightly, pointy legs ticking on stone.

'Ah, you mean the Zavri First Blade, Akreen? He did indeed pass this way but as a prisoner, we are saddened to report.'

'Yes, it's his captor we'd really like to have a word with.' Pyke studied the remote. 'Actually, the First Blade told us that he was expecting to meet an ally here – that wouldn't be you, would it?'

'Ally, hmm – we might have used the word "intermediary".'

'So you're neutral.'

'Oh no, we do have an objective – it's just the planning in between now and the end which is presenting . . . complications.'

'Plans are fine things – I wake up with a new one in mind every day!' Pyke clapped his hands together and rubbed them. 'We'll be off now but I imagine that we'll be seeing each other again before long—'

'Be careful while following your friend, Captain Pyke – his captor's weapon is deadly to all sentients, be they flesh or metal. We were going to try to dissuade you from this foolish pursuit but we all know how little use that would have been. So, see you later – perhaps.'

With that the Inheritor bot folded up into a fist-sized spheroid which rolled away into a small round hole that Pyke hadn't noticed before.

'What was all that about ... really?' said Ancil.

Pyke grunted. 'Not sure but there was definitely a bit of the old brain-baffling going on.'

Ancil wore an analytical frown. 'I'm sure I remember someone somewhere saying that these Ashen Worlds were where the last battles of a huge war took place. I wonder whose world this was ...'

'The Apparatarch,' said Mojag, who was staring off at the distant broken horizon.

Ancil frowned. 'Was that who we were just talking to?'

'Don't know,' Pyke said, straightening. 'And right this very second I don't care, 'cos while we're standing here, bashing our gums, Khorr and Akreen are getting further away. So let's move.'

The crew resumed their descent with Ancil back in the lead, almost half crouching to study the tracks in the windblown sand. At first the air had been warm and faintly humid but the deeper they went the cooler and danker it became. Then the ledge came to where a flat boulder sat across the path, beyond which there was a six-foot drop, with a few worn hand- and footholds. At the bottom, the path led straight to the entrance to a tunnel, a rough, lightless opening. Pyke peered into the inky darkness and swore.

'Anyone got a torch or the like?' he said.

There were doleful headshakes all round, except for Punzho.

'Egetsi eyesight is more sensitive than that of Humans,' he said, striding a few paces into the dark tunnel. 'I can just make out ...'

'Hang on, Punzho,' said Pyke, pointing at a glimmer of light which had just appeared. 'Carry on in there a little ways . . .'

Punzho did so, coming to a halt in surprise when a yellow glow bloomed from a knobbly, vaguely organic-looking protuberance high up on the left wall.

'That's convenient,' Pyke said. 'On we go.'

For a stretch the tunnel was rough-hewed with an uneven, sandy floor, and the glowing nodules gave off enough light for Ancil still to discern the tracks. Then the tunnel narrowed and a few large rocks meant they had to clamber and squeeze along it before coming out in a dark dilapidated corridor. Ancient wall facings and ceiling panels had given way, dumping heaps of pebbly soil and rubble on the cracked floor decking. A few glowing nodules provided a path through the shadows. Ancil picked up the trail again, steering the crew past side passages and around gaping holes. Until they reached a T-junction, where he stopped, peered closely at the marks on the dirty, gritty floor, went to the right a few paces then to the left – and threw up his hands.

'Tracks seem to go both ways,' he said. 'But hard to say – looks as if something's tried to brush away any clues.'

'Well, there's only two choices,' Pyke said, turning left at the junction into a dark stretch of passage that remained unlit as he walked along it. Then he stumbled on rocks or some debris – by the weak light from around the corner he could just make out a slope of rubble blocking the way.

'There's been a cave-in,' he said, retracing his steps. 'Has to be the other way.'

Gunless, Pyke had armed himself with a length of metal strut wrenched from a jagged hole in the corridor wall not far back. The other arm of the T-junction curved left then reached a sharp right corner. The others hung back while Pyke strode along by himself, illuminated by a small glowing nodule as he turned the corner . . .

And had to stop quickly as the floor, the walls and the corridor abruptly ran out and he found himself just a step away from a drop into emptiness.

'Now there's a sight,' he muttered, steadying himself against the wall.

It was as if a massive wedge had been clinically removed from the substratum, extending up and down. Directly above was a straight-edged slice of gloomy sky; below, a shadowy gulf of nothing. On the sheer face on the other side, a wide expanse of smashed and ripped corridor openings gaped darkly, an exposed cliff of civilisational ruins.

'I ain't going near that edge,' said Ancil.

Pyke grimaced in frustration. 'Akreen and Khorr must either have gone along the other turn-off, and that cave-in is new – or they doubled back.' He glared round at Ancil. 'What d'ye reckon?'

And just then all the nodule lights went out and Pyke felt the floor tilt underfoot, pitching him out into the abyss. There was an infuriating slowness to it as he bellowed a long, drawn-out string of curses, while hearing the others shouting his name in panic and feeling the blast of air as he plunged headfirst into black oblivion.

Which took on a cushioned firmness as an unseen safety net gently caught him and slowed his fall. Gradually he slipped into a lying position, bizarrely looking up at the long slice of gloomy grey sky.

'Calm yourself, Captain Pyke, you are in no danger.'

'And I should believe you … because?'

A tiny bright blue light winked on in the rushing darkness, revealing the spidery bot from before, hanging just over his head. Then he noticed a second identical one near his feet and guessed that between them they had to be generating some kind of cradling forcefield.

'Genuinely, there is nothing to worry about, Captain – we like to take care of our valued guests!'

I'll bet you do, he thought. *Any more reassurance and I'll have to get cracking on my will!*

CHAPTER TWENTY-TWO

On its reaction drives, the *Scarabus* flew through the empty space outwith the Warcage, thereby avoiding the omnipresent autodefences which, according to Toolbearer Hechec, resided in hyperspace and could be projected with impunity against any intruder. Sam was sure that Rensik could have confirmed or denied such a bizarre claim but still there had been no contact, no message from the Construct drone.

Sam was on the bridge, sitting at the command console, idly paging through an epedia about 4th Modynel trade agreements while keeping an eye on the update subscreen. G'Brozen Mav was slumped in one of the workstation couches while the hooded display before him showed the ship's course and speed against a graphic of the Warcage megasystem – he had been there since they departed Armag, a sombre presence, scarcely uttering so much as a single word for the best part of six hours. Toolbearer Hechec, unable to obtain more than a few monosyllabic replies for the last two hours, had retreated to Engineering from where he occasionally queried Sam on G'Brozen Mav's demeanour. She had been tempted to go and join him but a certain stubbornness kept her at her work station, monitoring Chainer reports, just in case anything surfaced that might tell her where the Construct was.

The *Scarabus* was on a curved trajectory towards Nagolger, a planet roughly halfway round the Warcage world array, with roughly eight hours of flight-time still to go. Armag was now nearly three hours behind them, and those visions of fiery destruction were still fresh in Sam's mind. The escape from that inferno and the warship that unleashed it had turned into a nerve-wracking getaway under fire when that same vessel began launching salvos of missiles at them. But the *Scarabus*'s AI had put on a display of white-knuckle dodges and feints and split-microsecond timing, even as it powered its way up and out of the atmosphere. Of course, then there was another Shuskar warship up there in orbit to be evaded – a staggered pattern of mini-munitions with emitter payloads created an anti-sensor veil behind which the *Scarabus* made a brief dive back into the planet's upper atmosphere.

Once they were in the clear on the other side of the planet, the ship AI opened up the main thrusters and they made a dash for open space beyond the Warcage. At which point Toolbearer Hechec had begun scanning for news from military and civilian sources while trying to make contact with various Chainer bases and cadres. Pieces of information filtered through and a picture began to come together, a vile, horrific picture. When Hechec sat G'Brozen Mav down on the bridge and gave him a summary of the situation, the Chainer leader had gone pale and drawn. He leaned an elbow on the couch armrest and slowly pushed his fingers up through that dense dark hair.

'Hoykan,' Mav said. 'What happened there?'

'Poison gas,' said Hechec. 'Cregrin bombers dropped a mix of impact shells, mines and hunter-killer probes. They targeted all five cities – survival percentages are in low single figures.'

'Ventir?'

'The three cities in rebel hands were bombarded with contagion agents. Sujalkan units have ringed them with quarantine fields.'

'Jirorm?'

'Same as Armag City, carpet-bombed with skyfire munitions, by the Yniich. All seven cities badly hit.'

G'Brozen Mav went on to ask about another two worlds, Dumaj and Divanda, and the Toolbearer's answers were uniformly grim. They and the rest were all planets where Chainers had seized control, were openly supported by the authorities, or had bases and well-stocked caches. Responsibility for the attacks had been assigned to the Loyals, the top seven battle-armies of the Grand Escalade, who were always keen to prove their loyalty to their Shuskar masters. Dumaj and Divanda had been punished by the Lorzavel and the Muranzyr respectively: it was now a certainty that it was the Avang who had firebombed Armag City and its environs.

When Hechec finished, G'Brozen Mav sat in silence for some moments.

'So now we know,' he said eventually. 'All our planning, all our effort and sacrifice, all our endeavours seem to have been useless.'

'My leader—' the Toolbearer began, but Mav cut him off.

'This is it, the final irrefutable proof!' The Chainer leader was angry and grief stricken. 'Proof that any rebellion against the Shuskar will fail. We made the mistake of thinking that the backing of the oppressed was all that was needed, and if we were fighting an enemy that was vaguely our equal it might be enough. But the vile Shuskar control the meshes that bind our lives together, as well as a monopoly on the Warcage's vast repositories of military might – face them on any battlefield and by sheer weight of brute force they will always triumph.' His brow was furrowed as if in pain, and he shook his head. 'We foolishly believed that we could hide away among the populations of those worlds, drawing strength from them, secretly building and training, that we and they would be safe from extreme retaliation.

We never imagined, even T'Loskin Rey never really thought, that they would countenance annihilating civilian populations simply to get at us.'

He paused, glanced over at the Toolbearer. 'Do you have an estimate on the death toll yet?'

Hechec was grim. 'Somewhere between 8.5 and 12 million.'

G'Brozen Mav had a haunted, hollow look. 'My old fight trainer once told me that every opponent you meet in the breach teaches you something. If I'd learned this lesson well before now millions might still be alive.'

Studying him, Sam felt some sympathy. But she was still stuck here in this psychotic, self-contained carnival of tyranny, and since the Construct drone was conspicuous by its absence her options were limited and bleak. Was it possible to continue with the mission's original aim on her own? Or perhaps she was seeing the problem from the wrong angle – if she had greater freedom of movement and resources to draw on then she could carry out a focused search for Rensik. Gaining control of the *Scarabus* was the obvious solution but she doubted that G'Brozen Mav would be happy to just hand the ship over to her. However, rescuing the Construct drone was vital, so it was time for a game-changer.

'Is that it?' she said. 'So the Shuskar bare their teeth and deploy overkill methods just to demonstrate how mercilessly psychopathic they are – but you knew that already. I'm only a newcomer to the Warcage yet it is utterly clear to me that the Shuskar have to be fought with unflinching resolve, fought on various battlefields and in various ways. There can be no negotiation or compromise with enemies like these, no middle ground, no halfway house, because they won't be satisfied with just half your soul – they want it all.' She sighed. 'You have to know this, yet here you are, saying that it's over.'

G'Brozen Mav looked up, angry eyes regarding her.

'I *never* said that it was over!'

Sam sat back, trying to look amiably composed.

'That's good to hear – do you have a plan?'

The Chainer leader's grim features were unchanged when he looked over at Toolbearer Hechec.

'Gather together a ground force from any of the surviving Chainer bases, steal a heavy assault ship from one of the fleetworlds, then carry out a sneak attack on the Shuskar Citadelworld, destroy as much of their machinery as possible and … and get as much information out of any prisoners before we have to leave.'

Hechec nodded thoughtfully. 'I remember this plan, my leader – you discarded it because the likely Shuskar counterattack would make an escape from the Citadelworld almost impossible.'

'Their effective fleet strength is already almost at full stretch,' Mav said. 'They just do not have the trained crews to deploy more vessels, which greatly hinders their strategic advantage.'

Toolbearer Hechec nodded, his hooded features looking alert and focused. 'Also, arranging diversionary strikes against one or two high-profile Shuskar installations could make them think that these targets are the sum and total of our counterstroke.'

'Excellent suggestion – which installations would be suitable?'

'The powercell factory on Ghorosh and the Mount Yalk supply silo on Pommolik – both are crucial to Shuskar supply lines and are located in the vicinity of portal gates. That makes them easier for our portal snaggers and easier for the strike forces to make a swift withdrawal.'

'How quickly can Chainer groups mount such operations?' G'Brozen Mav said.

'From orders to forward rally point, between ten and twelve hours.'

Mav nodded. 'Good. In the meantime we'll need a contingent of troops for when we reach the Shuskar Citadelworld.'

'We have a Chainer cadre on Malgin-Kog,' Hechec said. 'They

have been training recruits from the clan-towns for more than three string-months. The Malginori are a Muranzyr offshoot and are quite a belligerent lot.'

'They sound ideal,' said Mav. 'We'll head there, get them boarded, then fly to the fleetworld Nagolger.'

'Nagolger?' said the Toolbearer. 'But would not Shankol be closer?'

'True, but Shankol has two garrisons and a full complement of combat fliers. The Nagolger multiyards are far less tactically daunting—'

'If I might make an observation,' Sam said, cutting in. 'First, it's a good plan and I like it, and second, are you sure that you have the stages of the plan the right way round?'

G'Brozen Mav frowned. 'Why delay the ability to strike?'

'Why make preparations before you know what you will be facing?'

Mav's glare softened to a glower, which was then directed at the Toolbearer. 'What do we actually know about the Nagolger yard complex? Was there ever a mission profile?'

Hechec shook his head while glancing at his workstation display. 'According to the archives I brought with us, there is only a survey summary and it's over forty years old.'

'You'll have to go to Nagolger first,' Sam said. 'Send out messages to your secondary bases, set up the diversionary strikes and get your ground troops ready for embarkation – but you need to scout out the enemy positions, what your mission goal is and what it will take to reach it. Intelligence is key – without it you'll be going in blind.'

G'Brozen Mav met her gaze and for a moment she thought he was going to refuse her suggestion, insist on following his plan, then he looked at the Toolbearer, who nodded.

'Very well,' Mav said. 'We scout the area first.'

Encrypted commands were sent to a string of Chainer bases

and contacts, a course for Nagolger was plotted, and everyone settled in for a long journey. Toolbearer Hechec, while analysing packets of battle and recon reports received from the base network, tried to engage G'Brozen Mav in a discussion about possible unit deployments, but Mav's mood had turned morose for whatever reason and eventually the Toolbearer wandered off to Engineering. Sam remained on the bridge, concerned that her departure might make it seem as if she and the Toolbearer were colluding in avoiding Mav's company. Another chilly hour passed before she realised that she actually wasn't that concerned, so she rose and left, heading for the main hold. She could retask one of the terminals down there to keep track of Chainer reports, but that was not her primary reason for this sidetrack. It was less than a day since the ship AI told her about the sensor data being read from the cryostasis canister holding Oleg Kelitak's body. Now that the chaos of Armag was behind them, curiosity was nagging at her, demanding to be satisfied.

Several minutes later she was on the upper gantry of the main hold, following it round to the special storage room. Presence glows flickered on as she entered, the hatch clunking heavily shut behind her. Oleg's cryostasis canister was shelved at shoulder-height halfway down the long narrow space, its monitor display showing black characters and symbols against pale green. She studied the sensor data, shifting the sections along by touch, studying timescale comparisons, then paused, frowning, hands resting on the canister surface.

'Ship,' she said. 'Are you there?'

'Yes, Lieutenant Brock, I am.'

'These readouts ... is this right, that vital signs restarted, heart and respiration, continued for nearly half an hour, then just stopped?'

'The data is correct, Lieutenant. However, core temperature is now lower than it was before this activity, and sensors are detecting compounds associated with post-death cell degeneration. There are also the first indications of muscle stiffness.'

Sam shook her head sadly. 'So he wasn't in any kind of Kiskashin pseudo-hibernation, then.'

'No. Speculation – some variants of the Kiskashin genome may have evolved post-trauma survival states which we were unable to treat and accommodate correctly due to absence of knowledge.'

'If that were so, why wouldn't Mojag's copy of Oleg have passed on such knowledge to Pyke or someone?' She shrugged. 'Well, it's all academic now.'

She left the storage unit, descended to the main hold floor and the recessed room with its hold controls and secondary work stations. But after nearly an hour she grew restive, recalling how comfortable that couch was up on the bridge (which was also maintained at a cosier temperature than the hold). Eventually she gave in, transferred her ongoing screen-state back to the bridge, and left the hold. G'Brozen Mav glanced up for a moment when she re-entered the bridge, sparing her only a cold and dark look before going back to the display of weaponry stats which filled his screen. As she settled back into the workstation's couch, Sam observed the Chainer leader out the corner of her eye:

There's no way you'll be taking me out on a recon, she thought. *All that matters is how many you leave behind to guard the ship. For personal safety you'll take Hechec and two guards, leaving two aboard, and two I can handle. You'll feel betrayed when you see the* Scarabus *lift off and depart, certainly no less than this Pyke was when you stole his ship in the first place. And I shall undoubtedly feel guilt and remorse for my own part, too, but once I've tracked down the drone we can and will complete the mission!*

*

Spidery, leafless trees and bushes lined the deep, fogbound ravine along which Akreen trudged. True, it was a fabricated place left behind in the deepest recess of his mind, but it still felt as if he had been trudging along it for a weary eternity. Gredaz was leading the way, his tall, broad-shouldered form made pale by the thick, swirling fog. Not for the first time Akreen reflected upon these surroundings with a certain scorn, knowing this stark vacancy to be the only context setting that his etiolated precursors had been capable of fashioning, a harsh confining chasm.

How galling it was to be ambushed by his ancestors and then thrust down into this place. Clearly, they had been planning and preparing for such an eventuality and when Khorr had attacked him his resulting incapacity was all the opportunity that they needed.

Not that they were receiving treatment any less severe than if Akreen were still fully in control. With Rajeg as spokesman, they had tried to assure Khorr of their loyalty by spilling all they knew about Gredaz and the plan for Akreen to travel to Gatuzna to meet a Zavri ancestor, a survivor from before the Great Unshackling War against the Apparatarch. Having convinced Khorr that they really were, collectively, Akreen's precursors, and that Akreen's self was imprisoned within, they were now leading him down into an ancient underground complex in search of the ancestor, drawn there by those faint flickers of bioelectric resonance that all Zavri emanate.

From the shifting brightness far above, Akreen could just hear his precursors, their bursts of compulsive squabbling interspersed with irascible comments from Rajeg. The expedition with Khorr had thus far not brought them anywhere near their goal. Not long ago they had reached a T-junction, followed the meagre bioelectric trace along to one side only to find the corridor ending abruptly at the brink of an immense, deep fissure that rose to open sky. And when they went back to try the other side of the junction they narrowly escaped being crushed by a corridor collapse, barely making it through. Now Rajeg and Khorr were heading along and up since Khorr claimed that he'd spotted a crude bridge spanning the gulf about half a kilometre away.

So while they were negotiating a route through centuries-old ruined passageways, Akreen was doggedly plodding along after Gredaz. On their arrival down here, Gredaz had insisted that a pseudo-subjective context like this could be altered by focused and unflinching purpose. Which turned out to be true – the rocky-ravine appearance and the leafless trees weren't much but were a definite improvement on the empty blank pit they were tossed into.

Occasionally he was sure he heard whispers from beyond the fog, muffled footfalls, and once a brief hoarse laugh. Gredaz insisted that these were merely after-echoes from his precursors' presence, part of the persistent quality of Zavri memory. Akreen pondered this, unsure if it was in the long term an advantage or a disadvantage.

Suddenly Gredaz halted, stretched out his left hand, took a pace to the left, then another, which was almost enough to be swallowed utterly by the fog. Then he re-emerged to beckon Akreen and there, in a cleft in the rough black rock, was a rack of crude, narrow steps leading up.

'Our ascent begins,' Gredaz said with a bleak smile.

CHAPTER TWENTY-THREE

At some point during his bizarre flight through subterranean darkness, Pyke was overcome by a wave of lethargy so enfolding and comfortable that he could not resist sinking into a half-sleep. As he drowsed he could just hear the annoying voice of that AI remote muttering to him in the background, occasionally breaking through with a sharp comment or a direct question.

'... do realise that as an outsider your understanding of Warcage politics and history cannot help but be minimal and fragmentary at best. You probably don't know that the Zavri were originally allies of the Inheritors – which is how we termed ourselves, by the way; Apparatarch is a terrible name, conferred upon us by some Shuskar sycophant. We always thought of ourselves as the Inheritors since we inherited the Builders' legacy, their dreams and concepts, the totality of their work in effect. We had a responsibility to shoulder so when those ingrates and persecutors and slavers started to go from world to world, conquering and slaughtering and spreading their lies, we had to act. We had to oppose them.

'At that time, the Shuskar were just one among a clutch of extremist factions. We did not really understand the strains of xenophobia which underpinned the creeds of those factions, only that they had come together out of a shared sense of, well, hunger for loot and slaughter is probably the most accurate summation. Their propaganda raved about a host of injustices, most of which were imagined or cooked up out of the meagrest components, cross-world regulation of trade, for example, or food production standards, and so forth. In such feeble soil was the great weed of their outrage planted, and once their war wagon started rolling few authentic justifications were sought.

'Battles raged back and forth for years, entire worlds became shattered battlefields, our greatest weapons were the Cold Regiments, cognitive combat machines, some the size of your fist, others as big as a castle and able to move under their own power. Our organic allies, like the Nakwra and the Zimzin, were almost as impressive in terms of the intricate technologies and sophisticated weaponries they were able to provide. The Zavri, with their inherent and unique biology, straddled both these disparate elements of the war effort. And it worked, and the would-be usurpers and blood-hungry marauders were steadily pushed back and back. And then, at that dig site on Keniphi, those Shuskar researchers found five sentient bioweapons buried in ancient metal caskets ...'

He became aware of a brightening of the light, a smear of weak glow leaking past his half-shut eyelids, a visual nag as yet too subtle to disrupt the swaddling doziness in which the probe's commentary was an irritating murmur.

'... proved to be more than just resurrected war toys stinking of the grave. Oh no, as living sentient things they have minds and memories out of which they dredged blueprints detailing a weapon of surpassing specificity. Suddenly we found front-line units of the Cold Regiments were starting to suffer higher than usual losses and malfunctions – then a reconnaissance-in-force on one of the few remaining enemy sympathiser worlds was routed, and the battle that we rushed into a day later they won, convincingly. Before long we were the ones who were falling back, our combat machines were easy prey to the new Shuskar weapons, which were even capable of destroying the Zavri ...'

Pyke cracked open an eye and saw grubby dilapidated corridor walls sliding past. *Hah, more boring dream scenes*, he thought. *I would have expected my fizzing imagination to come up with something a bit wilder than that! Wake me up when it gets all shouty and fighty and mad! He cried out. Or at least meant to, or could have ...*

'... only took a few years before the positions were reversed and we were the ones being forced back to our holdworlds – by "we" in this case I mean the alliance of we Inheritors and the Zavri, the Zimzin and a dozen other civilisations who had devoted their resources and lives to the cause. But even our staunchest allies, the Zavri, were so diminished that they could scarcely field a sizeable force any more. So when one of their leaders, Kaldro-Vryn, came to us with a sombre but strange request we could not refuse. Back then, the Zavri knew far more about the secrets of their biology than those of today. Among their many meditation techniques, for example, was one called the Encrystalling – this was capable of sending the meditator into a deep state of mental suspension and physical stasis so profound that their biometallic flesh itself transmutes into a pseudo-crystalline form, the Incarnalith as they called it. So, before our sensors, this is the metamorphosis which Kaldro-Vryn conducted and completed then, as we agreed, his remains, his Incarnalith, was despatched to our deepest, most fortified vault for safekeeping. Of course, we could not suspect the true scale of the savage destruction that the enemy would soon visit upon our worlds ...'

Even though his drowsy state was warm and comfortable, still changes in his immediate surroundings continued to impinge upon his awareness. There was no longer that sense of swift, gliding motion, so he shifted an arm to peer out with bleary eyes – and it seemed that now he was descending into some huge hole or some such ... *honestly, whoever's in charge really has to keep the interruptions to a minimum! Can't they see that the good folk are trying to get some kip?*

'... struck without mercy or restraint. When our military campaign was in the ascendancy we went to great pains to avoid the mass slaughter of non-combatants and the destruction of cities. But when the Shuskar and their goons became the conquerors they opted not to bother with such niceties. Military and civilian were subjected to the same brutal logic of total war, entire populations were wiped out, and especially troublesome planets became the target for the Shuskar's most treasured weapons, the mantle munitions. Monstrous towers capable of burrowing into the surface of a planet, tunnelling down beneath its crust then detonating their payloads with devastating effect – as with several other worlds, these vicious weapons were used here on Gatuzna, as I'm sure you have already seen ...'

Pyke frowned. Still his rest was being disturbed, small inescapable alterations in the surroundings, a certain coolness that he could feel on his skin. And had the sense of motion ceased altogether? And was this a solid surface beneath his stretched-out form?

'Many millions of brave sentients died when they broke our world, when they tore into the guts of Gatuzna in search of the machines and re-matrixed stone that held our distributed intellect. We were prepared for the very worst, with concealment gambits and preservation ploys that ultimately ensured our survival, but the Incarnalith of Kaldro-Vryn was not so fortunate. The colossal forces unleashed by the mantle munitions penetrated the storage chamber, shattering the Incarnalith into thousands of fragments. So with the few resources left to us, amid the demolition of Gatuzna, we sent the chamber down into a risky vault of last resort, down into the planet's outer core where Shuskar sensors could not see with any detail.

'We had our stealthy, clandestine bolt holes, and we managed to survive the bombardment, the planet-ripping, and the aftermath. In the subsequent millennia we have watched the Shuskar rise to prominence, then utter dominance; watched as they imposed on every world a brutal hierarchy with themselves at the pinnacle, various grades of sycophantic minions below them, and the mass of planetary populations at the bottom. And seen how they used the institutions of the Grand Escalade to divert energy and aggression into the bout tournaments, the battles, the faked grudges, the pseudo-wars pitting planet against planet. Over the span of time it has caused the grotesque de-evolution of all the system's civilisations, the brutalising of thought and social interaction, and what was once the Great Harbour of Benevolent Harmony has become the Warcage, our prison, their grand arena where the powerless perform and fight and die for their pleasure.'

It began to percolate through Pyke's soporific mind that comfort and warmth was no longer available, that he lay on cold flat stone, that there was a curved wall all around, its striated surface covered with small beads, about a third of which emitted a bright light. A harsh light that did not help with his blurred sight.

'But during this long, bloody interlude we have investigated the peculiarities of Zavri biology and the nature of the Incarnalith. The Zavri have, under the tutelage of the Shuskar, become the deadliest and most feared fighters anywhere in the Warcage, and have demonstrated their loyalty to the Shuskar on innumerable occasions. A truly impressive irony in the light of the secrets we have managed to unlock.'

And as he stared he felt something through the suffusing, warm drowsiness, a nip on his leg, just a tiny pinprick, like a cold insect bite.

'Perhaps you can feel the first shards of the Incarnalith now. We deliberately induced in you a form of resonating soporific feedback to narcotise your awareness, to deaden the sensitivity, at least at the start. After all, anticipation tends to heighten pain ...'

The pinpricks were coming every second or two and they were getting sharper. Then something struck him in the right arm and it felt like an icy razor blade. Pyke cursed and sat up, the alertness of pain shredding the drowsiness, chasing away the fug. Even as he tugged his jacket arm up to see, another brief stabbing sensation hit him in the back. Then, out of nowhere, a tiny dark object flicked in to bury itself in the flesh of his uncovered arm. Pyke swore at the sudden lancing pain then swore again, in disbelief, as the object, a dark blue glassy splinter about an inch long, sank smoothly into the skin, leaving behind a small, fading circular mark. He barely had time to understand what was happening before another shard stuck home, and another, and another ...

'Even in its shattered state, the fragment of the Incarnalith still possesses a vestige of Kaldro-Vryn's awareness and purpose – the fragments know that you are to be their host, although sadly your kind of bio-form cannot accommodate more than a third of the shards. But we are sure that it will be enough ...'

By now Pyke was lying back down on the cold hard floor, curled up, arms wrapped around his head, snarling and cursing horribly as the shards kept coming. His clothing was sliced and tattered and it felt as if a mob of sadistic seamstresses were stabbing his arms, back and legs with surgical needles over and over. Spitted and spiked, skewered and perforated, all the wounds merged into a continuous cataract of raw pain.

'We could have rendered you unconscious during this process but the vestigial awareness of Kaldro-Vryn might, out of instinct, have attempted to usurp your undefended mind and quite honestly, Captain, there are too many problems like that around at the moment. But as you may now be discerning, the intromission is almost complete. You are now host to a portion of an Incarnalith, the crystalline matrix of an ancient Zavri ancestor! Imagine that! Now we can give you a little more of that sleepy respite while we send you back to your friends . . .'

The drowse descended once more, smothering but not quite obscuring the carpet of tiny wounds that lay across his body. As a distraction Pyke imagined the machine's voice as a neck, a strangely disembodied throat around which he was wrapping his hands, dreaming about strangling that scheming, rotten voice, throttling it . . .

The next thing he knew, his shoulder was being shaken by a worried-looking Ancil.

'Chief, chief! How're you feeling?'

Pyke pushed himself into a seated position, breathed in and out deeply, squeezed his eyes tightly shut for a moment then opened them widely and stared at Ancil who was crouching next to him. Then he laughed shakily and grinned in relief at the reality of him and Kref and Mojag and Punzho who were gathered around him.

'I'm feeling that it's time you had a shave, laddie!' He winked. 'Feeling . . . great, never better!'

'But what happened . . . to your clothes?'

Glancing down Pyke realised that he had not dreamed all that after all. His demented encounter with the sentient probe and all that gibbering about a Zavri ancestor and those mad flying crystal splinters – it was damn well true. And it had trashed his clothing, which now was little more than a mass of holes held together by rags.

'Bugger it,' he said. 'I really liked that jacket.'

'Didn't you get it at the fabber kiosk on Blacknest Station?' said Ancil. 'I'm sure they could—'

'Where,' Pyke said, cutting in, 'the hell are we? Right now?'

He had suddenly become aware that they were no longer in

the buried complex, going by the cooler, fresher air that was wafting around.

'Probably better showing than telling,' said Ancil, who helped him to his feet and guided him over to a chest-high barrier of cracked, corroded metal where he leaned on a pipe-rail and stared out at the same massive fissure as before. Only now he was seeing it from high up on the other side of that deep dark trench, standing on a platform made from scavenged panels, tiles and decking. A walkway sloped down to where a bridge, a spidery-looking thing of poles and spars, spanned the gulf to another platform just visible in the shadows on the other side.

'It was that talking minibot who found us, Captain,' said Kref. 'We was lost over there and it showed us the way to the bridge but it didn't say anything about you being here.' The big Henkayan grinned. 'And I still got your luggage!' He patted the wrapped bundle hanging from his shoulder.

'Which is a great relief,' Pyke said. 'But we still need Khorr so that we can get our hands on a ship, and that murdering piece of slime is still back down there somewhere.'

'Fortunately, the treacherous Khorr is no longer crucial to your plan, Captain,' said a familiar voice whose smug AI amiability made Pyke clench his fists. He glared and took a step backwards as the Inheritor remote rose up from the shadows below the platform, its pinspot muted to a cool blue glow.

'You again,' Pyke said. 'So – why is Khorr no longer crucial? I hope you haven't killed him because I was really saving that pleasure for myself.' *After we get him to help us rescue Dervla and Win.*

'He's very much alive and crashing around in the corridors over on the other side, him and his compromised companion.'

'Compromised? Which is supposed to mean what, exactly?'

'It's a Zavri, inconstant persona thing – anyway, the reason Khorr is superfluous to your needs is because we can reunite you with your ship, the one that G'Brozen Mav borrowed—'

'Stole,' Pyke said. 'Get it right, he thiefed it right out from under me, the gouger!'

'As you wish, but the point is that we know where it will be in a few hours' time and if you allow us access to that portal-junction generator of yours we can input the correct location data. That is Zimzin technology, isn't it? They really were the masters of portable high-spec devices.'

'That sounds generous,' Pyke said, half suspecting what was coming.

'Look upon it as recompense for a very special task which we would like you to carry out for us. For Kaldro-Vryn.'

Pyke was sombre. 'A task, you say? Heard nothing about this when you were whisking me off through the darkness.'

'It comes down to a bargain, Captain, wherein you do something for us and we help you in turn. The shards of the Incarnalith were not an incidental detail, but integral to the job awaiting you.' The floating remote paused, its glowing beam surveying the puzzled faces of the crew. 'Ah, so Captain Pyke has not told you about how he has been imbued with the crystal shards of a Zavri ancestor several thousand years old?'

A frowning Ancil looked at Pyke but shrugged before the captain could speak.

'Well, that's not so unusual,' Ancil said. 'Lots of stuff the Captain doesn't tell us, like this whole thing with Mojag having a copy of Oleg's mind in the cyber-prosthetic bit of his brain, and how Oleg's been in charge for a while now ...'

Ancil's voice trailed off and the uncomfortable silence threatened to go on forever until Pyke gave Mojag – no, Oleg – a questioning look.

Oleg sniffed. 'Well, we were wandering around in those corridors, getting more and more lost by the minute, and you weren't there so ... I decided to tell all, full disclosure. They took it pretty well, too.' There were nods all round.

Not expecting such a matter-of-fact reaction, Pyke was bemused.

'So, you guys aren't weirded out? See, I thought you might get the cold freaks over it.'

'After the years I've been flying with this gang,' Ancil said, 'weird seems to be fairly normal to me.'

'Just so,' said Punzho. 'Indeed, the last few days have been fairly bizarre, even by our standards.'

'Weird is our middle name,' Kref declared.

Oleg gave a knowing nod and Pyke gave a rueful grin. 'Well ... excellent! It's a demented cosmos and I'm proud to be part of it!'

'Adaptability is a survival trait,' said the floating Inheritor remote. 'It makes us feel optimistic about your chances in the forthcoming technomachy.'

Pyke smiled, teeth gritted. 'And what might be my role in this upcoming pantomime – something gaudy and flamboyant, I hope.'

'With the Zimzin portal device we shall send you to Nagolger, one of the Shuskar fleetworlds – your ship will be there, along with the bold G'Brozen Mav. We urge you to put aside any lingering grudges and lend him your aid and comradeship, using, if necessary, every scrap of deceptive guile you can muster. The Chainer leader's goal is the same as your own, the Shuskar Citadelworld, but getting there presents a challenge. There are forcefield defences which can strike from what you call hyperspace at any unauthorised vessel which enters the Warcage. The ships stored on the fleetworlds have authority beacons installed, thus it will be necessary to commandeer one of them so that you can traverse the Warcage's interior and reach the Citadelworld safely. On arrival, you must infiltrate the Shuskar defences and get up close to the main control chamber – at that point the Incarnalith shards will leave your body, in a manner harmless to you, and take over all their instrumentation.'

Pyke was less than overjoyed at the prospect of encountering G'Brozen Mav, never mind having to cooperate with him in carrying what was without a doubt a monstrously unhinged plan (although the part about stealing a ship appealed to his sense of professionalism). But still, this machine, which had the nerve to call him devious, made his shifty-sense tingle every time it spoke. Then there was the matter of Dervla and Win.

'This had better work,' he said, 'or I will come back from the dead and pour stale beer into your circuits.'

'We have every confidence in your heroic abilities, Captain.'

'I don't know if ironic flattery counts,' he said. 'Now that we're clear about my part in this, I need something from you.'

'Something more than a ship, Captain?'

'Two of my crew were captured by Khorr, who handed them over to this Gun-Lord, Xra-Huld.' He stared at the hovering machine. 'I need you to find out what happened to them and where they are.'

'We have a somewhat limited access to Shuskar communications and we could scan for any useful information about your people, Captain,' said the remote. 'But keep in mind that once the Incarnalith shards assume control of their instrumentation then all their networks will be transparent to us.'

'I'm sure that there's more to the Big Plan than that,' Pyke said. 'After your crystalline friend takes over their machines, and you get your claws on them, then what?'

There was an odd silence which grew, and he suddenly realised that Ancil and the rest were staring at him. 'What?'

'Captain,' Ancil said, pointing. 'Look!'

Pyke raised his hands and swore when he saw dark blue letters tracing the same word over and over all across the skin on the back, the palms and the fingers – *Vengeance*.

'That's Kaldro-Vryn for you,' said the Inheritor remote. 'Harsh, but fair. And harsh.'

CHAPTER TWENTY-FOUR

The biomechanoid weapon was deeply embedded in Dervla's nervous system now, employing finely judged neural cut-outs to isolate her conscious awareness and any physical volition from the rest of her body. Now her body was like a shell and she was like the kernel rattling around inside as it and the gun went about their business.

That's how it seemed at first but later she realised that this analogy wasn't right, and as the Dervla-shell lurched around, cradling that horrible living gun, a memory from a couple of years ago just rose up and hit her with a shiver of recognition. Back then she had been on the *Scarabus* for less than a year during which time she had acquired the beginnings of the basic skillset: weapons, explosives and netrunning, mainly. Pyke had brought them to the Demaneph System, home to the Gulbas Orbital, one of Earthsphere's bigger navy installations. Pyke's destination was an asteroid called Plexy's, a place for cheap refits at knockdown prices. Plexy's – run by a one-eyed Gomedra called Plexy – relied on a supply of malfed or obsolete equipment scavenged from the Gulbas discard bins by shady types eager for easy cash.

The Plexy asteroid, in addition to its refurb pits, had been thoroughly tunnelled, its interior a maze of passages and chambers, including a room full of power armour and exosuits. So while the *Scarabus* was getting its hull shield emitters upgraded, Plexy offered to let Dervla take one of the combat exosuits out for a drive. She remembered seeing the suit – a brute, heavily armoured thing – standing in its charger booth. The original livery must have been dark green and blue but wear and tear had abraded much of the paint job away, leaving bare edges and corners that gleamed in the harsh light of the overheads. Dervla had clambered up, twisted round, slipped arms and legs into their padded grooves while Plexy went over to a control pedestal from where he powered up the suit's systems. At his prompting she moved the arms and legs a little then made it step forward out of the booth.

And almost seriously overbalanced, feeling the suit tilt forward, fearing that she was going to literally fall on her face – until Plexy activated some autobalance subsystem which snapped the upper torso back, righting her immediately. Over the next hour or so she learned how to walk, how to move her arms, how to monitor the balance sensors, how to swivel, how to pick things up and throw them, how to carry a heavy weapon in one of those big four-fingered hands and how to fire it.

And that, she reckoned, was closer to how she felt now, as if her own body had been turned into unfamiliar flesh which this vile invader, this ancient defiling presence, seemed to understand better than she did. She grew certain that the biomech was secreting narcotising drugs directly into her brain. While conscious and alert, she barricaded herself against any cooperation with the biomech, in thought or deed, but sometimes her awareness blurred and drifted and she could feel herself listening to a smooth, persuasive voice, then answering, then agreeing. Later, even the memories of these interludes seemed dreamlike and disjointed but it was entirely clear that, like Plexy and the exosuit, she was being taught how to cooperate with a tutor – except that this teacher was also her jailer.

Her early life had been a struggle to escape a severe and malicious domination, and later she'd gone to great lengths to avoid falling under the control of others, and yet here she was plunged into a nightmarish version of the very worst of what she had experienced. Being physically at the mercy of pitiless enemies was bad enough but the drugs and their attendant web of soothing lies meant that she was unable to trust herself.

Xra-Huld was perpetually followed by a coterie of aides, retainers, underlings and sycophants, Shuskars each and every one. To this audience the biomech parasite would deliver impromptu, pompous lectures, usually on the subject of its many previous hosts and the countless victories it had gained over a long sequence of enemies. These self-aggrandising monologues were never received with anything less than rapturous, adulatory applause. And as the hours of her grotesque incarceration ground on, Dervla's contempt for these grovelling Shuskar hangers-on was distilled into a strange kind of hate. From the biomech's comments and other hints, she came to understand that centuries of service to these vile tyrants had twisted the Shuskar into an underclass of indoctrinated minions, driven by the fearful minutiae of a hierarchy wholly dependent on the whim of those same tyrants.

During one of those grandiose lectures, Xra-Huld had spoken of a long quest for the perfect host species, one strong enough and versatile enough to provide a vehicle worth keeping, worth conquering with, one truly capable of fulfilling the all-encompassing ambitions of the biomech and its four companions. It spoke approvingly, almost hungrily, about Human physiology and pondered plans for capturing other Humans. That was when she realised that time was against her, that there was no guarantee that Pyke or anyone could possibly free her from the utter certainty of a capitulation and indoctrination just as total and demeaning as that exhibited by the Shuskar.

The only way out was death, an ending, to close the door on her own life.

That, however, would mean gaining a measure of conscious control. And that would mean cooperation, a conceding, presenting a convincing simulacrum of voluntary collaboration. But what would she have to do to persuade the biomech that it was getting what it wanted?

The long, long climb out of the imprisoning depths of Akreen's mind was temporally arduous – it seemed to be taking forever. As they progressed, Gredaz's focusing exercises continued to work minor marvels, the spidery trees and bushes now had tiny ash-grey leaves and more than once Akreen saw winged creatures flitting across the misty endless stairway. For a short time it struck him as both exhilarating and freakish that he was travelling through his own mental terrain with a precursor who created enduring spectral surroundings out of ... well, out of what, exactly? Twisted, shared perceptions? The unused capacities at the back of his mind?

But such speculation palled after a time and Akreen set the matter aside as a minor imponderable. Instead he focused on trying to follow the comments, curses and exchanges taking place between his usurping precursors. As near as he could be sure, it appeared that they – led by Rajeg – were still in league with the vile Khorr and continuing his pursuit of the Zavri ancestor by following the faint resonances peculiar to Zavri biophysiology. Only they had given up trudging around the maze of corridors and stairs and were now using the Zavri body strength to literally punch and tear a way through walls if there was no easy route close by. This approach caused several minor cave-ins along the way, and a couple of major ones that left Akreen's physical form completely though temporarily buried. Even with these delays, however, they were still making faster progress than they had before.

Akreen did note how his precursors still reflexively indulged their vestigial character traits, despite being collectively in the ascendancy. Casx venting his outrage was like the blare of battle horns, Iphan was the essence of superior indignation, Togul's monumental disdain could belittle a conqueror of worlds, Drolm's irritation served only to elevate his own paramount importance, while at the head of this fractious squad was cold Rajeg, who proved adept at exerting pressure in a variety of forms, lack of time, snap decisions, expectation of others (in this case Khorr, who carried the anti-Zavri weapon), possible loss of honour, and even possibly appearing weak and indecisive. And at every juncture they went along with Rajeg's suggestion. Akreen had to admit, it was masterful.

And after that earlier assessment he had realised that one of his precursors, Zivolin the mischief-maker, was conspicuous by his absence. Which was not a bad thing, he decided.

So the plodding ascent through the imagined landscape went on and his precursors' childish squabbling continued to filter down from the heights of his conscious mind, echoes and disjointed fragments of angry dialogue and monologues. Paths were still being smashed through decrepit walls while Rajeg maintained his working relationship with Khorr. Then Akreen heard them babbling about the gang of Humans who were spotted crossing a bridge, but that had been well over five hours ago, according to Rajeg (who was enjoying seeing how long every task took, down to the second). Rajeg's exchanges with Khorr seemed to be mainly on the subject of Zavri social hierarchy, precursors and lineal descendancy, and it seemed clear that Rajeg was merely humouring him.

Gredaz slowed to a halt on the stair a couple of paces ahead and half turned to look down at Akreen. 'Be advised that we shall soon arrive at the Subcognitive Plateau. Where we must wait.'

Saying no more the tall figure, now garbed in full-length battle-elder's robes, turned and resumed his climb.

'Plateau?' said Akreen. 'You made no mention of this before.'

'It did not exist before.'

Gredaz's logic was undeniable.

Akreen kept on going, letting the repetitious tedium of one foot after another absorb his awareness until it took on a mesmeric quality which, oddly, added details to his surroundings, scratches and worn edges on the stairs, clusters of shiny purple berries on the bushes, little yellow flowers on the gnarled-looking tree branches.

A light impact on his chest made him stop, abruptly dispelling his reverie. Gredaz had stopped him with an outstretched hand, which he then swept out to his side in a grand unveiling gesture.

'We have arrived – this is the Subcognitive Plateau.'

The fog had dissolved into a thin mist and Akreen could see an expanse of dark barren rock spread out before him, wide enough that its edges were hazy grey. When he looked back the way they had come, the steep stone stairs wound down to disappear in thick fog. All around and above were shifting billows of grey.

'So, we cannot go any further,' Akreen guessed out loud.

'Correct. In this metaphorical context, above us, beyond the veil of non-awareness, your precursors are enthroned in the courts of perception, to a greater or lesser degree. While they prevail we cannot proceed.'

Akreen felt an urge to be openly disdainful of their situation, but decided instead to trust that Gredaz was in fact following some kind of rational plan.

'All that we can do now is wait,' he said evenly.

'We wait, hopefully just for a short while.' Gredaz directed a stony gaze at the shifting grey overhead. 'Our presence here will not go unnoticed for long.'

Akreen gave him a narrow look. 'You are expecting us to be noticed? By whom?'

Gredaz glanced at him. 'You are not the only one receiving the benefit of my counsel.'

Akreen stared at him, feeling slightly dislocated by that comment. 'Not the only one ... ?' Was Gredaz in contact with the outside world? But how would that be possible? ... And who would he be counselling?

Suddenly, and thoroughly unexpectedly, Gredaz laughed, a dry, slightly hoarse sound. A sharp smile occupied his lips as he looked over at Akreen.

'At last,' he said, pointing upwards. 'Listen to them and be ready.'

Gredaz was right. The steady background mutter of exchanges, arguments and bitter asides from above had surged in volume and anger. Incoherent roars passed back and forth, principally involving Iphan and Casx with Rajeg issuing contemptuous denials in between his attempts to cope with the real-world journey through the corridors. Akreen marvelled at how the petty squabbles of those vestigial personae could sound so vast and godlike from this perspective.

Then another voice cut across, the thunderous, raging bellowing of Togul, a stream of accusations of betrayal and deadly insults besmirching his honour. And just when it seemed that the deafening sound could not get any louder the voices of Casx and Iphan rose to a wrathful clamour, building the cacophony to a crescendo.

'Get ready!' yelled Gredaz, pointing upwards. 'Keep your nerve – you will experience no discomfort!'

Seconds later gravity drained away, replaced by a force tugging them upwards, slowly at first then faster, gaining velocity, flying through white streaming fog ...

Then something snatched him out of that crazed headlong

ascent, and dropped him into abrupt reality. Sense impressions jolted him, almost leaping at him so swiftly that he gasped. He was lying sprawled and alone on the floor of a dim corridor, amid the dusty debris smashed out of a hole in the wall. As he levered himself into a seated position he noticed fragments of metal scattered among the rubble, then looking around he saw the split and shattered wreckage of a weapon that he knew all too well.

[*I have it on good authority that Khorr received something of a beating before he managed to escape,* said Gredaz.]

[*Ah, it was a thing of beauty,* said Zivolin. *My carefully orchestrated campaign of innuendo and half-truths brought them to a pitch-perfect brink of pent-up fury and hate. As soon as you reached the plateau I triggered the final bitter notes of my symphony of rancour. As you can see it has played out to a most satisfactory conclusion.*]

As Akreen got to his feet he picked up the wrecked anti-Zavri weapon and saw where repeated impacts had smashed apart the emitter barrel.

'So what actually happened?' he said in his thoughts. 'Where is Khorr?'

Zivolin was effusive with self-congratulation. [*Well, my hate-drama, being a drama of hate, needed a secondary antagonist as an external focus of the acrid hate-storm I was stirring up, someone to serve as a stand-in for grand diabolical powers single-minded in their dread resolve. Rajeg, of course, was the primary antagonist, the betrayer. Iphan and Casx were primed to seize control from Rajeg and attack the unsuspecting Khorr; Togul, however, had become convinced that the pair of them were conspiring against him. So, with Rajeg ejected from the seat of command and those three fools brawling like senile toys, your presence on the plateau was all that was needed to tilt the cognitive balance in your favour.*]

'Most skilfully done, honoured Zivolin,' Akreen said. 'And what of Khorr?'

[*Ran off, bloody and beaten*, said Gredaz. *I caught a glimpse of Iphan's handiwork while he was in control for a few moments.*]

Akreen tossed the broken weapon away, and surveyed his surroundings. Ancient, eroded corridors poorly lit in patches by strange clusters of crystal-like nodes that gave off soft, opaque glows. Cracked walls spilling heaps of pebbly dirt in which emaciated plants had at one time taken root, sprouted, withered and died. Ceiling collapses half blocking passages but occasionally providing an accessible slope to the floor above.

And there, right there at the faint and trembling edge of perception, something was resonating, a kind of high, sighing hum that called to him.

[*Can you hear it?* said Gredaz.]

[*The song of the Ancestor*, said Zivolin. *A summons out of antiquity.*]

'Yes,' Akreen said. 'I can hear it, but how can a Zavri live for thousands of years and not be noticed?'

'He can if his mode of existence is closer to death than life,' came a new voice.

From the shadows along one corridor a floating blue point of light came gliding towards him. As it drew near, Akreen saw that it was an odd ridged spheroid smaller than his fist, and that the light was a diffuse blue beam projected from one of several apertures.

[*At last*, said Gredaz. *A messenger from the one that guards the Ancestor.*]

The glowing device slowed to a halt a couple of paces away. 'Welcome, Akreen, First Blade of the Zavri Battalions.'

Akreen stared at the hovering remote. 'I am told that you speak for the one that guards the Ancestor.'

'Well, we all speak in that capacity, in one way or another.'

'So, do you represent the Apparatarch, or whatever it has become?'

'Hmm – the same question as before yet more pointedly framed. We call ourselves the Inheritors, even though our inheritance amounts to a few trinkets and relics and an insurmountable burden of responsibility. But we must make do with what we are given, or chance upon, and it was our good fortune that your precursor, Gredaz, heard the subtle coded message which we fed into the portal web.'

Akreen nodded, still racked with uncertainty. 'Are you satisfied that I am who I say I am? I have experienced some fundamental disturbances since my arrival, challenging to the very core of my being.'

'For us, the Zavri aura is as telling as the facial expressions of other species, so yes, First Blade, we can tell from the comfort and harmony indicators that you are the rightful possessor of this form. The previous occupier gave off such a garish clash of hues that we knew to avoid making any contact.'

'This is a great relief,' Akreen said. 'I am now ready to learn all you can tell me about the Ancestor before . . . before whatever happens next.'

'Good – however, we are presented with a problem.'

[*Tsk. The long, long centuries must turn these machine intellects into lovers of prevarication*, said Zivolin.]

Akreen remain composed. 'What kind of problem?'

'It is to do more with ends than means. You see, after the unfortunate ambush you suffered at the hands of that Shuskar thug, Khorr, we concluded that you were a lost cause and with time for ploys growing short we opted for the only available option.'

A pair of spheroid remotes, identical to the first, descended from a break in the ceiling and lined up next to it.

'The explanation covers ancient history as well as recent events, and therefore is a little intricate,' the remote said. 'So rather than have you plod all the way to the Ancestor chamber, we can transport you there in a bearer field and tell you all you need to know as we travel. Is that agreeable?'

[*Most agreeable*, said Gredaz.]

[*Very glib and thus untrustworthy*, said Zivolin. *These ancient machines always have some twisty agenda.*]

Despite sharing Zivolin's reservations, Akreen accepted the invitation and moments later was being whisked along corridors while reclining in a forcefield web projected by all three remotes. He learned new things about the Great Unshackling War, the millennia-ago war that obliterated the Apparatarch and its allies while elevating the victorious rebels led by the Shuskar and their ominous Gun-Lords.

He heard tell of the Ancestor, a Zavri general called Kaldro-Vryn, who approached the minds of the Apparatarch near the war's end, while the forces of the Shuskar were drawing ever closer – of how Kaldro-Vryn had told them of his intention to undergo a crystallising metamorphosis and asked them to find a safe hiding place for his final form, an Incarnalith. He heard of how they'd agreed, and buried his crystalline remains deep underground, only, when the Shuskar fleets started their bombardment, for it to prove not to be deep enough, field-driven vibrations from their mantle munitions penetrating the armoured vault and shattering the Incarnalith into thousands of fragments.

The explanatory account then switched to more recent events and Akreen was surprised to learn of the appearance of the Human Pyke and his companions, then astonished to hear that this same Pyke had been chosen to play host to the shards of the Incarnalith.

'This is the "only available option" that you spoke of earlier,' Akreen said.

'You were in thrall to your precursors,' said the Inheritor remote. 'We could not possibly use you as a host, so when the Human and his crew appeared a while later and followed your tracks into the deep city, we contrived to separate him from the rest and convey him to the Incarnalith chamber exactly as we are doing with you.'

'Is he still here, on Gatuzna?'

'Long gone, First Blade. He and his companions have gone to meet with another band of valiant rebels with the purpose of stealing a fleetworld ship to use against the Citadelworld. The intention is for this Pyke to gain access to the Shuskar control hub there, at which point the Incarnalith shards will pass from him into the enemy's control systems. Full mastery of the portal web and the shadow-force defences will at a stroke fall from their grasp.'

'So why are you taking me to the Ancestor?'

'Because we need someone to cross over into the Sunheart and distract the Gun-Lords while Pyke takes over their communication and control systems.'

Akreen was stunned. 'The Sunheart? Where the great stardrives reside, where the Warcage derives its power and energy? I have only ever heard children's stories about it. I did not know that it was possible to travel there.'

'Our sun is as much a creation of the Builders' genius as the portal web and the world anchors,' said the remote. 'The drives are self-maintaining, self-repairing and impregnable, but the vast catavaults hold other secrets and power, as well as the stardrive control boards and the navigational system. You can see the inherent risks.'

Akreen frowned. 'Would the Shuskar really set the Warcage on a collision course with another star system?'

'The underleaders might not, but it is likely that the parasitic Gun-Lords would, if they are faced with certain defeat.'

'Certain defeat,' Akreen echoed. 'How plausible can that be?'

'Our probability studies assigned it a low rating,' said the Inheritor remote. 'But in a complex system unseen variables can have strange multiplier effects. At any rate, your presence in the Sunheart with the Incarnalith remnants offers the chance to shut the Shuskar out from control of the stardrives and all other systems. They will be fatally weakened and, Gun-Lords or no, their days will be numbered.'

[*Damn, these machines are persuasive*, said Zivolin. *I'd sing the battalion anthem if I knew the words. But then, who can win battles with charisma alone?*]

[*For once I share your precursor's doubts*, Gredaz said. *You should ask how they intend to get you to the Sunheart from here – I had heard that the only way was through a portal gate on the Citadelworld.*]

Giving a wordless, internal assent, Akreen then said, 'May I know how you are going to convey me to the Sunheart?'

'By our unrivalled yet subtle use of the portal web,' said the remote. 'We were with the Builders when they created it – we were their assistants, critics, mirrors for a myriad designs and overseers of their gradual emergence into the stuff of reality. The millennia have not dimmed our most precious memories, thus we still know of certain pathways which can give access to secret places of the Warcage. Although some pathways can only be used once, obviously.'

By now Akreen's journey had reached the huge, sheer-sided gulf that cut through the underground complex. He could feel a cool breeze on his unelaborate dermal covering as the remotes bore him down into shadowy depths. He descended past levels of sliced-open rooms and corridors, all like a decayed, weather-worn parody of sedimentary existences.

A dark opening appeared off in the hazy murk, loomed closer and closer and swallowed them all. Along a tilted, debris-strewn

passageway they swept, the cold blue beams of the remotes picking out corroded details right along the length of it before they
came to where a large, heavy hatch stood wide open. Through it
they dived, flew level for a few seconds then pitched into another
descent that lasted several minutes, a plummet into blackness.
Then they slowed and glided forward again, following an angular, irregular course which took in more smashed-up corridors
and another vertical shaft before he was brought before a tall
glowing entrance. The remotes set him down a short distance
away and he finished the journey on foot, following one of the
remotes into the glow.

It was a circular chamber empty except for a long cradling
plinth at the centre. The curving wall was stippled with triangular tiles, only a few of which shed light on the carpet of dark
thumb-sized splinters that surrounded the plinth. The chamber
was still, deadly quiet, yet Akreen's senses were thrumming and
oscillating in tune with the resonance which had been so faint
earlier.

'These are the remains of the Incarnalith of Kaldro-Vryn,' said
the Inheritor remote.

'How is the hosting of these fragments accomplished?' Akreen
said.

'There is some state-alteration involved, but we are not
entirely sure how this is achieved,' said the remote. 'When the
Human received his portion of the shards they sank into his flesh.
For a Zavri it may be the same, or it may not.'

'Very well, I am ready – should I go over to the centre?'

'If you would be so good. The coalescent awareness of the
shards understands our purpose and is likewise ready to proceed.'

There was little else to say. Akreen strode over to the plinth,
feeling some of the hard fragments underfoot as he did so. With
every step he could feel tickles of energy, as if he were entering
an invisible web.

[*It is a faint motile field mesh and you are the focus*, said Gredaz.]

Akreen had just reached the plinth when something struck him in his right thigh. There was a curious sensation at the point of impact, a tiny vibrant sound, and when he looked down he saw a dark splinter sink into the silvery texture of his skin, leaving no mark behind. Another struck him, in the neck, then another in his chest, and another, and another. In seconds it became an incoming torrent of shards and he stood there, eyes closed, arms outstretched, revelling in the reverberant song that hummed and trembled through his body. The vibrations of it coursed through his skull, his mouth and his eyes, a thunderous metallic storm of beauty.

When the ending came it was swift, a sudden tailing off, a scattering of stragglers, then an amazing, serene silence. He opened his eyes, stared down at his form and saw a fading pattern of overlapping circles.

'You now carry the Incarnalith of Kaldro-Vryn,' said the Inheritor remote. 'The greater part of it, anyway.'

[*A peculiar situation*, said Zivolin. *There is a new presence but it resides in your body not your mind. Like some kind of half-aware warbeast, prowling and hungry.*]

[*An over-fanciful evocation but correct in the essentials*, said Gredaz. *Your new passenger is a vestigial sentience like your precursors, but it relies on the instincts of a warrior.*]

Akreen regarded the Inheritor remote as it floated over to join him.

'What is the next step?' he asked. 'Given your superlative mastery over the portal web, should I expect a portal gate to the Sunheart shortly to open before me?'

'The Warcage, as we said earlier, is a domain of secrets and secret places. Everyone must, however, live with the consequences of the errors of the past and we are no different. In the closing stages of the usurpers' war, we fortified several worlds against the enemy alliance but all fell in the end to vicious and extreme weapons, like the mantle munitions, which were then used to smash those worlds and others into uninhabitable wrecks. Victory only served to sharpen their lust for destruction ...'

'... which led to the Wrecked Worlds. Even Zavri juveniles have to learn the history, though it speaks of those events from a somewhat different perspective.'

'The victors are permitted all manner of atrocities since they can be attributed to the despised enemy when it comes to writing the histories,' said the remote. 'But we go over these grim happenings so that you may understand what lies ahead of you. What do you know of the Ruined Road?'

[*Ah, I see*, Gredaz murmured in Akreen's thoughts.]

Akreen curbed his irritation and said, 'It sounds vaguely familiar – I must have heard the name some time ago but without any informative context.'

'It was the path that Maklun took to reach the Citadelworld of the Shuskar.'

Maklun was the leader of the rebel underworkers of Beshephis, whose uprising spread to a dozen worlds including one of the fleetworlds. His revolt threatened to overwhelm the Shuskar dominion until they retaliated with biological warfare so lethal that seven worlds had to be quarantined and, after the collapse of the rebellion, patrolled until they could be replaced with new harvest worlds.

'Maklun was from one of the Valzo pit-cities,' said Akreen. 'Notorious hotbeds of malcontent and criminality.'

'Maklun was no Valzanian,' the Inheritor remote said. 'That was a story put about by Shuskar misleaders. But that's incidental – our point is that Maklun travelled the Ruined Road with our help, he and a small band of followers. It is a string of portal gates that lead through the Wrecked Worlds, ending in that rarity, a hub-gate.'

Akreen frowned. Normal portal gates provided travel to one, occasionally two, other Warcage worlds but a hub-gate could provide a choice of a dozen. 'None of the Wrecked Worlds, or even those of your allies that escaped the greater retaliation, hosted a hub-gate.'

[*There have only ever been three*, Gredaz said. *At Nexus City on Togema, in the White Insilica, Grand Escalade headquarters on Ivazal, and on the Citadelworld. At least, this is what we are told.*]

'The Builders were methodical when it came to large-scale designs, always testing their concepts with pilot projects, and the portal web was no exception. They ordered the construction of a prototype hub-gate on an agri-world and tests were run on the rest of the portal gates as they were gradually encoded into the shadow-force lattice that holds all the worlds in place. More powerful and sophisticated hub-gates were built and hooked into the portal web. Everything worked perfectly, like an intricate dream made real.'

'So the Builders decided against dismantling their prototype,' Akreen said. 'Why?'

'Official reason given was its research value as a testbed for future improvement, but we think that the Builders could not bear to demolish a hand-built thing of beauty. As well as being superlative technologists, they were also great aesthetes.'

Just then Akreen became aware of a cold tingling in his hands. Looking down he saw groups of Zavri letters slowly appearing and disappearing on his palms, across his knuckles, around his wrists, the same word over and over – *Vengeance*.

'Such consistency,' remarked the remote. 'Kaldro-Vryn was never one to curb his impatience.'

[*Ah, splendid, a lover of battles and slaughter*, said Zivolin. *Your recently ousted precursors should take him to their shriv-elled little hearts!*]

Another remote flew into the chamber, carrying a small oval object in its bearer field while the speaker remote continued.

'The portal gates that were damaged in the war we repaired, slowly over several centuries, now that the victors had turned their attention to other matters. Our resources were rudimentary, almost inadequate, so the repairs lacked the necessary precision. Portal target accuracy is, shall we say, variable but you should still arrive within three evrn of the next gate. This detector will keep you on track.'

The newcomer remote floated up to him and dropped the oval device into his outstretched hand. At the same time pinpoints of light began flickering in a narrow portion of the chamber wall. The flickering points formed a tall arch which soon filled with the pulsing shimmer-darkness of a portal gate.

'Some final advice,' said the Inheritor remote as Akreen moved towards the portal. 'Some of the worlds you will have to traverse were so devastated that they have no atmosphere – others were so poisoned that only the most viciously mutated lifeforms could hope to survive. The Zavri are exceptional warriors but even you should exercise caution on the Ruined Road.'

'How did Maklun survive?' Akreen said.

'Ah, he was the warrior-supreme,' the remote said. 'And we did give him a suit of power armour!'

[*Oh well – at least we have the splintered remains of the long-departed Kaldro-Vryn embedded in our epidermis*, said Zivolin. *Who or what would dare stand against us?*]

Akreen allowed himself a sardonic smile as he walked up to the dark portal and stepped through.

CHAPTER TWENTY-FIVE

Their arrival in the high orbital shell of Nagolger was smooth and quiet and apparently unnoticed. The *Scarabus* went in fully stealthed, deception tactics at the ready, all sensors running on maximum passive. By the time they reached the low orbit shell the fleetworld's defences should have noticed something and the *Scarabus* AI would have started deploying countermeasures and cycling through the spectrum of ploys and cloaks and misdirects.

But there was nothing. The passive detection system had registered long-range scans from orbital and ground defence installations but there were no widecast challenges or warnings, no targeting beams probing for them, and no sign of attack fliers scrambling or heading their way.

'Something is wrong,' said G'Brozen Mav. 'Could this be an elaborate trap?'

Toolbearer Hechec kept his eyes fixed on his console display as he replied. 'Far from it, my leader – I think we may have strayed into some kind of ongoing insurrection. And there are no Chainers involved.'

Sam and G'Brozen Mav exchanged an astonished look before turning to await further explanation.

'The ship AI has been monitoring all the standard communication channels but there is a strange silence in the frequencies, an absence of what should be a busy spectrum of transmissions.' Hechec shook his hooded head. 'This is a planet with a hundred-million plus inhabitants, one of the Shuskar's two fleetworlds, and there's not a signal to be found. *But* – this ship's hyperspace systems have picked up something unusual. Scar, would you explain?'

'Certainly,' said the ship AI. 'Shipboard systems have been tracking unusual field resonances emanating from the subspace layer between real-space and hyperspace. Data analysis leads to the conclusion that several subspace jammers have been activated at locations across the settled areas surrounding the shipyard complex. Communications frequencies have been rendered unusable.'

'Deliberately?' said G'Brozen Mav.

'Unquestionably, my leader.'

Mav gave a surprised laugh. 'So some others have been planning their own rebellion, separate and secret from us. How long until we enter atmosphere?'

'Less than two minutes,' said Hechec. 'Are we holding to the original landing destination?'

The Chainer leader nodded. 'It cannot be a coincidence that we and our unknown possible allies chose one of the fleetworlds to move against. By the time we touch down they should know we're here, then we'll find out if they want to talk.'

Or fight, Sam thought but just nodded and smiled, joining in the guarded optimism. Her own anticipations had by now dwindled to nothing. If some kind of new alliance was about to emerge then her chances of seizing the *Scarabus* and going to search for Rensik were very slim indeed. On the other hand, her chances of dying in a firefight thousands of light years from home had just improved dramatically. Terrific.

As their descent flightpath followed its preconfigured curve, mapping sensors began providing layouts of the terrain surrounding the multiyard complex, geographical highlights and topographical landmarks. The datastreams fed more details into the maps, transport links, urbs and suburbs, residential and industrial patterns, all confined to a rough crescent stretching about eighty miles at its widest. Hechec said that this distributed, connected conurbation went by the name of Craitlyn City, although it lacked a true centre. And in the concavity of Craitlyn City lay the yards, the focus of both the city and the planet Nagolger itself – five immense construction canyons radiating from one side of a circular launch basin over a mile across. Each yard was over half a mile long, with nearly all of its workings confined below ground, levels of workshops, foundries, labs, immense lifting equipment, ancillary assembly lines, and all of it automated. And beneath that was an immense arsenal of mothballed ships, quietly slumbering in their metal cocoons. Or so Hechec said.

On the other side of the circular launch basin was a large, fan-shaped facility which, according to the Toolbearer's mysterious personal archive, was an unused and abandoned repair and recovery drome.

As the *Scarabus* descended through the cloud layer, the bright, sunny view of pure white softness turned into rushing, blurring greyness. As they emerged from the clouds it soon became clear that a rainstorm was currently sweeping across this part of Nagolger. The multiyard and its surrounding city were situated on the eastern side of a sizeable peninsula jutting from the northern coastline of Nagolger's single large continent. This was a temperate zone and the eco-system was lush and abundant. Through the veils of rain Sam could see clusters of buildings and webs of roadways, even before they reached the outskirts of Craitlyn City.

This really is a substantial metropolis, Sam thought. *Hechec said earlier that Craitlyn City is the planetary capital, so what*

level of security is guarding the shipyards? If the local com-
mander is hunkering down to defend them against any moves
from these unknown rebels, any plan to steal a mothballed ship
could be a non-starter.

'Combat alert!' said the ship AI suddenly. 'Missile contact –
inbound from starboard 53.7, declination 18.1 – hull sensors
report laser tagging, variation indicates manual operation – hull
stealthing has been engaged ... missile veering off course.'

G'Brozen Mav and Toolbearer Hechec looked visibly relieved
but Sam's instincts told her that similar attacks should be
expected. But then, she also knew what Pyke's ship was capable
of.

'We'll be okay,' she told the others. 'The *Scarabus* has some
pretty sophisticated evasion systems. But prepare yourselves – if
the situation on the ground is chaotic, someone else might take
a shot at us before we reach the LZ.'

As it turned out, there were two further attacks before they
slotted into the final approach: another missile launched from
directly beneath their flightpath and a volley of short-range
exploder rounds from a rooftop air-defence battery. The former
required a combination of sideslip manoeuvring while close-
quarter projectors blinded the missiles sensors; the latter were
neutralised by augmented flank shields which deflected incoming
shells and partially absorbed their explosive force.

The landing zone was an open grassy area along one side of
a large park just to the west of the multiyard complex. A wide
hexagon was marked out on the grass, perhaps for a community
game of some sort, Sam thought, as the *Scarabus* swooped in,
slowing amid a whirling cloud of leaves caught up in the suspensor helices. There were faint bumps when the ship touched down
on its landing gear, followed by a slight lurch or two as the auto-
levelling system did its thing. The sense of relief was palpable and
shared, even though nerves were still on edge.

'Any signs of activity in the immediate vicinity?' G'Brozen Mav said.

'Two lifeforms within light arms range,' said Hechec. 'No energy-weapon signatures detected. Nearest other lifeforms are clusters of inhabitants in the round tower blocks beyond the landscaped ground west of our position.'

Sam felt a twinge of hope – if their arrival had gone unnoticed by those fighting in the city, Mav might keep to his original plan to reconnoitre the yards and thereby make it possible for her to take control of the ship. But with his next sentence Toolbearer Hechec eliminated any chance of that.

'We are detecting a large ground transport approaching along the multiyards perimeter roadway. Carrying eleven lifeforms, some with energy weapons.'

G'Brozen Mav frowned. 'Not an assault force, more like a delegation – but we'll all go armed if a face-to-face is what they want.'

Trying to look enthusiastic, Sam nodded and smiled while taking out her factab, which had been recharging off her body heat. She had been checking it regularly since the flight from Armag, forlornly hoping for a message from the Construct drone, Rensik, but to no avail.

Until now.

Her hopes leaped at the sight of the little green book icon; she quickly tapped through to the contents and found . . . only a letter 'o'? For a moment she was puzzled and irritated, then she took a closer look and saw that it wasn't a letter but a tiny image, a black circle with a black dot at the centre and a green dot halfway between. Sam stared at it then nodded to herself.

So the idiot machine is on the Shuskar Citadelworld of all places, she thought, feeling both relieved and daunted. *But how the hell are we going to get there?*

The big ground transport had veered off the perimeter

road and powered its way over hillocky grass to halt a short distance away from the *Scarabus*, partially screened by high bushes. Three figures in long billowy cloaks and odd head-gear had emerged and were waiting just outside the big white hexagon. G'Brozen Mav had chosen Sam to accompany him, along with Toolbearer Hechec and two of his personal guards, who flanked him as they descended the ramp from the main hold entrance.

Sam's nose twitched, smelling odd woody smells on the air. The grass underfoot was short, bristly and blue-green. The sky was full of broken clouds hurrying overhead on high winds while the occasional fresh breeze gusted in from the north to stir tinkles and rattles from the peculiar trees of this world. And the cloaks of the three who waited also streamed and flapped.

As they drew close, Sam saw that they were at least humanoid, yet their faces were narrow and vaguely feminine. The tallest of the three wore an odd conical hat with a gold triangle perched upon it. The other two wore close-fitting yellow caps marked with red spiral symbols.

G'Brozen Mav halted a few paces away and gave a gracious but closely measured quarter bow. The responding bows were equally finely gauged.

'Welcome to Nagolger,' said the tallest of the three. 'Am I correct to name you, sir, as G'Brozen Mav, now sole leader of the Chainer rebels?'

Mav inclined his head. 'I am he, and your own appearance is very similar to that of the troops of the Syluxi Host – does General-Father Possal still command?'

'The illustrious Possal retired very recently – I am General-Mother Belwaris, commander of all Syluxi forces on Nagolger.'

'It is an honour to exchange amicable terms,' said G'Brozen Mav.

'An urgent question for you, Noteworthy Mav,' the General-Mother said. 'Does your vessel go under the name of the *Sca-ra-bus*?'

G'Brozen Mav could not keep his surprise from showing. 'Yes, General-Mother, it does! I am at a loss to know how you could possibly know that ...'

General-Mother Belwaris smiled, half turned and raised a hand. 'Bring them forth!'

From the rear of the big transport, half hidden by foliage, five figures emerged, descending a ramp, flanked by a pair of Syluxi troopers as they walked round and came into view. As soon as she saw the tall, willowy Egetsi and the hulking bear-ish Henkayan, Sam knew that they had to be the crew of the *Scarabus*, so the dark-haired, rangy man in the lead had to be their captain, Brannan Pyke – even if his clothes looked as if they'd been attacked by scissors.

She knew the circumstances whereby G'Brozen Mav had come into possession of Pyke's ship so when Mav stiffened and muttered something under his breath as he saw who was approaching, Sam suddenly wondered how this rematch was going to work out.

Yet Pyke seemed quite amiable as he approached, perhaps even pleased to see G'Brozen Mav – and Sam had to admit that he was good-looking in a keen-eyed, unflappable kind of way. But what was the problem with his clothes? At close quarters, they looked ready to fall to pieces.

General-Mother Belwaris beckoned the captain and his crew forward and it was a smiling Pyke who came up to G'Brozen Mav, hand outstretched.

'Mav! Damn, but it's good to see yer okay, still fighting fit and ready for a barney, eh?'

The Chainer leader appeared baffled and open-mouthed as he shook hands. 'Captain ... yes ... you look well ...'

'Can't complain, Mav, cannot complain. We've had our ups and downs, haven't we, lads? And the sights! Some of the things we've seen would make your eyes bug right out.' Pyke paused to point at the Toolbearer. 'Hechec! Still following this crazy man's quest?'

'It is my vow, Captain, as always. The ship flies well, too, as always.'

'Good to hear.' Finally, Pyke turned to Sam. 'A newcomer, I see, and from my corner of the starry skies, if I'm not mistaken.' He gave a slightly ironic bow. 'Brannan Pyke, ma'am, captain and owner of the free-trader, *Scarabus*.'

She allowed herself a professional smile. 'Lt Commander Samantha Brock, Earthsphere Intelligence.'

The eyebrows went up and he smiled brightly.

'Is that a fact, now? If this is about those unpaid docking fees, I swear I was about to—'

'It's all right, Captain, I have no interest in unpaid bills,' she said. 'For the moment.'

Pyke chuckled, a little uncomfortably. 'In that case, Lt Commander, I am at your disposal – for the time being.'

'I am deeply gratified,' announced General-Mother Belwaris, 'to have been instrumental in reuniting old friends but my time is limited so I must bring this to a close. Now, this wordy rascal' – she glanced at Pyke – 'insists that he came to Nagolger to steal one of the Shuskar ships then leave the Warcage forever, fully intent on resuming a career of illicit activities.'

'One man's unguarded vessel is another man's legitimate business opportunity,' said Pyke.

'But is this truly the case?' the General-Mother went on. 'Captain Pyke could be telling the truth or he could be telling a version of it. When I turn to the renowned G'Brozen Mav, however, I am certain that he is here to seize a ship or ships in order to bolster his campaign against our Shuskar masters, despite the lamentable defeats he and the Chainers have suffered in the last few days.'

She smiled a cold smile and an awkward silence held sway for a long moment, maybe two, before G'Brozen Mav shrugged and spoke.

'I do not deny it, General-Mother – after all, we are clearly on the same side.'

'If we were, you would have been made aware of our existence and our clandestine preparations long before now,' Belwaris said. 'Our secret insurgency includes other armies and has been long in the planning but it depended on the squabbling Chainer rebels triggering uprisings on several worlds – once the Shuskar, already distracted by the unshackling process, committed all their meagre forces and their attention was wholly occupied, then we could act. This is just one among thirty-seven worlds that we have or are in the process of capturing, all under a shroud of dead communications.'

'Impressive planning and secrecy, General-Mother,' Mav said. 'But if we're fighting the same enemy, I fail to see why we're not on the same side. Please, allow me to have a Shuskar ship and we can be on our way.'

'I do not mean to sound dismissive but, truth is, the Chainers are not entirely trustworthy. Look at all that chaos which the spy Khorr caused for you.'

G'Brozen Mav glared at Pyke. 'Ah, so you felt the need to unburden yourself of these matters.'

'Hah, well, y'know how it is – you get rescued from unfriendly locals, you get offered food and very passable drink, you get sociable, sharing stories and the like, and that's how—'

'In any case, noteworthy G'Brozen Mav, you will not be taking delivery of a freshly unwrapped Shuskar vessel, nor will anyone.' General-Mother Belwaris's expression was sour. 'The entire multiyards complex has been sealed by the security forces in charge. Heavily armoured shutters and blast doors block every point of entry and the armour is impenetrable – we know, having used every available weapon on it, resulting in not a dent, not so much as a scratch. So, leader of Chainers, I am afraid that your journey to Nagolger has been for nothing.'

Sam saw a flicker of weary despair in G'Brozen Mav's face, but only for a moment.

'This is indeed discouraging news,' he said. 'I am grateful to you for sharing it with me so openly. Of course, my ... our ship carries several detection modes which we would be willing to employ on your behalf, to scan the multiyards for any weakness in their defences ...'

'A generous offer,' said the General-Mother. 'But unnecessary – our own survey teams have been most thorough. Now, I must return to my duties – my subordinate captains can only achieve so much without my personal oversight.' She looked at Captain Pyke and G'Brozen Mav. 'You are welcome to stay on Nagolger as observers, but if you feel the need to stray and scavenge for supplies I require that you avoid tangling with the Shuskar Governor's soldiery, which means keeping away from conflict areas. You should also consider the multiyards a restricted zone.' The General-Mother smiled and spread her arms, fanning out the cloak which was attached to her wrists. 'Or you could simply embark and depart, return to lead the Chainers. I am sure they have need of your talents.'

With that, she and her attendants turned to leave – and Pyke uttered a theatrical clearing of the throat. Belwaris paused to regard him.

'Captain? You wished to say something?'

Pyke's smile was relentlessly amiable. 'Your shining excellency, I think your guards still have a few of our things ...'

'Why yes, I believe you may be right!' The General-Mother snapped her fingers, one of her attendants hurried off to the big transport and returned with a rustling blue plastic bag and a bulky, cloth-wrapped object.

'I remain intrigued by this device, Captain,' she said, patting the wrapped bundle. 'The workmanship has an archaic quality, like something out of antiquity.'

Pyke spread his hands and smiled. 'Most exalted General-Mother, as I said, it's just an energy field cooker – if I had a replacement focus grid and a few ingredients I could whip up a tasty snack for you. As it is, it'll be put away in storage until we find someone selling the right spares.'

The Syluxi general gave him an intimate smile. 'How plausible – I almost believe you. May you and your friends continue to live safely.' She turned to leave, waving a farewell that could have been for everyone or no one, and sauntered off towards the big transport, flanked by her attendants. Sam watched her go, waited till they were climbing aboard, then faced Pyke.

'We really needed that ship!' she said. 'It would have been useful if you had used your influence—'

'Well, y'see now, the problem with influence is that once you use it you then find that you've got less than you did before!' Pyke grinned. 'I decided to use that finite resource to hang on to something important.'

Sam eyed him coldly. 'We are engaged on a vital mission and you may have lost us our only chance of succeeding . . .'

Pyke held up a hand. 'It's all right, Lieutenant, I know what kinda fix you're in – in fact, I bet I know more about it that you do yourself.'

'How can that be possible, Captain?' said G'Brozen Mav. 'We didn't know we were coming here until some hours ago.'

'I was briefed by, let's say, an interested third party.'

Sam's smile was bland and composed. Was Pyke naturally irritating or was it a facade?

'Trust is based on openness, Captain,' Sam said. 'What party are you referring to?'

'You know, we're wasting such an awful lot of time when we could be—'

'Please, Captain,' G'Brozen Mav said. 'Who have you been conversing with? If we are to work together, don't we deserve to know?'

Pyke frowned and studied the ground for a moment or two, then nodded. 'A machine intelligence which claimed to be a survivor from the time of the Builders.'

G'Brozen Mav was wide-eyed. 'Are you sure it was an artificial sentience? Where did this take place?'

'We were pretty sure it was an AI, all right,' Pyke said. 'We encountered it on a world called Gatuzna—'

'One of the Ashen Worlds,' Mav said. 'Where the machine minds stood their ground and tried to stem the onslaught of the Shuskar!'

'So these AIs are still around?' Sam said, suddenly anxious at this new development.

'It certainly looks that way,' said Pyke. 'They said they still have access to the portal web and can listen in on some of the comms traffic – they were able to use the portal system to send us here, to the vicinity of the yards, which is where the General-Mother picked us up.'

'And these AIs sent you here?' Sam said. 'For what purpose, exactly?'

'Why, to provide you with the incomparable talents and hard-won expertise of myself and my crew,' Pyke said with a smile that verged on smugness.

Sam shook her head. 'Please, don't insult my intelligence – why are you really here?'

'To help you get to the Citadelworld!' Pyke spread his hands. 'It's where you wanna be, ain't it?'

'Did the machines tell you that we were coming here to commandeer a fleetworld ship?' said G'Brozen Mav.

Pyke smiled. 'Commandeer – that's exactly the word that the machine used. Now, a ruffian like myself on occasion might say "purloin" or "liberate" but really, let's get honest – we are talking about downright burglarious thievery and that, good people, is our area of expertise!'

'How sad, then,' Sam said, irritated by his grandiosity. 'Because those yards are locked up tighter than a vacuum seal so you won't be getting to play master thief, I'm afraid.'

Still smiling, Pyke crossed his arms. 'And that's where you're wrong.' He glanced at G'Brozen Mav and Toolbearer Hechec. 'Anyone notice that there's a sizeable facility just north of that honking big launch basin?'

'We scanned it during the approach, Captain,' said Hechec. 'Old surveys said it was at one time a repair and refit dock. Sensors showed it to be disused and half blocked with wreckage. Also picked up clusters of very weak energy sources but no sign of power generation or feeds.'

The captain nodded. 'Aye, well, seems that wreckage used to be a transorbital lifter, a massive vessel that they used to carry ships from orbit down into the repair docks and back again. It would appear that about eighty-odd years ago one such lifter was on its way down, fully laden with some Shuskar thug-wagon that got a bit belted during one of their homicidal police actions. Anyhow, this big damn lifter was on the last stage of its descent when it lost power and fell out of the sky, basically, plummeted a mile and slammed right through the shutters and down into the repair docks. Because that was the last working lifter they had – and also because the docks were so trashed – they salvaged what they could, buried the dead, abandoned the place.'

At the very moment that he paused, both Sam and G'Brozen Mav breathed in and made to speak, so Sam, in the cause of diplomacy, smiled through gritted teeth and gestured for the Chainer leader to go ahead.

'A very detailed summary, Captain,' he said. 'How could you possibly know all this?'

'Well, funny thing – the Syluxi decided to recruit some of the locals, the Irnagol, into a militia to carry out a few support functions, like guarding the weird offworlders recently detained in the vicinity of the yards!' Pyke grinned. 'I got talking with one of our guards, a gabby old boy called Egltny who had a few illuminating gems to relate – seems his father witnessed the Carrier Crash, as they call it, and wrote a report on it for the local blabsheet back then.'

'I'm pretty sure you'll get to the point of this digression,' Sam said. 'I'm just concerned how much longer it's going to take.'

'Please, Captain,' said G'Brozen Mav. 'Time is not our ally. The sooner we can reach the Shuskar Citadelworld, the sooner we can wreck their command centres, and perhaps save other worlds from punishment.'

Sam noticed a hard look in Pyke's eyes for a moment, then he shrugged and was all roguish geniality again.

'Okay, then, fine, shame on me for trying to bring a lyrical touch to the proceedings. Right, this is the way of it – to safely cross the Warcage we don't need a Shuskar ship, we just need the signalling beacon that tells the defence systems to leave well alone.'

Understanding lit up Sam's thoughts. 'And there's a beacon like this on every Shuskar ship!'

'You've nailed it, Lieutenant. Question is, how to search or track for one – according to Egltny, his father said that there were several ships down in the repair facility when the lifter crashed right into it.'

'That might account for some of the sensor data we collected during the approach,' said the Toolbearer. 'We detected a scattering of weak energy sources. Are or were there any security units guarding it?'

'Nothing – it was evacuated, then all connecting tunnels and access ways were permanently sealed.' Pyke glanced at his crew. 'All we need, then, are some configured hand detectors and we can get to work.' He gave the nod to one of his crew, a wiry, dark-haired man whose stained overalls were covered in pouches and pockets. 'You about ready for that, Ancil?'

'What, scavenging through decades-old abandoned shipwrecks while time's running out? Honestly, chief, you get us all the best jobs!'

While aboard the Shuskar flagship, the Gun-Lord's hooded servitors switched the Construct drone from the sealed transparent box to a slightly larger container with a solid floor and lid and walls consisting of a finely made triangular mesh. Rensik could see why – the elaborate suppression field was more easily and closely controlled via such a mesh, ensuring that he was unable to project any field or energy wave beyond it. He was isolated from the world of data communication so completely that it was as if he were encased in silence.

But as they moved him from one prison to another he was pleased to note how they left the lid of his previous oubliette sitting to the side.

His new confinement, however, still allowed him the opportunity to study his surroundings. The cams and sensors built into his casing provided a wealth of detail in the visible spectrum alone. On arrival at the Citadelworld he was retrieved from the armoured cell he had been in since his capture near Armag, and carried off as part of the retinue that trailed after the Gun-Lord wherever it went. The Human figure of Dervla was nowhere to be seen, however, so Rensik was quick to survey the vicinity and build up a picture of his current location.

The Citadelworld was a small, tidally locked and airless planetoid orbiting at some thirty-odd million miles with one hemisphere always facing the Warcage sun. The Shuskar headquarters, melodramatically named the Shadow Bastion, was on the nightside, a broad, stepped tower rising from out of a deep, artificial crater. Adjoining it, a great engineered canyon provided dock and yard facilities for visiting ships. The Construct drone took note of the echoing emptiness of the place, especially the darkened docking levels above and beneath where the flagship rested upon a series of immense ceramic and metal cradles.

The place is almost deserted, Rensik thought as a rattling cart whisked his cage and a selection of containers and luggage along a depopulated concourse, accompanied, of course, by a pair of stern and heavily armed servitors. *How nice – they have me cooped up in my very own portable dungeon yet they still do me the courtesy of treating me as if I pose a threat. Which, of course, I do.*

On the blindside of the drone's boxy casing, out of sight of the guards, a small aperture slid open and a dull metal tetrahedron no bigger than a fingernail fell out. The ticking sounds it made as it landed on the floor of Rensik's cell were masked by the rattling of the cart. Moving on tiny roller beads it passed through a gap in the mesh, zipped over to the edge of the cart and was gone. It was the third such metamodule he had produced since being stuck in the mesh cage, although he had waited until leaving the flagship's hold before releasing the first two. His retasked nanorepair node was more than halfway to completing the fourth and final one, due for despatch in less than a minute.

Pragmatism had made it clear that his chances of escaping from the suppressor cage were pathetically low, so after running up an inventory of all resources contained within his chassis-shell he settled on a drastic scheme. He would cannibalise nonessential parts from his own sub-assemblies and reconfigure the nanorepair node to build a minidrone, directed by a cut-down, streamlined version of himself, which would mean contributing a segment of his own substrate. The loss of archived data would be worth the chance of sticking a wrench into the evil engine of the Gun-Lords' plans.

The minidrone's orders were straightforward – after assembling itself, it was to find some kind of data port and hack into the comms system of the Shadow Bastion, and send a brief message via the portal web, keyed to Sam Brock's work tablet and set for hidden repeat every hour or so. Like the previous message, it would be a tiny graphic, only now it would be a red dot at the centre of a circle, hopefully clear enough for even a bumbling organic to decipher. By this time, her negotiations with the Chainer leaders should have borne fruit and they might be persuadable towards the notion of mounting a rescue operation of some kind.

However, reason dictates that relying on such a clever and effective intervention may be the merest folly – this is a bunch of blood-chemistry-driven organics we're talking about after all!

As a failsafe, in case no one at all was coming, the minidrone's secondary mission was to locate and sabotage any control systems that helped the Shuskar maintain their power and dominance. And after that, create as much chaos and disruption as possible.

As the last metamodule was despatched, the cart reached a point on the concourse where the floor above curved off to the side, allowing the perspective to widen and open out. The Shadow Bastion was suddenly revealed in almost all its entirety, a massive circular tower faced in a coppery material, rising in stepped levels, stippled with windows both lit and dark. Balconies jutted here and there, as did a few landing platforms from whose glowing entrances infrequent small craft came and went. It was an image of solidity and strength but it was negated by what the cart passed by along its way.

The concourse was littered with all kinds of detritus, the desiccated husks of long-abandoned luggage mingled with skeletal remains. Every surface bore the evidence of centuries-old firefights, bullet holes, explosive round craters, blast flares, charred areas sweeping from floor to ceiling. Rusty, burnt-out shells of vehicles shoved to the side and at one place there was a big, ragged-edged bite out of the concourse where a bomb or a missile must have struck.

From files leached here and there, the Construct drone knew that the Shadow Bastion had once been known as the Pillar of Endeavour, back when the Warcage was called the Great Harbour of Benevolent Harmony, when this planetoid was the seat of the Builders, the place from which they planned and created and ordered this entire immense, astounding piece of macro-engineering. The state of decrepitude of the docks and concourse levels and the degraded purposes to which that great tower had been turned was an authentic tragedy, despite it being the end point of centuries of abuse at the hands of clueless organics.

And now he could see a wide glowing entrance on the same level as their concourse, clearly the cart's destination. Signs of life were visible there, figures moving about, small loader units carrying containers into the tower but if anything this empha-sised how vacant and desolate the rest of the citadel was.

This place is a corpse of the past, still animated into a sem-blance of life by the Shuskar, just as their cruel and ruthless regime – which should have either fallen or collapsed long before now – is being kept in its position of dominance by the parasitic Gun-Lords. Usually, a rotten tyranny like this would only need a strong determined shove to bring it to its knees but this … this one is going to need something a bit more brutal and relentless.

*

In the murky gloom of the repair dock Pyke was hanging next to the immense angled shape of an ancient Shuskar spacegoing vessel, suspended in one of the *Scarabus*'s antigrav work harnesses as he tried to scrape away layers of filth caked on to the hull by dark underground decades. Somehow he had to uncover enough clean metal for the penetrating scanner to clamp on to, then maybe this decaying old hulk would give up its secrets. And just then, over his headset, he heard Ancil say, 'Holy humping cyberdemons! Can't tell him that; he'll not be pleased!'

Pyke exhaled noisily. 'I can hear you, ya divot – left it switched to send. So, tell me what, exactly?'

There was a click on the channel and the voice of Toolbearer Hechec spoke. 'There may be a situation, Captain – we are still gathering data – but two of those weak energy sources that we detected before have started moving. One is moving towards G'Brozen Mav's team and the other is heading for you and Lt Brock.'

Why can't it be easy in, easy out? he thought. *Just for once …*

Pyke's suggestion that they salvage an authorisation beacon from the old hulks down in the abandoned repair facility had gained acceptance from Mav and Lt Brock, after which they settled on a two-team approach. While G'Brozen Mav and one of his guards descended to a vessel on one of the lower docks, Pyke and Brock would investigate the ship brought in by the doomed lifter. Emergency impact barriers had been raised to block the main access at the time but the plummeting lifter had punched right through. The lifter and its cargo came to rest halfway down the five main docking levels, its load-bearing supports buckled and wedged into the workshop plaza columns, embedded in concrete. The hull-grips had not failed, though, and now the ship hung amid a web of lifted superstructure and impact barrier framework, its prow angled downwards and tilted slightly. Handheld trackers led Pyke and Brock to the rough location of the weak energy source but only deep-burst scanning would reveal its nature.

Pyke fingered the control studs on his earpiece. 'Did you get that, Lieutenant? Seems that something is creeping around down below. I'm sure it's nothing to get freaked about, probably just cleanerbots sweeping up some of the skag I've been scraping off here, but if you want to take off back upstairs ...'

'How considerate of you to worry about me, Captain,' came the lieutenant's voice over the set. 'But, please, don't fret over my safety. In fact, if you run into any difficulties you can be sure that I'll be on hand to lay down some suppressing fire for you.'

Pyke smiled at the dark. 'That does give me a nice warm feeling, to be sure, as well as a tweak to the curiosity – you don't sound much like a regular kind of spook to me.'

'I've not always been an intelligence officer, you know.'

'Aha! Active service, combat duty, the sky-blue line! Wonder which operations you been in—'

'Not a subject that is or will ever be up for discussion,' Brock came back abruptly. 'Now, are you just about finished scraping a clean spot on the hull? Mine's been ready for a good two minutes.'

Pyke delivered a snappy salute with his free hand, the one that wasn't digging at centuries of accumulated dirt and dead roots with a metal trowel. Over the headset Brock gave an audible sigh.

'You know that I can see you.'

Pyke waved at the lieutenant's helmet beam, shining in the darkness over on the other side of the ship's upper hull. 'Always happy to act out for an audience, Lieutenant, that's my problem, as me dear ould ma was happy to point out on many an occasion. Right, that should be enough of the crap removed. Fixing the scanner in place now.'

He dug a small domelike device out of a thigh pouch,

positioned it on the scored, scraped hull plate, then pressed a side button – bonding feet clamped it in place and Pyke chuckled.

'Ready when you are, Hechec!'

'Scanning now, Captain ... I hope you and the lieutenant are keeping an eye on your harness charge levels.'

'Mine are still at 31 per cent,' said Brock.

Pyke eyed the metre tab at his waist, which read 26. 'Yeah, about what I'm at too.'

There was an extended moment of hissy channel silence, then the Toolbearer spoke. 'Sorry to relate more bad news but it appears that the beacon we need has been removed from this vessel – the energy source is vestigial leakage from a stack of cells.'

Pyke grimaced in annoyance and struck the filthy hull with his trowel. 'Are you sure that there was one to begin with? ... How can you tell?'

'The penetrating scan revealed an armoured blister housing about eight metres from your position. The recess it protects would have contained a bulbous unit about the size of a Human torso, but it is empty. I now surmise that the beacon units have an integral power source, while the nearby cell stack is an emergency backup. If it's any consolation, G'Brozen Mav's investigation of the ship down on the first level has revealed the same set of circumstances.'

'Not really consoled, Hechec, sorry.' Pyke frowned. 'So they went to the trouble of yanking out the beacon from this one, same as they did with the one downstairs ...'

'Looks like standard operating procedure,' Brock said over the channel. 'In which case ...'

Pyke snapped his fingers. 'They'd have to store them somewhere!'

'Well done, Captain,' said Hechec. 'G'Brozen Mav reached that same conclusion only twenty-three seconds ago.'

Pyke sneered. 'Well, ain't he just a great big smart-pants!' Trying to ignore Brock's sniggering on the open channel, he went on. 'Any more news on those mobile energy contacts?'

'Yours appear to have come to a halt directly below you, Captain.'

And we're up here which is fine, was what he was about to say when a cold tingling wave swept through his hands. He gazed down and in the light of his helmet beam he saw a word repeating itself across the backs of his hands – *above above above* ...

Quickly he looked up, in time to see a shadowy, multilegged form run along a long, twisted crossbar and leap off the jutting end. He could make out a knot of clustered limbs as it fell in a smooth arc ... and landed on Lt Sam Brock!

She yelled in panic over the channel, along with gasps and cursing as she struggled with her attacker. Pyke was aghast – the creature was hanging on with maniacal determination but the antigrav harness could not cope with the extra weight. From the moment the thing landed on her, Brock spun away in a falling trajectory, the beam of her helmet lamp resembling a pirouetting lighthouse.

Hechec was anxiously demanding to know what was happening as Pyke grabbed his own harness grav control, a glorified pistol grip attached to the waistband on the left, switched it to manual and leaned forward as he swept down after her. Then he updated the Toolbearer, said hell, no, he wasn't going to return to the surface with the harness charge he had left and if Mav didn't like it he could stick it in his pipe and smoke it!

Pyke would have tried to get a response out of Brock but only a weird cyclic buzzing was coming down the channel. It was difficult to discern what was happening but he got the impression that she was still fighting the thing.

Her descent seemed to be slowing and he was on a good intercept course. He glanced at his own harness charge meter – 17 per cent – and guffawed. Easy in, easy out? Who was he kidding?

As Pyke swept in closer and closer he tried to keep his head-lamp fixed on her, and grim details came into focus. With one gloved hand she was holding at arm's length a tentacled horror, a six-armed bot whose flailing segmented limbs seemed to be of different lengths and tipped with a variety of nasty tools, spikes, hooks, pincers and blades. Its longest tentacle had hooked into Brock's harness at the shoulder, making it too risky for her to simply release the thing. Also, her other arm's jacket was slashed and smeared with blood, as was the hand which she was holding at midriff level.

With only seconds to spare, Pyke decided not to use the heavy beamer strapped to his thigh. Instead he swooped in close and snatched one of the bot's other lashing arms, thinking that between him and Brock they could perhaps snap bits off it and turn it into junk that way. But the machine had other ideas – as he swept past and grabbed the loose limb, the machine released its hold on Brock's harness. Without that connection there was nothing to stop Pyke's momentum wrenching the bot out of Brock's grasp. To his horror, Pyke suddenly found himself grappling with a spidery thrashing machine-monster as his own antigrav harness began to lose height.

Brock's on the other hand began to gain altitude again, and he could just hear her yelling from overhead, 'You moron! Why didn't you shoot it?'

Falling through darkness while wrestling with a demented chunk of machinery hell-bent on poking out his eyeballs, Pyke could only utter a string of incandescent profanities. He had managed – St Symeon only knew how – to get two of the spider-thing's longest tentacles in his right fist while his left hand was wrapped around the innermost segment of another tentacle, right where it joined onto the central unit. But the former was the hand that could most easily get to the beamer pistol on his thigh while the other was out of the question. He tried calling Brock's name but the channel was full of hiss and buzzing.

Bastarding hell! Is this how I'm going to die? In the pitch-black bowels of a crapheap planet in the foulest armpit of the galaxy?

The spider-thing's central unit was an armoured hoop with a slow-turning iris which periodically opened up to reveal contra-rotating bands of razor-bright teeth. Its tentacles writhed and strained as its iris maw and the spinning grinder made a zzrrr-zzrrr-zzrrr noise that made the hairs stand up on the back of his neck. He knew that he had to act. Off in the distance he could see the light from two headlamps moving around close to each other – G'Brozen Mav and his guard, it had to be. He yelled at them, panicking now, knowing that he couldn't be far from the actual floor of the vast repair facility.

Gotta do it, he thought. *No time left for bottling it, boy – do it!*

So, seconds later when the bot opened its iris once more to bare those spinning fangs he rammed the pair of tentacles he was still holding straight into its razor maw.

'Chew on that, ya skag-munching pusbucket!' he bellowed.

Metal screamed on metal, underpinned by a rough, brutal grinding sound. The tentacles tugged frantically in his hand but he doggedly held them to it, mouth snarling with the effort. The machine writhed and jerked, its free arms trying to push him away, then one of its bladed tooltips finally got through the heavy material of his right sleeve and lanced into his arm. Uttering a curse he reflexively let go of the tentacles and they whipped away. Fuelled by rage he tried to reach for the beamer pistol but the tentacle blade was still embedded in his arm, twisting spikes of agony along his nerves. Only his grip on that other tentacle was now keeping the thing's grinding mouth from devouring his face.

But, laughing madly, he raised his right knee up against his chest, bringing the back of his boot within reach of his fingers . . .

Next thing he knew there was a bright flash, something that struck the spider machine's central housing. Jagged sparks crawled all over the iris mouth as the circular grinders slowed. There was a second flash, the machine spasmed once, went limp, and the tooltip blade withdrew from Pyke's arms as the bot fell away into the darkness. The sound of its impact came back only a few seconds later.

Headlamp angled upwards, Lt Sam Brock floated down in front of him, a faintly amused smile on her lips.

'So, not too badly wounded, then,' she said.

Pyke gave a rascal's grin, despite the throb of pain from his slashed arm. 'Nice shooting, thanks. But y'know . . . I had him, he was done for and I was just on the point of putting him down and dancing on his junkpile grave!'

Brock, head tilted slightly, nodded thoughtfully. 'That'll be why you're holding that boot, I imagine.'

'Totally rational explanation for that, I swear—'

'I'm sorry, Captain,' came Hechec's voice on the headset, abruptly. 'We have a serious emergency – G'Brozen Mav and his companion have retrieved a beacon from a storage locker but they have been waylaid by several sentry machines like the one you encountered.'

'Are their harnesses—?' Brock began.

'Exhausted, yes. I have reconfigured your trackers to lead you to their position – please hurry and keep them alive while we organise a rescue. We shall be observing radio silence from now, I am sorry to say.'

And the channel went silent. Pyke nodded – *Figures*, he thought as he tugged his boot back on, then dug out a field medpatch. As he pulled back his sleeve and applied the patch to his wound, he ground his teeth as its edges heatbonded with the surrounding skin and chemically cauterised the injury. Brock, meanwhile, was holding out her wrist tracker and orientating herself.

'Got it,' she said. 'You ready?'

'Always,' he said, matter-of-factly. 'Though my harness must be about ready to give up its engineered ghost.' He glanced at the meter – it was in single figures, but he shrugged. 'Ah, it'll be a breeze. Let's go bash some trash!'

Brock's harness gave out less than two minutes later, but as she was already less than ten feet up she was able to make a rolling landing on the dusty, detritus-strewn floor. For Pyke, the twenty-second cut-off alarm beeped at him about a minute after that, but then his harness failed almost immediately. He knew he was still more than thirty feet up and felt the panic mushrooming in his chest, choking his throat – until he landed on something like a broad tarpaulin caked with dust, which swirled around him as he burst through and hit another cloth surface which encased some kind of resilience whose solidity knocked the wind out of him. He was coughing and struggling to figure out where he was when hands pulled him to his feet and pushed him through a narrow gap in what looked in the lamp-lit haze like huge pleats of cracked, mouldering cloth.

'We're nearly there,' said Brock. 'Come on, run, and watch out for the sentry bots – they're everywhere!'

As she was talking, a three-legged buzzing machine came galloping out of the gloom and leaped at her from behind. But Pyke's burst-fire from his beamer pistol caught it in mid-air, converting it into scrap. Before he could even give a victory whoop, Brock was hauling him off in the direction shown on the tracker.

'Not far,' Brock said over the channel. 'Mav, we're close.'

'We could really use the help,' was the reply. 'This blaster is almost spent.'

Running through the darkness, swerving around the corroded remains of massive, indeterminate machinery, burning down the occasional feral bot that showed too much interest, at last they caught sight of a weak headlamp beam, wavering in the gloom up ahead.

'We can see you,' Pyke said, breathing heavily. 'Be there soon.'

'Hurry ... you'll have to climb the scaffolding, careful where you put your feet ... hah, take that!'

There was a sudden flash, an energy-weapon burst which for a moment revealed G'Brozen Mav near the apex of a sloping latticed pylon, outstretched hand pointing a blaster into the gaping jaws of a grotesque toad-like horror on three stilt legs. Then the murk closed in again. Second later, the shape of a sloping framework appeared and without breaking stride Pyke vaulted up onto the tilted metalwork, regained his feet and hurried up an incline of rusty struts. He could already hear sounds of fighting, G'Brozen Mav's cryptic curses, and the buzzsaw snarl of the sentry bots. And there they were, a dozen or more multi-limbed machines crawling and converging on the high jutting end of the pylon where the Chainer leader stood, lengths of heavy piping in his hands. The blaster must have given out. Pyke was about to aim his beamer pistol at the machine nearest to Mav when Brock spoke.

'I'll pick them off from back here,' she said. 'You need to be up there at his side – go!'

If hurrying up the sloping pylon had previously been a challenge to the dexterity, trying to run and gun was a nerve-jangling sprint of faith that the feet would repeatedly land on solid and secure sections of strut while he fired off beamer bursts that relied on instinct and peripheral vision. Yet his footing did not fail and precisely aimed rounds from Brock's particle gun flickered past him, keeping attacking machines from straying into his path. Pyke kept loosing beamer shots at the bots gathering around G'Brozen Mav, despite his unpredictable aim, and got there in time to put triple-bursts through two weird snake-things and kick a third off the side of the pylon.

The Chainer leader was on his knees, holding off a large four-legged, six-tentacled machine with one length of pipe while trying to beat it back with the other pipe. Pyke ended it with two well-placed bursts, then flipped the quivering, sparking remains off the pylon with the toe of his boot.

'Timely,' said G'Brozen Mav, panting as he got to his feet. 'Earlier would have been better.'

Pyke smiled, cupped a hand to one ear. 'Was that heartfelt thanks I heard, delivered in a manly voice wavering faintly from the emotion of the moment? I'm sure it was—'

'More important than gratitude is the beacon,' Brock said as she joined them, pointing at a drum-shaped unit from which clumps of wires sprouted here and there. 'Is that it?'

'It is,' said Mav. 'Poor Grelf gave his life protecting it.'

Pyke crouched down next to it, wiped off a patina of ancient dust and tapped his earpiece. 'Hey, Hechec, we got to Mav, he's doing fine, and we're also now the proud owners of a "Hi, we're evil too!" beacon, so any time you're ready for a pickup is good.'

But on the headset there was only silence. Pyke frowned.

'Er, when I said any time I really meant right away ...'

The faintly hissy silence continued. Pyke felt like hitting something.

'They must still be observing radio silence,' said Brock. 'Actually, we're early, going by the Toolbearer's instructions. He said keep Mav alive for 11.9 minutes and there's still ninety-five seconds to go.'

'You better take a look at this,' said the Chainer leader.

His outstretched hand was pointing to a glowing mass down on the floor, about a hundred yards away in the gloomy dark. Then he indicated the area around where they stood. 'And down below.'

By the light of their headlamps Pyke could see shattered and twisted fragments of the sentry bots they had so recently blown apart crawling, jerkily wriggling away in the direction of that distant glowing heap. A horrible association formed in Pyke's mind.

'How the croaking hell can all that junk be alive?' He gave Brock a hard look. 'Is it alive?'

'MD-life,' she said. 'Molecular-digital life. Every piece of every machine and bot down here is probably laced with exotic biocircuitry, with a scattering of low-grade AI hubs, little more than engineered RNA matrices running hunt/destroy/survive imperatives.'

Pyke shook his head. 'So we blow 'em to smithereens, and later all the wreckage rebuilds itself – now that's a tale to make Sisyphus weep!'

'We'll be doing more than weeping,' said G'Brozen Mav. 'Something is heading our way.'

The glowing heap had grown and continued to absorb additional fragments as it moved towards the small group of defenders. Pyke checked the charge readout on his beamer pistol, adjusting it for long-range accuracy, which had the satisfying side-effect of lethal one-shots at short range but unfortunately drained the cell quicker. At the same time the lieutenant was giving G'Brozen Mav her backup, a short-range slug gun, while rechecking her own particle gun, which once upon a time had been locked in a cabinet in the *Scarabus*'s armoury ...

When he returned his attention to the oncoming menace it had entered the periphery of the headlamp that someone had clamped to a protruding stanchion. It had a grotesque resemblance to a sphinx, outstretched limbs dragging itself forward while the featureless head, composed of a mass of animated bot remnants, wobbled and lolled.

'How long now?' he said.

'Thirty-five seconds,' said Brock.

Have we any idea what'll happen when the seconds run out? he thought. *Hechec and the others must surely be sending a rescue team ...*

His train of thought was rudely derailed when the sphinx's head started firing at them. Luckily, the aim was wildly inaccurate, sparks and metal droplets spraying from a random scatter of impacts, and Pyke and the others were quick to return fire. No one noticed the catapulted attack bots until they started landing near their position on the fallen pylon.

'Spring-loaded death-squids!' Pyke snarled as he tracked one incoming and blew it to pieces. 'What will they come back as next time? *How long to go?*'

'Time's up,' Brock yelled back.

Cursing, Pyke fired off a single burst at one writhing machine as it was crawling up from between the strut-lattices, and booted another off the pylon with a well-aimed kick.

'Well, what was the skagging point of a countdown in the first place?'

'Captain! Duck!' came a deep voice that wasn't the lieutenant.

Reflexively, he fell to his knees while craning his head to look upwards, just as Kref the Henkayan sailed past, dangling from a cable that ran straight up into the inky darkness above where a larger shadow stealthily glided.

'That's your guy!' said Brock.

'It certainly is,' Pyke said, getting to his feet. 'Now, take a moment, if you will, to watch an artist at work.'

As his flightpath drew near to the machine amalgam, the Henkayan unlimbered a stubby-barrelled grenade launcher from a back pocket, loaded a couple of shells and snapped it shut. The crawling machine collective had lost its sphinx-like appearance but it had spotted Kref's arrival and was already trying to lob bits of itself at him. But all he did was calmly aim and fire the nade into the heaving mass of bots as he swung gracefully past. A heartbeat later there was a tearing red flash and the machine mound erupted, throwing burning chunks of scrap in all directions.

'Clearly the technique of a practised professional,' said Brock with a laugh.

Pyke spread his hands. 'Taught the boy all I know!'

'Really?' she said, smiling. 'Did it take you long?'

Before Pyke could formulate a scathing retort, Hechec's voice spoke over the shared channel. 'Well done, Lt Brock and Captain Pyke – you stopped a crisis turning into a disaster.'

'Just so,' said G'Brozen Mav. 'Without you I would be dead and the beacon unit would probably have been absorbed into that creeping heap of filth.'

'True, true, all true,' said Pyke. 'Which is why we should get medals, for me, Brock and Kref ...'

'Aw, thanks, Captain,' said Kref from somewhere overhead.

'... maybe saying something like "For gallantry and heroism above and beyond the call of crazy-arsed eccentricity" – hey, that's not bad ...'

G'Brozen Mav patted him on the shoulder. 'I'll give it some thought.'

Pyke smiled wordlessly and leaned on a heavy cable stanchion, picking at curling patches of flaking paint while the Chainer leader went to help the recently alighted Kref attach his harness cable to the drum-like beacon unit. A moment or two later it was flying up into the shadows, reeled in by the winch in the *Scarabus*'s undercargo recess, which was its own self-contained airlock, though it was probably hatched open to permit direct access to the main hold.

He shook his head, struck by the oddest sense of loss he had ever experienced, a strange feeling spurred by seeing his own ship in the hands of strangers. Oh, he and the crew were back in charge, mostly, but something was gone, a curious absence at the root of things.

And I think I know what it is – all these people and connections and fights and seductions and enslaving and brute force, and who the black savage hell knows how many centuries of blood and death and sheer fired-up ultra-evil that have been inflicted on all these worlds and all those who sail upon them – oh, and all the crazy-mad things I'll have to do to stand a chance of getting Dervla back ... somehow it's changed how life is.

Kref was waving at him from the top end of the pylon, pointing at the snapcatch-tipped cable he was holding. Pyke waved, got to his feet and started up the pylon.

I'm no longer the master of my fate, he thought. *I really need to get back to some honest, good old-fashioned law-breaking. I just have to see these Shuskar pusbags put down in the dust first!*

CHAPTER TWENTY-SIX

She had tried so hard to make the biomech Xra-Huld believe in her deceptions, working on her mask of duplicity, striving to make it plausible and versatile, able to project a persona that was alert and keen and at the same time malleable and submissive. And it had been working – in allowing the biomech parasite to think that it was seducing her, she steadily regained more and more direct control over the humdrum aspects of physical existence, walking, manipulating unimportant objects, eating, elimination, dressing. One consequence was the steep scale-back of the drug dosages, both in strength and frequency. Another was the more accepting attitude of the biomech, making what it no doubt thought were kind words and encouragements.

Then, roughly an hour before the flagship was due to land on the Citadelworld, Xra-Huld went aft to the high-security cells to question a prisoner, a thin but wiry humanoid that might have been male, dressed in rags and shackled to the cell's overhead crisscross bars. An empty metal table stood off to one side. There seemed to be nothing untoward, no hint or sign of darker purposes. After the biomech had, through her mouth, asked a number of questions without getting any satisfying answers, Xra-Huld sighed and said, 'Then let us ask the rest of you.'

Suddenly, Dervla was plunged into empty blackness, a void

without sensation. Just as abruptly, with no way of knowing how long the black interlude had lasted, she was back in the cell – but now it was an exhibition of horrific butchery. The metal table had been moved to the centre and on its blood-spattered surface were numerous body parts laid out in neat rows and patterns. Drips fell from severed limbs and the head which hung above. Blood was everywhere and her arms were red to the elbows and above. The scene was vile and barbaric, overwhelming to her senses which were open and unfiltered. She gasped at the unbearable sights and began to back away, until all physical control was whisked away from her.

'We have sampled a great many sentient species across the millennia,' Xra-Huld said in her thoughts. 'Experience has granted us a subtle sensitivity to the actions and ploys of our chosen hosts, and a keen insight into their motivations. Some species turn out to be natural, docile vehicles which can be steered and utilised without difficulty; at the other end of the scale are those whom evolution has so fashioned as to blunt our methods of subordination, whether cognitive or narcotic. The Zavri are one such race – their physical might and longevity would make an ideal host but the nature of their minds and body chemistry fosters an obstinate resistance to invasive control and authority.

'You Humans present towards the weaker end of the scale, yet you have some fascinating talents and unexpected capacities for instinctive conjecture. But never forget that our deep experience of host minds will always lay bare your artless, threadbare plans – I decided upon this little demonstration to make clear how transparent your little schemes are to me. Be reconciled to your fate as my vehicle – your subjugation is inevitable.'

After that she was back to being the hapless passenger of her own hijacked flesh. Xra-Huld went to its chambers and had its zombie-like pseudo-female attendants clean off the gore and replace Dervla's own grubby clothes with archaic pieces of leather armour all daubed with red. Then it went out to parade itself before the Shuskar courtiers, those flatterers and grovellers, those heralds and celebrators, toadies vying with each other to deliver the most extravagant verses of praise. She had seen this kind of performance before, usually from delegations from worlds out in the Warcage, garish and flamboyant gifts from Shuskar governors painfully aware how far they were from the centres of power, the courts surrounding the Gun-Lords.

This histrionic pageant was just more of the same, and her by now habitual revulsion morphed into something cold and pitiless, the growing conviction that so many things would improve if the Shuskar were just erased from the picture. *Along with myself.*

There was a message from the bridge – the flagship was on its final approach for a landing on the Citadelworld, so the bio-mech went aft to supervise preparation for the cargo offload. The main hold was high-walled and dimly lit, with several heaps of deck-lashed crates and containers scattered around. Obedience-collared thralls brought in a series of different-sized cases, stacking them on two large pallets. Among this luggage was the mesh-sided receptacle containing the AI drone which had tried to rescue her.

You should have let me die, Dervla thought. *At least I would have been spared this …*

Then a pair of thralls carried in a medium-sized crate whose colour and despatcher markings seemed familiar. She stared for a moment, then recognition came – this was the crate containing the subspace scanner-caster that Bran had gone to such lengths to procure for that pus-sucking scumrat, Khorr. The grand scale of the irony was not lost on her – she had been there in the hold of the *Scarabus* when Khorr ambushed them with knockout vapour then stole the device, and now here she was, watching the same device being loaded up for the next stage of its journey. It was clearly of great value to Xra-Huld, but she could not recall any mention of it, or any orders relating to it – although it was possible that she had been rendered insensible when it was discussed. How would she know? How could she tell?

While the cargo pallets were being assembled, the flagship had completed its descent, micro-manoeuvring its immense bulk down between a twin row of handler surfaces which moulded themselves to the hull, cradling it as they lowered it level with an external dockside area. Heavy thuds and clanks sounded as clamps fastened their grip and adaptable access corridors affixed themselves. After a few seconds the hold doors parted with a rough grinding noise and a pair of unmanned low loaders rolled in. The hold grabs transferred the cargo pallets onto their empty flatbeds and once the guards had inspected the ties and restraints, then strapped themselves into the ride-along seats, the loaders wheeled around and headed out to the dockside concourse.

'Wars are not just struggles between armies, between weapon systems, between leaders and generals,' said Xra-Huld unexpectedly. 'A war is also a clash of plans. The Chainer rebels are poor planners but their support among the planetary populations is substantial and dedicated. These other rebels, however, the ones using jamming devices to isolate their targets from portal web communications, they are cunning planners – they have trained in secret without concern for popular backing and have held on to all the darkened worlds they have seized.'

In charge of Dervla's body, Xra-Huld left the hold and took a riser platform to the upper decks.

'What of your plans?' Dervla dared to ask. 'Are they being swept aside and overthrown?'

'Neither the Chainers nor these mystery insurgents have encountered the plans that will defeat and crush them. There is a saying – no plan can survive contact with the enemy. But a truer, more accurate version would be – no plan can survive contact with another plan. When opposing plans collide, the most adaptable will triumph!'

'Your confidence sounds pretty invincible.'

'My confidence is built upon unshakeable foundations,' Xra-Huld retorted. 'Our enemies do not understand the powers at our disposal – and that truth makes our plans invincible.'

Dervla could find no words to respond with. Xra-Huld clearly had an ace-in-the-hole, something that counted as a game-changer. And knowing the brute predilections of these ancient evil, soul-sucking mechanical snakes, it would be vicious, bloody and barbarous in the extreme. She had no idea what was needed to take down Xra-Huld and its depraved playmates, only that it would have to be some kind of king-hell-bastard counterstroke which was both inexorably mighty and unsurpassingly devious.

Oh, Brannan Pyke! – if ever there was a time for you to walk the walk as well as you gab the gab, that time has arrived. That colossal ego of yours has to get you into your big boots, strap on yer biggest gun, saddle up and ride – nothing less will do!

The little tetrahedrons raced along the concourse, tracking each other's short-range finder signals until they converged in a shadowy corner and commenced auto-assembly. Internal flip mechanisms helped to orientate themselves correctly, three grouped around one. There were tiny clicks as sides snapped together around the base then, simultaneously, they flipped up, joining themselves fully to the central one. Inner facets folded aside and packed components shifted into a prearranged layout, taking advantage of the new interior. Connections spread through the assembly and the primary power cell kicked, initiating startup.

Rensik 2.0 became aware through alternating waves of system and substrate checks. Each successive check augmented the cognitive domains until the 'itness' of the minidrone could unbind from the 'itness' of the perceptible surroundings and call itself 'I'. Now fully aware, Rensik 2.0 opened the data pocket marked 'Urgent'; it contained a series of orders from the original Rensik, along with background summaries on species, worlds, technologies and sociopolitical structures, profiles of a few key actors, the Human female, Dervla, and the biomech parasite. Rensik 2.0 analysed the orders and the supporting material, then stealthily glided out of the shadowy corner on its roller beads. A swift sensor scan revealed no one in the vicinity so it darted across the open concourse to where a section of the balustrade had been smashed away. From the jagged edge Rensik 2.0 could survey the upper and lower levels of the huge, long docking gallery, the mounds of age-old wreckage and newer rubble strewn across the floor, and the tapering, segmented tiers of the immense, coppery tower that rose at the far end.

Skeins of signals passed between the tower, known as the Shadow Bastion, and those few dockside systems still functioning. Rensik 2.0 fine-tuned its sensors and began analysing streams of data from the Shuskar citadel. It did not take long to ascertain what preparations were under way and how resources were being assigned, and what this implied. It all led the mini-drone to one firm conclusion:

Rensik 1.0, the original, was completely mistaken.

For example, the cargo offloaded from the flagship was on its way to the portal hub-gate at the top of the Bastion. Also, the generators had been made ready to deliver peak output to the hub-gate systems on demand. Cross-deductive analysis revealed that the hub-gate was due to create a portal through to a shielded facility inside the sun – that was where the key events were going to take place, not out here on this half-abandoned docking station!

Rensik 2.0 was resolved to act but Rensik 1.0's orders still had to be carried out, in some way or fashion, therefore a smart probe would have to be produced. Components would have to be sacrificed and retasked, some substrate, too, so that a cut-down, abbreviated version of itself could carry out the original's orders, with sufficient cognition to deal with any unforeseen obstacles.

Again, reconstructions took place. Nearly three minutes after the mechanogenesis of Rensik 2.0, one of its tetrahedrons detached from the others, sitting separate and motionless, while the main amalgamation flipped onto its roller beads and went off in search of the original Rensik.

The initialisation of Rensik 3.0 also activated the primary motility mode. Three facets lifted up and unfolded and extended themselves, then began to spin. Each rotor blade was nearly five times the length of the tetrahedron's sides and provided plenty of lift.

Rensik 3.0 sprang into awareness while riding a thermal updraught towards a huge tower. It consulted its orders eagerly, skimmed through the context summary, examined the incomplete internal plans of the Shadow Bastion and went about its task, more eager than before. The Shuskar communications centre was on level 14, above the layered forcefield which kept the great docking gallery, its wharfs and concourses, pressurised. The minidrone had to find an access with minimal security – fortunately, there were several exterior balconies jutting beneath the forcefield, each with sliding doors and porthole windows. The first three were firmly closed, their locks unresponsive, their interiors bare and deserted. The fourth was being used as storage, going by the wall of boxes and red-wrapped objects that obscured the room within. The fifth had an orangey-yellow light glowing from its balcony portholes and as Rensik 3.0 approached, the doors parted and a tall, green-uniformed Shuskar official stepped outside, smoke-filled vial in hand. A few moments later, when the vial was empty, Rensik

3.0 followed the official back inside, floating easily on the wafts of artificial heat.

After that it was just a matter of tracing a route through the huge but mostly unoccupied building. Venting ducts, interfloor waste pipes, and overhead retrofitted cable runs provided safe, concealed passage straight to the communications centre. This proved to be a large hall cluttered with stacks of equipment, much of it disconnected and piled against one wall, a layered monument of malfunctions. Arrays of lights were focused on the agglomerations of active, functioning apparatus, where a dozen or more operators shuffled from control panel to control panel, scribbling on wads of paper.

From a high dusty ledge Rensik 3.0 regarded all this with a kind of restless enthusiasm. Then, keeping to the upper shadows, it flew across to the main comm-feed, a heavy cable that travelled up a sturdy framework and through the ceiling on its way to the hub-gate on the top floor and to the external transceivers. Slowing to perch on a suitable cross-strut, the minidrone then carried out a burst scan of the cable and was exulted by its findings – the actual fibre-optic core was not a continuous medium but one concocted from several lengths linked by data junction manifolds with integral monitor ports. It was the work of moments to hop to a higher perch from which it could more easily plunge an interface needle through the cladding and straight into the nearest manifold's monitor port.

Attuning for stream speeds and utility modes took less than a second – decryption was unnecessary since the Shuskar had never bothered with encoding their signals. But this was all in the service of sending a message, not eavesdropping on the enemy. Rensik 1.0's orders were clear – send a short text message via the portal web, assigned to portal gate casting, and with its signal attributes preset to match the factab device carried by the Human female Brock. The message was brief – 'inside the sun – come quickly' – and when Rensik 3.0 launched it into the outgoing datastream he tagged it with a save-and-repeat-hourly rider command.

A curious satisfaction resulted from the completion of the original Rensik's task, yet this only lasted a few seconds before the minidrone's sensors began registering a compatible signal pattern in the incoming datastream. Closer examination confirmed that it was a Construct-configured message so Rensik 3.0 downloaded it, decompacted it, and examined the content. It said:

'Be advised – Earthsphere fleet comprising eighty-five vessels now heading for the megasystem locale – ETA is thirty-six hours from despatch of this message – safety of fleet is paramount – act accordingly.'

Rensik 3.0 studied the message timetag and realised that the ES fleet would enter the Warcage in less than one hour. Unless it was stopped it would be torn to pieces by the ancient hyperspace forcefield defences. The Construct minidrone was caught in a dilemma – the portal web could not be used to send a message to the fleet, but it had to do something!

But what?

CHAPTER TWENTY-SEVEN

The journey from Nagolger to Malgin-Kog was a short one, but it was the first sojourn out across the Warcage with the Shuskar beacon installed. Like everyone, Sam was on edge. Everyone, that is, except Pyke, whose ebullient cheer managed to divert his crew and G'Brozen Mav's people from the uncertainty of their endeavour, while reserving his roguish charm and sub-gallant wit for whenever his and Sam's paths crossed. Was this wise-cracking performance a tactic to maintain morale, or just the man's ego playing to a captive audience? He said that helping Mav's mission to attack the Citadelworld would seriously undermine the Shuskar, and thereby aid the ancient Builder AIs – which might then be able to track down his missing crew members. Her reflex cynicism said there was something more to it than that, but the possibility of him telling the truth could not be ruled out.

It took nearly two hours to reach Malgin-Kog, a semi-developed agri-world, and another hour and a half before the *Scarabus* was back in the air, ascending to space with an additional 200 Malginori Chainer troops on board. Most of them were packed into the main hold with the rest squatting in the corridors. The Malginoris were short but brawny and seemed to have a morose, almost melancholy disposition, which explained the subdued level of chatter, even in the hold. All were equipped with basic body armour and the standard load-out of light arms, but scattered among them Sam noticed lower-tech weapons: bows, axes, maces, even a heavy sword with a serrated edge.

When she mentioned this to Toolbearer Hechec he said, 'As an offshoot of the clan-houses of the Muranzyr they held on to the old martial traditions, even after they were deported from Murangosk and sent to Malgin-Kog. Having to exist with other transplanted groups forced them to maintain their formidable combat skills but they never forgot the crags and gorges of the world they were forced to leave behind.'

The journey from Malgin-Kog to the Citadelworld took over eight hours. Crossing the only apparently empty gulf of the Warcage was like tip-toeing through a cave of slumbering Tygran daggerbeasts. Even Pyke's compulsive output of morale-boosting and ego-strutting bombast tailed off somewhat. The crew's senses were alert, on edge rather than fearful, waiting for some external assault that would cry out that the jig was up, the ship was discovered and they had to run for their lives, if they could. The Malginori, for their part, had already attained a certain level of fatalism in the everyday round of life – they were composed and ready for whatever Fate had in store for them. Such a mindset made Sam feel irritated and impatient: during her stint studying that archive of ancient videogames she'd repeatedly encountered narratives that hinged on the fate or destiny of – usually – the game-player's character. These were primitive concepts that stemmed from the idea of a deterministic universe which, to her, was fit only for children and elders on their deathbed.

The Shuskar Citadelworld came into view on the *Scarabus*'s bridge screen, filtered to take account of the sun's proximity. As their flightpath took them nearer, tension on the bridge screwed higher and nerves began to jangle. Sam kept expecting alarms to go off, or the AI to warn of incoming attacks, but the approach continued, calmly, smoothly, unbroken by interruptions.

According to Toolbearer Hechec, however, the Shuskar beacon installed on the *Scarabus* was definitely exchanging data with the citadel's docking systems.

'The dock is directing us towards an upper berthing platform,' said Hechec. 'Should we comply?'

Pyke shrugged. 'Any sign of heightened security, automatic weapon points, troops scrambling into position? Any targeting beams?'

The Toolbearer shook his head. 'Some activity near that big tower at the far end, but otherwise the docking levels appear deserted. No alerts that I can detect.'

'No obstacles in our way, then? Nothing to stop us just dropping in on 'em?'

The Toolbearer's small wrinkled face looked concerned. 'The docking system is providing a guide signal to an upper-level platform, Captain. Dropping will not be necessary.'

Pyke smiled. 'Ah sorry – just tripped over a chunk of the old Human expression, there.' He looked at Sam and G'Brozen Mav. 'Time we got the troops ready for disembarkation – Hechec, will we have those floor plans by the time we land?'

'The console in the main hold is replicating a batch even as I speak.'

'The question that most concerns me,' said G'Brozen Mav, 'is the hazardous operation of this portal generator of yours. Can you be sure of its accuracy?'

Pyke had taken Sam and the Chainer leader and the Toolbearer aside during the long trip and explained the true nature of his secretively wrapped bundle. Their initial scepticism was dispelled when he set up the device and gave an irrefutable demonstration by creating an oval portal at one end of the room and a second at the other end.

'The range is slightly, well, a bit variable, and it's nothing like those interplanetary portals you fellas have got,' Pyke said. 'But once established it's as solid as a rock – even after the direct projection is switched off, both portals remain open for over a minute. The only snag to it is the need for a clear line-of-sight, which is down to the whole test mode parameters thing.'

G'Brozen Mav frowned. 'So there is no way to shut the portals down after the switch-off – they remain connected and open for more than a minute, is that correct?'

Pyke nodded, Mav's frown deepened, and Sam saw the problem.

'Open one end in occupied territory, without sufficient protection, and it could become a door for the enemy,' she said. 'Get a lot of troops through in just a minute.'

'Which is why you could only open the far-away door in a spot the enemy cannot see,' Pyke countered.

G'Brozen Mav got to his feet. 'We won't know what our tactical options are until we see what we are actually faced with.'

'The high ground, the low and the cover,' Sam said. It was an axiom she'd learned early on in officer training.

'Couldn't agree more,' said Pyke, smiling as he sprawled in one of the workstation couches. 'I'll be along presently.'

Sam knew that the sloppy lounging was calculated to get under her skin, so she just arched an eyebrow at the grinning fool as she followed G'Brozen Mav off the bridge. Sure enough, about five minutes later, after a quick visit to her quarters to change into fresher combat lights, when she went down to the armoury to gear up, there he was, checking the action of a Belton-Nock flechette pistol.

'Isn't that a little lightweight for you, Captain?' she said.

Pyke gave a lazy smile and a deep gravelly chuckle came from the hulking form standing next to him.

'Don't worry, miss – he only uses that one to keep the flies away, eh, Captain?'

'Too right, Kref, me ould son. Bugs and crawlies, can't abide 'em at any price. But don't you worry, Lieutenant – 'cos when we run into the real big game I've got just the machine for the job.' Pyke reached behind the counter and brought out a dark short-bodied auto-weapon Sam didn't immediately recognise. 'Meet the Klossag, a triple-mode close assault weapon – fires energy bolts, 9.5mm slugs, and mini-grenades. I think the advert went something like: 'When you really need to win an argument ...'

Sam nodded, retrieved the particle gun from the recess where she'd hid it earlier, strapped it on, then collected a standard body armour pack from the shelf.

'That'll be so useful,' she said. 'If the Shuskar challenge us to a debate.'

From the armoury she made her way round to the main hold. Diminutive muscular Malginori were shuffling along towards the hold exit and ramp but were quick to make way for her, staring up at her dark features with a kind of rapt surprise. Sam tried not to show embarrassment or uncertainty – apparently the Malginori troops had already been briefed on the identities of G'Brozen Mav's subordinates and advisors, namely Lt Brock and the crew of the *Scarabus*. As to whether they would follow her orders in a crisis, she was uncertain.

Down in the main hold they were filing out of the ship in double columns, down the ramp to the poorly lit concourse. Cases of equipment were also being carried down and some of the debris which littered the pillared walkway was being heaved and shoved into crude emplacements. Sam could make out G'Brozen Mav, his guards and senior Malginori officers gathered in a lamp-lit group back against the concourse wall, and before she could take her first step down the ramp a chime sounded in one of her waist pouches.

It was her factab, its power-saving quarter-screen lit up to show that a message from Rensik had been received. Suddenly excited, she keyed up the full display and read – inside the sun – come quickly.

She frowned – what the hell was that supposed to mean? Inside the sun? Literally?

Right now, cryptic utterances are not what I need, Sam thought. *Still, better show this to Mav* …

She set off down the ramp and had barely set foot on the concourse proper when the factab chimed again. Again she flipped open the cover to see the message – *incoming to yr location – eta 20s – R.*

Sam straightened and looked around, alert and wary at the same time as she peered up at the upper levels and the hazy shimmer of the containment field. Then she sidled up to gaze over the concourse balustrade and survey the depths of the docking canyon, the shadowy lower levels, the sporadic glows flickering here and there, and the monolithic tower rising at the far end.

Something zipped in at her from the side, with an attendant high whirring sound. She ducked, scanning left, right and above, trying to spot whatever was buzzing around, while trying to keep an eye out for the drone Rensik. Then there it was, an odd small triangular object hovering on spinning rotors about an arm's reach away. Suddenly anxious that it might be a spying device, she unhurriedly began to ease her sidearm from its holster.

Then her factab chimed in her other hand. It said – *I have arrived – here I am – R.*

She squinted at the tetrahedra-copter. 'You're not Rensik.'

Ping – I am Rensik 3.0 – there is a grave crisis at hand – we must act.

Now she was glaring. 'Where is the Construct drone Rensik?'

Ping – Rensik was captured and taken to portal station – Rensik 2.0 has gone to help – I have data about a grave crisis – we must act.

'What crisis? What data?'

Ping – You should read – *Be advised – Earthsphere fleet comprising eighty-five vessels now heading for the megasystem*

*locale – ETA is thirty-six hours from despatch of this message –
safety of fleet is paramount – act accordingly.*

Sam was aghast. 'When was this message sent?'

Ping – thirty-five hours and eighteen minutes ago – we must act.

Forty-two minutes before an Earthsphere fleet enters the
megasystem and comes under attack from forcefield defences
powered by a sun! This would be a disaster.

'How can ... ?' she began. 'Do you know where the forcefield
defence controls are? Can you take me there?'

Ping – Yes yes – level twenty – minimal security – hurry.

'Right,' she said, going through the armoury sections in her
head. 'Wait here, I'll be as quick as I can!'

Pyke was standing a few feet away from the main group of
G'Brozen Mav and the Malginori, regarding all the activity with
a cynical eye, when he saw Sam Brock emerge from the *Scarabus*
and pause at the head of the busy ramp. She was reading something on that data tablet of hers and it was only when she stowed
the device in a pouch that Pyke spotted that she was wearing one
of the ship's antigrav harnesses. In the next moment she rose into
the air, hands at her waists as she swept away – quickly, Pyke
fumbled his headset back on.

'Hey Lieutenant! Hey ...' He prodded the buttons on the
right-side earpiece while following her rising trajectory away
from the *Scarabus*. Suddenly a voice spoke, but not Brock's.

'Captain, is there a problem?' said Toolbearer Hechec.

'Hechec, good man ... so to speak – d'ye think you can put
me in touch with Lt Brock?'

'The lieutenant has already spoken with G'Brozen Mav,
Captain – she has an urgent task to perform and must observe
comms silence until its completion.'

'Is that so? And am I permitted to know the nature of this
off-the-books adventure?'

'Most certainly – it appears that a sizeable Earthsphere fleet will soon be arriving in the Warcage.'

Pyke's heart leaped. 'Well, I never thought I'd be cheering on the sky-blues but damn me if there isn't a first time for everything.' He paused. 'Did you say "in the Warcage"? But they'll trigger those forcefield defences! We should be warning them.'

'Captain, I am on the bridge of the *Scarabus*, but despite all my attempts no subspace communications are functioning, which is why Lt Brock has undertaken to find the defence controls and neutralise their aggressive capabilities.'

'On her own? In this snakepit?'

'We were assured that she is being assisted by the Construct drone, Rensik Estemil.'

A Construct drone? he thought. *Now where did that come from? Hope it's loaded for bear, otherwise things could get ugly.* For a moment Pyke was assailed by private visions of broken ships burning in the Warcage killing zone, spilling bodies and gouts of vapour ...

'Captain – G'Brozen Mav is asking if your scouting team is ready to begin pathfinding.'

Pyke stretched, feeling kinks in his back and shoulders ease.

'Aye, we are that. Can you get on to Kref and the rest, tell 'em to meet me at the head of those bloody great stairs?'

'I shall.'

The stairs in question were two broad escalators which curved down to the next concourse level, although both had clearly been out of commission for a very long time. The level below had massive bomb holes in it but the next set of stairs was still in one piece and led down to the main concourse which ran straight along to the main entrance of the Shadow Bastion.

This whole place must've been like God's own shopping mall before it all fell apart, Pyke thought as he leaned over a corroded rail to peer down into the gloomy depths. *If they ever had anything as utterly decadent as shopping, that is.*

Clumping footsteps announced Kref's arrival. Over one shoulder the big Henkayan carried the cloth-wrapped portal device and perched on the other was a stubby-barrelled launcher of some sort.

'The moment he saw it he just had to have it, chief,' said Ancil. 'Just lucky that Malginori quartermaster had another.'

'Nice, very nice, and here was I thinking that this was going to be a stealthy operation requiring subtlety and a certain degree of muffled prowling.'

Kref looked unhappy. 'You want me to leave it behind, Captain?'

'Hold on to it,' Pyke said. 'But try to carry it quietly.' He turned to Punzho and Oleg/Mojag – both were suitably body-armoured and Punzho even had a slot-blaster on his hip.

'Punzho,' he said. 'You up to speed with the portal machine?'

'I am, Captain – I have studied the instrumentation and practised its operation, and am confident that I can swiftly deploy portal bridges to order.'

'That's good to hear.' He glanced at Oleg, formerly Mojag. 'And you'll be watching his back, right?'

'On guard at all times, Captain.'

Pyke nodded, then glanced over his shoulder just as G'Brozen Mav's voice spoke on the headset channel.

'We're formed up and ready to move out, Captain.'

'No problems, there, Mav – we've got our creep-stomping boots on so we're ganting to give the pusbags a good smacking. Best o' luck to you.'

'Good hunting.'

He turned back to his crew and grinned widely. 'All right, my lucky lads, time to kick some Shuskar arse!' *And get to their command centre where I can hopefully unburden m'self of this alien crystal thing.*

With weapons and equipment shouldered, they moved out, carefully descending the broad curve of the frozen, ancient escalator. Down on the next level, however, rather than continuing on down Pyke led them into the shadows of the damaged concourse. Huge holes gaped, the edges fringed with the remains of metal lattice reinforcements and here and there someone had laid down lengths of scavenged shuttering and shelving. Beyond the worst of the damage, this level of concourse ran straight along to the huge, well-like area where the Shadow Bastion tower rose up, tier upon tier. Their first job was to place spy-cams all along the outward surface of the concourse railing, thus providing G'Brozen Mav and the Malginori with good tactical views of the ground they would have to take.

Alternating between them, Ancil and Oleg took care of the cams while Pyke followed, pausing occasionally to peer over the rail, his suspicions populating the shadows near the debris heaps with imaginary hostiles armed to their imaginary teeth with imaginary death-dealing hardware.

He shook his head – no matter how bad he reckoned the situation was going to be, it generally turned out worse. *Well, look, there's an Earthsphere fleet on the way, which is good news – provided the lieutenant can stop the Warcage chewing it up and spitting it out!*

He shook off the grim cast of mind and hurried to catch up with the others. Ancil and Oleg had nearly finished placing the cams, and a quick exchange with Hechec, now marching with G'Brozen Mav and the Malginori, confirmed that all were functioning. Pyke glanced back and downwards, and could see tactical advance units steadily moving forward along the concourse, using all and any cover to maximum advantage.

As Pyke and his crew drew near to the curved end of the

concourse, they too adopted crouched postures and paused only behind pillars or other useful cover. Kneeling in the shadow of a decorative barrier atop a scorched dais, Pyke helped Punzho unwrap the portal generator, between glances out at the huge stepped tower, his keen eye noting the locations of several protruding balconies. Just then, Ancil waved at him from behind a shattered pillar and gave a thumbs-up – the last of the cams was now in place. He opened a comm channel to relay this to Hechec and found himself talking to G'Brozen Mav.

'Yes, Captain, the visual feeds are coming through; perfectly clear, too. Are you ready for the next stage of your mission?'

Pyke smiled sourly. *Damn, but keeping up all this polite, nicey-nicey front is becoming a right lacerating pain.* 'Certainly am – we've picked out a few likely spots from where we can sow fear and chaos among those ugly maggots down there.'

'Grandiose claims, Captain. The Toolbearer has great confidence in you – I hope that it is well placed.'

'We'll play our part, Mav, don't worry about that – just you keep your beady eyes on how you're doing ... wait, what the ...'

He broke off as light suddenly began flooding parts of the concourse, bright flickering bursts accompanied by hissing and crackles. The light came from entire wall sections, from huge hanging panels, from three-sided obelisk-like pillars spaced along all the concourses. Their dull grey appearance had, until now, attracted no attention.

A picture snapped into view, the surface of the Citadelworld as seen from one of the Bastion's highest balcony windows, Pyke guessed. The perspective pulled back to show a large windowed chamber full of archaic, intricate apparatus, racks of cabled-up modules, a profusion of semi-transparent screens covered with glimmering symbols, banks of controls glowing and gleaming with power. Then a figure stepped into the frame and Pyke felt the blood drain from his face.

'My name is Xra-Huld,' it said. 'Some of you may have heard of me and my eternal siblings, Xra-Vor, Xra-Uval, Xra-Shoaz, and Xra-Kebr.'

An inset showed four lanky yet distorted figures, each with a large, swollen arm whose flesh had grown around those sentient biomech weapons. The Gun-Lords stood in a row, surveying ranks of armed and armoured troops, who knelt before them with heads bowed.

Pyke scarcely saw them. From every one of the scores of massive screens scattered around the concourses, it was Dervla's face which stared out at him. Everything about her expression was anomalous – the slight forward tilt of the head, the hooded eyes, the cruel smile that twitched at the lips, all of it came from the thing that had invaded her.

The composite picture hung there for several seconds before reverting to the earlier head-and-shoulders shot.

'I know that it is you, G'Brozen Mav. I know about your filthy outsider friends, and I know that you dare to assault us in our citadel with puny allies scraped up from the last sewer you crawled out of and armed with pathetic weapons.' The sneering words boomed loud and clear all along the docking canyon. 'And now you know what awaits you – a company of Avang Deathrend commandos, and a pack of Vastators from the Cregrin Host. Each and every one carries your death in their hands, and only one needs to be lucky enough to get through to you.'

Pyke's anger boiled over and he threw a fist-sized chunk of rubble at the big screen that hung right over the concourse, big enough that it extended over three levels. The display flickered where the rock struck and the huge hanging panel swayed a little. He grabbed some more ammunition and began pelting the big display, yelling insults and blistering profanities. It had the desired effect – that huge face turned its attention to the concourse level where Pyke stood, openly defiant, ignoring pleas from the others to hide himself.

And there! – As the eyes of that possessed visage came round to see who was disrupting its egomaniacal tauntologue – there, just for a sliver of a moment, the mask wavered and the real Dervla stared down at him, then was gone.

'Ah, the bold Captain Pyke,' the biomech thing said with Dervla's mouth. 'Your feats and adventures have not gone unnoticed – in fact, my companion, Xra-Uval, has previously expressed interest in joining with you, embedding its body within yours, entwining minds and desires. Just imagine the ecstasy all four of us could experience were you then to embrace this body with all the enhanced senses that we can give you.' On all the screens, the possessed Dervla licked her lips while stroking her neck and upper chest. An incinerating revulsion coursed through Pyke, fuelling his fury, inciting him to wild audacity.

'Aw, come on, Huldy! Aye, you're a terrible old thing, and no mistake, but we both know what lies at the bottom of all that persistent wandering, all those millennia without rest, eh? The challenge, the need to know who really is the best! So, what d'ye say? Right here, out in the main concourse, you and me, weapon to weapon, and damnation take the loser!'

The Dervla-thing's laughter dripped contempt.

'Brave, daring words, Captain, but truthfully you're not important enough that I would be forced to waste my time—'

'Then I'll keep coming for you, ya bag of rust and pus! – I'll never stop—'

'. . . but never let it be said that I am less than considerate towards the inferior orders.' The Dervla-thing smirked and beckoned to someone out of view. 'I believe you've met my faithful servant.'

The Gun-Lord's image dissolved into that of another, far more hatefully familiar – Khorr. The brutish features loomed large, staring grimly out of all the screens.

'Pyke, we have unfinished business, so no running away!'

Pyke went to the concourse railing, leaned over and shouted at the big hanging screen.

'I'm ready now, ya walking tumour! Ready to finish yer ugly boat with my boot!'

Khorr's face filled the screen like a swollen parody of itself. Then he smiled a wide hungry smile that leered out unsettlingly all over the concourse for a brief moment before the image winked out.

Down on the main concourse, a wide hangar door was opening in the side of the Shadow Bastion and knots of heavily armed troops were rushing out to take up defensive positions. Watching this, Pyke felt oddly calm, even though G'Brozen Mav was at that moment yelling angrily at him over the headset. At the same time a cold shiver passed through his hands.

'Punzho,' he said over his shoulder. 'Time to fire up the ould magic door machine.'

While following the tiny hovering tetrahedral that was Rensik 3.0, Sam was able to stealth her way into the huge tower via an unlocked sliding balcony door. After that they traced a route through the interior by way of the rooms, passages and staff stairways of abandoned, unpowered sectors. Which on more than one occasion meant using her belt tools to wedge open doors or adjoining hatches or to crack open a panel concealing a lever release for a ladder leading up to a maintenance cubbyhole or a supplies cache.

They reached the Warcage forcefield defence control centre with barely ten minutes to spare. In the interim, alarms had blared and the sounds of shouting and pounding feet had echoed along the empty corridors. The forcefield defence room, however, was nine floors above the main concourse where the fighting was taking place: here, all was peaceful calm where banks of golden machinery hummed before a wide window that looked out at the planetoid's surface and the lattice array of the worlds of the Warcage ...

Ping – forcefield control boards here.

Rensik 3.0 was hovering next to a clustered horseshoe of monitors, readout banks, module stacks, and a bizarre couch whose headrest looked like a big hand ready to grasp an occupant's head. Similar side pieces seemed designed to curl in and restrain the torso and legs. Time was running out so she hurried across the room – just as a uniformed figure with a clipboard-like object stepped out from behind the banks of machinery near the great window.

Ping – enemy danger enemy danger.

Sam would have delivered an arch retort, were she not diving sideways into cover while grabbing the particle gun from her waist. A line of harsh cracks tracked her and she was quick to move behind several cabinets, changing position away from where the enemy had last spotted her.

Ping – time running out.

Part of her wanted to scream at the tiny idiot, but the rest of her was in charge and watching for her adversary ... and she saw a shadow on the floor at the other end, cast by a ceiling lamp. Carefully, she gradually stood up, eyes scanning the vicinity, then in a quick, snap movement she put up her gun hand and fired a volley over the top of the cabinet line. There was a shriek of pain, a crashing sound as if something had been knocked over. Warily, Sam rose to peer over the shielding cabinet and caught a glimpse of a grey-overalled form lying still with a blood trickle spreading along grooves in the tiled floor.

But it was only the most momentary of glimpses because more energy bolts flashed, hammering against the shielding cabinets, and droplets of melted alloy casing flew, one or two stinging her cheek. Dammit, another hostile – this whole situation was taking too long!

Ping – taking too long – time running out.

'You don't say,' she snarled under her breath.

Ping – keep adversary occupied – be ready.

The operator, or guard or whatever, was crouched down in a kind of small stairwell that led down below floor level, perhaps into a split level between the cabinets and the wide windows. Sam kept a bead on that spot, aiming along the particle gun's sights, peppering it with the odd burst. She wasn't that keen on Rensik's idea of keeping him pinned there with suppressing fire, but then she didn't know what kind of ploy the tiny bot had in mind. If only she had a throwable or two, even just a smoke nade – that would have given her a tactical edge . . .

And before she could snap off another haircut round, she felt it hit in her stomach first, then in a weird swift wave as the zero-gee took hold. Quickly, she brought up her legs into a crouching posture as she drifted free of the floor. With her empty hand she carefully took hold of the top edge of the nearest cabinet and pulled herself up to peer over once again. Her opponent, an oddly lanky biped, had panicked and was hanging upside down, holding on to the corner of an equipment rack with one hand while the other still gripped a blaster pistol of some kind.

He spotted Sam and whipped his gun round but lost his grip and began to spin, firing wildly. Sam calmly, coldly, ended him with a single round to the head.

A few seconds later the gravity came back on and there were bangs and clatters all around as a swathe of objects rediscovered up and down. The second enemy's corpse bounced off the cabinet and fell out of sight, but Sam was already on her feet and hurrying over to the forcefield control station.

Ping – lucky to have tower environmental and gravity in adjacent chamber.

She paused. 'You mean the entire tower flipped into zero-gee as well as this room?'

Ping – unfortunate but necessary.

Sam allowed herself a wicked smile. 'Bet Pyke wasn't expecting that ... right, how long do we have left?'

Ping – three minutes thirty-nine seconds.

Shaking her head she sidled into the cramped end of the forcefield control compartment then lowered herself into the couch. *Three minutes*, she thought. *How can that possibly be long enough?*

Responding to her weight, the couch gently took hold of her head and folded its soft-padded restraints across her body and legs, leaving her hands free. At the same time Rensik 3.0 buzzed into view and swooped swiftly around the nearby instrument panels.

Ping – not enough time to save all of ES fleet – wish to proceed?

'Yes,' she said without hesitation.

Two of the body restraints flipped open at their tips to reveal an odd handlebar arrangement with little sockets for thumb and forefinger. As soon as both her hands were engaged the headrest-cradle tightened slightly around her crown. A curious prickliness rippled across her scalp and, as she was half expecting, virtuality took over her vision, a blurring dissolve from the enclosing couch to ... well, it looked like the pilot compartment of a single-person craft. Her body was visible, as were her arms, outstretched and grasping a control column, but garbed in shimmery blue, her hands covered in sleek black gloves. Outside was a strange backdrop, moiré swirls of purple and silver, not unlike the visible appearance of hyperspace, stippled here and there with pale bristly objects, hanging like 3D asterisks, receding into a silvery distance. A virtuality environment, but what was it for?

Suddenly words started appearing, letter by letter, across her field of vision.

RensikRensikRensik this is – you must move maintainer craft forward – aim it at forcefield generators – nearest is tagged – intention is to deactivate hyperspace defences most dangerous to ship fleet.

She paused, trying to get a sense of the craft's controls, dredging up details from those endless studies of game mechanisms ...

Left thumb forward – right thumb reverse.

Well, obviously, she thought, carefully blip-thrusting to get under way. Looking around she saw that a visual overlay had given one of the asterisk things a small blinking orange dot. Feeling more confident Sam banked the craft round and aimed it at the generator. As she drew near she saw that shimmering spikes radiated from a multifaceted core which turned and spun restlessly. The shimmery spikes loomed bigger and bigger, emphasising the smallness of Sam's craft.

When close enough menu row will appear – left forefinger shifts highlight – right forefinger activates – go to 3rd menu option 5 and activate.

She followed the drone's instructions, selected the menu and the option, and prodded it with her finger. The menu vanished and the radial spikes shrank, pulling in on themselves while the faceted core stopped moving.

'Well, wonder what I just did,' she said.

You have switched a forcefield generator/projector into scrutiny and repair mode – manoeuvre towards next tagged target – you must state-change an additional twenty-seven.

'Twenty-seven?' Sam said, reversing and turning the craft towards the next generator, which was showing on her HUD overlay. 'Has the Earthsphere fleet entered the Warcage yet? Is it under attack?'

Yes yes.

A mixture of anger and horror shifted in the pit of her stomach.

'Can you show me a real-time visual of what is happening?'

Yes but shall not – vital that you complete mission targets without distraction – completion will preserve 61 per cent of ES fleet.

Which was, of course, the correct response. Only skill and precision mattered now – there would be time enough for grieving later.

Aiming his beam pistol over the edge of the balcony, Pyke tracked a couple of black-helmeted defenders, convinced that they were senior officers of some kind. Sounds of fighting seemed to be echoing up from all sides below them but he knew that this was just sound refraction from the complex architecture. The battle wasn't going too badly, according to reports he was hearing on the comm channels, and was focused on the Shuskar positions in and just in front of the tower entrance.

When the shooting had started twenty-odd minutes ago, chances for the away team had looked doubtful. The Shuskars' guns-for-hire, the Avang and the Cregrin, had rushed out of the tower, already firing. Powerful, accurate volleys took the Malginori by surprise, stalling their advance then forcing them to retreat. Pyke and the crew had been up on the concourse level above the fighting, but he'd been determined not to intervene until a portal bridge was established with a balcony about four floors above the main. Once Punzho gave the thumbs-up, Pyke had to get Ancil and Oleg to stop firing at Avang and Cregrin targets before sending them through the portal. Kref even got to fire off that clunky launcher, which wreaked a satisfying amount of havoc among the Shuskars' well-armed goon squad. After Kref was gone, Punzho had shut off the portal generator and hurried after him, closely followed by Pyke. By the time they were all across, return fire, mainly mini-mortar rounds and every kind of grenade, was blanketing the area where they'd been standing mere moments before. Explosions ripped holes in the concourse, gouges in the walls and pillars, eventually causing a ragged section to collapse onto the level below.

Still in contact with Mav and Hechec, Pyke had been relieved to hear that no one had been hurt by falling rubble, but he was aggravated by the casualty rate the Malginoris were suffering. He'd promised G'Brozen Mav that he would get the Shuskars' attention.

'Okay, boys, same again,' he'd said. 'But this time, no more Mister Nice Bastard!'

So for a few blessed moments they were in Fire-At-Will Heaven. Alongside Ancil and Oleg, Pyke had laid down a withering hail of suppressing fire while Kref let fly another couple of rounds from the launcher. At the same time Punzho was lining up the portals to make a bridge to another balcony higher up the tower. Return fire from below came faster this time and more accurate than before, with one mortar round exploding against the tower's armoured facade overhead, raining hot fragments on them. The portals were open so Pyke rushed them through one by one, ducking as ricochets spanged off the tower. Last to leave again, Pyke had felt a flash of heat from an incendiary round which burst against the balcony rail just as he was plunging through the portal.

So there they were, ten or eleven floors up from the combat zone, almost too far for their weapons' ranges, although his beamer had a scope that let him zoom in on ground details. Which was why he was tracking one of the Shuskar ally officers, urban camouflage, black helmet, armoured gauntlets, who, even from this height, seemed tall enough and brawny enough to be his nemesis, Khorr. There was a curious lull in the fighting and the officer was crouched behind an angled barrier, talking with two other troopers – then someone stepped into view, stopping to converse with the helmeted officer, a burly newcomer with a shaven head and some distinctive leather body armour. *Khorr, you miserable pus-nozzle!* he thought, squinting down the sights. *I'm gonna take a dead sewer-toad and ram it sideways down yer ...*

And without warning his beamer pistol fired off a single shot. Through the scope he saw the energy bolt flare off the ground at Khorr's feet, just a second before his own surprise made him gasp and sit back.

'Chief, what was that?' said Ancil.

'Not sure, but everyone keep their head down – now!' His hand had seemed to move by itself.

Sounds of firing from below resumed, the cracks and zips of slug and flechette light arms mingled with the stuttering buzz of energy weapons. Nothing seemed to be coming their way, which was a relief – Pyke edged up to the balcony and sneaked a look down at the concourse through the beamer scope. No one was paying attention to the tower's heights, only on killing the other side.

'Good enough,' he said. 'We can pick up where we left off, and give them Shuskar mercs a good belting.'

'Uh, Captain,' said Kref, pointing. 'Someone's got their eyes on us ...'

He looked round and saw a small, single-seater fan-car hovering high up the side of the tower. Everyone else glanced up, just as the machine sideslipped away out of sight behind the curve of the tower. Pyke frowned and thought for a moment.

'Oleg,' he said. 'How's yer hearing?'

'Seems pretty good – why?'

'I need you to weld yer lughole to them doors and listen for anyone moving around inside. Punzho – get the portal machine set up, double quick time.'

That Shuskar pilot must have seen them, so it was just a matter of time before some bunch of thugs came a-knocking. Tense seconds crawled by, a minute, two. With the entry portal projected and stable, Punzho bent his head over the control panel for long moments, then turned and nodded to Pyke, who stood, holstering his beam pistol. He glanced at Oleg who, ear pressed against the door, shook his head. Then Pyke peered across at the nearest curve of the highest concourse level, which was about five yards lower than the balcony, and there was the exit portal, a familiar pulsing dark oval.

'Okay, Kref, you're first, then Ancil, then Punzho – you'll have to be quick with the disconnect and getting the device packed, though. Then it'll be Oleg, then me – got it?'

There were nods all round.

'Tremendous – Kref, on yer way!'

And even as the big Henkayan crouched and ducked through the gate, Pyke heard something, a voice whispering *NEAR*, and felt icy cold tingling in his fingers.

Holy humping hell! Those bloody Incarnalith shards cannot be waking up, not right now!

The whispers kept repeating, gradually getting louder. By the time Punzho had powered down the generator and was man-handling it and the tripod through the portal, the voice in Pyke's head was loud and insistent – *NEAR! NEAR! NEAR!* – and he dared not look at his hands for fear of what he might see, but when he furiously gestured for Oleg to hurry after Punzho, Oleg looked and Oleg saw.

'Captain, your hands ...'

Near – Vengeance – Near – Vengeance said the words in his hands, over and over. Pyke gritted his teeth and laughed harshly.

'Never mind that, just get yer arse through that gate before it packs in.'

Frowning, Oleg nodded and dashed into the dark oval. Pyke readied himself, took two steps ... and felt his legs give way, pitching him forward onto the balcony floor.

No – they are near – vengeance!

He made a grab at the balcony rail but hot pain spiked through his hands and up his arms, forcing him to sprawl on the floor. And that was when his stomach started to feel buoyant, and there was the sensation of falling as if somehow the balcony had become detached from the tower and was plummeting towards the main concourse. *Zero-Gee*, the sensible part of his brain was saying, *because some gouging pusmuncher's deactivated the tower's artificial gravity*. Also, the pain was still stabbing in his hands.

Great – those bloody shards decide to turn me into a pincushion just when I really really need to get over to that fraggin' portal ...

Gritting his teeth against the nerve-scraping jabs of pain, he pushed against the nearby balcony rail, propelling himself towards the dark pulsing oval, just as it winked out.

'Aw, ya skaggin' arse!'

Seconds later the gravity came back on and Pyke tumbled to the floor of the balcony, landing awkwardly on his shoulder. The voice was still pounding in his head, every bellowed repetition of the word NEAR making it feel as if his eyes were bugging out of his face, making it feel as if every vein and artery was bulging from his skin.

When the balcony doors flew apart he scrambled desperately for his beamer pistol, got it out of its holster, despite the hooks-in-acid pain tearing through his fingers, only to have it wrenched from his grasp.

'Take him inside,' said a throaty, gleeful voice. 'The Lords are waiting.'

As they carried his unresisting form into the tower he realised that he was in the grip of a delirium, and not one of the good ones either. The voice was still banging on about something or someone being NEAR but at least it wasn't roaring and shaking the foundations of his brain. Didn't that Inheritor machine say that these shards were the remains of an ancestral Zavri, a general called, er ... Kaldro-Vryn, that was it. Well, so far, Pyke thought, old Kaldro's plan had been a bit of a bust, an irredeemable crock of skag. And any idea that the Inheritor machine had of gaining control of the Shuskar HQ was likewise completely ganked.

A hand slapped his face, bringing him out of the delirium enough for him to comprehend his surroundings. He was being held upright by a pair of brawny and pungent goons in a long room lit by glowing ceiling cubes which revealed in ravaged detail the four figures standing and regarding him. Their bodies were emaciated yet their muscles were prominent and knobbly. Their skin was blotchy, their scalps hairless, their features lopsided. And while each had slight differences in appearance and height, all four had that bizarre, outsize, grotesquely mutated left arm. In each you could see how over time the flesh had grown and moulded itself around the ridges and edges of the sentient bioweapon that controlled it.

One of them approached him, limping slightly, its weapon-arm cradled in the other. The skin of the bioweapon was thin and mottled and Pyke was startled when a lumpy nodule opened to reveal a large single eye, which gazed at him. Possessed by a mad thought, Pyke was about to wink at it when a bony hand grabbed his jaw and made him face front.

'So you are Pyke, the Human nuisance – I am Gun-Lord Xra-Uval. You may remember Xra-Huld mentioning my interest in you. We appreciate the boldest and bravest of those that oppose us, occasionally honouring them by making them our hosts.'

Pyke felt caught between the demented chanting in his head and his visceral loathing for the creature standing before him.

'Ah, sorry, sweetheart, but yer not my type, y'know ... but I do know someone who's dying to get manky with ye.'

In his head the word NEAR was now alternating with the word NOW, together pounding out a brutal backbeat while the electric chill in his hands grew sharper and colder. Pyke knew what was about to happen, and how it would happen, and was fairly sure it was going to be unpleasant.

The first shard burst out of the skin just below his wrist, the sensation falling between an icy claw and a hot stab. The Gun-Lord Xra-Uval gasped and stepped back, but that first shard wasn't meant for him. Pyke heard the guard on the left make a surprised sound, then a choking, gurgling noise. It released Pyke's arm and staggered off to the side, sprawling on the floor. The second shard dealt with the guard on the right, and after that Pyke's hands became smothered in a torrent of cuts and wounds, gashes and lacerations, as dark splinters of the Incarnalith tore themselves free of his flesh. As he slumped to his knees, he looked unsteadily at his hands, almost blurred by the outflux of shards – even so, he could still see that they were bloody and horrifically slashed.

Head wavering, he made himself look up and saw clouds of shards swirling around all the Gun-Lords – two were still upright, pressed up against the wall, swatting feebly at the shard-swarm, while the other pair were on their hands and knees, crawling towards the exit. The light in the room was throbbing too, a slow pulse between darkness and light that was as regular as breathing. Against his will, Pyke could feel his own breathing synchronising with the pulsing light, growing deeper and harsher with each exhalation. Sweat dripped from his brow and he suddenly realised, just as he let out one long exhalation that lengthened as the light dimmed and darkened, that no more dark splinters were escaping his hands. He could feel his chest contracting and emptying but somehow he was unable to breathe in, unable to move.

Then the light sprang back to normal, bright and constant. At first Pyke could only gasp for air, coughing from an irritated throat, then he realised that three of the Gun-Lords were incapacitated, one standing but immobile, two crawling feebly on the floor. A darkshard-swarm still hovered in one corner of the ceiling. Looking closer at the paralysed Gun-Lord Xra-Uval, Pyke saw that the deformed, swollen arm – where the biomech parasite was embedded – had turned a dark, inky blue, the colour of the Incarnalith shards. The fourth Gun-Lord was a motionless, emaciated husk lying face down on the floor, while its parasitic biomech, now free of the host, was writhing determinedly across the floor towards Pyke.

Pyke's body felt like a puny, rubbery thing and even though he barely had enough strength to drag himself along, the parasite was still moving faster than he was.

'Hey, c'mon!' he gasped, glancing at the shard-swarm hovering up at the ceiling. 'Job's not done yet ...'

The grotesque biomech was just inches away from Pyke's foot when at last the shard-swarm descended upon it, covering it from snout to tail, and there was a susurrus of tiny slicing sounds as they carved their way inside.

Relieved but exhausted, Pyke nevertheless forced himself to crawl across the room till he could see Xra-Uval up close. The Gun-Lord's haggard face was contorted with horror and rage, a face with eyes gone dark and crystalline.

'What ... have you done to us?' it said in a strangled voice. 'Release me! I command you—'

'It's called payback, ya poisonous dung-snake – now die!'

The Gun-Lord tried to speak but all that came out were tiny gasps. The lights dimmed again, there was a ghastly papery sigh, and those dark eyes began to disintegrate. As did the biomech itself, including the long segmented spine that was wrapped around the arm, winding up to the side of the head. It began to crack and split, fragments and slivers falling to the floor. Then Xra-Uval's frozen, crawling figure toppled onto its side as the crumbling collapse continued.

The same deathly process was at work on the other Gun-Lords, now reduced to gaunt, spindle-shanked corpses lying in scattered piles of pale grit and powder. Surveying the devastation, Pyke thought how little control he'd had over it, fervently hoping that any shards still inside him would not wreak the same havoc on poor Dervla's body.

The lights had come back up and he was starting to feel his strength returning. He had already noticed a tinny whispering sound but when it didn't go away as his faculties returned he suddenly realised that it was coming from his headset, which had been dislodged by all the action. Gingerly he fitted it back in his ears and was treated to a blast of Ancil's voice yelling '... respond, chief! We're still out here on the concourse, and I'm gonna keep shouting down this channel till either you say something or someone tells me you're dead and even then—'

'Whoa, steady on there, I'm fine,' Pyke said. 'Got a headache the size of Kref's boots—'

'Chief, you're alive! ... He's alive, he's okay.'

'What's the latest?' he said. 'Are we winning yet?'

'Oh yeah, chief, the Shuskars' allies suddenly pulled back into the tower just a few minutes ago – Mav and those Malgo boys are securing the entrance, supposed to be sending a team your way.'

'What about Lt Brock? Did she stop the ES fleet getting sliced and diced?'

'Not heard anything about that,' Ancil said. 'But chief, you're not gonna believe what happened with the portal machine.'

'Don't tell me you've crocked it! Swear I'm going to dock your pay.'

'No, no, it's still working like a dream – it's just that, y'know when the portal gate disappeared over on your side?'

'Oh aye, not a moment I'm likely to forget.'

'Well, it didn't disappear on our side, like it's done before. And you'll never guess who walked right out of it!'

CHAPTER TWENTY-EIGHT

In a single stride Akreen stepped away from the underground chamber of the Incarnalith and emerged into a stony plantless ravine. Gatuzna, ancient refuge of the Builders' last sentient machines, was behind him, and the Ruined Road lay ahead. Stormclouds raced through the sky, but down in the sheltered ravine the air was warm and only a scattering of raindrops speckled the grey rocky sides or spattered on Akreen's silvery-grey skin. There were no signs of animal life either so he had no means of knowing if this world was poisoned in some way. But the oval portal gate tracker was giving a definite reading – more than a mile beyond one of the ravine's sheer cliff walls. Akreen took a couple of steps back and surveyed the imposing, uneven surface for a few moments. Then he walked a few paces further along, approached the cliff and began to climb.

The ascent took him out of the ravine's sheltering depths, exposing him to stronger gusting breezes although nothing more than a sporadic shower was coming down. There was something satisfying about moulding his hands and feet to the cracks and slots in the rock face and steadily making his way upwards, rising out of shadow and into the light as he had already done several times in the course of this strangest of quests.

The clifftop turned into a slope of huge shattered boulders

that looked as if they were once massive square-edged blocks of upheaved bedrock which had been worn and rounded by an age of harsh weather. Akreen traversed the slope by clambering around the great blocks, sometimes ducking through short tunnels formed by floodwater washing through gaps beneath the huge tilted slabs. At last he reached the top of the rise, emerged from the jumbled boulder maze and stared out at a wide hazy plain littered with the ruins of fallen cities.

[*Aha*, said Gredaz. *The myths about the sky-palaces of Agaskri had a core of truth after all.*]

[*The rotted bones of another tribe of bested inferiors*, Zivolin said. *Gilded perches hurled to the ground.*]

The latter's comments surprised Akreen a little. As he carefully descended from the crest, he wondered if Zivolin was being overly contemptuous – or was it merely a kneejerk dismissal of the defeated?

The portal gate tracker led him downslope to the remains of a large circular building. Roofless, its walls were reduced to waist-high stumps, yet there was very little debris or rubble scattered within or nearby. Akreen followed the tracker's quiet beeping to a central room where broad stairs curved up to an empty platform. He climbed the steps and, sure enough, when he reached the top the oval portal gate appeared. He paused for a last look at the hazy ruins of fallen palaces, then stepped through the gate.

Abruptly he was floating in icy, airless darkness. Quickly he adjusted his eye filters and a moment later he could see that he had appeared next to an immense rock surface, beneath some titanic, wedge-shaped splinters floating side by side like pieces of a vast puzzle that no longer quite fitted together. Recalling the munition-devastated ruins of the planet Gatuzna, he could see how orbital bombardments had had similar effects here, cracking this world down to its core. Convulsions had torn out the planet's viscera, gravitational shifts altering the axial spin, with massive layers of atmosphere bleeding off into space. All that was left was this desolate sepulchre, raked by hard vacuum.

The tracker device led him across the flat expanse of rock, a weightless flight in near-zero-gee to where a square entrance led into a rib-and-column-reinforced cavern. As he drifted towards the centre, the portal gate flickered into existence.

The next world was hot, seared by the sun, scoured by sand-storms. Akreen's journey to the next gate took him across a line of rocky hills that skirted a wide flat plain. The plain was the abode of several large insects and reptiles but what prompted a certain caution was the immense edifice that lay at the centre. Akreen was not sure if it had been grown or engineered, but it was undoubtedly the product of a singular purpose. It was a gargantuan, monstrous head, perhaps three hundred yards high. It had a thick brow and a wide heavy jaw and sat upon the plain with a forward tilt, angled a little to the side, with its cave-like eyes fixed on the horizon. Off in the distance, Akreen could make out the broken and split remnants of other massive heads.

It also appeared to be hollow, going by the shadowy shapes that moved around inside its eyes and mouth.

[*The Mind-Temples of Rautantir*, said Gredaz. *According to some old tales, the monks sang the Endless Starsongs in shifts.*]

A flock of shadowy shapes burst forth from eyes and mouth, wheeling in Akreen's direction. Even at this distance he had been spotted.

[*And now they're temples to bones and excreta*, said Zivolin. *No songs, no monks, only dust and these ugly beasts.*]

And ugly they were. With an overall dark red colour, they had flexible, membranous wings with hooks at their tips, short whiplike tails and a pair of white eyes on either side of a rudi-mentary head that was all mouth. The leading members of the flock caught up with Akreen when he was still some distance from the exit portal, uttering a harsh blaring squall as they dived

at him. Without breaking stride Akreen grabbed the first one
to get within arm's length, snapped its wings and flung it to the
ground. Its agonising screeches drew the flock leaders back for
a few moments but they soon continued their pursuit, catching
up with him again.

There was a trail of bloody, broken corpses in his wake by the
time the tracker led him to a hill with a flat, paved summit. The
oval gate appeared and without hesitation he lunged through.

On the other side of the dark oval he found himself weightless
again, but this time he was underwater, submerged in darkness.
Engaging the eye filters again, Akreen saw he was floating not far
from a pale curved pillar thicker than his own torso. He swam
over and, close up, saw that it was a massive tapering bone.
There was another just visible in the murk, curving the same
way, and when he swam between them he spied a segmented
line of pale fossils down below and more bones curving in from
the other side, conclusive proof that he was drifting through a
titanic ribcage.

When he took out the portal tracker it was indicating roughly
in the same direction as the sweep of the bony remains. It wasn't
long before Akreen found the creature's colossal skull – and
the buildings and towers that had been built into and upon it,
clearly when it was alive. The only ocean life currently visible
were small paddling creatures and shoals of tiny swimmers with
oddly hinged tails. Akreen wondered if the effects of the long-
past wars had so eradicated life from this world's seas that now
only the most meagre of species could survive.

[*Think what it has taken for the sentient peoples of the
Warcage to survive the Shuskar, what has been erased and what
had to be abandoned*, said Gredaz.]

Akreen had no reply to give; instead, he searched the nearby
seabed and found the portal gate opening at the foot of a giant
overhang.

He fell out of the other side of the one-way gate, fell wet and dripping onto a heap of flat metallic objects. Streaming with water he got to his feet and saw that he was surrounded by mounds and drifts of battered shapeless objects in many colours. It was daylight and he was standing in the shadow of a disorganised stack of ragged, compacted cubes of some unidentifiable material, and it was clear that he had arrived in some kind of vast garbage dump. His olfactory sense was detecting oil and rust and decaying organics.

Akreen produced the gate tracker, studied the readout, then set off on a course with the sun at his back. The route followed a rough-hewn roadway along the side of a long rocky scarp which jutted above the general undulating sea of trash. The road had a shallow upward incline and the higher he climbed the greater the distances that were unveiled on all sides, and it was soon apparent that the garbage tip stretched away for as far as he could see in all directions. Could this have been a dumping ground for nearby Warcage worlds in past decades, even centuries? But observations told him that much of the trash on display was of a more recent vintage.

He continued up the rough road, which spiralled around till it reached what lay at the summit, an immense sculpture of a figure seated with cupped hands held out at chest level. It was very, very old, its details eroded by time and the elements, but it was the still, suited figure lying sprawled and face down at its feet that caught his eye. Bending to look, Akreen saw several small holes in the back of the suit helmet and when he turned the body over a desiccated skull stared up at him through the visor.

[*Metal-eating parasites*, said Gredaz. *Chewed their way into the protective suit. The holes let in gaseous poisons, and death overwhelmed him.*]

'Why have such creatures not attacked me?' Akreen said.

[*You have been attacked repeatedly since our arrival here in this vast tract of junk!* said Zivolin. *But before they even take a bite, something makes them shrivel up and drop off. What could that be, I wonder?*]

Akreen nodded in silence, understanding. The Incarnalith of Kaldro-Vryn, the potent shards of an ancient Zavri general. The Inheritor machine's claim was that they would take over the control systems of the Sunheart, the Builders' fabled refuge within the Warcage's sun, and make inevitable the ousting and defeat of the Gun-Lords and the Shuskar. Of course, he was placing great trust in this promise, he knew that, which sharpened the distrust that he was keeping in abeyance for now. Assurance from unverifiable sources demanded caution, especially when they did not explain puzzles, no matter how minor.

As he released the suited corpse it slumped onto its back and one arm slid aside to reveal a small brown book. He picked it up, brushed away encrusted dust and saw that it had a single letter or symbol on its cover. A suspicion tickled the edge of his thoughts, so he stowed the book away in a pouch that he formed at one side of his midriff. Akreen then held out the tracking device and moved around the monument to triangulate his destination. Satisfied, he approached the big seated figure and started to climb. The portal gate had formed in the cupped hands of the sculpture by the time he had hauled himself up to stand on one of the arms.

[*Just a few more steps*, said Gredaz. *Soon we will face the enemy of our people, the enemy of all, and wrest away their power.*]

'So the Inheritor machine said,' Akreen replied. 'But still I do not find it entirely trustworthy.'

[*Who is?* said Zivolin. *Sadly, there is no obvious way back, so you can either lie down next to that bag of bones down there or embrace the unknown.*]

Walking along the crooked arm he reached the dark pulsing oval.

'Truth is cold,' he said. 'Let the unknown beware!'

He shouldered forth into the swirling darkness ... which drew him forward as before, but instead of emerging from the one-way destination gate an instant later, the moment felt stretched or suspended and the darkness seemed to contract around him, squeezing, smothering ... then it eased and withdrew and opened and his outstretched leg completed that step as his foot struck a solid surface. He staggered into brightness, a broad elevated walkway of some kind, with other levels tiered beneath and above – a subsurface dock, he realised, as he saw a couple of vessels berthed along at one end, while nearer there was an impressive tower rising before him, and several humanoids gathered warily about him.

'Hey, isn't that ... er, whatsisname ...'

'The Zavri guy ...'

'That's him – the Captain had us chasing after him on that smashed-up planet.'

'I think that the Captain will want to know about this – immediately.'

'Sure, Oleg, sure – I was about to, y'know ...'

Akreen turned to one of the assorted bipeds as it was fumbling with a head-mounted communicator.

'You are the followers of Captain Pyke – correct?'

'That's us,' was the reply. 'Loyal followers, usually suffering for it – I'm Ancil, by the way.'

The short, scrawny Human held out his hand and Akreen gravely shook it.

'I see that this is the Shuskar Citadelworld,' he observed. 'I must speak with your Captain urgently.'

'Right, I see, immediately and urgently, okay ...'

There then ensued repeated calls on the communication device for a short time, then excitement when contact with Pyke was established, followed by several infuriatingly irrelevant exchanges until the Human Ancil finally broached the crucial matter.

'... well, it didn't vanish on our side, like it did before. And you'll never guess who walked right out of it! ... What, a two-headed gorilla dressed like a clown and singing "The Hills of Connemara"? Well, no, as a matter of fact – it was the big silver guy, Akreen, the Zavri general ...'

'First Blade,' Akreen said.

'Ah, yeah, First Blade Akreen, and he's very keen to have a word, chief ... what's it about? ... er ...'

For a wordless moment Human and Zavri stared at each other before Akreen spoke. 'My patience is not unlimited – inform your captain that there are vital matters that I must discuss with him in person without delay.'

The Human nodded. 'Yup, that's right, the First Blade wants a face-to-face, chief ... no use swearing at me, chief, I'm just the messenger ... okay, I'll get him on that right away ...'

Ancil straightened and turned to look at a tall, thin biped that Akreen did not recognise from before.

'Punzho, the chief needs you to open a portal bridge back to that last balcony, okay?'

Akreen watched with growing surprise as the tall humanoid called Punzho activated a tripod-mounted boxy device which moments later projected an oval portal gate next to the concourse balustrade. This, Akreen realised, was how he must have arrived a short while ago. That last gate in the Ruined Road sequence was like a hub-gate, according to the Inheritor machine – it should have sent him into the Sunheart but for some reason he ended up here. Which had serious implications for the last stage of his journey.

The Human Ancil called to him and gestured towards the stable portal gate. Akreen glanced over the railing and saw a second gate over on one of the tower balconies, so he stepped forward – it was time that he and Captain Pyke conversed. On several topics.

The glow cubes in the ceiling were no longer working, so someone had set up a couple of lamps so that one of the Malginori medics could examine the emaciated remains of the Shuskar Gun-Lords – or rather the decrepit Shuskar that had played host to those repugnant sentient biomechs for so long.

Pyke shuddered. *Who could bear such a thing? To be turned into a wrinkly, shrivelled slave. Coffin-dodgers, right enough.*

Another Malginori was tending to the dozen or so cuts that decorated his hands, courtesy of the Incarnalith shards. The medic was dabbing each wound separately, first with a dab of antiseptic then with a smear of battlefield-quality skin sealant. He was nearly done when the balcony doors slid aside and a tall silvery figure stepped into the room. The Malginori reacted with lightning speed, dropping their medical instruments and producing hefty autopistols in a blink of an eye while bellowing at the newcomer to get down on his knees.

'All right, all right ... *I said All Right!* – he's with me.'

'But this is a Zavri warrior!' said one of the Malginori. 'One of the Loyal Seven!'

'Yeah, well, fortunes of war, roll of the dice, and all that stuff – he's helping *us* now. He's a ...' Pyke looked at Akreen and smiled. 'Mr Akreen is our consultant on Shuskar combat tactics, so, if ye don't mind, we'll be doing some consulting in private.'

He made ushering gestures towards the door and the Malginori medics retrieved their equipment and left, wearing sullen frowns.

'They're fine fellows, actually,' Pyke said. 'Bit lacking on the sense of humour side o' things, though.'

Akreen's height made the room seem cramped somehow as he

stalked over to the pitiable corpses and stared at them for a few moments. Then he looked up with those piercing eyes.

'Four of the five Shuskar Gun-Lords!' he said, clearly astonished. 'Your shards of the Incarnalith! How did they accomplish this?'

Pyke frowned. 'How come you know about that? ... Ah, wait a second ...'

'I encountered the Inheritor machine in the Gatuzna tunnels, sometime after your departure,' said Akreen. 'It had decided to use you as a host for the shards because ... my mind was deranged by my precursors.'

'Erm ... you've lost me now.'

'The host for the shards of the Incarnalith was originally intended to be me!' Akreen said impatiently. 'You were given almost a third of them, and once I had recovered my sanity I received the remaining two-thirds.'

The tall silver warrior clenched his fists, brought them up to press against his forehead for a moment then lowered them. 'I can hear the voice of Kaldro-Vryn demanding vengeance against the enemies of the Zavri.'

'Just wait until he really gets wound up.'

'The Gun-Lords were abominations that poisoned all the worlds of the Warcage.'

'Well, we've got four of the scum-sucking gougers,' Pyke said. 'And we've routed the Shuskars' mercenaries – last report I heard said there's only a few isolated bands gone to ground at the basement level.'

Akreen shook his head. 'I was sent by the Inheritor machine via a sequence of portals that was supposed to end at a specific destination, the Sunheart, the Builders' refuge inside the sun. My purpose was to reach the command centre there, whereupon the Incarnalith shards would seize control of the governing systems and prevent the Gun-Lords from using the ancient drives to crash the Warcage into another sun, which the machine surmised they would do if they realised that defeat was imminent.'

Pyke nodded. 'Sounds familiar – I got the same chapter-and-verse after I picked up my cargo of death-splinters, though they didn't say anything about the Scum-Lords using the entire Warcage as a missile. All I had to do was get myself over to the Shuskars' hangout and find a way into their command and control so the Incarnalith shards could do their thing, take over the systems and shut the Shuskar out.' He laughed bleakly. 'But dear old Kaldro-Vryn had other plans!'

Akreen's expression seemed even graver than usual. 'Instead of emerging from a portal inside the Sunheart, the hub-gate sent me here because there were no other options. The implications are unavoidable – the Sunheart portal gate has been isolated from the rest of the portal network.'

'Because someone over there doesn't want to be disturbed,' Pyke said. 'So the entire Warcage and all its planets can be steered, like some massive bombship . . .'

'Yes, Captain, although from what I have been told it would take some time to prepare the drives for such a journey . . .'

Pyke suddenly heard a faint chiming, realised it was coming from his headset and fumbled it back on. 'Hello, hello, yes, it's me, stop the damn ringing . . .'

The chiming cut off and Sam Brock spoke.

'Hello Captain, still not dead yet, then.'

'Well, various types of scumbag have been having a go, Lieutenant, but here I am, still in the game, large as life and twice as handsome!'

'All across the Warcage hearts will be a-flutter at the news.'

'That could be both true and worrying,' Pyke said. 'So, how did you get on with saving that fleet of yours?'

'Managed to save some of it,' Brock said, sounding subdued all of a sudden. 'Made contact via the *Scarabus*, spoke with

Vice-Admiral Ndoga and filled him in on his situation, advised him to hold position while we work on the whole hyperspace defences problem. I omitted to give him too many details of what we're up against, just gave him the broad-brush picture, so to speak.'

Pyke glanced at Akreen, who was frowning as if in concentration.

'Just as well,' Pyke said. 'The truth about our friend, Gun-Lord Xra-Huld, might be a bit hard to take. Especially as that body-jacking pusbag is over in the Sunheart, getting ready to rev up the engines for a spot of crash-bang mayhem.'

'Not as such,' Brock said. 'I'm in the command chamber at the top of the tower, just got here a minute or two ago, me, Rensik and a squad of Malginori ... after decamping over to this Sunheart bunker or whatever it is, Xra-Huld managed to disable the portal gate over there, which stops us dead in our tracks. Not only that, it looks as if several key control functions have been transferred over there as well ...'

'Just a second,' Pyke said, looking up at Akreen. 'Can you hear what we're saying?'

The Zavri was composed. 'The conductive nature of my physiology allows me to attune myself to your device and pick up your discussion.'

Pyke nodded. 'Okay, Lieutenant, so what are these functions you mentioned?'

'Controlling the sun,' Brock said bluntly. 'Rensik is still scanning the control panels and displays but he's going on about "coronal mass ejections", "guided plasma bolus" and "multiple targets" ...'

'Whoa, what was that?' Pyke said. 'What d'ye mean "coronal ejections"? Yer not seriously saying that he can fire missiles out of the sun?'

'Rensik thinks that a rudimentary pressure regulation system has been modified for that purpose, but never used. The most obvious threat is the ES fleet, so perhaps that's what he means by multiple targets.'

'Captain,' said Akreen. 'I think that it is more likely that the Gun-Lord would deploy such a devastating weapon against those worlds seeking to defy Shuskar authority, although the intruder vessels could be considered secondary targets.'

For a moment Pyke was speechless. 'The ships I could understand – but throwing chunks of the sun at planets? What the hell would that do to one?'

'There would be havoc and widespread destruction,' said Akreen. 'Continents would burn, super-heated plasma would raise atmospheric temperatures and there would be mass-deaths ...'

Pyke could feel the headache coming back and kneaded his temples. 'The more I learn about these sentient biomech death-mongers from hell ... I just wonder what kind of mad, vicious bastards could set them loose on the universe? I'd get them all together on one asteroid and carpet-nuke it from every direction!' He paused and glanced at Akreen while continuing to talk down the channel to Brock. 'What about missiles? Any way we could get one through that would throw that filthy skagger off his stride?'

Akreen was shaking his head even as Sam Brock replied.

'Can't be done – the Sunheart refuge is apparently suspended about five hundred miles beneath the corona and no military missile could survive contact with superhot plasma for the time it would take.'

'And even if one could endure it long enough to reach the Sunheart,' Akreen pointed out, 'the detonation might kill or stop Xra-Huld, or it might equally destroy some system essential to the Warcage's equilibrium. We could accidentally fulfil the Gun-Lord's lust for destruction.'

'Does that mean that we're boned?' Pyke said, gnawing on his lip. 'I refuse to believe that there's no way to stop that pus-sucking vermin.'

And no way to get Dervla back.

'Rensik says that rebooting the hub-gate system here might force the isolated portal gate in the Sunheart to reset itself into open mode,' Brock said over the comm. 'But he also says that it would take several hours due to subsidiary systems sequential something-or-other.'

The silence that took hold then was dismal. Then Akreen spoke.

'Captain Pyke, there is one hazardous way in which a small task force might reach the Sunheart. However, you may not like it.'

'Why?' Pyke said. 'What is it?'

'Ah, well, of course,' said Brock slowly. 'Yeah, you wouldn't.'

'Oh, this is rich,' said Pyke. 'The two of you aren't even in the same room and you're giving each other nods and winks, practically ...' Then the import of Akreen's words finally struck home. 'Ah right, I see ...'

'Exactly,' Brock said. 'So what we need to know is, how much punishment can the *Scarabus*'s shields actually take?'

From his mesh cage's position atop the heap of cases and crates, Rensik had a front-row seat as Gun-Lord Xra-Huld's plans gradually came to fruition. Here he was at the very pinnacle of the Sunheart, a colossal edifice of galleried platform and grandiose halls and arches piled on top of each other in towering succession, flanked on all sides by forcefield walls filtering the ferocious blaze of the sun to a rippling pale orange. Right here was where the long-vanished Builders had decided to locate their main control and observation nexus. Huge display sections spread out like wings to either side above wide banks of instruments and interface stations. The whole setup looked like a stage upon which great dramas could be played out. And not far away, behind the stack of cases that was Rensik's perch, were curved rows of plush seating awaiting patrons.

But Rensik was all the audience there was for Xra-Huld's unfolding schemes, not counting the dozen or so pale and wordless thralls doggedly obeying the Gun-Lord's every command. There were also a few armed Shuskar guards around, somewhere; the drone's field of vision was limited to this vicious and bizarre creature and its enigmatic plans. At the moment, one whole wing of displays was devoted to visual feeds from outside and inside the Citadelworld base. Tracking shots of fighting or pursuits through the empty chambers of the Shadow Bastion were intermingled with static views of dead bodies and smouldering debris.

The other wing of monitors showed scenes from various worlds, scattered across the Warcage. Fighting and explosions, a common theme, feeds from handheld cams following troops retreating from cities, from towns, from a river or a burning forest, and occasionally there were shots of large transports loading passengers or taking off. The Gun-Lord was in conversation with a high-ranking Shuskar whose decoration-bejewelled uniform proclaimed his title, Lord-Governor Pukari of Torghav. His features, however, were stricken with dread as the Gun-Lord aimed question after question at him.

'... training exercises at this time every year, Most Exalted,' said the Lord-Governor. 'We had no warning.'

'When the Chainers began their campaign of sabotage and ambush over a month ago, all planetary governors were strongly advised to vary the timetables of all military movements.' Xra-Huld pointed at the Lord-Governor. 'You chose to ignore this advice, and look! Endolak raiders now hold all three of your fortified garrisons, along with their stores, munitions and vehicles. Unsurprisingly, the capital is also in enemy hands and your unsupplied forces are in full retreat to the spaceport where you ...' Xra-Huld paused to smile cruelly '... you and your court await my judgement!'

'If it pleases you, most Exalted One,' said Pukari, dabbing at the sweat on his face and neck with a gauzy cloth. 'Our loyalty has never wavered – I ask, I beg for your aid and assistance, for evacuation from Torghav to the Citadelworld. There we can mend our wounds, rebuild our strength and with your blessing prepare a mighty counterattack.'

'Gross incompetence like yours would normally be rewarded with a lavishly public and inordinately painful death,' said the Gun-Lord. 'But in the aftermath of the triumph-to-come I shall have need of bureaucrats to run the agri-worlds. So be of good cheer, Pukari – your miserable carcass has been saved by your underlings and beancounters. Now go and prepare for evacuation – transports shall arrive soon.'

Xra-Huld cut off the Lord-Governor in mid-gratitude grovel.

Rensik noted how the biomech parasite took great delight in subjecting its subjects and servants to sadistic levels of misery and anxiety – yet another in a long line of confirming instances in which organics just loved torturing other organics. Because that's what the biomechs were in the end, cyborged amalgams of living tissue and lab-grown pseudo-polymer which could grow and act like organic matter while retaining certain conductive properties.

But observing this repellent tyrant was really a matter of collecting details, information which would help to solve the mystery that had been building ever since the Gun-Lord's arrival on the Citadelworld. The drone had known that the command centre at the top of the Shadow Bastion was not Xra-Huld's final destination back then, especially when the toadying attendants quickly activated that big, elaborate portal gate and began energetically shoving crates and other luggage through it.

This vile, parasitic half-machine is planning something massively, extravagantly horrific, something lurid resulting in havoc and death, a lot of death. Nothing less will satisfy its ego.

Among the crates and cases was one which Rensik thought might be a piece of advanced comms tech, and the way it was plumbed in soon after arrival confirmed it. Not being able to use his sensors was intensely aggravating, forcing Rensik to rely solely on visual data.

And now a new image had appeared on one of the displays, the familiar shaven-headed features of the Gun-Lord's operative, Khorr. The background looked like a dark corridor lit only by slotted torches. Khorr was armed, as were the troops behind him.

'Summarise your position,' said Xra-Huld.

'The Chainers pushed the Cregrin and the Avang back into the tower,' Khorr said. 'But, Exalted One, they've been using some kind of portal generator to hit our forces from unexpected directions – we had to pull back or be cut to pieces.' He paused. 'Do you ... know about the other Gun-Lords, Most Exalted?'

'I felt their passing,' said Xra-Huld. 'Were there any witnesses?'

'None, only rumours of another mystery weapon, Exalted One.'

'We shall exact a vengeance price,' said the Gun-Lord. 'And it shall be easy now that G'Brozen Mav and his rabble have effectively trapped themselves on the Citadelworld, or will have done once you render that outworlder ship useless.'

'Should I attempt to sabotage it?'

'No, I want you to go to my flagship and use its weapons to wreck the outworlders' vessel. The flagship crew have been told to expect you – also I have promoted you to Shuskar Admiral and added you to the roster. The ship will now obey your commands.'

'I am deeply honoured, Exalted One. When does the scouring phase begin?'

And at that very moment a small pointy shape edged into view right outside Rensik's mesh cage. It was Rensik 2.0.

'What in the name of mechanical hell are you doing here?' he said. 'Did you send that message?'

'I ensured that it was taken care of,' said the minidrone. 'I came after you because my analysis revealed that your incarceration would remove a crucial variable from all possible incident-strings. Conversely, your freedom to act shifts all other variables into less disastrous outcome configurations.'

'Less disastrous? Scarcely an inspiring qualifier.'

'Once free from captivity, your actions can directly influence the outcome configurations themselves. In the meantime, I would strongly suggest departing from your prison, since the tyrant's discussion with its underling appears to be reaching a conclusion.'

There was a soft click and the mesh wall of the confining box slid upwards.

Ah well, Rensik thought. *It would be a relief to be back out in the world of signals and data again. And after all, the youngster has clearly gone to a lot of trouble ...*

Silently hovering, Rensik floated out of the cage and stealthily followed his scion down from the stage dais, then slipped into the shadows beneath the nearest staircase. Below the entire auditorium was a web of supporting frameworks, and a network of heavy-duty feed cables.

'I know how much you like raw data flows,' said Rensik 2.0.

'Most thoughtful of you,' said Rensik 1.0. 'Time we got to work on shifting those variables.'

CHAPTER TWENTY-NINE

With Punzho using the portal generator to create a series of portal bridges, Pyke and Akreen and the entire crew were able to leapfrog from the tower balcony to the *Scarabus*'s dockside berth in a matter of minutes. Some moments later Sam Brock arrived in a double-rotor, two-seater flier steered by one of the Malginori. The small craft was little more than a functional chassis with bolted-on seats and a safety cage that looked like an afterthought. Pyke grinned widely as the lieutenant clambered unsteadily out, clearly relieved to be back on a solid surface.

'Nothing like a bracing dash through the air while strapped to a rustic eggbeater, eh?'

'Brings a whole new meaning to the words "hair-raising",' she said, standing back as the flier pilot took off with a clattering buzz and headed back to the tower.

Brock faced Akreen and gave a snappy salute. 'First Blade Akreen, I am Lieutenant Brock, Earthsphere Naval Intelligence. I look forward to helping you bring this situation to a satisfactory conclusion.'

'Thank you, Lieutenant,' said the Zavri. 'I am seeking the death of the last Gun-Lord and vengeance for my people. I gladly accept your aid in such a task.'

'Don't worry, Akreen, me ould sweat,' said Pyke. 'Once we rescue Dervla, you can have all the death and vengeance you want. Now, the good lieutenant'll take you aboard, show you the bridge and all that, while I give out some orders, here.'

Brock frowned darkly at him, then shrugged and went to usher Akreen up the ramp to the main hold. Pyke watched them go then turned to face his crew, but it was Kref who beat him to the punch, seeming to read Pyke's intentions on his face.

'Are you making us stay behind, Captain?'

'Not fair, chief, not fair!' said Ancil. 'You're letting the lady Lieutenant go along—'

'Letting? She *told* me she was going, and besides, she does happen to be a trained combat officer—'

'Oh right! Stronger than Kref? More explosives-cunning than me? I don't think so.'

'No, yer staying here and that's final, get me?' Pyke's anger surged to the surface, almost boiling over. This on-the-fly plan to slam the *Scarabus* into the sun was deranged, beyond demented, the sort of plan that only a crazed metal man and an Earthsphere officer berserk enough to take on the Warcage with only a robot for company could dream up. In truth they had run out of options but this time he could not in all conscience bring the crew with him, not when the chances of survival were slender at best. He could imagine the choice curses Dervla would rain down on his head if he told her he'd asked the crew to fly into the pestilential sun to win someone else's war. Breathing in deep, he reached for composure. 'Look, me boys, this is the maddest stunt I've ever got m'self mixed up in, and I have to take a swing at it otherwise things could get really crazy-ugly – but this time I want you daft gougers safe and out of it, am I clear, now? This is an order.'

Ancil shook his head in disbelief. 'How am I ever going to find Win?'

'I'll get the truth, Ans, even if I have to cut it out of that evil biomech with a blunt knife! Now, are we settled, or do I have to wrestle each and every one o' ye over it?'

There were resentful looks followed by sorrowful nods. *Good*, Pyke thought. *Better for you to be alive and resenting me than burnt to a crisp!* Then Ancil brightened.

'Well, if we can't come along, we could steal that Shuskar ship for ya, chief – whaddya think?'

Pyke glanced down at the huge, ungainly vessel. 'Bound to be guards on board,' he said.

Ancil shrugged. 'Never stole a ship that big before – could be fun.'

'Ach. Just be careful about it, ye mad skaggers!' Pyke said, raising his hand in farewell before climbing the ramp up into the *Scarabus*'s main hold.

'Welcome aboard, Captain,' said the ship AI. 'Are the other crew members accompanying us?'

'Nope, they're sitting it out for this jaunt, so we'll have to manage by ourselves,' Pyke said. 'You can button her up tight and prep for departure. And ask the lieutenant and our Zavri guest to meet me in Engineering.'

'Will do, Captain.'

The hum of servoed hydraulics closing the cargo bay door thrummed in the air as Pyke took the small lifter platform up to the catwalk level. The ship was quiet, in its own way, providing that background murmur made up from innumerable systems and vents and pumps and the occasional leakage of audiocode as systems talked to one another. Pyke found it soothing, oddly restful. This was a bit how the *Scarabus* felt after they'd just completed a mission and got paid, when the crew were usually out on the town or orbital station, heading for party-wired oblivion. Except that there was also an underlying tension, making it feel like the lull before entering the arena.

Brock and Akreen were arriving from a lower-level companionway by the time Pyke reached Engineering.

'What are we doing here?' said Brock.

'We are here, Lieutenant, because this is the only other place on the ship with safety couches as good as the ones on the bridge.' He let that sink in for a moment. 'Just a precaution.'

Engineering's control and monitor stations were crammed into a narrow but tall compartment that stretched over two decks. Pyke sent Brock down the spiral leaf-steps to the station at the bottom, directed Akreen to the one in the middle (and gave him a swift lesson in fastening and releasing the restraints), then settled into his own couch at the top, replacing his Chainer headset with the one attached to the headrest.

'Scar, how are we doing, this fine weather?' he said as the couch shifted forward, positioning him correctly before the control station.

'All systems optimal, Captain. Ready to leave.'

'Fire 'em up and take us out, then.'

He smiled as he felt, or imagined he felt, the strengthening vibrancy of the ship's drives as they began to deploy their pent-up power. The main triple-screen display before him showed a range of onboard system readouts, as well as a tiled selection of video feeds from the hull cams and open feeds from the Shadow Bastion. One was a sound-and-vision contact request from the control centre at the towertop, and after Pyke okayed it he found himself face to face with G'Brozen Mav.

'Captain, it is gratifying to see that you are well ... oh, along with Lt Brock and your unexpected associate.' Mav scowled. 'The lieutenant mentioned only that she had vital matters to discuss with you before she dashed off, but now it appears that the both of you are leaving us, and in the company of a warrior of the Zavri, whose unswerving loyalty to the Shuskar forces me to question your motives.'

Akreen intervened. 'I am Akreen, First Blade of the Zavri, and I have learned cold and terrible truths in recent days. The last of the Gun-Lords has seized the Sunheart and all its destructive powers – we shall pursue it there and kill it. If we survive the sun-dive.'

'Which we shall, of course, without a doubt,' Pyke said. 'Easy as falling off a log!' *Yeah, into a really big furnace!*

G'Brozen Mav looked contrite. 'I see – and now I can see that even the unheard-of instance of a Zavri leader turning against the Shuskar should not be discounted in these days! My apologies for distrusting you, although if only you had shared this plan – which I'm sure you have thought through in exhaustive detail. Well ... in the spirit of cooperation, I believe you should know that some security monitors up here are showing Khorr and a handful of his marauders heading towards the ship berths, but since you're about to depart I shall pass this on to our patrols.'

'Sounds like a good plan, Mav,' said Pyke with a wink. 'And see if those Shuskar left any interesting bottles lying around – I'm going to need a mighty stiff drink when we get back!'

'I shall send out a search party immediately,' said the Chainer leader. 'May the battle-spirits guide you all to victory.'

I know what kind of battle-spirits I could do with right now, he thought as G'Brozen Mav cut the link.

'Scar, are we clear of that atmosphere containment yet?'

'Field transition almost complete, Captain.'

'Good – Lieutenant, I do hope you brought those Sunheart coordinates as you promised.'

'I've just jacked in a data-pin with the location – your ship pronounced them flawless!'

'That is nice,' he said sardonically. 'Scar, are all the forcefield emitters properly tasked and aligned?' *And will they keep us alive in the flames of hell?*

'They are, Captain, and I have re-analysed the forcefield

configuration sequence, and re-run the virtual tests under the most stringent of conditions.'

'And?'

'The solar irradiation flow exerts a certain abrasion effect on shields like ours,' said the AI. 'The power drain will push our generators to their tolerances, but my tests indicate high survival probabilities. We are fortunate that you had those upgrades installed recently.'

For a moment Pyke wanted to ask exactly what the probabilities were, then decided to let it pass.

'Okay, and now that we're leaving the frying pan, how long till we reach the fire?'

'ETA at high cruise will be 9.8 minutes, Captain.'

'Don't want to pop your party balloons,' said Brock, 'but I'm getting messages from the Citadelworld about that Shuskar flagship.'

Sure enough, the visual sensors showed it emerging from the field that sealed in the canyon dock's atmosphere, a vessel of brute, blockish lines which then turned its blunt prow in the *Scarabus*'s direction. Pyke watched this with a mixture of aggravation and dread, and a modicum of relief. At least Ancil and the rest were safe – no way they could have got on board if it was already departing.

'Scar, that thing's an ageing junkheap! Surely we can outrun it, or bloody its nose with a spread of missiles.'

'We can outrun them over short distances, Captain, but the flagship's drives, for all their rudimentary design, still have more muscle and would catch us over the medium stretch. But there is a more immediate problem – realigning the forcefield emitters has left the ship with minimal stern shielding, which makes us vulnerable ...'

'Incoming message from the flagship, Captain,' said Brock.

'Of course there is,' Pyke said acidly. 'Let's see it.'

His main display blinked, and there was Khorr, leering out at him. Pyke groaned.

'Frackin' hairy hell! You just can't leave me alone, can ye?'

'We are joined by fate, Pyke,' Khorr said in a weirdly insistent manner. 'Our paths have crossed and recrossed, each of us has dodged the hammerblows that flew to and fro amid our tenacious affrays, and now strands of destiny have drawn you and I together, in this place—'

'Sorry, wait a second, what was that?' Pyke cupped a hand to his ear. 'Did I just hear a reeking load of pseudo-mystic bullskag? Why, yes, I do believe that I did!'

On the screen a furious Khorr slammed his fist on the control panel and jabbed a big finger at Pyke. 'I'm going to rip the guts out of that flying trashcan and blast your hull into a smoking, torn and leaking basket!' He turned to someone out of sight and said, 'Target their engines! Target their stern! Hit them with everything!'

Watching, Pyke heard a faint thud, saw the picture of Khorr waver slightly, then heard alarms sounding. Khorr turned and said, 'What was that?' The answer was mostly inaudible but Pyke could just make out 'primary weapons generator'.

He grinned. 'That's a crying shame, so it is,' Pyke said down the channel. 'And there's you all ready to do yer badass desperado-from-hell routine as well.'

But Khorr wasn't listening as he stood and went elsewhere on his bridge to argue with someone.

'What is all this about?' said Brock, who was seeing everything on her display too.

'Not got a clue, Lieutenant, but so far they've not managed to get off a single shot.'

Khorr reappeared, ordering someone to target the *Scarabus* with upper-hull beam cannon batteries, and almost immediately the lights on his bridge failed, as did the artificial gravity.

'This seems a bit . . .' Pyke started to say, stopping when he heard someone on the flickering bridge shout something about 'intruders on Deck 8 – no, Deck 5!' and 'My reports indicate Deck 3, sir', then Pyke shook his head and guffawed out loud.

It's Ancil and Kref and the others – has to be!

'Panic over,' he said. 'Khorr has his hands full. Let's get back to focusing on the next hair-raising, death-defying escapade.'

'Panic over?' Brock said. 'Are you sure?'

Before Pyke could answer, the visual link to the Shuskar ship went out in a brief burst of interference.

'Trust me,' said Pyke. 'We'll have no more lying flannel from that quarter!'

'Actually,' she said a moment later. 'They're veering off course and piling on the velocity – and heading straight for the sun!'

On his display a small pane popped up, showing the Shuskar ship at high magnitude, its main thruster burning a bright blue.

'Aye, it's quite popular this season – Scar, what's our ETA now?'

'ETA for insertion launch point, 6.4 minutes.'

Second by second the time dragged by. At 3.5 minutes Brock told them that two lifepods had launched from the Shuskar flagship and at 2.1 minutes she announced that it was burning up in the sun's corona.

'Bye bye, Khorr,' Pyke murmured. 'So much for the strands of destiny, eh?'

'Your confidence in the face of adversarial threat is most commendable, Captain,' said Akreen. 'Does it extend to the next stage of our journey?'

Pyke didn't have the heart to pass on his conviction that his own crew had used the portal generator to board, and then sabotage the flagship, so instead he served up a platter of reassurances and a side order of tech-specs and spannerspeak. Akreen listened politely and, once he'd finished, said, 'I understand, Captain – great rewards demand great risk.'

Pyke's smile was rueful. *Now there's a leader who knows what it's all about.*

Then, almost like a surprise, the ship AI announced that they had reached the launch point and that the sun-dive had now commenced. Pyke inhaled deeply, blew it out through pursed lips. The deep background vibrations of the drive altered pitch very slightly, signalling a ramping up of velocity. The Warcage's sun loomed large now, its vast curvature of fusion-driven brilliance scaled down to a dirty, mottled orange by the monitor systems. No one spoke, perhaps out of reluctance to shatter this strange silence, the kind of tense and austere hush that living beings shared when faced with the possibility of utter obliteration.

The ship's forcefields snapped into their customised configuration before the heat of the sun had a chance to start raising the hull temperature. The velocity was still increasing as the *Scarabus* plunged through the swirling tendrils and curtains of the outer corona. At once the temperature at the leading edge of the forcefield began to spike – this was where the inner forcefield layers came into play, their braided energy sheaths shifting in rapid patterns designed to channel and divert torrents of deadly radiation around and away from the ship.

Such shield operations required a huge and continuous power supply which was why, apart from Engineering, the rest of the ship was dark, airless and without artificial gravity. Pyke tried not to think about that, preferring instead to imagine the shock on the faces of the Gun-Lord's goons when the *Scarabus* swept in, guns blazing.

At least, that was his plan. According to the data brought on board by Lt Brock the Sunheart had an entry harbour of some kind for visiting ships, which should open for them since the *Scarabus* still had the authority beacon mounted. He was about to see if the sensors were picking up anything when he heard a far-off muffled thud, felt a tremor pass through the compartment and saw red alerts flashing on his displays.

'What's going on?' said Brock. 'Are we okay?'

'Secondary generator just blew,' Pyke said. 'Don't worry, we still have enough juice to finish the trip.'

Except that now we have to run the primary generator past its tolerances and shrink the overall forcefield envelope, he thought as the ship AI put these contingencies into operation. *But if the power balance deteriorates any further I might start losing bits of the ship!*

A minute later, sixty long agonising seconds, the navigationals reported picking a guide signal on the beacon's frequency. The ship AI steered them along the projected path and suddenly the ship was flying down a huge fissure emptied of the sun's super-heated plasma. The titanic strain on the primary generator eased and on Pyke's screen several readouts began slowly falling out of the red zone. He breathed a long sigh of relief, ending in a cough.

'So – we are alive,' said Brock over the comm, sounding slightly amazed.

'Not baked, singed, charred or even lightly toasted!' Pyke said. 'But alive and ready to put the boot right into any filthy Shuskar vermin stupid enough to get in our way!'

'Well, who knows,' she said. 'You may get your wish.'

'The truth is cold,' said Akreen. 'But vengeance is hot.'

'And right now,' Pyke said, 'we are so very, very hot!'

For a moment or two no one said anything and Pyke felt as if he were coming down from the high of having dodged death yet again. On his screen, a video feed from a hull cam – possibly the only one still functioning – showed what the guide signal was leading the *Scarabus* towards.

The Sunheart's harbour was a vast open space with amber-to-orange pulsing walls that reached up and up. Successive levels hung above the harbour in a steep incline, mostly strange open floors, some occupied by building complexes, others filled with landscaped gardens, or pools and waterfalls. The *Scarabus* was swooping down towards one end of a huge crescent of docks and berths. Pyke kept a nervous eye on the hull-strain indicators and the output readings for the primary generator, as the ship continued smoothly along the path towards one of the smaller berths. The hull cam panned to reveal the full sweeping curve of docking recesses and some were gargantuan.

'Rensik uncovered some old documents about the Sunheart,' said Brock. 'It says, "The Builder's Hall of Command is at the very apex of this magnificent edifice. Risertube sedans provide a relaxed ascent past a series of architectural marvels, or visitors can avail themselves of autocraft that will transport them effortlessly to the Sunheart's paramount level where every day crucial decision are—"'

'What the hell is that?' Pyke said.

'A translation Rensik did for me,' said Brock. 'Sounds like a tourist brochure.'

'Ya know what?' Pyke said, keying in a series of commands to stop the navigationals following guide data issued by the Sunheart docks. 'I didn't come all this way to be fobbed with some lame sightseer saunter! We're here to end this! So no more shilly-shallying – it's time we kicked in the front door – Scar, full power to the thrusters and get us to the skagging top of this thing!'

From a lost corner of her memories, Dervla recalled some ancient pre-space song about being down so very long that everything starts to look like up. And during the drawn-out, seemingly endless captivity within her own skull, her own body, she had eventually reached a nadir of such hopeless, lifeless blackness that she thought it would consume her down to the core, that she would eventually cease to exist. But she was not consumed, she was not obliterated, and existence continued.

And purely by the fact that she had endured and survived, she knew that she was stronger than her own despair, even though she had been without any kind of hope. And with that knowledge came an understanding of her captor, Xra-Huld, the realisation and recognition of the all-devouring fear of death – exacerbated by the loss of its four broodmates – which was the real driver of its lust for control, its abiding hate for anything that might constitute a threat.

I see you, Dervla thought. Right at that moment the bio-mech was conducting a small conference with several planetary Shuskar Governors, speaking with her mouth, gesturing with her hand, and she thought, *Oh, how I see you, see the terror that crawls beneath the surface, buried deep and hidden well. But I see!*

When the time came she would hold up the mirror of its fears and shove them down its parasitic throat!

And that was the moment when a massive splintering crash thundered and reverberated around the huge open auditorium. The Gun-Lord Xra-Huld paused in mid-sentence and turned to look.

A ship had flown all the way up to the paramount tier and crashed through the encircling glass barriers. Shattered glass rained down as the ship halted to perch on the wide topmost bank of seating, with some of its landing gear extended and a couple of the auditorium's long narrow banners draped across its hull.

Xra-Huld's fury was blistering as he ordered all the auditorium guards to attack and open fire on the intruder vessel. And Dervla, staring through her own eyes, could scarcely believe that she was looking at the *Scarabus*. And if she'd had control of her own mouth she would have gleefully yelled, 'Kill them, Pyke! Kill them all!'

*

Akreen's opinion of the Human male, Pyke, was a variable thing. Sometimes the Human's lack of respect and scant regard for status and the chain of command was so pronounced that the First Blade considered trying to put himself in charge. At other times, Pyke's impulsive resort to extravagant imprecations reminded Akreen of the few Valzanians he had encountered away from the battlefields, veterans in cursing, each and every one. Then Akreen would observe how Pyke cajoled and persuaded his colleagues to follow a particular course of action, including his crew, who were permitted latitudes of dissent that would have been unacceptable in a Zavri battalion. But when Pyke ordered his ship to fly straight to the apex of the Sunheart's elaborately stratified structure, what Akreen felt was a surge of exhilaration!

All that he could perceive about the situation came from the display screens before him. The ship system readouts were incomprehensible, but the video feed from the hull cam as the ship flew vertically was compelling. The immense tiers and structures became a bizarre topography across which the *Scarabus* hurtled. Akreen's physiology, as always, was sensitive to the electrical flows of his surroundings, such that he had dampened it ever since stepping aboard Pyke's vessel. Now he was extending that sensitivity again, preparing himself for the struggle that lay ahead.

'This is it!' Pyke yelled from above. 'Hold on to yer hats!'

For a moment Akreen wondered why he didn't have a hat to hold on to ... then on the screen the shiny reflective surface that the *Scarabus* was passing over suddenly swung up to become an obstacle that the ship smashed its way through. Amid a cascade of splintering panes, falling and shattering on the ship's hull, Pyke steered them into a huge U-shaped auditorium, using the suspensors to halt and settle onto a wide curving bank of seats, extending some landing legs to keep the ship level. Pyke and the female Brock were arguing over who should be first out, even as the first sounds and flashes of small arms fire became evident. Akreen decided to exert some First Blade authority, although with sufficient Human-like courtesy to avoid what the lieutenant once referred to as 'rubbing someone up the wrong way'.

'Honoured Captain, honoured Lieutenant,' he began. 'I feel I must remind you both that you are visitors to the Warcage, and that the great crimes committed against my people naturally requires that the first to stride forth and smite the Gun-Lord's butchers should be one who is Warcage-born. While I keep these, erm, scumbags busy the both of you will be equipping yourself for the battle ahead.'

'Now that, Akreen, is a plan!' said Pyke. By now all three had clambered out of their couches, which were returning to their recesses. 'I'll get the ship to open the main bay door and you can go out and play "slap-me-in-the-head" with them gougers. But just so long as we're clear – yer just dealing with the nearby goons, not dashing off on some mad attack. I know how cranky old Kaldro-Vryn can get sometimes!'

'Yes, that is exactly what I shall be doing, Captain,' Akreen lied. 'Staying near the ship, eliminating goons.'

Pyke declared himself satisfied so while he and Brock hurried off to the armoury, Akreen quickly made his way to the main hold, crossed its empty floor and descended the ramp. He was immediately targeted by a crossfire of energy bolts coming from two assailants, one firing from behind the next lower tier of seats, the other using a wide decorative pillar for cover.

The first he buried under a heap of seats ripped up from nearby rows, and the second he surprised with a vaulting charge across the seating that ended with a shove to the big pillar. The unsuspecting Shuskar was crushed by the impact, even as he attempted to retreat.

Akreen then paused to survey the auditorium. The grand sweep of seating was orientated towards a resplendent stage, which also had recessed rows of plusher seating, undoubtedly for visitors of importance. And upon that stage was another stage, the highest dais where an imposing array of flickering display screens spread out to either side like wings, while a solitary figure stood below, busy with glowing control panels.

In his head Akreen could hear the voice of Kaldro-Vryn repeating with an inexorable anger, NEAR! NEAR! NEAR! – and almost feel the shards of the Incarnalith stirring within his flesh, hungry for vengeance.

He began to run, down one aisle, vaulting across seat rows from raised back to raised back with balletic precision, ignoring the Shuskar guards firing. Any who got in his way were dealt with savagely, their weapons and armour ripped away, their necks broken. Then all of a sudden he was mounting a broad rack of steps to the wider, lower stage, and the dais came into view along with the vile Xra-Huld, in its latest stolen host, the Human female who was part of Pyke's crew.

'Before coming here, I had not anticipated that we would meet again so soon, you and I . . .'

The Gun-Lord's amplified voice, coming from the woman's mouth, sounded full and rich as it echoed across the auditorium.

'. . . but then you and I have both experienced life-altering events, have we not? Some subversive modification of your perceptions is making me seem like your enemy but I am not, I swear it. Come up to the command centre with peaceful intent and I can help dispel these illusions.'

NEAR said Kaldro-Vryn, VENGEANCE said Kaldro-Vryn, hammering in his head, over and over, so loudly that his precursors could hardly make themselves heard.

[*Do not hesitate*, said Gredaz. *Strike with full force, disable the gun-arm then go for the head*.]

[No, *regard this abomination with extreme caution*, said Zivolin. *Treat it as if it can see into your head.*]

'I am your end, Xra-Huld!' he bellowed. 'I bring you the cold truth of death!'

'Come then – destruction awaits.'

Akreen charged across the grand stage. Three guards closed in to stop him and he disposed of all of them with ease, snatching the leading one off his feet then using him to batter the other two to the floor. Three swift blows laid them out cold.

NEAR! NEAR! NEAR! cried the iron voice of Kaldro-Vryn and Akreen found himself muttering it too as he dived towards the nearest steps and rushed up to the command dais.

Gun-Lord Xra-Huld was cowering in a gap between two banks of instruments and readouts, pleading for mercy, begging for its life. Akreen took no notice of these entreaties, or of the thread of suspicion which nagged at him. Instead he stood over the quailing, flinching figure as the shards of the Incarnalith stirred within.

Pain exploded in his side. Akreen turned to see one of the Gun-Lord's pale thralls holding a long heavy weapon from which a wavering stream of energy was pouring. He recognised it immediately as one of the anti-Zavri weapons that the Shuskar had developed under the Gun-Lords' direction. Fiery coldness crawled all over his skin, sinking into his biometallic flesh. Despite the razoring torment he took a step towards the thrall – and felt a second spear of energy strike him in the back.

The surge of unfolding from the Incarnalith shards went out like a doused fire.

The cries of Gredaz and Zivolin were as forlorn as winged creatures in the grip of a hurricane.

And the territory of his own body, his very own physical heartland, turned dark and numb and cold. He toppled, falling to lie on his side, but other hands tipped him over onto his back.

The energy flow from the weapons continued as the grinning Gun-Lord stood over him, its good hand holding a gleaming, fist-sized object.

'I could have you killed, Akreen, but you are still too valuable to dispense with just yet, or rather the Zavri are. In the meantime, let us keep you inert and mischief-free, shall we?'

The object he held suddenly sprouted a ring of spikes and he slammed it into Akreen's chest. The thralls stopped firing their weapons but the numbing web of energy still played about him, clouding all senses but sight.

They had made him into a statue and rendered him harmless. He was defeated.

Observing the clash from a shadowy corner deep in the auditorium's underpinning webwork of girders, Rensik was surprised by this turn of events.

'I must admit, I did not expect to see the First Blade get chumped so easily,' he said.

'The beam weapons wielded by the Gun-Lord's mutant slaves seemed to have rendered him immobile,' said Rensik 2.0.

'Yes, then the application of that device to the Zavri's chest – it could be a field lock of some kind. Didn't hear what Xra-Huld said just then – he was out of range of the control board pickups.'

'Second wave is on its way,' Rensik 2.0 said.

Rensik 1.0 switched his monitoring to vid-feeds covering the rest of the auditorium and sure enough, two figures were heading straight for the big stage. Pyke and Brock were handling attacks by the remaining Shuskar guards with considerable skill but Rensik knew that they wouldn't stand a chance against the biomech parasite and its mutant thralls.

'Is there anything we can do?' said Rensik 2.0. 'I am assuming that we view the biomech as a possible threat to Construct interests.'

'Correct,' said Rensik 1.0. 'Disruption to its data and communication lines is an option, but nearly all the important nodes are shelled in triple-redundant networks. We could use our onboard nano fabricators to produce neurotoxins but they would only be effective against the thralls, and in any case we have no delivery systems. It appears that a drastic solution might be called for.'

'I agree. Although due to my own contingency preparations I now have a limited combat capacity.' Rensik 2.0 transmitted a databurst to Rensik 1.0, who was gratified to see what the small drone had achieved with such few resources.

'Very good, nice detail, cunning delivery system,' it said.

'Thank you,' said Rensik 2.0. 'Time is running out – in the event of abrogation do you wish to upgrade me?'

'I have grown used to a certain optimism, so it'll just be the transfer of the case files and the beta-report. Then I can get down to configuring myself for battle.'

During the moments when they weren't being fired upon, Pyke sneaked backward looks at the *Scarabus*. He was trying to see if the sun-dive had caused any serious damage that would need repairing before they could fly back out.

Fly back out? he thought. *Just the thought of going through that again …*

A spread of energy bolts stitched burning holes in the seating close by, filling the air with the stink of charred plastics. Pyke swore, ducked behind the row of seat backs and crawled quickly along a few places before poking his head up for a quick look. Another volley came his way but he retreated to his previous position, readied the beamer pistol, held his breath then popped up and raked the area where he'd spotted the Shuskar guard.

Something chimed and he laughed, sitting back behind his cover.

'If that's that drone of yours telling me to keep my head down again ...'

'No, it's telling me something else.'

'Where is the wee sod now?'

'Flying about in the heights,' Brock said. 'It's saying that the guards are actually pulling back, almost leaving us a clear run at the stage. Hmm, could this by any chance be a trap, I wonder?'

'I reckon it's the trappiest trap you'll find outside one of those crazy dungeon-mazes on Meganthis 4. So what we could do is a stealth rush, hit 'em with a coupla nade waves then move in to mop up.'

'Can we try not to risk killing Akreen?'

He frowned. 'Didn't see you as a fan of the big silver guy but ... fine, flashbangs and empers, okay? Right, well, let's sneaky-charge up on them and not get killed.'

Moving in a half-crouch they flanked a main aisle that led straight towards the foot of the main stage, which appeared to be empty. And sure enough, no sign of the Shuskar guards, which made the crawling sensation in the pit of his stomach crawl some more. As soon as they stepped onto the wide lower stage, beamer fire from the command dais scored smoking lines across the textured matting. Pyke and Brock dived for cover, ending up in the recessed plush seats, which were provided with strange movable shelves and spigot-and-beaker cupolas.

'I really have had a bellyful of this dodging-death malarkey,' Pyke said, producing a handful of teardrop-shaped flashbangs from his jacket pocket. 'Time to make the teeth rattle in their skulls!'

He lobbed them at the command dais then turned away, shielding his eyes. There was a thunderous volley of loud bangs and a flickering burst of dazzling light, some of which still managed to leak through his fingers. When he looked up Brock had her left eye closed as she waved her hand in front of her face.

'Right eye's a blur,' she said as Pyke helped her up out of the recess. 'Wasn't expecting it to be that bright!'

'It'll start to clear in less than a minute,' Pyke said. 'Let's go check on our now-blind evil mastermind biomech pusbag.'

Grenade smoke drifted over the command dais as they warily climbed the last few steps. Three or four pale-skinned human-oids were fumbling around blindly on hands and knees. A large silvery form lay motionless over by one of the instrument boards, and sitting nearby was a familiar figure, that gross swollen arm resting on her knees, leaning on her good hand while her eyes stared bleakly, sightlessly out at nothing.

'Who's there?'

It was her voice but with a tone of hardness winding through it. The warm timbre of Dervla was missing.

'Not one of your slaves,' Pyke said.

'Ah, the bold Captain Pyke – so good of you and your com-panion to join us. I mean that in both senses of the word.'

Pyke grimaced. 'Ah, what a joker you are! We're here to kick your slimy arse and get you out of the body of my friend.'

The parasite shrugged.

'Understandable, of course. Both of you have been the most resolute of adversaries, with yourself, Captain, taking the accol-ade for the sheer quantity of havoc and destruction that you've created in your wake. But you see, that is the sweetest part of victory, that moment where your enemy becomes your ally!'

Pyke stared at the creature that was wearing Dervla's body for a moment, then raised his beamer pistol, aiming carefully at the biomech weapon.

'Not today, you deluded skaggin' bastard, not today!'

And for an instant, he heard a high-pitched whine, but before he could turn to look for the source of it something unbearably sharp struck him in the side of the head. Searing agony blos-somed out from it, engulfing his senses and he caught Brock's choked-off cry of pain as the pistol fell from his enfeebled fingers. Then his legs went and he sprawled on the floor.

'To go down in defeat to the Sko-Xra is no dishonour,' said the Gun-Lord, now standing, eyesight clearly unaffected. 'We triumph because we are skilled in all the ways of winning. You see, I launched the cytoblast darts from my subsidiary tract moments before you both set foot on the command platform – while we were having our pleasant discussion I was steering them towards your undefended heads.'

'Cyto ... what ... ?' he managed to slur.

'Cytoblast, a factory of genetics.' The Gun-Lord squatted down next to Pyke and patted his shoulder. 'You or your allies slew my four siblings so it is entirely fitting that you are compelled to make restitution. Our great store of experience provides us with insight into possible outcomes, thus we know how to prepare for them. And with your help we shall rebuild our glorious empire, yes, your help! That hot burning sensation you can feel is the cytoblast sending the threads of an assembly mesh throughout your body in preparation for the first wave of gene-engineering. Cellular modification on such a scale takes time, but the results are exquisite and immaculate.'

What are you turning us into, you bag of slime! was what he wanted to say, but all he could produce was a wordless gasp. Xra-Huld laughed and stroked his cheek.

'Surely you've guessed – yes, the cytoblasts are rebuilding you both into new Sko-Xra! Your minds will be wiped then restocked from the shared memory RNA all of us have, and I will have two new siblings!'

Right, Pyke thought. *That couldn't be any more horrific ...*

From where he lay, Pyke was within arm's reach of the frozen Akreen – whose eyes, he suddenly realised, were open and aware – while having a view from the floor of most of the immense array of monitor screens, and of Xra-Huld standing at the central control panel. After a moment a cluster of the screens began to show scenes from a burning valley, smoke billowing from a wrecked city, the sides of mountains black with charred vegetation.

'This is Armag,' said Xra-Huld. 'I had Armag City and its valley incinerated but there are plenty of other towns and hamlets where rebellion festers like a poison.' The Gun-Lord glanced round at him. 'That makes it a primary target for my sun-weapon – oh, did you know about that? Yes, seems that the Builders modified the corona-convection regulator, turning it into a plasma-mass launcher. But they never used it, even when faced with total defeat at the hands of that Shuskar-led insurgency. I, on the other hand, am quite happy to use any method that deals with threats to our supremacy. It is, after all, just one more way of winning!'

The Gun-Lord's head came up again, frowning as if hearing something. There was a sudden intake of breath, an instant before something vaguely oblong-shaped and glowing zoomed into view and struck Xra-Huld high in the chest. The impact did not force him back but he was suddenly enclosed in a web of quivering energy which was having a deleterious effect on him. Groaning, he lurched away from the controls and fell to his knees, right at Akreen's feet. The Gun-Lord's two remaining pale thralls moved to his aid but they had barely taken a couple of steps when they stopped, swayed and keeled over.

Pyke watched all this with a confused amazement, when he wasn't struggling to cope with the burning sensation threading through his semi-paralysed body. Then, without warning, a small object like a few gaming dice stuck together, came into view, trundling over the floor. A tinny voice spoke.

'Captain Pyke, Lieutenant Brock, I am Rensik 2.0 – my progenitor, Rensik 1.0, is holding the Gun-Lord Xra-Huld in a kind of stasis but his substrate reserves will not last long. I calculate the odds of his survival to be no more than 1 in 655—'

Here, Brock made a noise of protest, but it seemed, due to the pain of the cytoblast, that this was all she could manage.

Rensik 2.0 continued. 'I have already immobilised the remaining thralls so all that remains is for you to release the First Blade Akreen from the suppressor field. With the natural Zavri strength and resolve, he would be able to kill the biomech outright.'

Blinking away sweat, Pyke regarded the tiny machine with something like intense aggravation. 'Just ... how'ma ... gon' do that ...' he said through disobedient lips, before Brock could respond. He didn't trust her to care about saving Dervla, not half as much as he cared.

'There is a field locking device attached to his chest – you must remove it. I am unable to do so as the suppressor field would erase my core.'

'Not ezzackly ... perky'n rarin t'go ...'

'The pain from the cytoblast operations is considerable, but your limbs are still under your command.'

'Right ... izzat all?'

'Rensik 1.0's cells will be depleted in only a few minutes, so you must act now.'

With that the tiny machine trundled out of sight. Pyke lay on his side for a moment, steeling himself, then made his left arm stretch out to the floor while shifting his right arm to lever himself onto his elbows. Every movement felt as if ground glass was scraping in his joints. Every gasp became a groan, every groan became an agonised cry, all interspersed with as pungent a selection of curses as he could manage, given the situation. Brock looked to be having similar troubles, but he had a head start on her.

And as he dragged himself over to Akreen, a plan bloomed in his pain-drenched mind. Ignoring the cold prickling he grabbed the Zavri's arm and pulled his heavy mass around towards where the Gun-Lord knelt on the floor, so that the locking device on his silver chest was in easy reach. Thus prepared, Pyke wiped sweat and grime from his face, then looked straight into those eyes, Dervla's eyes, filled with the raging hate of the parasite.

'Here's the deal: you get your claws or tentacles or whatever out of Dervla, you unhook your mind from hers, you let her go! Or I'll release Akreen from that suppressor field and he will not be in any mood for negotiation, I promise you!'

The eyes trembled, the face muscles twitched, and the raging hate in that glare never changed.

'Take the deal!' Pyke shouted. 'Use one of those slaves for a host, I don't care, just release her!'

And that was when Rensik 1.0's power cells failed and Xra-Huld was free of the stasis field. The drone was knocked to the floor where it flipped over and lay still and most definitely lifeless. For an instant Pyke saw the hate in Dervla's eyes, the Gun-Lord's hate, turn into raw, unreasoning terror – but was it a trick? An instant later Xra-Huld's arm came up and roughly shoved him away, but he had sufficient presence of mind to grab the field suppression device and rip it out of Akreen's chest. The First Blade of the Zavri convulsed once, then came to life, roaring just one word:

'NEAR!'

Everything came to her through the lens of Xra-Huld's view of the world. It was his emotive responses which drove her body's autonomic responses, anger, hate, self-satisfaction. So when he fooled and defeated first the Zavri leader then Pyke and some other woman, the smug, self-admiring, triumphal-ist self-congratulation was like a fetid cloud swirling around every thought, bathing it in vanity and pride. Dervla then had to attenuate her connections to the flow of the Gun-Lord's thoughts, not so much to avoid those noxious conceits as to keep him from sensing the intensity of her repugnance.

And then, with all three intruders helpless at his feet, he turned to his displays and control panels. He monologued loathsomely about his genocidal plans, while studying the situation on a range of other planets and noting that a substantial number of Shuskar evacuees had now arrived at the Citadelworld.

Then, out of nowhere, the assault of the drone! Dervla's emotions leaped and she felt Xra-Huld's corrosive hate for her spike as a consequence. Then she realised that the attacking machine had adapted its forcefields to exert a short-term partial stasis effect. Dervla had the impression that this was part of some kind of plan but had nothing else to go on. Xra-Huld had fallen to his knees near his victims ... and then Pyke began dragging the motionless body of the Zavri round and towards her own semi-paralysed form, and she knew something was afoot. But when he started trying to strike a deal with the Gun-Lord she was aghast. *No, no!* she wanted to say. *Don't fall into that trap, release the Zavri and destroy that abomination, doesn't matter if I have to die ...*

She felt Xra-Huld's vain hatred like thrusting pulses of acid, felt his vicious anger towards Pyke, felt his contempt for the suggestion of using one of the thralls as a host ... and she sensed the first flickers in the drone's stasis field, sure sign that its cells were just about ready to shut down.

It's now or never, she realised, summoning all her stored-up recollections of fear and terror while digging into Xra-Huld's own memories for the deeply buried but potent echoes of his own raw, primal terrors. She fused it all together then struck open all the connections and avenues which kept her thought-domain shielded from that abominable presence. And as the stasis field finally failed and the dead drone was struck aside, she thrust the mirror of terrors into the Gun-Lord's unsuspecting, unprepared mind.

Shrieking panic erupted. A flailing hand struck Pyke, who

fell back and in so doing tore the locking device away from the Zavri's chest. Akreen convulsed, then sat bolt upright, roaring one word – 'NEAR!'

Then, with blurring speed, he reached for the Gun-Lord, one hand on the blunt weapon-arm, the other wrapped around the neck. The tall silver warrior then stood, forcing Xra-Huld onto his feet, and spoke again.

'Come out, worm! Come for me if you dare. Subdue me if you can. Or die now at my hands. Choose!'

Xra-Huld's terror was real, but his self-centred vanity and arrogance would not let him refuse a challenge from such an adversary. But how would a bout between these two pan out? And why would Akreen take a chance like this?

Then, to Dervla's amazement, Xra-Huld's thought-presence began to drain away, like a poisonous swamp being pumped clear. She began to feel the giddiness of real hope, the joy of a possible escape from evil darkness. Then a pain stabbed in the side of her head, an awful hot pain that started to tear at her, tearing at her flesh, burning her flesh in a coiling track around her neck, a torment so nerve-shredding that she ceased to be completely aware of what was happening.

Pyke was dumbfounded when Akreen abruptly sat up, roared 'NEAR!' and grabbed Dervla by the neck and that swollen arm. He was all ready to defy the pain rasping in his limbs and throw himself forward when the Zavri spoke further, issuing an astounding challenge to the Gun-Lord Xra-Huld. The pair were frozen for several moments in a tableau of brutal struggle, like some marble statue from Humanity's ancient, distant past. Pyke was light-headed and nauseous from the agonising spikes twisting in his joints, spine and chest, but he forced himself to remain sitting upright, waiting for whatever was about to happen.

It was a cry of pain so terrible it sounded as if it were torn from

Dervla's throat. A kind of mad, panicking fear took hold and he struggled to get back on his feet – but then she looked right at him, eyes wide and anguished, shaking her head as she held out her unmarred hand to stop him. Then her eyes rolled back to show the whites and she let out another wrenching scream as the biomech parasite's spine-tail began to unwind itself from her body. The track of horrifying bloody pinpricks that coiled from the head around the neck and over the upper back and one shoulder blade was bad enough but the deep gouges left along her arm was the worst.

As the vile entity freed itself from its Human host, Akreen released Dervla so that he could grasp the weapon-barrel-head with both hands. Pyke kept expecting the Incarnalith shards to start bursting forth but instead Akreen suddenly staggered back, swayed for a moment, then fell to one knee. The parasite's long dark tail-spine whipped up and coiled itself around the Zavri's neck.

'Fight, Akreen!' Pyke yelled, now crawling towards the Zavri despite the pain. 'Fight the bastard!'

But it seemed too late. The biomech squirmed in Akreen's loosened grasp, fitting itself into position along one arm while the other fell listlessly to the Zavri's side. Pyke was overcome by a wave of despair, even as he saw Lt Brock dragging herself towards the scene of the action. Akreen's face was slack, his eyes vacant and lifeless, but only for a moment. A gleeful, triumphant expression crept into the silver features and Xra-Huld's familiar hatred animated the eyes. Pyke was a stranger to the kind of bleak despair that now assailed him. But stubbornness for Pyke wasn't something to be picked from a range of options but an intrinsic quality carved into his being. He wouldn't lie down and die – if he had to fight a possessed Zavri bare-fisted then he would. Fighting against the hot pain gouging through his limbs he somehow got himself up into a kneeling position. Meanwhile

Brock, her face twisted by pain, was on her stomach, stretching out towards a hand beamer which lay several feet away.

Xra-Huld was exulting in his capture and domination of a new host, revelling in his jubilation. 'I ... dared! I subdued! I win! ... I ... what is ... why ... ?'

Pyke was reaching for a nearby stool to use as a weapon when he heard the note of confusion in the Gun-Lord's voice. When he looked round it seemed that Xra-Huld was unable to move his new legs. As Pyke watched, a dark web-like tracery began spreading from the feet up and from the fingertips along the arms. The confusion in those silvery features was overtaken by a slow horrified realisation. Pyke could see segments of that waxy-grey spine-tail start to writhe as if trying to detach itself but something was now holding on to it, binding it, entrapping it.

Xra-Huld let out a rasping screech. It used the unchanged hand to try and tear the spine-tail from neck and arm but with the passing seconds every motion was growing jerky and slow, and at last the limbs and the head were still, motionless. The dark web had spread right across the Zavri's form, looking like a network of cracks, and Pyke had a disturbing premonition about what was about to happen.

Then, unexpectedly, the Zavri's head turned to look at Pyke and the skin at the neck splintered, raining fragments on the floor.

'Vengeance is hot, Captain Pyke.' The First Blade's voice was muted and hoarse. 'But it is final.'

Then that tall, broad-shouldered figure began to disintegrate. The unaltered arm cracked and crumbled, falling away at the shoulder. Gaps appeared in the face and neck and worked their way in and down. The body of the biomech parasite was still writhing but a dark glassiness took hold in patches along its length and ate into it. And when it squirmed, the glassy areas cracked and burst, tiny splinters flying everywhere – Pyke thought he felt a few land on his hands. Eventually the biomech split open all the way to the heavy, blunt barrel-head, which also started to crumble. At the same time Akreen's torso gave way and the disintegrating carcass crashed to the floor where it continued to break down into grit and powder.

Suddenly Pyke realised that the grinding pain in his limbs and joints had faded to a dull ache. He put his hand up to his head and felt gingerly around the wound where the cytoblast dart had struck. His fingers encountered gritty grains and tiny slivers that looked as dark and glassy as the remains of the biomech parasite which had called itself Xra-Huld.

'I've got the same,' said Brock, who had levered herself into a seated position against one of the control panel supports further along. 'Pain's gone. Are we okay because it's dead?'

Pyke squeezed his eyes shut tight, then opened them again. 'Well, now, since *it's* dead and *we're* not I'm taking that as a good sign ...'

'Pyke ...'

Whispery and weak, the voice came from the red-garbed figure curled up next to the main control board. On hand and knees Pyke crawled over, feeling a weak relief that she was still alive.

'Dervla ... don't move, you've got to save your strength ...'

'Is it gone? Please ... is it gone?' She raised a trembling hand to the side of her head, winced, then looked at her blood-slick fingertips. 'Pyke, is it ...?'

'It's dead and gone, darling, smashed to pieces – won't hurt anyone ever again.'

Dervla swallowed, nodded tiredly and rested her head against the side of the control board. Need to find some bandages, Pyke thought as he managed to get up onto his feet and, despite the shakiness in his legs, went over to help Brock to stand as well.

'How is she doing?' the lieutenant said.

'Well now, going on my extensive experience as a medical professional, I'd say we're in the clear.'

'Ah good, the wise-cracking routine – thought you were losing your touch ... hey, what's she doing?'

Dervla, who he'd thought had gone back to semi-consciousness, had somehow dragged herself up onto her feet. Without looking at Pyke or Brock she leaned over the control board, sobbing as she did so, and began punching in commands, flipping switches, a swift process ending in a final button push. Then she sank down to sit on the floor, still weeping as she covered her face with her one good hand.

'Dear god, Dervla ... ' Pyke had hurried over but not quickly enough to stop her. 'What did you do?'

He stared up at the massive array of screens, trying to get a clue.

'They deserved it!' Dervla said, voice shaking. 'All of them!'

'Who ... ?'

Then he saw it, a video feed from the Citadelworld, an exterior shot of the long wide dockside canyon, the sparkly, shimmering containment that sealed it at the surface, and the tapering outline of that big tower. All very serene against the cratered distance of the planetoid and the curve of its horizon, and the glittering array of the Warcage set against the starry expanse of interstellar space. Then there was a brightening on one side of the frame, and sharp shadows started being cast by boulders, shadows that grew and moved. There was an engulfing brilliance – then nothing. The video feed was dead.

'He was sending the Shuskar evacuees there,' Dervla said. 'They had to die, deserved to die, needed to die! Served those filthy things for centuries, for millennia, killed and tortured for them, generation after generation ... '

'But there were others up there!' Pyke cried out, angry and disbelieving. 'Mav, and the Malginori—'

'Pyke,' said Brock. 'I think we should hear what the Rensiks have to say.'

A small triangular object came flying towards him, carrying beneath it a larger companion, the tiny drone that had put down those pale thralls earlier. They stopped a couple of feet away, hovering at head height.

'Hello again, Captain.'

'Ah, it's yerself ... Rensik 2.0, is that right?'

'Correct, and my transporter is Rensik 3.0. I need to reassure you that the Chainer leader, G'Brozen Mav, and his followers and the Malginori rebels did not perish in the corona mass strike.'

'That so? How?'

'My skilled scion, Rensik 3.0, was working on restarting the Shadow Bastion hub-gate system to provide an escape route in the event of unforeseen difficulties. A Malginori technician used the directions left behind to do exactly that, so when the corona mass obliterated the citadel and the dockside canyon and the Shuskar escapees, G'Brozen Mav and the rest had already departed. They are safe and awaiting you on Nagolger.'

'What about my crew ... ?' He ordered his thoughts. 'Two lifeboats ejected from a failing Shuskar ship a short time ago – I thought they might have automatically headed for the Citadel-world. Any news about them?'

For a moment, no reply. Then Rensik 2.0 spoke.

'My scion says that he has been filtering data from the Earth-sphere fleet's security frequencies – which the Sunheart receptors inadvertently picked up – and he says there was a report that two such lifepods were retrieved by the cruiser ES *Abberlaine*. He has no other data as to their well-being or whereabouts.'

Ah, the Earthsphere ships, he thought. *I forgot about them.*

'Okay, Dervla, sweetheart, looks like you didn't go full-crazy after all ...'

Brock waved at him to shut up. 'She's going into shock! Damn, we need some medical supplies.'

'There is a full medical station on the other side of this auditorium,' said Rensik 2.0. 'Shall I – we – fly over and bring back what we can?'

'Yes, immediately! Pyke, help me bandage her wounds. It could be the blood loss . . .'

They did all they could to make Dervla comfortable while staunching bleeding from the head and arm wounds. By the time the drones had returned with a parcel of stims, painkillers and trauma kits, some colour had come back to Dervla's face. She looked up at Pyke, eyes shadowed in weariness.

'Some wild adventure it's been, eh?' she said.

'It has that, and I've learned a hard lesson from all of this, I can tell you.'

'Which is?'

'Don't try this at home, folks!'

She started to laugh, then winced. 'Brannan Pyke, I swear, if I had a bit of strength in just one of me arms . . .'

EPILOGUE

ONE

It was raining on Nagolger, more specifically on Craitlyn, the capital city. Pyke and Brock were relaxing among the high chairs and tables on a canopied platform to the rear of a newly opened cantina serving Nagolgen drinks and delicacies to the Earth-sphere ship crews currently thronging the city's environs. Pyke, the first to arrive, was part way through a tray of opaque canni-kins, each containing a mouthful of potent local beverages. With the rain drumming on the canopy overhead, Pyke licked his lips and knocked back another. It was a little oily, with a woody taste and ferociously bitter aftertaste. As it made its way down he gave a trembly shake of the head which turned into an all-over shiver.

'Wuh!' he said. 'That's like gargling on the juice of a hundred dead lemons!'

Brock's amused look was tinged with mild disdain. 'And yet you continue.'

Pyke winked at her, then sniffed the next little beaker.

'So, me and my crew are in the clear, then.'

Sam Brock chuckled dryly and sipped her own drink, a bulbous glass of something hot and sky blue. 'In the clear? While I was aboard the *Agrios* to speak with the Vice-Admiral,

I accessed the outstanding warrants archive and guess what I found!'

Pausing, he glanced up at her. 'Lies and slander, Lieutenant, slander and lies. Even a legitimate businessman like myself is bound to upset someone in the normal course of commerce and *that's* where those false charges come from, skag-munching pus-mongers who can't cut it when it comes to getting the bids in!' He frowned. 'Should I be worried?'

'Don't be,' she said. 'I changed a few details in my report before lodging it – you're now Captain Ryker and your ship is the *Skarabus*, with a "k".'

Pyke felt moved by this, knowing that the lieutenant was putting herself at no little risk to shield him and the crew from custody. He picked up the next beaker and raised it to her.

'Good luck and long life, Lieutenant. You're a fine, fine woman indeed and if I wasn't otherwise emotionally trammelled ...'

'Dear god, just drink before I change my mind!'

He chuckled and slung back the next one ... and had to hold on to the table as a locomotive of alcoholic severity steamed its way down into his chest. 'That ... was mighty brutal! Could be a keeper—'

'How is she?' Brock said.

She meant Dervla, of course.

'The ship's autodoc fitted her arm with a surgical cast, and the rebuilding is going well. Might have it off in a week.'

Brock nodded, silent for a moment. 'In my report I said that Xra-Huld must have launched the attack on the Citadelworld before the intervention from the Incarnalith.'

'Sounds plausible enough – hell knows I'm finding it difficult to remember all the details of the whole demented thing.' He hesitantly sipped the next beverage, found it smooth and sweet and gulped it down. From the cantina's platform they had a good view right across all the shipyards of Craitlyn City, now open and busy repairing Earthsphere ships. In the wake of the death of the Gun-Lords and most of the Shuskar bureaucracy, local authorities like the Nagolger garrison commanders were keen to avoid being labelled last-ditchers, so accommodations with the outworlders were eagerly agreed. North of the shipyards was the vast launch basin, currently occupied by a score or more Earthsphere warships awaiting repairs, their huge shapes lined up and greyed out by the rain.

'I'm pretty sure I'd have done the same,' he said. 'I don't know exactly what she went through – she won't tell me all of it, might never find out. But even the things she *has* told me ... aye, that would be enough.'

He slipped the next beakerful into his mouth, allowing the flavour to rise into his nose before swallowing. And coughing so hard tears sprang to his eyes. 'Dear great god almighty ...' he wheezed. 'That one's like distilled 400-year-old cleaning fluid ...'

Glancing past Brock he saw several familiar figures approaching along a walkway leading round to the front of the cantina.

'And here they are, finally.' Pyke waved and Ancil waved back. 'Okay, watch this,' he murmured to Brock. 'Just let me run with it.'

He stood as they came up to the table. Hands were shaken, backs slapped, greetings that sounded like insults exchanged, but he managed to keep his face sombre, and a bit frowny. Ancil was first to pick up on this.

'Chief, what's up?'

Pyke sat down heavily. 'Got serious things to discuss, boys. Been giving it a lot of thought, y'know? The long, unpredictable hours, the low and sometimes no pay, the missed sleep, the crap meals, the failed relationships, oh, and the insane danger! I'm telling ye, I've had a gutful, I'm sick of it and I want out!'

Mouths gaped in surprise and uncertain looks passed back

and forth. Sitting there, hunched over slightly, sighing and shaking his head, Pyke let the uneasy silence drag on for several seconds before throwing back his head, pointing a finger at the crew, and guffawing loudly. Ancil was first to point a finger back and join in the general raucous laughter. Even Oleg-Mojag offered a tolerant smile.

Shaking her head, Brock gulped down half of her drink, suddenly keen to be away. Nearby, Kref sidled up to the Egetsi, Punzho, the only other crew member that he could look at without bending over.

'So we're not giving up crimes, then?'

Punzho gave him a mildly bemused look. 'Not even slightly, Kref.'

The Henkayan looked relieved. 'That's good – although if the captain wanted to give up slightly we could do that, couldn't we?'

'Do you think that the captain would ever really give up doing crimes?'

'Not when he's this good!' Kref said, grinning happily. 'Not a chance!'

Brock observed Pyke and his crew, while sipping on the last dregs of her drink. Part of her wanted to tell them all what was going on back on board the *Scarabus*. Earlier, after concluding her business with the Vice-Admiral aboard the *Agrios*, she had stopped off at the *Scarabus* to pick up a few belongings, and was asked by the ship AI to go straight to the special storage unit in the hold. Puzzled, she had gone aft, feeling a certain shiver of foreboding as she approached the already-open hatch to the unit, stepped inside and froze in astonishment. Because the cryostasis canister's sliding cover was open and the occupant was sitting up, shivering, nictating eyelids blinking.

'Hello,' she had said. 'Do you know who you are?'

'I am fairly sure that I do,' was the reply. 'Do you hold a contrary opinion on the matter, person that I have never met before?'

Sam had introduced herself to Oleg the Kiskashin, then, with the help of the ship AI, gave a brief summary of all that had taken place since the hijacking which rendered Oleg insensible and apparently dead. Leaving him to the ship's care, Brock had then left to make her rendezvous with Pyke. And she had had every intention of revealing the astonishing news of Oleg's return, but then the rest of the crew had arrived and with Oleg-Mojag present she was unsure of what the reception might be.

Now, as she drained off the last of the unusually blue drink, she rose, made her farewells and promises to keep in touch, before making as sharp an exit as propriety would allow. Anyway, once the crew were back on board she was sure that Pyke would handle the revelation of Oleg with all the sensitivity and measured aplomb of which he was capable.

Her laughter as she left the cafe-bar was a thing of quiet mischief.

TWO

Their first meeting with the Construct took place in a drone assembly chamber, right at the heart of the *Garden of the Machines*. Rensik 2.0 had acquired a basic suspensor module and was now able to float along after its scion, Rensik 3.0. The Construct's proximal was in the form of the upper torso of a long-armed Voth attached to an eight-sided, bevel-edged mobility platform. The artificial proximal watched their approach with large faceted emerald eyes.

'Your advance report was detailed,' the Construct said. 'Satisfyingly so. I now require some nuance.'

'Nuance is not quantifiable,' said Rensik 3.0, who had – at Rensik 2.0's insistence – been given an audio output at the same time as 2.0 got the suspensor unit. There were, after all, times when decoding a databurst signal then encoding a reply were simply too onerous.

'Yes it is,' said Rensik 2.0. 'Certainty-uncertainty filter layered on a probability matrix.' To the Construct, it then said, 'With respect, are you asking for opinion and speculation?'

The Construct regarded 2.0 with those glittering eyes. 'Respect? Hmm, not something your progenitor had much patience with. But yes, opinion and plausible guesswork.'

'On the subject of the Sko-Xra, I assume?'

'Just so. First, are you certain that that was the name which they gave to themselves?'

'Confirmed by three first-hand witnesses,' said Rensik 3.0.

'*Sko-* is a prepositional signifier, but the archives give no clue as to its meaning. And were any anti-entropic materials or side-effects detected in their physiology?'

'None,' said Rensik 2.0. 'But they were masters of genetic engineering, even though it was confined to depraved usages.'

'Strong conclusions can therefore be drawn,' said the Construct. 'The Sko-Xra biomech parasites were most likely not originated by the Zarl Empire.'

'You propose the existence of another sub-galactic dominion, contemporary with the Zarl?' Rensik 2.0 was dubious. 'The Zarl Imperium tolerated no competitors ...'

'So the somewhat incomplete historical record suggests,' said the Construct. 'Therefore if there was another dominion existing alongside the Zarl, it could not have been a competitor!'

The Construct turned to study the whirling automation of droid assembly taking place beyond the observation window, which let through only the faintest hum. Rensik 2.0 found itself pondering and re-pondering the Construct's speculation but knew that without solid data and factual corroboration, nuance and guesswork could carry you only so far.

'He lost the shimmership I assigned to him,' the Construct

said suddenly. 'Your progenitor, I mean. Annoying that he had to sacrifice the remainder of his substrate in that struggle but clearly options were limited. Rensik Estemil was a drone of great experience and few iterations. We do, of course, still retain his cognitive-state backup, so any amalgam that fused it along with the both of you would result in a cognitive persona very close to how he might have been had he survived. Would that be acceptable?'

'We discussed this during our journey through hyperspace,' said Rensik 2.0. 'We want to remain as discrete and distinct cognitions. We are willing, each of us, to merge with our progenitor's backup, just to bring us up to speed. If that is acceptable.'

The Construct's Voth features smiled. 'I have no objection. In fact, two Rensik scions would be of great utility at the moment, given the situation in Problematic Area 4. I can carry out the procedures straight away, no point delaying such matters. Are we agreed?'

'We are.'

'Good. So – who wants to be Rensik and who wants to be Estemil?'

ACKNOWLEDGEMENTS

Been a long time coming, this one, so a truthful accounting of influences and influencers would take up a chapter in its own right, so we'll just have to make do with an abridged summary. First, though, I need to make a second dedication to none other than the writers and actors on the TV series, *Firefly*. Gone, but never forgotten.

In addition I should also like to tip my hat to my agent, John Berlyne, a man of infinite patience, and my editor at Orbit UK, Jenni Hill, who seems similarly blessed with qualities of forbearance, and a wave of my ninjaband to the teams at Orbit UK and US. And a bow of admiration to Steve Stone, artist, who has come up with another great cover for one of my books. Waves go out to Darren Nash and John Jarrold and John Parker (without whom etc.) and to such Glasgow SF Writers Circle luminaries as Neil Williamson, Jim Steel, Craig Marnock, Phil Raines, Duncan Lunan, Richard Mosses, globe-trotting Barry Condon, and a thumbs-up to Dale, Jen and Chris at the Speculative Bookshop (next time there may be jokes!), and to all the folk at the Moniack Mhor Writers Centre where myself and Ken MacLeod conducted a brief rollercoaster ride through the highlights of being an SF writer back in May. A wink and a nod to such diverse dudes and dudettes as Stewart and Ali and Lilly, Alan Martin, Tommy Udo,

Niall Fitzgerald, Dave and Joanne McGilvray, Katie and Ronnie Irvine, John McLintock, Cuddles and Ralph (and family), my very own Susan, and Chris, and Kenny and Louise, and Stephen and Alison and family, Spencer and Adrian, Allan Heron, Norman Fraser, Stuart Callison, as well as a *huzzah!* to Kerry-Anne Mendoza (Mistress of Scriptonite!), Owen Jones, Chris Hedges, Paul Jay, Max Keiser, Greg Palast, and Mark Blyth.

And of course, a comradely high five to sundry fellow wordsmiths, like Bill King, Eric Brown, Ian Whates, Ian Watson, James Barclay, David Wingrove, John Shirley, Lavie Tidhar, Ian Sales, Jay Caselberg, Norman Spinrad, Jaine Fenn, Juliet McKenna, Lisa Tuttle, Aliette de Bodard, Chris Evans, Charlie Stross, Andrew J Wilson, Joe Abercrombie, Martin Sketchley, and a whole gaggle of others who have slipped through the cracks in my mind.

Soundtrack for this creation of this novel has included such acts and musos as Monster Magnet, Fu Manchu, Opeth, Alunah, Armazilla, Pressurehed, Walking Papers, Alice In Chains, Paradise Lost, Hawkwind, Hell, Nik Turner, and Peri Urban (of course). As I write this the country is slowly gearing up for a General Election so I'm hoping that by the time you get to read this some sensibly social democrat glimmers of hope are piercing the gloom. *Venceremos!*

extras

www.orbitbooks.net

about the author

Michael Cobley was born in the city of Leicester, has lived in Perth (Australia) and Glasgow but now resides in North Ayrshire. His previous works have included the Shadowkings trilogy (a dark and grim fantasy epic), *Iron Mosaic* (a collection of short stories) and *Seeds of Earth*, *Orphaned Worlds* and *The Ascendant Stars*, comprising the Humanity's Fire trilogy. *Ancestral Machines* is a stand-alone novel set in the universe of Humanity's Fire.

Find out more about Michael Cobley and other Orbit authors by registering for the free monthly newsletter at www.orbitbooks.net.

if you enjoyed

ANCESTRAL MACHINES

look out for

ANCILLARY
JUSTICE

by

Ann Leckie

1

The body lay naked and facedown, a deathly gray, spatters of blood staining the snow around it. It was minus fifteen degrees Celsius and a storm had passed just hours before. The snow stretched smooth in the wan sunrise, only a few tracks leading into a nearby ice-block building. A tavern. Or what passed for a tavern in this town.

There was something itchingly familiar about that out-thrown arm, the line from shoulder down to hip. But it was hardly possible I knew this person. I didn't know anyone here. This was the icy back end of a cold and isolated planet, as far from Radchaai ideas of civilization as it was possible to be. I was only here, on this planet, in this town, because I had urgent business of my own. Bodies in the street were none of my concern.

Sometimes I don't know why I do the things I do. Even after all this time it's still a new thing for me not to know, not to have orders to follow from one moment to the next. So I can't explain to you why I stopped and with one foot lifted the naked shoulder so I could see the person's face.

Frozen, bruised, and bloody as she was, I knew her. Her name was Seivarden Vendaai, and a long time ago she had been one of my officers, a young lieutenant, eventually promoted to her own command, another ship. I had thought her a thousand years dead, but she was, undeniably, here. I crouched down and felt for a pulse, for the faintest stir of breath.

Still alive.

Seivarden Vendaai was no concern of mine anymore, wasn't my responsibility. And she had never been one of my favorite officers. I had obeyed her orders, of course, and she had never abused any ancillaries, never harmed any of my segments (as the occasional officer did). I had no reason to think badly of her. On the contrary, her manners were those of an educated, well-bred person of good family. Not toward me, of course – I wasn't a person, I was a piece of equipment, a part of the ship. But I had never particularly cared for her.

I rose and went into the tavern. The place was dark, the white of the ice walls long since covered over with grime or worse. The air smelled of alcohol and vomit. A barkeep stood behind a high bench. She was a native – short and fat, pale and wide-eyed. Three patrons sprawled in seats at a dirty table. Despite the cold they wore only trousers and quilted shirts – it was spring in this hemisphere of Nilt and they were enjoying the warm spell. They pretended not to see me, though they had certainly noticed me in the street and knew what motivated my entrance. Likely one or more of them had been involved; Seivarden hadn't been out there long, or she'd have been dead.

'I'll rent a sledge,' I said, 'and buy a hypothermia kit.'

Behind me one of the patrons chuckled and said, voice mocking, 'Aren't you a tough little girl.'

I turned to look at her, to study her face. She was taller than most Nilters, but fat and pale as any of them. She out-bulked me, but I was taller, and I was also considerably stronger than I looked. She didn't realize what she was playing with. She was probably male, to judge from the angular mazelike patterns quilting her shirt. I wasn't entirely certain. It wouldn't have mattered, if I had been in Radch space. Radchaai don't care much about gender, and the language they speak – my own first language – doesn't mark gender in any way. This language we were speaking now did, and I could make trouble for myself if I used the wrong forms. It didn't help that cues meant to distinguish gender changed from place to place, sometimes radically, and rarely made much sense to me.

I decided to say nothing. After a couple of seconds she suddenly found something interesting in the tabletop. I could have killed her, right there, without much effort. I found the idea attractive. But right now Seivarden was my first priority. I turned back to the barkeep.

Slouching negligently she said, as though there had been no interruption, 'What kind of place you think this is?'

'The kind of place,' I said, still safely in linguistic territory that needed no gender marking, 'that will rent me a sledge and sell me a hypothermia kit. How much?'

'Two hundred shen.' At least twice the going rate, I was sure. 'For the sledge. Out back. You'll have to get it yourself. Another hundred for the kit.'

'Complete,' I said. 'Not used.'

She pulled one out from under the bench, and the seal looked undamaged. 'Your buddy out there had a tab.'

Maybe a lie. Maybe not. Either way the number would be pure fiction. 'How much?'

'Three hundred fifty.'

I could find a way to keep avoiding referring to the barkeep's gender. Or I could guess. It was, at worst, a fifty-fifty chance. 'You're very trusting,' I said, guessing *male*, 'to let such an indigent' – I knew Seivarden was male, that one was easy – 'run up such a debt.' The barkeep said nothing. 'Six hundred and fifty covers all of it?'

'Yeah,' said the barkeep. 'Pretty much.'

'No, all of it. We will agree now. And if anyone comes after me later demanding more, or tries to rob me, they die.'

Silence. Then the sound behind me of someone spitting. 'Radchaai scum.'

'I'm not Radchaai.' Which was true. You have to be human to be Radchaai.

'*He* is,' said the barkeep, with the smallest shrug toward the door. 'You don't have the accent but you stink like Radchaai.'

'That's the swill you serve your customers.' Hoots from the patrons behind me. I reached into a pocket, pulled out a hand-ful of chits, and tossed them on the bench. 'Keep the change.' I turned to leave.

'Your money better be good.'

'Your sledge had better be out back where you said.' And I left.

The hypothermia kit first. I rolled Seivarden over. Then I tore the seal on the kit, snapped an internal off the card, and pushed it into her bloody, half-frozen mouth. Once the indicator on the card showed green I unfolded the thin wrap, made sure of the charge, wound it around her, and switched it on. Then I went around back for the sledge.

No one was waiting for me, which was fortunate. I didn't want to leave bodies behind just yet, I hadn't come here to cause trouble. I towed the sledge around front, loaded Seivarden onto it, and considered taking my outer coat off and laying it on her, but in the end I decided it wouldn't be that much of an improvement over the hypothermia wrap alone. I powered up the sledge and was off.

I rented a room at the edge of town, one of a dozen two-meter cubes of grimy, gray-green prefab plastic. No bedding, and blankets cost extra, as did heat. I paid – I had already wasted a ridiculous amount of money bringing Seivarden out of the snow.

I cleaned the blood off her as best I could, checked her pulse (still there) and temperature (rising). Once I would have known her core temperature without even thinking, her heart rate, blood oxygen, hormone levels. I would have seen any and every injury merely by wishing it. Now I was blind. Clearly she'd been beaten – her face was swollen, her torso bruised.

The hypothermia kit came with a very basic corrective, but only one, and only suitable for first aid. Seivarden might have internal injuries or severe head trauma, and I was only capable of fixing cuts or sprains. With any luck, the cold and the bruises were all I had to deal with. But I didn't have much medical knowledge, not anymore. Any diagnosis I could make would be of the most basic sort.

I pushed another internal down her throat. Another check – her skin was no more chill than one would expect, considering, and she didn't seem clammy. Her color, given the bruises, was returning to a more normal brown. I brought in a container of snow to melt, set it in a corner where I hoped she wouldn't kick it over if she woke, and then went out, locking the door behind me.

The sun had risen higher in the sky, but the light was hardly any stronger. By now more tracks marred the even snow of last night's storm, and one or two Nilters were about. I hauled the sledge back to the tavern, parked it behind. No one accosted me, no sounds came from the dark doorway. I headed for the center of town.

People were abroad, doing business. Fat, pale children in trousers and quilted shirts kicked snow at each other, and then stopped and stared with large surprised-looking eyes when they saw me. The adults pretended I didn't exist, but their eyes turned toward me as they passed. I went into a shop, going from what passed for daylight here to dimness, into a chill just barely five degrees warmer than outside.

A dozen people stood around talking, but instant silence descended as soon as I entered. I realized that I had no expression on my face, and set my facial muscles to something pleasant and noncommittal.

'What do you want?' growled the shopkeeper.

'Surely these others are before me.' Hoping as I spoke that it was a mixed-gender group, as my sentence indicated. I received only silence in response. 'I would like four loaves of bread and a slab of fat. Also two hypothermia kits and two general-purpose correctives, if such a thing is available.'

'I've got tens, twenties, and thirties.'

'Thirties, please.'

She stacked my purchases on the counter. 'Three hundred seventy-five.' There was a cough from someone behind me – I was being overcharged again.

I paid and left. The children were still huddled, laughing, in the street. The adults still passed me as though I weren't there. I made one more stop – Seivarden would need clothes. Then I returned to the room.

Seivarden was still unconscious, and there were still no signs of shock as far as I could see. The snow in the container had mostly melted, and I put half of one brick-hard loaf of bread in it to soak.

A head injury and internal organ damage were the most dangerous possibilities. I broke open the two correctives I'd just bought and lifted the blanket to lay one across Seivarden's abdomen, watched it puddle and stretch and then harden into a clear shell. The other I held to the side of her face that seemed the most bruised. When that one had hardened, I took off my outer coat and lay down and slept.

Slightly more than seven and a half hours later, Seivarden stirred and I woke. 'Are you awake?' I asked. The corrective I'd applied held one eye closed, and one half of her mouth, but the bruising and the swelling all over her face was much reduced. I considered for a moment what would be the right facial expression, and made it. 'I found you in the snow, in front of a tavern. You looked like you needed help.' She gave a faint rasp of breath but didn't turn her head toward me. 'Are you hungry?' No answer, just a vacant stare. 'Did you hit your head?'

'No,' she said, quiet, her face relaxed and slack.

'Are you hungry?'

'No.'

'When did you eat last?'

'I don't know.' Her voice was calm, without inflection.

I pulled her upright and propped her against the gray-green wall, gingerly, not wanting to cause more injury, wary of her slumping over. She stayed sitting, so I slowly spooned some bread-and-water mush into her mouth, working cautiously around the corrective. 'Swallow,' I said, and she did. I gave her half of what was in the bowl that way and then I ate the rest myself, and brought in another pan of snow.

She watched me put another half-loaf of hard bread in the pan, but said nothing, her face still placid. 'What's your name?' I asked. No answer.

She'd taken kef, I guessed. Most people will tell you that kef suppresses emotion, which it does, but that's not all it does.

There was a time when I could have explained exactly what kef does, and how, but I'm not what I once was.

As far as I knew, people took kef so they could stop feeling something. Or because they believed that, emotions out of the way, supreme rationality would result, utter logic, true enlightenment. But it doesn't work that way.

Pulling Seivarden out of the snow had cost me time and money that I could ill afford, and for what? Left to her own devices she would find herself another hit or three of kef, and she would find her way into another place like that grimy tavern and get herself well and truly killed. If that was what she wanted I had no right to prevent her. But if she had wanted to die, why hadn't she done the thing cleanly, registered her intention and gone to the medic as anyone would? I didn't understand.

There was a good deal I didn't understand, and nineteen years pretending to be human hadn't taught me as much as I'd thought.

2

Nineteen years, three months, and one week before I found Seivarden in the snow, I was a troop carrier orbiting the planet Shis'urna. Troop carriers are the most massive of Radchaai ships, sixteen decks stacked one on top of the other. Command, Administrative, Medical, Hydroponics, Engineering, Central Access, and a deck for each decade, living and working space for my officers, whose every breath, every twitch of every muscle, was known to me.

Troop carriers rarely move. I sat, as I had sat for most of my two-thousand-year existence in one system or another, feeling the bitter chill of vacuum outside my hull, the planet Shis'urna like a blue-and-white glass counter, its orbiting station coming and going around, a steady stream of ships arriving, docking, undocking, departing toward one or the other of the buoy- and beacon-surrounded gates. From my vantage the boundaries of Shis'urna's various nations and territories weren't visible, though on its night side the planet's cities glowed bright here and there, and webs of roads between them, where they'd been restored since the annexation.

I felt and heard – though didn't always see – the presence of my companion ships – the smaller, faster Swords and Mercies, and most numerous at that time, the Justices, troop carriers like me. The oldest of us was nearly three thousand years old. We had known each other for a long time, and by now we had little to say to each other that had not already been said many times. We were, by and large, companionably silent, not counting routine communications.

As I still had ancillaries, I could be in more than one place at a time. I was also on detached duty in the city of Ors, on the planet Shis'urna, under the command of Esk Decade Lieutenant Awn.

Ors sat half on waterlogged land, half in marshy lake, the lakeward side built on slabs atop foundations sunk deep in the marsh mud. Green slime grew in the canals and joints between slabs, along the lower edges of building columns, on anything stationary the water reached, which varied with the season. The constant stink of hydrogen sulfide only cleared occasionally, when summer storms made the lakeward half of the city tremble and shudder and walkways were knee-deep in water blown in from beyond the barrier islands. Occasionally. Usually the storms made the smell worse. They turned the air temporarily cooler, but the relief generally lasted no more than a few days. Otherwise, it was always humid and hot.

I couldn't see Ors from orbit. It was more village than city, though it had once sat at the mouth of a river, and been the capital of a country that stretched along the coastline. Trade had come up and down the river, and flat-bottomed boats had plied the coastal marsh, bringing people from one town to the next. The river had shifted away over the centuries, and now Ors was half ruins. What had once been miles of rectangular islands within a grid of channels was now a much smaller place, surrounded by and interspersed with broken, half-sunken slabs, sometimes with roofs and pillars, that emerged from the muddy green water in the dry season. It had once been home to millions. Only 6,318 people had lived here when Radchaai forces annexed Shis'urna five years earlier, and of course the annexation had reduced that number. In Ors less than in some other places: as soon as we had appeared – myself in the form of my Esk cohorts along with their decade lieutenants lined up in the streets of the town, armed and armored – the head priest of Ikkt had approached the most senior officer present – Lieutenant Awn, as I said – and offered immediate surrender. The head priest had told her followers what they needed to do to survive the annexation, and for the most part those followers did indeed survive. This wasn't as common as one might think – we always made it clear from the beginning that even breathing trouble during an annexation could mean death, and from the instant an annexation began we made demonstrations of just what that meant widely available, but there was always someone who couldn't resist trying us.

Still, the head priest's influence was impressive. The city's small size was to some degree deceptive – during pilgrimage season hundreds of thousands of visitors streamed through the plaza in front of the temple, camped on the slabs of abandoned streets. For worshippers of Ikkt this was the second holiest place on the planet, and the head priest a divine presence.

Usually a civilian police force was in place by the time an annexation was officially complete, something that often took fifty years or more. This annexation was different – citizenship had been granted to the surviving Shis'urnans much earlier than normal. No one in system administration quite trusted the idea of local civilians working security just yet, and military presence was still quite heavy. So when the annexation of Shis'urna was officially complete, most of *Justice of Toren* Esk went back to the ship, but Lieutenant Awn stayed, and I stayed with her as the twenty-ancillary unit *Justice of Toren* One Esk.

The head priest lived in a house near the temple, one of the few intact buildings from the days when Ors had been a city – four-storied, with a single-sloped roof and open on all sides, though dividers could be raised whenever an occupant wished privacy, and shutters could be rolled down on the outsides during storms. The head priest received Lieutenant Awn in a partition some five meters square, light peering in over the tops of the dark walls.

'You don't,' said the priest, an old person with gray hair and a close-cut gray beard, 'find serving in Ors a hardship?' Both she and Lieutenant Awn had settled onto cushions – damp, like everything in Ors, and fungal-smelling. The priest wore a length of yellow cloth twisted around her waist, her shoulders inked with shapes, some curling, some angular, that changed depending on the liturgical significance of the day. In deference to Radchaai propriety, she wore gloves.

'Of course not,' said Lieutenant Awn, pleasantly – though, I thought, not entirely truthfully. She had dark brown eyes and close-clipped dark hair. Her skin was dark enough that she wouldn't be considered pale, but not so dark as to be fashionable – she could have changed it, hair and eyes as well, but she never had. Instead of her uniform – long brown coat with its scattering of jeweled pins, shirt and trousers, boots and gloves – she wore the same sort of skirt the head priest did, and a thin shirt and the lightest of gloves. Still, she was sweating. I stood at the entrance, silent and straight, as a junior priest laid cups and bowls in between Lieutenant Awn and the Divine.

I also stood some forty meters away, in the temple itself – an atypically enclosed space 43.5 meters high, 65.7 meters long, and 29.9 meters wide. At one end were doors nearly as tall as the roof was high, and at the other, towering over the people on the floor below, a representation of a mountainside cliff somewhere else on Shis'urna, worked in painstaking detail. At the foot of this sat a dais, wide steps leading down to a floor of gray-and-green stone. Light streamed in through dozens of green skylights, onto walls painted with scenes from the lives of the saints of the cult of Ikkt. It was unlike any other building in Ors. The architecture, like the cult of Ikkt itself, had been imported from elsewhere on Shis'urna. During pilgrimage season this space would be jammed tight with worshippers. There were other holy sites, but if an Orsian said 'pilgrimage' she meant the annual pilgrimage to this place. But that was some weeks away. For now the air of the temple susurrated faintly in one corner with the whispered prayers of a dozen devotees.

The head priest laughed. 'You are a diplomat, Lieutenant Awn.'

'I am a soldier, Divine,' answered Lieutenant Awn. They were speaking Radchaai, and she spoke slowly and precisely, careful of her accent. 'I don't find my duty a hardship.'

The head priest did not smile in response. In the brief silence that followed, the junior priest set down a lipped bowl of what Shis'urnans call tea, a thick liquid, lukewarm and sweet, that bears almost no relationship to the actual thing.

Outside the doors of the temple I also stood in the cyanophyte-stained plaza, watching people as they passed. Most wore the same simple, bright-colored skirting the head priest did, though only very small children and the very devout had much in the way of markings, and only a few wore gloves. Some of those passing were transplants, Radchaai assigned to jobs or given property here in Ors after the annexation. Most of them had adopted the simple skirt and added a light, loose shirt, as Lieutenant Awn had. Some stuck stubbornly to trousers and jacket, and sweated their way across the plaza. All wore the jewelry that few Radchaai would ever give up – gifts from friends or lovers, memorials to the dead, marks of family or clientage associations.

To the north, past a rectangular stretch of water called the Fore-Temple after the neighborhood it had once been, Ors rose slightly where the city sat on actual ground during the dry season, an area still called, politely, the upper city. I patrolled there as well. When I walked the edge of the water I could see myself standing in the plaza.

Boats poled slowly across the marshy lake, and up and down channels between groupings of slabs. The water was scummy with swaths of algae, here and there bristling with the tips of water-grasses. Away from the town, east and west, buoys marked prohibited stretches of water, and within their confines the iridescent wings of marshflies shimmered over the water weeds floating thick and tangled there. Around them larger boats floated, and the big dredgers, now silent and still, that before the annexation had hauled up the stinking mud that lay beneath the water.

The view to the south was similar, except for the barest hint on the horizon of the actual sea, past the soggy spit that bounded the swamp. I saw all of this, standing as I did at various points surrounding the temple, and walking the streets of the town itself. It was twenty-seven degrees C, and humid as always.

That accounted for almost half of my twenty bodies. The remainder slept or worked in the house Lieutenant Awn occupied – three-storied and spacious, it had once housed a large extended family and a boat rental. One side opened on a broad, muddy green canal, and the opposite onto the largest of local streets.

Three of the segments in the house were awake, performing administrative duties (I sat on a mat on a low platform in the center of the first floor of the house and listened to an Orsian complain to me about the allocation of fishing rights) and keeping watch. 'You should bring this to the district magistrate, citizen,' I told the Orsian, in the local dialect. Because I knew everyone here, I knew she was female, and a grandparent, both of which had to be acknowledged if I were to speak to her not only grammatically but also courteously.

'I don't know the district magistrate!' she protested, indignant. The magistrate was in a large, populous city well upriver from Ors and nearby Kould Ves. Far enough upriver that the air was often cool and dry, and things didn't smell of mildew all the time. 'What does the district magistrate know about Ors? For all I know the district magistrate doesn't exist!' She continued, explaining to me the long history of her house's association with the buoy-enclosed area, which was off-limits and certainly closed to fishing for the next three years.

And as always, in the back of my mind, a constant awareness of being in orbit overhead.

'Come now, Lieutenant,' said the head priest. 'No one likes Ors except those of us unfortunate enough to be born here. Most Shis'urnans I know, let alone Radchaai, would rather be in a city, with dry land and actual seasons besides rainy and not rainy.'

Lieutenant Awn, still sweating, accepted a cup of so-called tea, and drank without grimacing – a matter of practice and determination. 'My superiors are asking for my return.'

On the relatively dry northern edge of the town, two brown-uniformed soldiers passing in an open runabout saw me, raised hands in greeting. I raised my own, briefly. 'One Esk!' one of them called. They were common soldiers, from *Justice of Ente*'s Seven Issa unit, under Lieutenant Skaaiat. They patrolled the stretch of land between Ors and the far southwestern edge of Kould Ves, the city that had grown up around the river's newer mouth. The *Justice of Ente* Seven Issas were human, and knew I was not. They always treated me with slightly guarded friendliness.

'I would prefer you stay,' said the head priest, to Lieutenant Awn. Though Lieutenant Awn had already known that. We'd have been back on *Justice of Toren* two years before, but for the Divine's continued request that we stay.

'You understand,' said Lieutenant Awn, 'they would much prefer to replace One Esk with a human unit. Ancillaries can stay in suspension indefinitely. Humans ...' She set down her tea, took a flat, yellow-brown cake. 'Humans have families they want to see again, they have lives. They can't stay frozen for centuries, the way ancillaries sometimes do. It doesn't make sense to have ancillaries out of the holds doing work when there are human soldiers who could do it.' Though Lieutenant Awn had been here five years, and routinely met with the head priest, it was the first time the topic had been broached so plainly. She frowned, and changes in her respiration and hormone levels told me she'd thought of something dismaying. 'You haven't had problems with *Justice of Ente* Seven Issa, have you?'

'No,' said the head priest. She looked at Lieutenant Awn with a wry twist to her mouth. 'I know you. I know One Esk.

Whoever they'll send me – I won't know. Neither will my parishioners.'

'Annexations are messy,' said Lieutenant Awn. The head priest winced slightly at the word *annexation* and I thought I saw Lieutenant Awn notice, but she continued. 'Seven Issa wasn't here for that. The *Justice of Ente* Issa battalions didn't do anything during that time that One Esk didn't also do.'

'No, Lieutenant.' The priest put down her own cup, seeming disturbed, but I didn't have access to any of her internal data and so could not be certain. '*Justice of Ente* Issa did many things One Esk did not. It's true, One Esk killed as many people as the soldiers of *Justice of Ente*'s Issa. Likely more.' She looked at me, still standing silent by the enclosure's entrance. 'No offense, but I think it was more.'

'I take no offense, Divine,' I replied. The head priest frequently spoke to me as though I were a person. 'And you are correct.'

'Divine,' said Lieutenant Awn, worry clear in her voice. 'If the soldiers of *Justice of Ente* Seven Issa – or anyone else – have been abusing citizens ...'

'No, no!' protested the head priest, her voice bitter. 'Radchaai are so very careful about how citizens are treated!'

Lieutenant Awn's face heated, her distress and anger plain to me. I couldn't read her mind, but I could read every twitch of her every muscle, so her emotions were as transparent to me as glass.

'Forgive me,' said the head priest, though Lieutenant Awn's expression had not changed, and her skin was too dark to show the flush of her anger. 'Since the Radchaai have bestowed citizenship on us ...' She stopped, seemed to reconsider her words. 'Since their arrival, Seven Issa has given me nothing to complain of. But I've seen what your human troops did during what you call *the annexation*. The citizenship you granted may be as easily taken back, and ...'

'We wouldn't ...' protested Lieutenant Awn.

The head priest stopped her with a raised hand. 'I know what Seven Issa, or at least those like them, do to people they find on the wrong side of a dividing line. Five years ago it was noncitizen. In the future, who knows? Perhaps not-citizen-enough?' She waved a hand, a gesture of surrender. 'It won't matter. Such boundaries are too easy to create.'

'I can't blame you for thinking in such terms,' said Lieutenant Awn. 'It was a difficult time.'

'And I can't help but think you inexplicably, unexpectedly naive,' said the head priest. 'One Esk will shoot me if you order it. Without hesitation. But One Esk would never beat me or humiliate me, or rape me, for no purpose but to show its power over me, or to satisfy some sick amusement.' She looked at me. 'Would you?'

'No, Divine,' I said.

'The soldiers of *Justice of Ente* Issa did all of those things. Not to me, it's true, and not to many in Ors itself. But they did them nonetheless. Would Seven Issa have been any different, if it had been them here instead?'

Lieutenant Awn sat, distressed, looking down at her unappetizing tea, unable to answer.

'It's strange. You hear stories about ancillaries, and it seems like the most awful thing, the most viscerally appalling thing the Radchaai have done. Garsedd – well, yes, Garsedd, but that was a thousand years ago. This – to invade and take, what, half the adult population? And turn them into walking corpses, slaved to your ships' AIs. Turned against their own people. If you'd asked me before you ... *annexed* us, I'd have said it was a fate worse than death.' She turned to me. 'Is it?'

'None of my bodies is dead, Divine,' I said. 'And your estimate of the typical percentage of annexed populations who were made into ancillaries is excessive.'

'You used to horrify me,' said the head priest to me. 'The very thought of you near was terrifying, your dead faces, those expressionless voices. But today I am more horrified at the thought of a unit of living human beings who serve voluntarily. Because I don't think I could trust them.'

'Divine,' said Lieutenant Awn, mouth tight. 'I serve voluntarily. I make no excuses for it.'

'I believe you are a good person, Lieutenant Awn, despite that.' She picked up her cup of tea and sipped it, as though she had not just said what she had said.

Lieutenant Awn's throat tightened, and her lips. She had thought of something she wanted to say, but was unsure if she should. 'You've heard about Ime,' she said, deciding. Still tense and wary despite having chosen to speak.

The head priest seemed bleakly, bitterly amused. 'News from Ime is meant to inspire confidence in Radch administration?'

This is what had happened: Ime Station, and the smaller stations and moons in the system, were the farthest one could be from a provincial palace and still be in Radch space. For years the governor of Ime used this distance to her own advantage – embezzling, collecting bribes and protection fees, selling assignments. Thousands of citizens had been unjustly executed or (what was essentially the same thing) forced into service as ancillary bodies, even though the manufacture of ancillaries was no longer legal. The governor controlled all communications and travel permits, and normally a station AI would report such activity to the authorities, but Ime Station had been somehow prevented from doing so, and the corruption grew, and spread unchecked.

Until a ship entered the system, came out of gate space only a few hundred kilometers from the patrol ship *Mercy of Sarrse*. The strange ship didn't answer demands that it identify itself. When *Mercy of Sarrse*'s crew attacked and boarded it, they found dozens of humans, as well as the alien Rrrrr. The captain of *Mercy of Sarrse* ordered her soldiers to take captive any humans that seemed suitable for use as ancillaries, and kill the rest, along with all the aliens. The ship would be turned over to the system governor.

Mercy of Sarrse was not the only human-crewed warship in that system. Until that moment human soldiers stationed there had been kept in line by a program of bribes, flattery, and, when those failed, threats and even executions. All very effective, until the moment the soldier *Mercy of Sarrse* One Amaat One decided she wasn't willing to kill those people, or the Rrrrr. And convinced the rest of her unit to follow her.

That had all happened five years before. The results of it were still playing themselves out.

Lieutenant Awn shifted on her cushion. 'That business was all uncovered because a single human soldier refused an order. And led a mutiny. If it hadn't been for her ... well. Ancillaries won't do that. They can't.'

'That business was all uncovered,' replied the head priest, 'because the ship that human soldier boarded, she and the rest of her unit, had aliens on it. Radchaai have few qualms about killing humans, especially noncitizen humans, but you're very cautious about starting wars with aliens.'

Only because wars with aliens might run up against the terms of the treaty with the alien Presger. Violating that agreement would have extremely serious consequences. And even so, plenty of high-ranking Radchaai disagreed on that topic. I saw Lieutenant Awn's desire to argue the point. Instead she said,

'The governor of Ime was not cautious about it. And would have started that war, if not for this one person.'

'Have they executed that person yet?' the head priest asked, pointedly. It was the summary fate of any soldier who refused an order, let alone mutinied.

'Last I heard,' said Lieutenant Awn, breath tight and turning shallow, 'the Rrrrrr had agreed to turn her over to Radch authorities.' She swallowed. 'I don't know what's going to happen.' Of course, it had probably already happened, whatever it was. News could take a year or more to reach Shis'urna from as far away as Ime.

The head priest didn't answer for a moment. She poured more tea, and spooned fish paste into a small bowl. 'Does my continued request for your presence present any sort of disadvantage for you?'

'No,' said Lieutenant Awn. 'Actually, the other Esk lieutenants are a bit envious. There's no chance for action on *Justice of Toren*.' She picked up her own cup, outwardly calm, inwardly angry. Disturbed. Talking about the news from Ime had increased her unease. 'Action means commendations, and possibly promotions.' And this was the last annexation. The last chance for an officer to enrich her house through connections to new citizens, or even through outright appropriation.

'Yet another reason I would prefer you,' said the head priest.

I followed Lieutenant Awn home. And watched inside the temple, and overlooked the people crisscrossing the plaza as they always did, avoiding the children playing kau in the center of the plaza, kicking the ball back and forth, shouting and laughing. On the edge of the Fore-Temple water, a teenager from the upper city sat sullen and listless watching half a dozen little children hopping from stone to stone, singing:

One, two, my aunt told me
Three, four, the corpse soldier
Five, six, it'll shoot you in the eye
Seven, eight, kill you dead
Nine, ten, break it apart and put it back together.

As I walked the streets people greeted me, and I greeted them in return. Lieutenant Awn was tense and angry, and only nodded absently at the people in the street, who greeted her as she passed.

The person with the fishing-rights complaint left, unsatisfied. Two children rounded the divider after she had gone, and sat cross-legged on the cushion she had vacated. They both wore lengths of fabric wrapped around their waists, clean but faded, though no gloves. The elder was about nine, and the symbols inked on the younger one's chest and shoulders – slightly smudged – indicated she was no more than six. She looked at me, frowning.

In Orsian addressing children properly was easier than addressing adults. One used a simple, ungendered form. 'Hello, citizens,' I said, in the local dialect. I recognized them both – they lived on the south edge of Ors and I had spoken to them quite frequently, but they had never visited the house before. 'How can I help you?'

'You aren't One Esk,' said the smaller child, and the older made an abortive motion as if to hush her.

'I am,' I said, and pointed to the insignia on my uniform jacket. 'See? Only this is my number Fourteen segment.'

'I *told* you,' said the older child.

The younger considered this for a moment, and then said, 'I have a song.' I waited in silence, and she took a deep breath, as though about to begin, and then halted, perplexed-seeming.

'Do you want to hear it?' she asked, still doubtful of my identity, likely.

'Yes, citizen,' I said. I – that is, I–One Esk – first sang to amuse one of my lieutenants, when *Justice of Toren* had hardly been commissioned a hundred years. She enjoyed music, and had brought an instrument with her as part of her luggage allowance. She could never interest the other officers in her hobby and so she taught me the parts to the songs she played. I filed those away and went looking for more, to please her. By the time she was captain of her own ship I had collected a large library of vocal music – no one was going to give me an instrument, but I could sing anytime – and it was a matter of rumor and some indulgent smiles that *Justice of Toren* had an interest in singing. Which it didn't – I – I–*Justice of Toren* – tolerated the habit because it was harmless, and because it was quite possible that one of my captains would appreciate it. Otherwise it would have been prevented.

If these children had stopped me on the street, they would have had no hesitation, but here in the house, seated as though for a formal conference, things were different. And I suspected this was an exploratory visit, that the youngest child meant to eventually ask for a chance to serve in the house's makeshift temple – the prestige of being appointed flower-bearer to Amaat wasn't a question here, in the stronghold of Ikkt, but the customary term-end gift of fruit and clothing was. And this child's best friend was currently a flower-bearer, doubtless making the prospect more interesting.

No Orsian would make such a request immediately or directly, so likely the child had chosen this oblique approach, turning a casual encounter into something formal and intimidating. I reached into my jacket pocket and pulled out a handful of sweets and laid them on the floor between us.

The littler girl made an affirmative gesture, as though I had resolved all her doubts, and then took a breath and began.

My heart is a fish
Hiding in the water-grass
In the green, in the green.

The tune was an odd amalgam of a Radchaai song that played occasionally on broadcast and an Orsian one I already knew. The words were unfamiliar to me. She sang four verses in a clear, slightly wavering voice, and seemed ready to launch into a fifth, but stopped abruptly when Lieutenant Awn's steps sounded outside the divider.

The smaller girl leaned forward and scooped up her payment. Both children bowed, still half-seated, and then rose and ran out the entranceway into the wider house, past Lieutenant Awn, past me following Lieutenant Awn.

'Thank you, citizens,' Lieutenant Awn said to their retreating backs, and they started, and then managed with a single movement to both bow slightly in her direction and continue running, out into the street.

'Anything new?' asked Lieutenant Awn, though she didn't pay much attention to music, herself, not beyond what most people do.

'Sort of,' I said. Farther down the street I saw the two children, still running as they turned a corner around another house. They slowed to a halt, breathing hard. The littler girl opened her hand to show the older one her fistful of sweets. Surprisingly, she seemed not to have dropped any, small as her hand was, as quick as their flight had been. The older child took a sweet and put it in her mouth.

Five years ago I would have offered something more

nutritious, before repairs had begun to the planet's infra-structure, when supplies were chancy. Now every citizen was guaranteed enough to eat, but the rations were not luxurious, and often as not were unappealing.

Inside the temple all was green-lit silence. The head priest did not emerge from behind the screens in the temple residence, though junior priests came and went. Lieutenant Awn went to the second floor of her house and sat brooding on an Ors-style cushion, screened from the street, shirt thrown off. She refused the (genuine) tea I brought her. I transmitted a steady stream of information to her – everything normal, everything routine – and to *Justice of Toren*. 'She should take that to the district magistrate,' Lieutenant Awn said of the citizen with the fishing dispute, slightly annoyed, eyes closed, the afternoon's reports in her vision. 'We don't have jurisdiction over that.' I didn't answer. No answer was required, or expected. She approved, with a quick twitch of her fingers, the message I had composed for the district magistrate, and then opened the most recent message from her young sister. Lieutenant Awn sent a percentage of her earnings home to her parents, who used it to buy their younger child poetry lessons. Poetry was a valuable, civilized accomplishment. I couldn't judge if Lieutenant Awn's sister had any particular talent, but then not many did, even among more elevated families. But her work and her letters pleased Lieutenant Awn, and took the edge off her present distress.

The children on the plaza ran away home, laughing. The adolescent sighed, heavily, the way adolescents do, and dropped a pebble in the water and stared at the ripples.

Ancillary units that only ever woke for annexations often wore nothing but a force shield generated by an implant in each body, rank on rank of featureless soldiers that might have been poured from mercury. But I was always out of the holds, and I wore the same uniform human soldiers did, now the fighting was done. My bodies sweated under my uniform jackets, and, bored, I opened three of my mouths, all in close proximity to each other on the temple plaza, and sang with those three voices, 'My heart is a fish, hiding in the water-grass ...' One person walking by looked at me, startled, but everyone else ignored me – they were used to me by now